PIECES
OF THE
PAST

PIECES
OF THE
PAST

(Trilogy - Part 1)

G. P. Schumacher

DISCLAIMER

This novel is a work of fiction. Names, characters, and events are products of the author's imagination. Any resemblance to real people, living or dead, and actual events is purely coincidental. Certain long-standing institutions, agencies, public offices, and places are mentioned in this novel, but the events happening and the characters involved are entirely imaginary.

Copyright © 2024 by Greta Schumacher

Title: Pieces of the Past

ISBN: 979-8-89109-774-2 - ebook

ISBN: 979-8-89109-775-9 - paperback

Cover design by: Joice Panilagao

Book design by: Richell Balansag

Line edits and proofreading by Motif Edits — www.motifedits.com

Interested in learning more about the author?

Follow me on Facebook: GP Schumacher

Reach me via email at gpschumacher.author@gmail.com

To my two wonderful kids, Maila and Ayden,
whom I love more than anything!
Ich hab euch lieb!

PROLOGUE

EGLIN AIR FORCE BASE (AFB) MAY 2003

The fog hung deep over Eglin AFB that fateful night. The happy couple sat arm in arm on the old couch in a TLF, one of the temporary lodging facilities right by the water, talking about their day. He told her all about his in-processing, the new bosses he'd met, and the team he would be working with. They had just PCS'ed to the beautiful base located in Florida's panhandle and were still waiting to move into their new house there. He was a young captain in the U.S. Air Force and was always excited to start a new job, meet new people, and excel at everything he did.

However, he couldn't do it without her—she was his rock, his stability in a rough and ever-changing military life. She was always there for him with a listening ear, open arms, and her beautiful smile that was contagious even on a bad day. She had given up everything for him, everything for *them*—her career, her friends, her family. She had left it all behind when she moved from Germany to the U.S. to be with him, finally together after years and years spent in a crazy long-distance relationship throughout college and the start of his military career.

They loved each other. Their love was mature and true, the kind all of humankind strives for. They were best friends, awesome lovers, amazing partners, great roommates. Their love was perfected in the form of their beautiful little almost-two-year-old daughter, Moana, who was fast asleep in a lower bunk bed inside her own kid's room. Her name meant "ocean" and stood for all the years her parents had been separated by the Atlantic.

Not anymore. Here they were at Eglin AFB, together forever. Or at least that's what they thought.

After he was done telling his wife all about his day, he asked about hers. She smiled and told him again that life with him was crazy, but worth it. He kissed her gently on the forehead before they sank into a deep, passionate kiss. She giggled, and he paused and looked at her, wondering what she was laughing about.

"Guess what our daughter said today when I gave her a big kiss right before she ran off to play on the playground?"

"I don't know, tell me." He was always interested to hear another funny anecdote about his daughter.

"'Eeee, Mama, kiss too wet,'" she mimicked the words of their toddler. "'Like a doggie.'"

He burst into laughter, joined by his wife. "Where did she get that from?"

She just shrugged her shoulders. "Maybe from a book that talked about *animals*?"

He had to smile again—he loved her accent. It was faint, almost nonexistent and he'd learned never to bring it up as she got very offended when he did, but he thought it was just so cute. The way she said "animals" sounded very close to "anemia," which just cracked him up. Instead of mentioning her little pronunciation trouble, he gave her a big kiss. "Our little miss is so smart! And you're an amazing teacher, role model, and mommy for her!"

His words warmed her heart and they got lost going on and on about their little daughter's wit. "Remember a few nights ago at the laundry facility when Moana noticed the TV show the cleaning lady was watching? She picked up the Spanish words right away. Even the cleaning lady was amazed."

She nodded. "Moana still knows that lady's name. She has a great memory."

"Yep, our little one. So smart, already bilingual, extremely social, very strong willed, and just as beautiful as her mommy." He leaned over to kiss her.

She smiled. "Nicely said, hun. But to be fair, she has your exotic eyes and kissable lips."

"Yes, but she got your wavy hair, bubbly personality, and contagious smile. . . ."

They kissed and got lost in their love, still as passionate as young lovers.

They were still cuddling on the couch when they heard a sound. Was it their little girl? They both looked at each other, then sat up to listen. The sound stopped. They sighed.

"Remember the times we used to cuddle all night long without having to fear a toddler walking in on us?" she said with a laugh, and he agreed.

When he went to pick up his uniform jacket off the ground, he suddenly remembered he didn't have any more clean uniforms. Most of their household goods were still packed away in containers, waiting to get delivered to their new house as soon as it was ready for move-in.

"Well, I can wear this one again, I suppose," he said as they both inspected it.

She pointed to a stain. "You better not, unless you want your new boss to yell at you."

"Oh dear . . . Any other clean ones around?"

She shook her head and started toward their bedroom. Within a minute she came out with the laundry bag, took the uniform out of his hands, and stuffed it in with the other dirty laundry, then headed for the door. "I'll go throw this in a washing machine at the laundry room. It's only nine p.m. Should be done in an hour or so."

She peeked inside the bedroom to check on their daughter and saw she was still deep asleep. When she turned around, her husband was putting on civilian clothes. "What are you up to?"

"It's dark and foggy out there, a little rainy. I don't want you to go alone."

She laughed and reminded him they were on an Air Force base, probably one of the safest places in the world. Still, he insisted on going with her. Mainly because he wanted to be close to her, hold her hand, talk to her.

"And Moana?"

"She's in a deep sleep," he assured her. "What could happen in the five minutes it'll take us to do a load of laundry? We'll lock the door, and she'll be fine. You said it yourself: 'one of the safest places in the world,' right?"

She didn't have a good feeling about this, but was flattered that he didn't want to leave her side. They checked on their daughter again, listened to her even breathing, stroked her head, and gave her a kiss, then left their little apartment, locking the door behind them. Hand in hand, the full laundry bag draped across his strong shoulders, they jogged through the fog and now-light rain to the laundry facility only a block away from their apartment. Their key card unlocked the door, and they said "Hello" to the soldier in there folding his laundry. They quickly got the load started and were back at their apartment door within eight minutes.

As he raised the key card to open the door, the wind picked up and all of the sudden the door opened by itself. "What the heck?"

They both stared at the now-wide-open door to their apartment. All color washed away from her beautiful face. "We locked the door, didn't we?"

"I think so. . . .Regardless, let's not panic."

He quickly scanned the living room as they walked in. All the lights were still on, the bedroom door was wide open, the door to their daughter's bedroom was half closed—just as they'd left it.

"See, nothing's disturbed, all is good—"

He had his back to his wife and before he could turn around, he heard it: a scream, an awful, ear-splitting scream that only a mom in distress can make. There she was, clutching the doorframe of their daughter's room, sinking to her knees before he could even react.

"She's gone! She's gone! Our daughter is gone!" Tears were running down her face.

Panicked, he stepped over her to search the lower bunk. He found his daughter's favorite stuffed toy, two pacifiers, her pink pillow—but not Moana. He checked the upper bunk, underneath the bed, then ran to look over the other rooms while his wife dialed 911 on her phone.

"Who are you calling?" His voice had gone deep, the voice of a hardened soldier rather than a dad whose daughter was suddenly not in her bed anymore.

"The police! Somebody took her!"

"We need to check everywhere outside before calling the police," he barked. "She must have walked out!"

"She doesn't know how to open this kind of doorknob yet! She can't unlock a door by herself. Just think about it!"

While she talked to the police, he ran out and frantically looked all over the area surrounding the TLF, calling his daughter's name. The rain grew heavy. It was only when he noticed it mixing with his salty tears that he realized his wife was right.

He had probably just seen his daughter for the last time.

He ran back inside the apartment and found his wife sitting on the very couch they'd made love on only half an hour before. She just sat there, cell phone in hand, tears dripping down onto it.

She raised her head to look at him, and the accusations started. "It was your idea! We should *never* have left her alone! Never ever! What have you done? What have *we* done? I'm a terrible mommy! I belong in jail for abandoning my child!" Her whole body was shaking, racked by deep, awful sobs. It was hard to look at her, to see her like this.

Another realization hit him in that moment—he would never see her smile again. Things would never be the same. He had just lost the two girls in his life, two girls he loved more than anything.

In just eight minutes, he had lost it all.

His life shattered into pieces.

CHAPTER 1

DAYTONA BEACH
20 YEARS LATER

Her smart phone on loudspeaker, Maria leaned toward the mirror in the tiny bathroom of her college dorm, getting ready for the special evening. She put on makeup that was subtle yet perfectly underlined her beauty, especially her exotic hazel eyes. She stared at her reflection and saw a mosaic of golden-and-emerald-green flecks in the dark-brown center encircled by a blue rim.

"Sí, Mamá," she babbled into the phone in perfect Spanish, as she started fixing up her stubborn wavy hair. "I will be careful. You know Aaron. He's a perfect gentleman. He'll bring me home safely after the ball."

She only half-listened to all the things her mom had to tell her—her concerns, her motherly advice, everything else. She was twenty-one years old, a junior in college dating a guy she'd met back when she was a freshman. Her mom shouldn't be concerned at all. But Maria knew she always was whenever she went out and about, regardless of the circumstances. Still, she had to admit, it was great to have such a wonderful relationship with the woman who had given birth to her and raised her all by herself. She promised her extremely nervous mom that she would text when she got home and tell her tomorrow all about how the night went, then hung up.

She slipped on the red dress that hugged her body like a glove and brought out the reddish streaks in her brown hair. After a quick look in the mirror, she became convinced that her new bra made her boobs look bigger than they were. But it didn't feel like enough.

Why can't I have Mamá's rack? I just had to take after my dad's side. . . . She sighed, but then admired her perfectly rounded butt in the mirror. Her confidence surged. *Good to go!*

The doorbell rang. She quickly grabbed her sparkling brown purse, slipped on her brown high heels, and opened the door after an impatient second ring.

"Wow." The tall, handsome young man standing on her apartment's welcome mat gaped at her. "You look amazing, Maria. I mean, you always do. But especially tonight. We better leave before we get stuck right here in your apartment." He grinned, then leaned in and kissed her on the cheek.

"Oh, a kiss on the cheek? Why so shy, Aaron?"

He peered down at her with his killer blue eyes that perfectly matched his blue Air Force cadet uniform. "Well, I heard girls don't like it if you ruin their lipstick before the party gets started."

Maria stepped closer to him and shut the door behind her. "It's *kiss-proof,* you fool," she said, then gave him a big warm kiss on the lips.

"Okay then," he smiled. "We better get going or we *will* wind up stuck here."

"Too late, door's closed." She laughed and they walked away, hand in hand, to his old car in the parking lot.

"Hey girl, there you are!"

Maria heard Keisha yell to her from across the beautifully decorated grand foyer in the fancy building where the Reserve Officers' Training Corps (ROTC) Air Force Ball was in full swing.

Maria waved to her and took Aaron by the hand. "There they are."

"Oh yeah, there's the gang. I see Nick made it. He wasn't even dressed when I left our apartment."

Maria laughed. "Well, your roomie sure is dressed now—and somehow beat us here. He's already sipping a beer. Come on! ¡Vamos!"

They walked over to the group. Aaron high-fived Nick and their friend Jim, then gave a hug to both Keisha and Brandy.

"Hey y'all, you finally made it," Brandy said. "You look stunning, Maria! I see you went shopping with your bestie. Y'all look amazing!"

Keisha and Maria stood arm in arm in their beautiful red dresses and smiled. "Thanks, Brandy," Maria said. "We wanted to find a dress that works for both our skin types."

"Yeah, girl, we're both rocking the dress," Keisha said before starting to sing "*Doesn't matter if you're black or white.*" All the girls burst into laughter and joined Keisha in singing while trying to moonwalk.

"I see it's a party already," Nick smiled, and gave Brandy a big kiss. "And your friend Maria here doesn't even have a drink yet."

"Who needs a *drink* to dance?" Maria teased Nick and flashed Jim a look. They both turned red.

"Well, we bust our best and *only* moves when there's alcohol flowing. So, if you want all of us to dance later, enjoy Social Hour, and let's party," Jim said, and raised his glass. "Cheers, everyone! Oops. Someone still doesn't have a glass to cheer with."

Maria smirked, then whispered to Keisha, "I suppose your boyfriend won't rest till I get that booze."

Keisha just rolled her eyes.

"Yep, better get yourself a drink, darlin'," Brandy said, and took Maria's arm to guide her toward the bar. "See, even your boyfriend is in line already, honey."

"Okay, fine, let's go, Brandy," Maria said, and let her friend whisk her along. "By the way, you look stunning. Love the baby-blue dress. Really brings out your eyes."

"Aw, thanks, darlin'," Brandy said. She batted her sparkling blue eyes, swirled around her blonde hair, and led them to the bar.

Aaron met them with two drinks in hand. "No need to get in line, girls. I already got Maria her favorite drink."

Maria looked at him and smiled, then took one of the fancy plastic cups out of his hands. "Thanks, Aaron. Rum and coke! You know me well."

"Hold on! That's *my* drink." Aaron took the glass out of Maria's hands and gave her the other one he'd been holding. "*This* is yours."

She frowned. "Looks the same."

"Yeah, but mine is coke minus the rum."

Brandy raised her eyebrows. "You're not drinking tonight? But it's your senior ball, Aaron! And Nick's. And Jim's. Come on, at least one drink?"

Aaron shook his head. "Nope, I'm Maria's designated driver. Always at her service." He grinned.

"Y'all could just take an Uber," Brandy said as they all turned around to head back to the group.

"I guess. But I want to drive Maria tonight."

"That's true. He insisted on driving me. Not sure why," Maria said.

She looked at him, studied his face while they all said "cheers" and laughed together. Aaron seemed a little spacy tonight. Nervous.

"You okay?" Maria whispered in his ear as they walked to their assigned table.

"Sure, I'm fine, why?" he answered a little bit too quickly.

Suppressing her surprise, Maria looked on in approval as Aaron pulled out and presented a chair for her—one of many gentlemenlike traditions the Air Force taught their cadets that she really enjoyed.

The ball started with the "Positioning of the Flags" that Maria always thought was a little stiff, then came the national anthem, sung by an amazing young female cadet. Aaron stood at attention next to her while she put her hand on her heart. The "Remembering of the Fallen and Prisoners of War" was next and gave Maria a big knot in her throat thinking of Aaron and potential upcoming deployments.

The first course started—a salad as usual.

"Nick, darlin', pass the salt and peppa, please," Brandy said, and looked at her boyfriend. "But honey, don't forget which hand to use and which way to pass it." The others giggled. Every ROTC ball they had attended, they always got a kick out of the strict etiquette rules and called out their friends if something was done incorrectly.

"Hey girl, will you pretend to use the bathroom first, or should I?" Keisha asked Maria. They grinned at each other; all the guys had to stand up whenever a woman left the table.

"Brandy said she'll go first," Maria whispered to Keisha, and gave a nod to Brandy, who immediately announced she had to use the restroom. All the guys stopped eating and got up. The girls suppressed their laughter.

"¡Vamos, Brandy!" Maria said, and Brandy looked at her, confused.

"Maria, that was Spanish. We don't speak it," Nick said with a straight face.

Maria looked at them all. "Come on, everybody! Everyone knows *vamos*!"

"Ha, she fell for it, guys! We boys gotta get in our teasing tonight too, don't we?" Nick said, and winked at the other guys who were still standing up, waiting for Brandy to leave. Jim grinned, but Aaron just stared straight ahead.

"Y'all tease her about this stuff," started Brandy, "but I would love to learn more about a different culture. Look at her—she knows so much about Venezuela and speaks two languages fluently. It's just fascinating."

"Maybe so," Nick said, "but also a hassle for your security clearance. Right, Aaron?"

"What?" Aaron looked at him with a blank stare on his face.

"Oh no, Aaron fell asleep while standing up! That *must* be against the rules."

Everyone laughed, except for Maria, who raised her eyebrows.

The salad plates were cleared and the speaker of the evening took the microphone. "Now, ladies and gentlemen, I'd kindly like to ask you to direct your attention to a little video of our senior class."

Applause from all sides as the video started, footage of the ROTC senior class training throughout their time at Embry-Riddle Aeronautical University. One part of it showed the boys in the sunrise on the beach, all in their PT clothes.

"Man, I remember that morning," Jim commented. "Do you?"

"I sure do. That run, ugh," Nick said. "I got so sick."

"Yeah, you sure did . . . all over Aaron's foot." Jim laughed and held his belly. "Remember, Aaron?"

Aaron looked up from staring at his feet. "What? Oh, yeah, yeah."

Keisha elbowed Maria and whispered, "What's wrong with your boyfriend tonight?"

"Not sure."

The video clip ended. Suddenly, a huge beam of light shone down on their table, pretty much right on Maria and Aaron.

"And now, ladies and gentlemen," the speaker said, "this young cadet here has the word of the evening!"

Maria looked at Aaron, astonished.

He rose to his feet and started his speech by welcoming everyone, then turned directly to Maria. "This beautiful young woman, ladies and gentlemen, is probably wondering why I didn't tell her I'd be giving this important speech today because I tell her everything—well, everything not classified, of course." Laughter from the audience while Maria raised her eyebrows.

"She's my best friend, and a great girlfriend, if you know what I mean—the best arm-candy ever—and most importantly, my rock, the person who brought me through college so far. Long study nights, early ROTC mornings, boot camp, all the other things we do to become Airmen. Maria has always been by my side, supporting me, even fighting with me over the things worth fighting about, and I cannot imagine a life without her. Everyone in the Air Force needs a wingman. Well, I choose a wing*woman*, and so here's the reason I didn't tell her about this speech—it would've ruined the surprise!"

The audience sighed, and Maria's heart started pounding. Her jaw dropped as Aaron got down on one knee and pulled out a little blue satin box. "Maria, I cannot imagine going anywhere without you, being without you and your support, not having my best friend next to me everywhere I go. You're my better half; you make me whole." Aaron swallowed and continued in broken Spanish, "Me has robado el corazón. ¿Te casarias conmigo?"

The audience oohed and awed as Maria stared at Aaron. *How does he know Spanish? He learned French in high school. Where will we live? Aren't we too young to get married? What will happen to my career if I follow him around in the military? Will I be a good military wife? Can I be his wingwoman?*

It seemed like minutes went by in silence. Aaron wiggled nervously on his one knee, then saw a single tear drop down in front of him onto the carpet. He looked up into her exotic eyes, she met his ocean-blue ones, and Maria got lost in the intense blue of his eyes as one might get lost in the ocean. She got down on her knees and leaned forward to whisper something in his ear.

The whole room seemed to hold their breath.

"She said yes!" Aaron jumped up and pulled her up into a long kiss in front of the eyes of hundreds. A standing ovation followed. As he put the ring on her finger, she noticed the diamond reflecting the beam of light in all directions, and started crying.

"I love you so much and always want to be with you, no matter what," she whispered, and they hugged again.

He seemed taller in her arms; relief had lifted the weight off his shoulders. They got lost in the moment until Keisha hit Aaron's arm. "Okay guys, show's over. Congrats, but dinner is served, and we're hungry!"

Aaron and Maria quickly sat down. While Aaron went back to his normal self and was able to finish his whole plate, Maria was too nervous to eat and barely touched her food. She had so much to tell her mom tomorrow. *Maybe I should do it now?* Maria looked for her phone in her purse.

Aaron gently touched her arm to stop her. "No, Maria, please don't call your mamá now. It's the guest speaker's turn—a general, high up. Besides, your mom already knows."

He pulled out his phone and showed her a message he'd sent to her mom that simply read: *Yes.*

Maria's jaw dropped for the second time that night.

"Why do you have my mom's phone number? You've only met her twice."

Aaron winked at her. "Not true. I spent a whole weekend with her, went through an interrogation more intense than any military one when I asked her permission to marry you. Remember that weekend I had training down in Miami and your mom invited me to dinner?" Maria nodded, remembering that had been a few weeks ago. "There was no training. I just visited your mom. Sorry I didn't tell you, but you were suspicious enough as it was."

"You told me a little white lie." She smirked. "But you're not good at lying. I knew it was just too odd you couldn't tell me what you were training for."

They smiled at each other.

Applause interrupted their little conversation, and the guest speaker took the stage. He was a good-looking man, well-built, and had an immediately likable smile and personality. His eyes sparkled as he took the mic. "Thank you, ladies and gentlemen, for the warm welcome—and I'm not just talking about the weather here." Laughter. He seemed like a fun, charismatic gentleman who knew how to work a crowd.

"He's a two-star general working at the Pentagon," Aaron whispered to Maria. "Very cool guy. I've only heard good things about him—he'll make chief of staff of the Air Force one day, I bet."

The general's voice boomed from the stage. "First of all, thank you all for having me tonight, and congratulations to the newly engaged couple. I'm afraid my speech may come across a little boring compared to that young man's, but let me start by saying: I was once in your shoes. I was there once—an ROTC cadet who wasn't sure what to make of the Air Force, thinking it was only a way to pay for college. But luckily I wasn't a Van Wilder who went to college forever, meaning I obviously refined my plans."

Laughter again. Somehow, Maria was fascinated.

"When I was a young man, I also asked my wife to marry me in a foreign language that I knew nothing about—no offense there, cadet!"

Laughter in the audience. Aaron's face turned bright red.

"She used to say I spoke at the level of a two-year-old."

Giggles, some applause. Maria stared at the older man, captivated by his presence.

"Well, things changed, I learned better language skills and definitely made a career of the Air Force—a choice many of you can make as well. Let me tell you, it's a great life, wonderful opportunities, but it will also mean sacrifice, sometimes more than you will personally want."

He paused; the audience waited.

Nobody but Maria seemed to notice the strange sadness in the general's eyes. She suddenly had a strong urge to run up on stage and hug him, then brushed that silly thought away and tried to listen again. *Stupid me! Who thinks like that? What's wrong with me tonight? Well, for one thing, I got engaged. . . .*

She looked at her ring and off she went, her thoughts somewhere else. She barely noticed the end of the general's speech and was only woken out of her deep thoughts when the rest of her table rose in a standing ovation.

After dessert, Maria realized that she actually had to use the bathroom, no prank this time. She got up, as did the rest of the men at the table, and walked out of the fancy room in search of the restrooms.

Where am I? Such a big, confusing place. Shoot. I'm lost!

While still walking, she turned her head to see where she had come from when she suddenly bumped into a gentleman in uniform who had been drinking from a water fountain in the hallway. The unexpected bump made her take a step forward again, but her high heel got caught in her long dress and she tripped over her own two feet. Luckily, she caught herself just in time and stood up tall, her back to the person she had bumped into.

"Oh, never walk backwards. Always look at where you're going and be aware of your surroundings," a familiar voice said.

Maria turned around mumbling sorry and stood face-to-face with the general. "Oh, my goodness, I'm so very sorry, sir!"

"It's alright," he said in a friendly voice, and she dared to look up.

She saw his exotic hazel eyes, a mosaic of golden-and-emerald-green flecks in the dark-brown center, a blue rim on the outside. He returned a firm but friendly gaze. They stared at one another, then all of a sudden he blinked, shook his head, and looked down. "Well, young lady, you better watch where you're going from now on."

"Yes, sir, I promise I'll be aware of my surroundings!" Suddenly, she felt like a child even as the words left her mouth.

He stared at her, then looked back down. "Well, ahem, you're forgiven tonight, as you just got engaged. Congratulations!"

"Thank you, sir! And sorry again. I was just looking for the restroom."

The general's security detail motioned for him to follow. He quickly pointed to the left and gave her a wink. She raised her hand to wave goodbye, then followed his directions.

There they are. She walked into the restroom, feeling a little dazed for some unexplainable reason.

CHAPTER 2

For some unexplainable reason, he felt a little dazed and kept thinking about the night.

"Sir?" The driver's voice interrupted the general's deep thoughts. "We've arrived at the Orlando airport, sir."

The general looked up at the AF captain who had served as his driver for the past hour. The captain walked around the car and opened the door for him. "You alright, sir?"

"Yes, sure, yes. Just a long night. I'm ready to be on that plane heading home."

"Sure, sir, just follow me, I'll take you to the gate," the captain said, and handed the general his bag. He took it and followed the captain into the airport to catch the plane that would bring him back to Washington, DC.

"Holy cow, did something happen, Cave Man? You alright?"

"Oh, did I wake you up, Drew?" The general looked at his watch and realized it was almost midnight. "I'm sorry for calling this late."

"Heck yeah, you should be. It's super late. All of us are, uh, asleep."

The general smirked. "But it's Saturday night, Drew. Thought you'd still be up. And I'm sure not *all* of you are asleep."

Drew sighed. "Well, not Simon, I suppose. But he'll sleep in. You know those teenagers can turn day into night. Both Sylvia and I couldn't even if we tried. We always wake up early. Just like the article we've read together said: it's called 'senile bed flight' meaning the older you get, the earlier you wake up and you just can't help it. Remember?"

He laughed. "Yeah, I remember that article. Amusing, but true. Yeah, I suffer from 'senile bed flight', too, even at night."

"No, Cave Man, at night, that's something else." He heard Drew laugh on the other end of the line. "That's just called 'giving up on sleep'. But you're the only person I know that can actually function after only four or five hours of sleep."

He laughed again. "Well, that's how I get stuff done, though."

"Yeah, I suppose so. But I assume you didn't call to discuss sleep patterns, did you?"

"No, I just got back from Florida. I hate Florida."

Drew sighed. "I know, Cave Man. I know. But Daytona Beach must have been a *little* fun, right? I know you enjoy crowds celebrating you like you're a rock star."

"Well, Drew, I didn't exactly walk in with my flight suit on. You know I don't actively fly much anymore."

"Yeah, *I* know. But those young cadets don't. To them, you're still the cool fighter pilot. Everyone wants to be like you."

The general frowned. "Yeah, I suppose. But you know me well enough to realize I'm only playing the role of the cocky pilot."

"Come on, Cave Man. Don't go back in your cave. Once a pilot, always a pilot."

"Just because you still use my call sign? Right, Screw?"

Drew now laughed a warm laugh. "I'm retired, man. Nobody uses my fighter pilot call sign anymore. Those wild days are over. Now, I'm just your civilian colleague Mr. Markas."

The general sighed. "Yeah, I know. You deserve to enjoy your retirement with your family. Glad you still work with me, though. Helps me make all those important decisions."

"Yeah, I love working with you, man. We sure make a good team. Even though we all know you love hiding in that cave of yours to contemplate those important decisions all by yourself."

"Come on, Drew. I always consult you and ask for your opinions."

Drew smiled. "Yeah, mostly. But I assume you didn't call your best bud to discuss work, did you?"

"You know me well, Drew."

"Of course, I do. That's what best friends are for. So, spill it, Cave Man."

The general sighed. "Tonight, at the ROTC ball, a young cadet proposed to his girlfriend. In Spanish. And, you know, it reminded me—"

"—of your wife, I know," Drew interrupted. "But Cave Man, she left you!"

"I know. But it wasn't her fault. And I miss her."

"Brad, you have to let go. She just packed her bags and left you. A long time ago!"

"I know."

"So stop thinking about her. She's your ex-wife. She won't come back. You got to move on. You have to forget her. Understood?"

"Yeah, I know. But tonight was strange. Brought back so many memories."

"You have to let go, Cave Man. I told you that years ago. She's gone. She left you. Packed her bags for good. You have to forget her! And I gotta sleep, man. Stop moping around and go to bed yourself. It's late."

"Yeah, you're right. I'll try harder to forget her."

Brad hung up and already knew that he was lying to his best friend, and to himself. After tonight, he knew he had to pick up the search again, the search for his ex-wife. Because he knew he couldn't forget her, or their past.

He just couldn't forget.

CHAPTER 3

"**F**orget it, boy," Keisha teased Jim. "They're not coming to Mai Tai's."

Jim, Nick, and Brandy looked at Keisha, then at Aaron and Maria. "Yeah, we're just going to head back to my place," Maria said.

"But we need to celebrate your engagement," protested Brandy, while Nick nodded enthusiastically.

"Let 'em go," Jim answered for the couple, "and celebrate in their own way."

Nick burst out into laughter as Jim winked at the group of friends. Maria just rolled her eyes. "Grow up, boys," she said, and pulled Aaron toward the parking garage.

The friends laughed, and parted ways for the night. Maria and Aaron strolled toward his old car, arm in arm. He opened the car door for Maria, who gave him a kiss and sat down.

He walked around the car and got into the driver's seat. She looked at him. "Can I finally call my mamá now?"

Aaron grinned and nodded, then drove them home while his new fiancée chatted away on her phone. He listened closely but barely understood a word the love of his life was saying to her beloved mom.

Maria cuddled close to Aaron and watched his chest rise and fall. She listened to his slow, content breathing and smiled. *I'm so lucky. Aaron is such a good-looking guy, a wonderful friend, lover, and listener—well, when he isn't asleep, of course.* She giggled.

Yeah, I'm ready to spend my whole life with him, have a family with him some day, and be a part of his. Grace, his mom, is so sweet, his little sis Emma so much fun. And Jack is nice also. And I guess Jack will be my father then, too. Well, father-in-law.

She sighed and felt the sparkling engagement ring on her finger. *But who will walk me down the aisle? I don't have a father. He just . . . left. Didn't even want to get to know me. I don't even know his name. I know nothing about him. Not that I want to, anyway.* She frowned. *Guess I'll just walk down the aisle by myself!*

Her thoughts kept wandering until she finally fell asleep.

She slowly opened her little eyes to see where the swaying came from. She was being carried by strong arms, and contently snuggled up closer to them. She started sucking on her pacifier and dozed off to sleep again.

But what's that? She felt wet drips on her little face.

Why is it wet in my bed? Wet bed? Did I have an accident? Maybe go potty?

She opened her eyes and realized she was still being carried.

That's right. I'm still being carried. Where is Daddy taking me? Another road trip?

Now she was curious and not tired anymore. She perked up, but immediately was tucked in tighter.

What's that all about?

She tried to move her head to look up, but it got pushed down again.

I don't like that.

The wetness got worse, lots of drips now.

Rain?

She wanted to see and wiggled, but again was grasped so tightly that she almost couldn't breathe. As she struggled, she lost her pacifier.

No, not my Schnulli! I want it back.

She tried to turn her head to speak, but she got pushed into the strong arms that carried her, now more hastily. Her little mind was uneasy; she suddenly didn't feel safe in the big arms anymore.

Daddy? Please let me go.

All of the sudden, the wetness got worse, it was surrounding her, she tried to sit up, but was held down and suddenly swallowed a mouthful of water.

How can rain be that much? How long does it take to carry me to the car? Why doesn't Daddy let go? She looked for her pacifier. Where is Schnulli? I need it. Now.

More water. She gulped in another big mouthful. It tasted awful, like nothing she'd ever tasted before. She tried to speak, but the water kept coming. She panicked, kicked, screamed as the water surrounded her.

She couldn't breathe.

Mama? Daddy? Help me, help me!

Water was all over, swallowing up her little body as she was sinking deeper.. . . .

"Maria! Maria! Wake up!"

Maria opened her eyes, breathing heavily. It took her a few seconds to realize she was in her own bed in her college apartment, next to Aaron.

"Are you okay?" He looked at her, his eyes full of worry. "You must have had a nightmare." He pushed her wild hair out of her face. The hair stuck to her forehead, which was damp with sweat.

"Are you okay, Maria? I've never seen you like this."

Her eyes stared at him in bewilderment. "There was water, so much water. . . ."

"What? Water? You need water? Sure, I can get some water."

And before she could say anything else, he had hopped up to get a glass of water from her little kitchenette. Her eyes were well-adjusted to the darkness now. As she watched Aaron fill up a glass for her, she finally calmed down. When he came back and handed her the glass, she took two big gulps and felt better.

"Thank you. It was just a strange dream. Nothing more. Just a dream."

CHAPTER 4

Just a dream! It was just a dream! I dreamed about her again. My ex-wife.

The sun was just rising as Brad rolled out of bed. He had always been an early bird and loved getting up with the golden sunlight. *The world looks so peaceful, so bright and golden in the mornings.* He was tired after his trip, but knew that a strong cup of black coffee would definitely help. Once it was brewed, he grabbed the steaming cup of coffee and walked out to sit on the front porch, just enjoying the quiet and the start of a new day.

A big, bright ball, the sun rose up over the bushes in front of his porch. The golden sunlight blinded him and he had to close his eyes. As usual, a picture formed behind his eyelids from a long-ago time, a picture of pure happiness.

He was sitting outside with his wife, watching the sunrise, one hand intertwined with hers, the other one holding a steaming cup of coffee, her head on his shoulder . . . just enjoying the moment.

The picture in his mind faded. He opened his eyes again and stared into the bush in front of his porch. His porch with just one chair. A beautiful porch to a big, empty house. Nothing in there, nothing but books, papers, and awards that had started to dust over. The golden sunlight shone down on him.

Mocking me. Just mocking me. I know the world isn't as peaceful as it looks! Look at everything: My life. All the wars. All those innocent little lives being destroyed every day. Have I really helped make the world a better place?

The general thought of all his deployments to both Iraq and Afghanistan. He had seen a lot: Poor, innocent civilians who could barely survive inside their own war-torn country. Families who had lost their children due to war or starvation, or were forced to give them to the Taliban for indoctrination.

He felt those families' pain. And those kids always got to him; their stories haunted him. He'd needed at least one success story involving kids. So, he had started many projects that gave little boys and girls the opportunity to stay with their families and live a better life. He'd even managed to get some young boys out of the Taliban camps and returned them to their families—he had a gold-star medal to prove it.

But I'm a failure. An empty shell playing a role. Nothing more. I'm a failure.

The sun shone down on him, trying to warm his heart, but it was broken, never to be fixed again. As with so many mornings before, he'd tried to start his day in a positive way, desperately trying to feel normal.

He'd failed again.

The coffee cup slipped out of his hand, hit the hard concrete floor of his front porch, and broke into a million pieces. Black coffee splattered over everything.

"Damn it!"

He got out of his chair and kneeled to clean it up, but as he stared at the broken pieces in the black, hot liquid, he broke down himself, sobbing like a little child.

His head bobbed up and down with each deep sob. *I miss her. I miss them so much.*

As the golden sun rose higher in the sky, shining down on him, he looked up again and suddenly found hope. As if giving one of his pep talks, he started encouraging himself. "Drew was right, it's been too long, way too long since she left. I can't forget her, but I *can* do something about it. Get it together. Yes I can!"

Over the years, he had googled her, saved every detail of information about her. About Elisabeth. He knew he had to contact her.

It's been twenty years. It's time. I have to apologize to her.

More determined than ever, Brad picked up the pieces and went inside.

CHAPTER 5

Hours and thousands of miles away, Elisabeth was sitting on her tiny balcony with a steaming cup of black coffee in her hand. She looked sternly into the blue sky lit by the high sun. Her tiny apartment's balcony overlooked a park and she saw people biking, walking, running, roller-blading, and enjoying picnics this lovely day.

Will I ever enjoy doing anything again? Like a picnic in a park. Just hanging out? It's been years since I've enjoyed my free time. I love teaching, though. Love those little first graders. But they move on, grow up, and then are gone. So fast. Like my current class. Soon, they won't be my kids anymore. They'll move on after summer break.

She sighed and sipped her coffee. A small family caught her eye, a family of three: a husband, a wife, a little toddler. The little one skipped ahead, her pigtails bobbing up and down. Elisabeth watched in delight as the little girl went further and further ahead of her parents and turned a corner right by a big bush.

Suddenly, she saw an older guy standing right behind the bush. Elisabeth stood up. She hadn't seen him in the park before. Her hands started trembling.

Oh my goodness, little girl! No, watch out little girl! He's going to get you! He'll take you!

Sweat formed on her forehead as the little girl hopped right on ahead around the bush; her parents were oblivious. That's when the man stepped right in front of the little girl. Elisabeth screamed. Her coffee cup slipped out of her hand and fell to the floor.

"Opa!" the little girl yelled with a big grin on her face before she bounced into the man's arms. Elisabeth saw her parents catch up with their little one and watched as they greeted the elderly man with a hug.

Oh my gosh, it's just her Opa. Her grandpa. Just her grandpa. She's alright. She's okay.

A tear ran down her stern face and dripped off her elegant nose, right onto her bare foot. The wetness on her foot made her look down, and she finally noticed the coffee cup. It had broken into a thousand little pieces with black coffee pouring off the balcony's ledge. As she bent down to pick up the pieces, she started sobbing.

I wish I still had a family. I wish. Maybe it could have been, maybe? But you *didn't believe me. You didn't. You threw yourself into your work, kept flying and flying, far away from our problems, high above the clouds, far away from me. I had to leave. I had to leave you. But maybe you were right. Maybe. Maybe everyone was right.*

She's dead.

Elisabeth sank down to the floor and cried next to her broken coffee cup, broken into a thousand little pieces.

CHAPTER 6

A big cup of black coffee clutched firmly in hand, Maria sat by the window in her small apartment and watched the sunrise. She loved the early mornings, the quietness of them.

I definitely want a porch and a balcony when I get my own house. Or both.

She smiled and sipped her steaming cup of coffee. A glimmer caught her eye and she glanced down at her left hand; the new engagement ring, sparkling in the morning sunlight.

I guess I'll need to make sure that's what Aaron wants as well. She turned around and looked over her shoulder. Aaron was still in a deep sleep this Sunday morning. *He deserves it. He's usually up so early for his ROTC training. Poor guy. My sweet Aaron. My fiancé. Fiancé. Wow, that still sounds so strange.*

The golden sunlight passed through the diamond of her ring and threw a thousand little bright spots all around her. Maria sighed.

Wish I could show Mamá not just on FaceTime but in real life. My sweet mamá. She's so excited. She likes Aaron, I know she does. She's only met him a few times, but I know she approves. Told her everything about him. Glad I don't need to keep anything from her. No, not from Mamá. We have a special bond. Just us two my whole life. We share everything; we don't have any secrets.

Maria felt a hand on her shoulder and flinched.

"Good morning, my love," Aaron said, laughing, and leaned in to give her a kiss on the cheek. "I'm sorry I startled you. Remember me, your fiancé?"

"Of course I do, silly. Do you want some coffee?"

"Yes, please. Do you need a refill?"

"Sure."

He took the cup out of her hand. "I'll get it. No need to get up. I know you love watching the sunrise. Enjoy."

She gave him a big kiss. "Thanks, my love."

He walked over to the little kitchenette, filled up her cup with coffee, and poured himself half a cup. He opened the fridge and started searching. "Hey, Maria, do you have any creamer?"

"Creamer? For what?"

"My coffee, of course," Aaron said, "Most people can't drink it black like you." He shook his head in disgust. "Black bean water. Ugh. I need it nice and creamy."

"Ah," she sighed, "you're just like Mamá. Creamer is not good for you in the long run. A bunch of sugar. Sorry, I don't have any, but I do have some regular milk. Just make sure you don't have a big cup of milk with a little coffee for 'creamer.'"

"Ha, ha, very funny!"

He walked back over to where she was sitting and looked out the window. She took the cup from him, and he plopped down onto the soft blue carpet next to her desk chair.

"Oh, we can sit at the table. You don't have to sit on the floor."

"I don't mind, Maria. This carpet is beautiful. You're lucky to have your own place."

"I know. Housing allowance sure is a great thing!" She smiled.

He winked at her. "Yeah, for sure. Guess a full-ride scholarship for your human factor studies is quite convenient, isn't it?"

She laughed. "It sure is. And after that first year in those crowded dorms, I just had to get out of there."

He smirked. "Yeah, I get it. Dorm life is *quite* the experience."

They both laughed.

"But you found a nice place too, though. You can't really complain—the Air Force is paying for your housing. You just chose to have a roommate. Luckily, Nick is a great roomie."

"True, he is. I think I'd get lonely without anyone around."

Maria looked at him and pouted. "Aw, poor lonely Aaron."

"Ha, ha, very funny. I'm just not as independent as you."

"Very true," she laughed. "Well, it's certainly super helpful having my own place whenever I'm tutoring. The high schoolers just love coming here instead of hanging out at their parents'. And it's less stressful. Whenever I'm at their homes, their parents constantly peek in to make sure they're learning something."

Aaron sipped his creamy coffee and nodded. "But who makes sure they learn something when they're *here*?"

"I do! You know I do," she protested.

He winked at her. "I know, I know. Just kidding. I know you're a good teacher. And responsible. And you really care about their success."

She smiled her biggest smile at him. "Yeah. Guess I get that caring gene from my mamá." She looked at her ring again.

"You wish you could see her and show off that new little ring of yours, don't you?"

She looked up at him and nodded.

"I figured. Well, better finish that coffee and get ready quickly then."

"What?"

"I just so happen to have an invitation for eating quesillo and catalinas!"

Surprised, Maria looked at him. *Why is he talking about Venezuelan desserts?* "What are you talking about?"

Aaron jumped up and grinned. "We're going to Miami, silly! Ready to see your mamá and the rest of the family and show them that ring in person?"

She looked at him. *No way! He actually organized all this behind my back with Mamá? My cousin Stephanie was right; he's quite the catch.*

She grinned and looked at her handsome fiancé. She gave him a big, warm kiss.

"Alright then," he said, "I'll take that as a 'yes.'"

Maria started singing. "'I'm goin to Miami, welcome to Miami.'"

"Here we are," Maria yelled. She rolled down the window and started waving frantically. Her mom was waving back from her apartment balcony. "Just park here on the street."

Aaron looked around. "I'm trying, but it's busy. Cars everywhere."

"Well, it's Miami. What do you expect, it's a big city."

"Yeah, big city with tiny streets and even tinier parking spaces." Aaron slowed way down, searching for a parking spot along the street. Someone honked at him.

"Just calm down, idiot. I'm trying to park here!"

Maria giggled. "Aw, little Aaron isn't in Montana anymore, is he?"

"If I were, I would just use a big, fat pickup truck and push all these tiny cars out of the way."

Maria laughed. "No, you wouldn't. Because you're Mr. Nice Guy."

He nodded and managed to squeeze into a small spot on the side of the road opposite Maria's mother's home. By now, both of Maria's aunts, her two uncles, and the three cousins had all joined her mother on the balcony and were waving frantically.

"Wow, everyone's here?"

"Sure. When I told your mamá I was going to propose, she told me I had to bring you back here first thing to celebrate with family. You shouldn't be surprised at all." Aaron smirked and looked at her, then took her by the hand. "Come on, it's clear now. Run!"

They crossed the street and rang the doorbell.

"What made both of you so sure I was going to say yes?"

The door buzzed open.

"Because we both know you well."

He grinned and raced up the two flights of stairs. Maria followed, and before they had even arrived, the apartment's front door opened.

"¡Hola! Finally you are here!"

"Hola, Martina," Aaron greeted Maria's mom.

The small, round little woman with sparkling brown eyes and curly brown hair gave Aaron a big hug and one kiss on the cheek, as was custom in her home country. Maria's relatives lined up by the door.

"¡Hola, Aaron! ¡Hola, Maria!" The pair got hugged and kissed over and over again until they finally reached the couch.

"Let's see that ring, mija," Maria's mom said.

Maria lifted her left hand and showed it to everyone.

"¡Maravilloso! What a beautiful ring," Tía Monica exclaimed, and everyone agreed, except for the three high schoolers who sat on the couch staring at their phones.

Tía Monica and Tía Mariella sighed. "Niños, at least acknowledge your cousin Maria's wonderful ring!"

They briefly looked up. "Yeah, maravilloso," they said in unison. Maria's aunts rolled their eyes while everyone else laughed.

"Aaron, how is the military training going?" Maria's uncle Mauricio asked.

"Oh, it's going well, thank you. We just did a sunrise formation run on the beach on Friday."

"Wow, that's cool," Maria's cousin Rolando said.

"Ha, look at that. Now you're listening?" Maria teased him. "Thought you were too busy with your phone."

"Well, military training stories are much cooler than a ring."

They all laughed and Aaron told them more stories about his ROTC training. Maria left the boys to it and walked into the kitchen to join her mamá, Tía Monica, and Tía Mariella, who were busy getting all the treats together. They chitchatted eagerly in Spanish while making coffee.

Back in the living room, Tío Mauricio, who sat next to Maria's other uncle Eduardo at the table, asked impatiently, "¿Cuando está lista la comida?" But the women in the kitchen were talking too loudly and couldn't hear him.

Aaron got up. "I'll go ask when the food will be ready, Mr. Santos."

"You speak Spanish?" Mauricio seemed shocked that Aaron had understood his question.

"Well, I'm a self-taught beginner," Aaron explained with a smile and walked toward the kitchen.

"Mmmh. . . .He might be okay, I think," Mauricio whispered to Eduardo. "I kinda like him."

"Me, too. So far, so good! Should be alright for our little Maria," Eduardo said.

Before the two uncles could finish their secret conversation, the ladies returned with platters full of famous Venezuelan-style desserts and goodies. A pot of coffee was brought out and Maria's mom Martina happily poured everyone a cup—half a cup, to be exact—leaving enough room for plenty of creamer.

"And one full cup of just-black coffee for our mija Maria," Martina said, amused.

"I know, I know, I'm very different. But I like black coffee."

"Ugh, yucky," the majority exclaimed, and they all laughed.

"Please, everyone, eat up!"

Maria's mamá proudly put a plate full of every type of dessert together for Aaron. He ogled the plate heaped with sugar then politely took it. "Gracias, Martina."

Maria giggled and whispered in his ear: "I hope you're hungry; it's rude not to finish it all. But make sure to leave a little bite on there unless you wanna be served seconds."

"Got it, thanks for the warning," he whispered back.

"And now, time for cocuy!" Maria's mom held up a bottle of liquor.

"Cocuy? What's that?"

"It's the only liquor native to Venezuela. A very special drink," Maria explained.

"Sí, especial," Maria's mom said, her eyes sparkling. "For a very special occasion! For our newly engaged couple! We are so excited!"

Maria's mom poured everyone a shot of liquor, and Aaron once again looked a bit puzzled. "Your cousins are underage," he whispered to Maria.

"Well, they're close enough to eighteen. Besides, a drinking age of twenty-one is totally silly! My cousins are learning to drink responsibly and enjoy it rather than binge-drink at a party."

Aaron nodded, then raised his glass with everyone.

"¡Salud!" they all toasted.

Aaron poured it down his throat. It was strong, but tasty.

"¿Uno mas?" Tío Mauricio asked Aaron, inviting him to sit with the uncles. Aaron nodded and joined them, and Mauricio poured him another shot.

"Gracias, Mr. Santos."

"No 'Mr. Santos,'" he said to Aaron, "Mauricio. Please, call me Mauricio!"

Aaron smiled and cheered with both of Maria's uncles.

"¿Uno mas?" Eduardo asked.

Aaron thought for a bit, then nodded.

Maria looked at him, then at her uncles. "Don't make him sick, tíos."

"Ah, no," they smiled in unison, "Gringo and us are drinking buddies now. He can handle it!"

The guys all laughed. Maria rolled her eyes and went over to the kitchen to help her mom and aunts with the dishes.

When the ladies finally returned from the kitchen, Aaron and the two uncles were busy poring over important-looking papers.

"What's this?" Maria asked.

"La autorización de seguridad," Tío Eduardo explained. "This young man of yours needs information from us for his job."

"What? Really?"

"Well, now that we are engaged," Aaron explained, "I need to collect your relatives' personal information for my security clearance with the Air Force. I need to put down all my close contacts. Remember when I told you I'd need your birth certificate for the clearance?"

"Oh yeah, I remember we briefly talked about it. But I thought it was just *my* information. This is a lot to ask of my family, Aaron!"

"I'm sorry, Maria. But everyone here's now considered a close contact."

"It's alright, mijo," Maria's mom said. "Here, Aaron, here's Maria's birth certificate."

"Gracias, Martina." Aaron quickly packed it into a neat folder.

"Aaron, I don't like that they need all this information."

"Maria, I'm sorry, but it's protocol. Like I said, the government considers your whole family close contacts now that we're engaged."

Maria walked over and inspected the paperwork. "Oh my gosh, this looks intense. More than I thought. You really need everyone's social security number? That's kinda private."

"Maria, mija, we don't mind helping this young fella," the uncles said. "He's a good one, Maria. We like him."

She looked back and forth at her uncles and then at Aaron. Maria's mom came over and put her arm around Maria.

"Sí. He's a good guy. Good for our mija. We don't mind helping."

Embraced by her mom's hug, Maria calmed down. *I'm glad everyone approves of my choice. Yeah, Aaron is a great guy.* But as she watched Aaron and her uncles fill out the security clearance paperwork, she still didn't have a good feeling about it.

"Can I have another cup of coffee before we hit the road?" Maria asked her mom while washing the dishes from their dinner.

"Sure, mija," her mamá said and started brewing some. "Will you drive tonight?"

"I better. I'm not sure how much liquor Aaron actually had. And the Air Force doesn't cut the cadets any slack when it comes to drinking and driving. A DUI is usually a career-killer. And you know Aaron— he doesn't bend the rules or take any chances."

Her mom nodded and poured Maria a big cup of black coffee. Together, they walked outside onto the balcony and joined Maria's aunts. While the older women talked, Maria looked at the coffee.

Finally, she said, "Did my dad like black coffee?"

The three ladies stared at her in bewilderment. Her mom threw up her hands. "¡Naguará! We do *not* talk about your father!"

"But Mamá, I just want to know. I don't know anything about him."

"No! Let the past be the past."

"Mamá, it's a simple—"

"No, I told you, no!"

Her aunts looked down at the floor.

"Mamá, I don't know anything about him and we—"

"*No.* Just you and I. Hear me? Just you and I. Leave it."

Martina stared out into the distance at nothing, her features stern.

"Mamá, I have a right . . ."

"No, Maria, no." The elderly lady's voice was loud and cold; the spark in her beautiful brown eyes was all but gone. She quickly grabbed the half-finished cup out of Maria's hand. "¡Vamos! Time to go. You better drive back now. It's a long trip." She hurried inside with the half-finished cup of black coffee.

Maria stared in disbelief, then turned to her aunts. "Tía Monica, Tía Mariella, why can't we talk about my father? I don't even want to meet him, but I know nothing. Not even his name. Why is it such a bad topic?"

"Maria," Tía Monica said gently, "your mamá was badly hurt and—"

"I know, it wasn't easy being abandoned and having to raise me all alone."

"No, Maria," Tía Mariella explained, "your mamá wasn't hurt by him leaving. The leaving was actually a good thing. But let the past be the past and don't bring back those memories to her. It'll hurt her all over again."

Maria stared at her aunts. *I have so many questions. But I better leave this topic alone for now.*

She sighed, got up, and went inside to find her mom. She found her in the kitchen, pouring the coffee down the drain.

"Mamá, I was still drinking that!"

"No, not anymore." Martina's face was flushed. She put her hands on her hips. "You need to go now. You have class tomorrow. Vamos."

Maria stared at her mom, hardly able to believe how she was behaving. The small, little woman pushed her out of the kitchen, grabbed Maria's purse from the hanger by the door, and handed it to Maria.

Maria started protesting.

"No, Maria, no," Martina said and yelled across the room, "Aaron, it's time to go. ¡Vamos!"

Aaron looked up from the middle of his conversation with the uncles, one of his eyebrows raised. "We're leaving? Now?"

The uncles looked at Martina, then at Maria. "Maria, mija, why are you guys leaving already?"

"Well, Tío Mauricio, I wasn't going to—"

"Because it's late and they both have class tomorrow," Martina interrupted. "Come on, Aaron. Pack up. ¡Vamos!"

Puzzled, Aaron picked up the paperwork spread across the table and put it in his blue folder. He walked over to Maria, handed her his car keys, and put the folder in her purse. "Okay, let's go then." Maria sighed. "I guess." She looked up at her mom as she put her shoes on. "Mamá? Must we really go now?"

"Sí, it's late!" She quickly squeezed Maria, then gave a long, warm hug to Aaron.

Maria rolled her eyes. *This is unbelievable.*

The rest of her family gave her a warm embrace, and when Maria received a hug from her Tía Monica, she felt her press something cold into her hands. She looked down to see a travel mug.

"Coffee for the drive. Don't let your mom see, okay, mija? I'm sorry," Monica whispered in her ear.

Maria smiled at her aunt, took the mug, and kept it out of sight as they ran across the street. Maria took the wheel of Aaron's car. Looking out the windshield, they saw Maria's whole family crowded in on the tiny balcony, waving to them. Only her mamá was missing. Maria sighed, then rolled down the windows, honked loudly, and waved goodbye until they turned the corner.

She glanced over at Aaron. "You okay?"

"I think so. Just a little sick. Stuffed from all the food and, man, those tiny drinks have more alcohol in them than you'd believe." He looked a little green.

She laughed. "Well, you're drinking buddies with my uncles now. They're quite the drinkers when they want to be!"

"No kidding." Aaron closed his eyes. "Thanks for driving tonight. I did have fun. And got a lot done on my security clearance paperwork. It's due this week. Now I just need all of your information."

"Let's go over it after class tomorrow," Maria suggested.

Aaron nodded and looked at Maria. "You okay? What happened with your mom? She seemed upset with you. I thought she was excited about us?"

"She *is* excited about us. She just got mad at something I said. No worries, she sure loves you."

Aaron let out a sigh of relief. "Oh, okay, that's good," he whispered before dozing off to sleep.

Maria chuckled. *Knew he had way too much to drink. Well, he'll feel better soon.*

She turned on the radio and settled in for the long drive home, the ring on her finger sparkling in the moonlight. She took a sip of her black coffee and sighed. *Mama's reaction tonight was odd. Why can't I talk with her about my father at all? Don't even want to know much about him. I just know nothing. Why can't I even ask a simple question about him?*

She wasn't sure, but by the time they got home she'd become determined to find out.

CHAPTER 7

Maria and Keisha were sitting in the little café on campus with some treats and an afternoon coffee. Their school day was over and they were waiting for the boys' to be done as well.

"Girl, what's up?" Keisha said.

Maria looked at her. "What do you mean?"

"You're quiet today. What's going on? Everything alright?"

Maria took a sip of her coffee. Her *black* coffee. She snorted. Keisha looked at her, surprised.

"Well, I guess I shouldn't drink black coffee."

"What? You always drink black coffee. So do I. Why? What's wrong with that?"

"I'm the only one in my family who drinks black coffee."

Keisha still didn't understand, so Maria told her all about the engagement party and the silly fight with her mom.

"Seems like your mom overreacted, girl."

Maria nodded. "Yeah, but why?"

Keisha shrugged her shoulders. "Well, ex-husbands are a bad topic for anyone. My mom doesn't like to talk about my dad much."

Maria nodded. "Yeah, I know. But you *know* him. You spent weekends with him. You got to grow up with him."

"Yeah, with him and his new family. Wasn't always fun."

"I know that, Keisha. I'm sorry. It's just . . . I just . . ."

"Don't know anything about him? Is that it?"

"Yeah, I guess."

"Girl, I thought you don't want to know him. You always said you don't need him. You said he was an idiot."

Maria nodded and took another sip of her coffee.

"Why now, girl? What changed?"

Maria shrugged her shoulders, then took two big gulps of her coffee. "I guess it's just strange to know I'll have to walk down the aisle by myself."

Keisha looked at her. Then took her hand. "Oh, Maria, that's okay. I know you like silly traditions like that, but I think it's much cooler if the bride walks by herself. Or maybe dance down the aisle? Like with your best friend, for example?" Keisha moved her shoulders to a silent beat.

Maria couldn't help but laugh. "Yeah, that would be fun. But you know . . ."

"What?"

"I can't stop thinking about my aunts' comments last night. Said my dad leaving was actually a good thing. Do you think he was abusive?"

The color left Keisha's face. "I don't know, girl."

Maria stared at her. "Think about it. That would totally explain why Mamá doesn't want to talk about him at all. She must have been totally scarred by the experience. Survivors of abuse often cope by trying to forget about it, bury it deep down in their brain and not think about the pain the abuse caused. 'Let the past be the past.' Mmm. I guess that would make sense. Why didn't I think of this sooner?"

Keisha's face regained its color. "I don't know, girl. But if that's the truth, your mamá probably needs therapy to really get over it. Depending on how bad it was."

"Keisha, how can I find out what really happened?"

"I have no idea."

The girls both sighed and sipped their coffees, each of them lost in thought.

"Hey, ladies," Nick greeted the girls. "We've got big news!"

Startled, Maria and Keisha turned around to find the three boys standing before them in their handsome cadet uniform. They were each clutching an important-looking paper in their hands. "We got our assignments!"

Keisha and Maria looked at each other, their prior conversation immediately forgotten.

"Oh my gosh, that *is* big news! Let's hear it," Maria said.

Nick shook his head. "I can't tell you guys before I speak to Brandy. I better wait until she's done with class. I'm gonna go pick her up."

"That's sweet, Nick," Keisha said, then looked at Aaron and Jim. "But you guys can tell us, right?"

The boys all looked at each other and nodded. Nick left, and Jim and Aaron sat down with their girlfriends.

Jim went first. "I got a fighter pilot spot!" The girls clapped and congratulated him. "That means I have to go to pilot training for a few months. It's in Texas."

Keisha looked upset—*very* upset. "Texas? That's like a thousand miles away!"

"I know, baby," Jim said, "but it's only for a few months. Then I get to go to the special forces base in Tampa, Florida for more training the next three years." He grinned a big grin.

"Wow, Tampa, that's great, Keisha," Maria told her bestie, who immediately relaxed a little bit.

"Tampa isn't far from here at all." Keisha smiled and hugged Jim tightly.

Maria was happy for them. She looked at Aaron. "So, what about you?"

"Well," Aaron started, "I didn't make it to pilot training, but I will be going into maintenance. Working on jets and so on."

Maria studied his face. *Aha, that's why he's upset. He wants to be a pilot, but his slight color-vision problem is an issue with the Air Force.*

He looked at Maria. "I'll be stationed at Eglin."

"Eg . . . what?" None of the girls knew where that place was.

"Eglin Air Force Base. It's close to Fort Walton Beach, in Florida's panhandle."

Maria's eyes lit up with a glimmer of hope. "That's not too far from here either, right?"

Aaron smiled. "No, only about a six-hour drive."

Maria hugged him tightly, gave him a big kiss, and whispered in his ear, "I'm proud of you, Aaron. Maintenance sounds like a fun job for you. You majored in engineering, so it's perfect. Don't be upset. You'll always be my hero."

He hugged her tighter. "Thank you."

Jim and Keisha were already looking at a map that the boys had brought with them. They chatted away, comparing how far apart the different military bases were.

Maria stared at the little dot on the map of Florida's panhandle. *Eglin AFB*, it read.

Eglin AFB? That sounds familiar. I've heard it before. Did Aaron talk about it? She couldn't quite remember. *Have I read about it before? Learned about it in school? Possibly. But when? Huh. Eglin AFB. Sounds fun. And not too far from here. Eglin AFB.*

Her brain repeated the words over and over and over again. Got stuck on them. *Why do those unusual words seem so familiar? Eglin AFB.*

"It's right on the water, you know. Surrounded by water, actually," Aaron explained when Maria finally focused on the conversation at hand.

"Eglin has beautiful white beaches," Jim told the group, "And the AF even owns their own little patch of beach there. Families seem to like it a lot. Shallow water for miles."

Keisha giggled. "Families, did you hear that, girl? Shallow water will be great for having a good time with a little baby maybe?"

Aaron raised his hands. "Whoa, whoa, hold your horses. We just got engaged!"

Jim and Keisha giggled, but Maria was far away in her own thoughts. *Eglin AFB. Surrounded by water. Little baby girl. Surrounded by water. Help!*

"Maria? Maria?" Aaron's voice eventually made its way into her ear. "You okay? Daydreaming away here." He gave her a little elbow knock.

Maria looked at him absentmindedly. "Sure, yes, I'm okay. Just processing information here. Eglin sounds great, Aaron. I can't wait to check it out."

But despite her words, for some reason the name sent chills down her spine.

CHAPTER 8

Elisabeth stared at the old crumbly picture of a dad and his daughter walking together on a wide beach with white sand. She studied the emerald-green water in the background and sighed, then took another sip of her wine. Two, three, a big gulp. It was late, but she often sat out on her balcony whenever the weather allowed. She enjoyed seeing the night sky and the faint lights in the park below almost as much as she enjoyed the mornings.

At least there's a few things I still enjoy. Ah, but those beaches were so pretty. Likely still are, I imagine. Beautiful spot. But it's in the past, and I will never return.

She clenched her elegant wine glass and went to take another big gulp, only to realize it was empty. She had drunk too much. She remembered the days when she got giggly after one glass; now a whole bottle made her feel nothing.

In training, I'm a well-trained drinker by now. She shook her head. *Sad. Isn't the kind of training I should be proud of. No, definitely not. I should be ashamed. It's just so hard. So hard to go on without them. So hard to hate him. But hating him is easier than admitting she's dead.*

Elisabeth looked at the old picture again, then at her empty glass. Suddenly, the doorbell rang shrill. It startled her so much that the wine glass slipped out of her hand and broke into a thousand pieces.

"Oh nein!"

She stared at the broken glass and sighed. *Not again! More broken pieces that I can never fix.*

She got up to clean the mess when the doorbell rang again. *What in the world? Who's coming to visit me at this hour? It's after ten p.m.*

The doorbell rang a third time, startling her once more. The picture slipped out of her hand and fell to the balcony floor without her noticing. Quickly, Elisabeth ran inside to see who was at the door.

"Sarah, what are you doing here?"

"Hallo Elisabeth, I have a surprise for you!"

"A surprise? For me?"

"Of course *for you*. A fun surprise for my best friend," Sarah said, and pushed past her into the little apartment. She then noticed the open sliding door. "Oh, you were just sitting outside on the balcony?"

Elisabeth nodded.

"How lovely, let's sit there," Sarah decided for both of them, and made her way toward the sliding door.

"No, wait! There's broken glass all over. You really startled me with that doorbell."

Sarah looked at her and laughed. "You want me to slip in quietly next time?"

"No, that would startle me even more!"

"Exactly."

Elisabeth smirked.

"Ha, got you to smile," Sarah said, and went into the small kitchen to find a broom and dustpan. "I'll help you clean up."

They grabbed the cleaning supplies they needed and headed toward the balcony. Sarah had started sweeping when she found a piece of paper in the broken glass. She picked it up and looked at it.

"Elisabeth, oh Elisabeth. You have to move on."

Elisabeth came over and quickly grabbed the picture out of her friend's hand. "You know I can't do that," she snapped.

Sarah and Elisabeth silently finished cleaning and then sat on the balcony, each sporting a fresh, unbroken glass of wine in their hands.

"So, what's your surprise?"

"How many glasses have you had already?" Sarah asked instead of answering.

Elisabeth thought about it.

"Don't know. Four, maybe five."

Sarah sighed. "Well, that makes me even more sure this surprise will be in your best interest."

Elisabeth raised her eyebrows. She was a bit curious for sure, even though she really didn't enjoy surprises. Her friend took a deep breath, then blurted out, "We're flying to America next month!"

Elisabeth stared at her. The wine glass slipped, but she caught it this time. "I'm not going. Definitely not."

"Yes, you are. Already have your ticket." Sarah pulled a piece of paper out of her purse. She showed it to Elisabeth. It was a printout of an e-ticket.

No way. That's my name there on it.

"How did you get my passport information?" Elisabeth wondered aloud. All her info had been filled in on the ticket.

Sarah took a neat red passport out of her purse. "Borrowed it." She handed it back to Elisabeth.

"I didn't give you permission to take my passport. That's important information on there. You stole it!"

"Oh, come on, Elisabeth. You didn't even notice, did you? After all, you've never used it. Well, now you will. With me. Next month. Already booked. Two weeks. During Pentecost break."

Elisabeth stared. She couldn't believe it. *It's all planned out already. But I can't go. Not to America. The United States. Land of the free. Land of thieves. Thieves that stole my life away from me.*

56

Then she noticed the destination. VPS.

Her hands started shaking. *I don't have to google that. I know what it stands for. I'll never forget those three letters. VPS. Valparaiso Airport. Destin-Fort Walton Beach. Right next to Eglin Air Force Base.*

She threw the paper at Sarah. "No, I'm not going! Hear me? I am *not* going! Never again! I'm not going back!"

"Elisabeth, it's been twenty years. *Exactly* twenty years. It's time to move on. You *have* to let go. Have to let go of all of your pain over the past. I'll go with you, I'll be there for you. We will face it together. I'll be there, holding your hand."

"Nein, nein, nein! I should be holding *her* little hand. Hers, not yours. Should've been holding her hand for the last twenty years. But I'll never hold her again, my sweet baby girl. Never. Cuz she's *dead*."

Sobbing, Elisabeth slipped out of the chair onto her knees. She looked into the night sky, the stars above; grief overcame her. She pulled out the picture again, the picture of her ex-husband and her little girl. The one that she had lost in just eight minutes. Her heart had broken, never to be healed again. She sobbed loudly.

Sarah sank down next to her, put an arm around her, and held her frail frame tightly. She rocked her gently back and forth.

"You have to let her go, Elisabeth. Keep the memories, but let the pain go. Bury the pain. Right there, on that sandy white beach. I'll go with you. We can bring whatever you want, and we'll bury it there. You can't live like this forever. None of them would have wanted you to live like this." Sarah pointed at the picture. "They'd want you to be happy."

Elisabeth looked at the picture, big tears running down her beautiful, freckled nose. "Do it for them," she heard her friend urge her.

For them. For my family.

"Okay, I'll think about it," she whispered quietly. "I'll think about it."

Sarah nodded and hugged her tightly and they sat there, watching the stars late into the night.

Elisabeth waved goodbye to Sarah and slowly closed the door to her apartment. She went back to the balcony to clean up the glasses. The unused red passport was still laying there, the e-ticket inside. She glanced at it as she brought in the wine glasses, then returned to the balcony to pick up the passport and the old crumbly picture. She took both inside, then closed the door and drew the curtains.

It was pitch-black now, but her eyes adjusted to the darkness. She walked over to her office and turned on the desk lamp. It shone on the many books she owned, and illuminated a bunch of papers with scribbles of first graders on them.

She smiled. *I love my kids. Yes,* my *kids. When I teach them, they're all my kids.*

She found an empty space on her desk to put the passport, e-ticket, and picture on. She was about to turn off the lamp when she saw it. The bright light was shining directly on the picture, illuminating the emerald-green water, and it suddenly dawned on her. Her fingers touched the picture, touched its emerald-green water, touched his face, and she started talking to the man in the picture, her ex-husband.

"Oh, Brad. I see it now. I finally understand why we weren't able to talk anymore. Why we weren't able to communicate. Why you were always flying, always working. I see it now, Brad. The emerald green. The emerald green your eyes turned to permanently, right after she disappeared. I'm an idiot. The color of your eyes should've told me how much you were agitated and disturbed. You drowned with her—in that emerald-green water."

A big tear ran down her face. She saw the ticket to America and suddenly knew what she needed to do. *I have to email him, let him know I'm not mad anymore. Let him know I finally understand why he threw himself into work rather than support me in my search.* She sighed. *And I need to tell him that he's right. She's dead. Gone forever.*

Determined, Elisabeth pulled out a drawer—the drawer where she kept all the information on him, on her ex-husband. She had printed it out a while ago. Had followed his career. She knew he'd never remarried. The evidence was clear on that.

I still love him. So much. Need to see him again. Tell him I'm sorry, tell him I miss him. Maybe he can meet me in Florida? It'll be exactly twenty years later—twenty years since our divorce, twenty years since her disappearance. We can bury her there together, bury the past there together.

She turned on her computer and pulled out his email address, hoping he hadn't changed it. Then she started writing to him. Her ex-husband. The love of her life.

CHAPTER 9

Maria was gazing at the love of her life when she caught her engagement ring sparkling in the sunset. She grinned. They were walking to the campus parking lot, hand in hand.

He looked at her. "So, what's your plan for tonight?"

"I still have to go over my notes from class."

Aaron looked disappointed. "I thought we could talk more about my assignment? Maybe fill out my security clearance? Since I'll be working on F-35s, I'll need a higher one. So that's kind of cool."

"What do you mean, 'a higher one?'"

"Top secret security clearance instead of just secret," he said proudly.

Maria burst into laughter. "Okay then, Mr. Top Secret, let's head over to my place. I suppose I did promise you we'd go over your paperwork."

Aaron smiled and gave her a big kiss. "Yes, you did, ma'am. Well, hop into my car and let's go."

Aaron searched his bag, then pulled out a bunch of paperwork that he laid out on the kitchen table. Maria looked at it while he explained the different parts to her.

With a serious look on her face, she asked Aaron, "Are we holding you back?"

"What do you mean?"

"My family. All immigrants, all those former ties to Venezuela. Is that a problem for your job? Most of my family falls under 'foreign contacts' since they weren't born in the United States. So, is that an issue?"

"Well," Aaron mumbled, "Not really. . . ."

Maria studied his face. "'Not really' means 'yes' here, I think."

"Maria, don't worry about it. All of you are citizens now, which really helps, and you're the most important contact of the bunch. And you're actually American. And *just* American, right? Not a dual citizen?"

Maria thought for a bit. "I don't think so. Mamá never wants to go back to Venezuela, so I don't think she got my birth registered over there."

"Okay, good." Aaron marked something on his paper. They continued, filling in her social security number and other information.

"'Spouse-like relationship with Maria Sullivan?'" she asked, surprised. "That's weird wording."

"I know, but it was prefilled out by the security people."

"Prefilled?" Maria couldn't believe it.

"Yeah, I guess they know we've been dating for a while."

"Oh my gosh, is someone spying on us?" Maria walked to her window and looked out.

Aaron laughed out loud. "Come on, don't be silly. They just know certain things about their cadets already. Not that it's a secret. Pretty obvious you and I are dating. And now we're engaged. So, no worries, nobody is watching us!"

Aaron went over and hugged her. She relaxed a little bit, and they went back to the paperwork. Once the final form was complete, she noticed two colorful papers at the end.

"What's that?"

"Oh, they're our birth certificates," Aaron explained. "Mine and yours."

Maria pulled them out and looked at them. His was a bright blue while hers was more yellowish and faded. Maria felt them then compared them side by side.

"Mine seems so thin compared to yours."

"Yeah, I noticed that, too. But I guess, just like the different background colors, each state uses different kinds of paper. The most important thing is that there's an official seal printed on it."

Maria nodded. *I've never seen my birth certificate before. Mamá did that part of my college application.* She looked at it again. Black ink jumped out at her. *There it is. "Father: Jonathan Eric Sullivan." Wow. So my father's name is Jonathan.*

"Aaron, how can I find out more about my father?"

He stared at her. "You want to find out more? I thought you said you didn't want anything to do with him?"

"I know I did, and I don't. I just need to find out why Mamá got so upset with me last night when I asked about him. Is there any way we can find out if he was abusive?"

Aaron gawked. "*Abusive?* You think he was abusive? You never mentioned that."

"I know. Not sure if that's true, but my aunts mentioned something yesterday that made it seem like a possibility."

Aaron let out a deep breath. He packed away his security clearance paperwork and pulled out his laptop.

"Hey, I'm trying to have a conversation here. Why are you getting on your computer?"

"So we can look him up in the state's database. If your mom has ever brought charges against him, his name would show up on court records. And if not, we can at least google him."

Maria sat down, excited and nervous. *Duh! Google him! That's so obvious. Why didn't I think of that? Well, I didn't know his name up until just now. And I've never had the urge to do much research. But I'm curious now.*

It felt to her like hours passed as Aaron slowly typed her dad's name into the Florida Cases Database. He started his search and the loading circle spun, showing that the computer was searching for something. This second wait seemed even longer to Maria. She stared at the screen. So did Aaron.

"Oh my," he finally said as the search results flashed on the screen.

There were four different entries. All of them from over twenty years ago. Three of the entries shared the same caption; the words seemed to jump out at Maria like a slap to the face.

Domestic Abuse.

All color flushed out of Maria's face; her mouth went dry. "Oh my gosh, Aaron. My dad really *was* abusive. He hurt Mamá. Badly. So bad that she had to call the police?"

Aaron looked at her. She was ghostly white. "Well, at least someone called the police. Maybe the neighbors?"

"Maybe. Oh my. Poor Mamá, my poor, poor Mamá. She left Venezuela to find a better life, to be safe in the United States, the land of the free. And yet she was being hurt."

Maria's face regained color and flushed red. "What a jerk! Such an asshole! What did he do to her? What?"

Maria grabbed Aaron's laptop out of his hands and clicked frantically on the words *Domestic Abuse.* Aaron was irritated. "Maria, I've never heard you swear before. And what the heck are you doing now? I know it's concerning, but we have to stay calm."

Maria grumbled something else in Spanish and kept clicking frantically on the words.

"Maria, stop! The database only tells you who's in there and what offense category they fall under, not the details of what they've done."

Maria looked at him. "So I can't find out what this jerk did to my mom?"

"I'm afraid not. You can't. I'm sorry."

He put his arm around her and joined her in studying the entries. He raised an eyebrow. "Look at this." He pointed to the dates that followed the listed offense. "This was all way before you were born."

Maria followed Aaron's hand and saw it, too. In fact, it went back many years before she was born. The last entry read: *Legal Divorce.* A date followed.

Both of them stared at the date in disbelief.

Aaron found his words first. "Didn't your mom tell you your dad left her when she was pregnant with you?"

Maria nodded.

"Well, obviously that can't be true. According to this entry, Jonathan Sullivan divorced his wife three years before you were born."

"They must have got the date wrong."

Aaron raised an eyebrow again in that way only he could. Maria looked at him. *I've never met anyone who can actually raise just one eyebrow. But he can. Only when he's expressing deep disbelief.*

She ignored him and crossed her arms. "They must have put the wrong date. They must. Sloppy workers."

"Maria," Aaron said in a slow, calm voice, "I don't think they got the date wrong. It lines up with all the other dates shown here."

"But not my birthdate. So it can't be true."

"Unless . . ."

"Unless what? There's no explanation other than that the silly bureaucracy got the dates wrong."

Aaron took a deep breath. "Unless your mom lied and—"

Maria stood up abruptly, wrenching out of his arm. "My mom *never* lies to me. We have a wonderful relationship. She would never—"

"She didn't even tell you *why* you should 'let the past be the past!'" Effectively, Aaron used her mom's saying that Maria had often been discouraged about. "She didn't want you digging in the past to hide that he was abusive. Maybe she's hiding something else and therefore lying about—"

"Mamá wouldn't lie to me! Ever! She was just bending the truth to hide he was abusive. She just didn't want me to know." She was crying now, big tears dripping out of her exotic eyes.

That's ridiculous. Everyone knows that "bending the truth" pretty much equals lying. But why, why would Mamá lie to me about my dad? Why didn't she just tell me that he was abusive? And how in the world could he be my dad if they got divorced three years before I was born?

Her tears suddenly dried up as the horror of her thought washed over her face. Aaron knew immediately that she had come to the same conclusion. Again, Maria turned ghostly white, her hands trembling.

"Oh my gosh, he came back, came back and . . ."

She couldn't finish the thought, couldn't say her horrible conclusion out loud. Maria slipped out of the chair and sank to the floor sobbing, big tears streaming down her face and pooling in her hands as she covered her eyes. "I'm a product of violence. Violence and pain."

She sobbed even louder. *No wonder Mamá never wanted to talk about my dad or even wanted to hear his name.*

Aaron sat down next to her, hugging her tightly, swaying her back and forth like a little child. Maria had never been this horrified, this sick to her stomach due to sheer horror. *I'm not what I thought I am. How can Mamá love me so much when I must remind her of that horrible night every time she ever looks at me?*

There were so many thoughts, restless thoughts, and her brain began to ache from the terrible weight of them. She went far, far away, and wasn't sure how long they sat there on the floor until she realized Aaron's head had grown heavy on her shoulder. He had fallen asleep upright sitting right next to her on the carpet. She looked up and found the computer had run out of juice and powered down. It was after midnight.

Time to stop thinking. Time to sleep.

She gently shook Aaron awake, who was confused for a second but then wide-awake.

"You okay? I'm sorry I fell asleep, I'm a terrible—" he started saying, but she put her finger over his soft lips.

"You're wonderful, Aaron. I love you. Let's get some sleep."

As soon as Aaron's head hit the pillow, he was fast asleep once more. Maria checked her cell phone. She had missed a call from her mom. She sighed. She hadn't talked to her or texted her since that silly fight yesterday.

Oh, Mamá, poor Mamá! I'm sorry, Mamá! I understand now. I'm not mad anymore. I'm so sorry, Mamá.

Maria saw her mom had also written a text message hours ago wondering if she was alright. Maria knew she was worried about her and replied to the text immediately.

Her mom was still awake and texted back right away: *Buenas noches, mija! It's okay. I forgive you. Te amo. Abrazos y besos.*

Maria stared at her phone and thought, *Mamá, I love you too. So much. You gave me unconditional love even though you must feel pain whenever you look at me. Whenever you see me. Yet you still love me. I'm sending hugs and kisses your way, too. My mamá.*

Even though her head was full of things she wanted to tell her mom, her text message was simple: *Gracias. Te amo también.*

Then she put her phone on the nightstand and cuddled up close to Aaron. *What a day. Crazy day. So much has happened. My engagement. Aaron's assignment. The truth about my father. I don't want to be like him at all.* She had a bad feeling her love of black coffee was because of him. *Abuser! Asshole! Tomorrow, I'll start drinking coffee with creamer.*

She finally drifted off to sleep.

She was holding a cup of coffee. Steaming black coffee. The way she liked it. She looked into it and suddenly, the cup got bigger and bigger. She screamed.

What's happening?

The dark liquid was threatening to swallow her up, and she felt herself being pulled in by a magic force, a strong force. She fell into the giant cup.

She splashed about and began to struggle, desperately trying to hold on to the rim of the huge cup, the cup of dark liquid she had fallen into. She swallowed water—it was all around her, that dark, deep water.

Water? It isn't coffee? No, it's dark water, all around me. So dark.

She gulped another mouthful and tried to get up to the surface to get some air. But strong arms were holding her. Arms so strong. They clutched her tightly and she couldn't free herself from them. She felt small, so very small. Small like a toddler, lost in those big arms. She wiggled, trying to get out, scratched the strong man's uniform, but he wouldn't let go, wouldn't let her go up to the surface as he waded into the dark, deep water with little her in his strong, big arms.

Her eyes widened as she tried to breathe and found she couldn't; she just got swallowed up by the dark, deep water. It surrounded her, carrying her further away from the beautiful beach with the white sand, the beach she had played at just the day before.

Goodbye, sandy beach, goodbye. I'll go far away now.

She kept swallowing that dark water, was dragged through it by those strong arms.

Goodbye beach.

The water swallowed her up and wouldn't let go. . . .

"No, no," she screamed, and suddenly found herself staring into a bright light—a bright, blinding light.

Oh my gosh, I'm with the angels now. Am I dead? Did I drown? I must have drowned.

Maria felt herself being shaken. It took a few seconds before she realized she was staring into her own bright nightstand light, next to her bed in her college apartment.

Aaron was shaking her, looking her straight into the eye. "Maria! My goodness, Maria! Are you okay?"

Foggy-brained, she stared at him. He hugged her tightly. "It's okay, Maria. You're safe here. You had a nightmare again. Just another nightmare."

Maria nodded and, after drinking a glass of water, felt better. She turned off the light and cuddled close to Aaron.

I feel safe in his arms. Can't wait to marry him and be with him all the time. Move into a new home. A home with him as soon as I graduate next year. Move in with him at Eglin Air Force Base. That sounds fantastic.

Yet, for some reason, that thought once more sent chills racing down her spine.

CHAPTER 10

The alarm on Aaron's cell phone shrilled loudly. He quickly hit it, then pulled the bed covers back over his head.

"No, sir, no, no. Time to get up." Maria pulled away the pillow beneath him.

"Please, a little more time? For the love of everyone who's not a morning person, please!"

"Morning person or not, time for your PT session! Get up, Aaron!"

"No, I don't want to go jogging. . . ."

Maria gave him a big kiss. "But you have to. Come on."

Slowly, Aaron got up and readied himself for his ROTC physical training while Maria made coffee. He grabbed a cup and poured in milk. Maria stared at her own cup of coffee, then at the milk. She raised her hand to grab it, but Aaron stopped her.

"What are you doing?"

"Well, I thought I would just try to see. . . ."

"Maria, come on. You tried it before and hated it. Don't change your morning routine just because you *think* your father might like black coffee as well. Even if it's true, your personal tastes don't have anything to do with him."

Her mouth dropped and she looked at him.

Aaron grinned. "I knew that's what you were thinking. I know you well, Maria. So please don't change. You are you. Black coffee is the way you drink it, the way you chose it. Nobody else can tell you how to drink your coffee. It's your choice, your preference. Stick with it. It's the way I know you. The way I love you."

That speech was exactly what she needed. "I love you, too, Aaron." She gave him a big kiss.

"You're perfect the way you are! So don't change. I love you for who you are—my Maria, my fiancée. I'm a lucky guy!"

She smiled her bright, beautiful smile that could make anyone's day brighter, even on a bad day. "And you have no idea how lucky I am to have found you!"

She put down her coffee cup and gave him a big hug that almost made him spill his coffee.

They parted ways once they arrived on campus. Aaron headed to the athletic fields for his morning PT session while Maria walked over to the library to look over her notes from yesterday. She found a nice little area, set up her laptop, and pulled up her notes. Before she could really get into it, though, her thoughts started wandering back to last night, back to her father. *My mean father. My abusive father. I'm a product of violence.* She sighed. *Forget studying.*

Instead, she pulled up Google, determined to find out more about her father. Slowly, Maria typed in his name. She clicked the search button and a bunch of hits came up in the search engine, everything from a LinkedIn profile to a picture of a law firm called Sullivan and Sullivan. There were a bunch of "Jonathan Sullivans" out there.

She sighed. *It's impossible to tell which is my actual father. Mamá never really spoke of him. She only said they met at her tailor shop and he helped her out with the "floating" dresses. Wait a minute. Floating dresses? I never questioned what that meant back when I was a kid. . . .*

Maria thought about it for a while.

Maybe a pipe broke inside the tailor shop? If so, Mamá would have needed a plumber to fix it. A plumber!

She looked at the different "Jonathan Sullivans" and kept scrolling down. There! One of them was listed as a plumber. And in Florida, too. Sullivan's Plumbing, in Jacksonville, Florida. That could be it!

Maria's face went red as she thought back to what they had found in the database, but tried to keep her emotions in check. *Sullivan's Plumbing in Jacksonville.* She clicked the link, which led her to a website with all kinds of credentials and a listed address.

An address.

I could drive there easily. But why would I want to? What would I even say?

She shook herself and tried to focus on the website. *There! A picture. Guy with a plumber's tool belt. Is that my father?* She stared at it. The picture was tiny and not a very good one, but it definitely showed a man that appeared to match what her father's age should be.

Must be the guy that owns the business, Jonathan Sullivan. My biological father.

She clicked on the image, but when it opened in a new tab, it was still just as small and pixelated. She could make out that the man in the picture had wide shoulders and was of regular height, like the average white American. Brownish hair, blue eyes.

He looks nothing like me. She sighed in relief. *But neither does Mamá.*

Suddenly, Maria's phone buzzed. It was Aaron. She saw the time. *Oh my, it's super late. Time for class.*

Maria rushed into the huge auditorium and looked around and saw Keisha waving at her. She'd saved her a seat.

"Thank you," Maria whispered as she slid along the row of chairs and plopped down to Keisha's right just as the professor started speaking up front. She hastily opened her laptop to take notes. Keisha suspiciously eyed her.

"What?"

Keisha continued to stare at her, eyebrows raised.

"*What?* I just ran a bit behind."

Keisha whispered, "Aha, sure."

Maria shook her head and focused on the professor's lecture. She opened up a new note and saved it inside the class's folder. She still felt Keisha's stare boring into her.

She finally looked at Keisha, feeling annoyed. "You gotta stop this, you're distracting me."

"Sure, girl," Keisha said, and looked at her own laptop. For a while, the friends just listened and took notes, until Maria noticed Keisha staring at her again.

"Gosh, what's going on? Do I have toothpaste stuck on my face or what?"

"Oh no, girl, you don't."

"So what then?"

"It's your face," Keisha replied nonchalantly.

"My *face?* What about it?"

Instinctively, Maria touched her face. Nothing stuck to it.

Keisha gritted her teeth. "Spill it! You gotta let me know what in the world's going on with you. What are you hiding? And don't give me that 'Nothing, girl!' I know you. I can see it in your face."

Maria's hand froze on her laptop keyboard. She stared straight ahead.

"You gotta tell me. You okay? I'm worried."

"I'm fine," Maria whispered without looking at her friend.

"Oh no, girl, you're definitely not okay."

Keisha clicked a button on her laptop, then leaned over to click "save" on Maria's laptop.

"What are you doing?"

"Let's get out of here and talk about whatever you don't want to tell me. Come on, I'll let the professor know." Keisha was about to raise her hand, but Maria stopped her.

"*No*, Keisha. We need to stay here and concentrate. Come on. Finals are coming up soon."

Keisha sighed, her eyebrows raised, her eyes resting on Maria. "You're sure you're alright?"

"Yes," Maria said quickly, and looked at Keisha, withstanding her stare. "Let's focus on class, please."

Keisha didn't say anything further, and both girls focused on listening to the lecture and taking notes.

The two girls sat underneath a giant, shady magnolia tree on one of the many beautiful open fields on campus. Keisha was still giving Maria a weird look, but Maria played it off as well as she could. Nick, Brandy, Jim, and Aaron showed up and Keisha waved them over.

"Hey, ladies. What's up?"

"Not much," Keisha said. "At least not with me." She gave Maria a strange look.

Maria stared back at her friend, then turned to the others. "Yep, not much going on. Just enjoying a nice spring day."

"Really, 'not much?'" Aaron knew better. "Come on, what's going on?"

Maria's face flushed. She stared at the grass. Keisha shrugged her shoulders. Neither said anything, and the silence grew uncomfortable.

"Hey y'all, what should we do tonight?" Brandy said, oblivious to the situation.

"Guess it depends on what's going on with the girls," Jim said, and smirked. "And whether they'll let us in on their little secret."

Keisha gave him the evil eye.

"What?" He gave her a kiss on the forehead. "Can't be *that* bad."

"I don't know. Gotta ask Maria. The girl's acting strange, not telling me anything at all."

Maria now stared at Keisha, who put up her hands in defense. "What? Don't be mad at me, girl. You're the one acting strange here."

"Maria," Aaron asked now, "what's going on?"

"Nothing!" Maria got up, grabbed her bag, and started walking away from the group.

"Hey, what's going on? Wait up," Aaron said, perplexed, but Maria just kept walking.

"Still have to study," she said and waved goodbye to her friends sitting on the grass.

I'm not ready to tell everyone I'm a product of violence. I don't want to be pitied or looked down upon. I don't want anyone to know. And I certainly can't tell anyone I'm going to drive to Jacksonville to confront Mamá's abuser.

"Well, y'all, that leaves us five then," Brandy said. "Obviously, Maria still has to study. So what are we going to do?"

Everyone ignored her, staring after Maria.

"That was odd," Nick concluded.

"Too odd," Aaron mumbled. He quickly said goodbye then ran after her.

"Keisha, are you sure everything's alright?" Jim wondered.

Keisha sighed. "Honestly, I don't know."

Brandy had finally caught on to the strangeness of the situation. "She's not getting cold feet, is she?"

"No, I don't think so. Aaron and Maria are meant to be together. They're perfect for each other," Keisha said, and all of the friends looked over to where Maria and Aaron were standing on the open field. They could clearly see the couple were having an argument.

"Puh, that doesn't look like the perfect couple," Nick said.

"Let's give 'em some space," Keisha told the others. "Not sure what's going on, but they'll be fine. Let's get something to eat, shall we?"

The friends agreed and left the arguing couple right there on the grassy campus field.

"You can't just do that. Drive to Jacksonville, and then what?"

"I already decided that's what I'm going to do," Maria pouted, now wishing she hadn't told Aaron about her plan of confronting her father in his plumbing shop.

"You aren't even one hundred percent sure this is the guy we're looking for!"

"I know," she said, "but it's very likely. Pretty sure he's the one. It lines up with the plumbing issue my mom had at her store before I was born."

"Pretty sure is not one hundred percent sure."

"Oh my gosh, Aaron. No, I'm not one hundred percent sure, but I have a feeling he's the guy."

"A *feeling?*" Aaron scoffed. "That's not enough. You need to be sure. You can't just walk into his plumbing business and say, 'Hey, you, I'm pretty sure you raped my mom, and that makes you my father!'"

Maria looked at him—at Aaron, the guy she loved—and could only feel anger toward him. "I don't even know yet what I'm going to say. I just want to *see* him. I'll wing it from there. See how I feel."

"Jeez, Maria, you can't just 'see how you feel.' You need a plan. Do you know what you're doing? You're accusing someone of a crime without having any kind of evidence! Where's your evidence? This is serious. A serious crime. But if he's not the guy, if you're wrong . . . I don't wanna think about it. Look, you need evidence."

"Evidence? *Evidence*? How will I find evidence? It's been twenty years and Mamá won't talk. She won't tell me. So I have to figure it out myself. Just see the guy, look him in the eye. See how he reacts. You and your stupid evidence. Most crimes get solved when people get confronted with something shocking, something unexpected. Not with evidence. Get too clinical and they won't talk. They'll only confess based on how they feel. That's what's important. Screw your evidence."

"Maria, come on. You can't even lock anyone up without evidence."

She was crying now. "You just don't understand. I need to do this. Need to do this *for me*. To find out more about me. How can I marry you if I don't really know who I am anymore?"

She looked into his beautiful ocean-blue eyes and felt the tears streaming down her face. She turned around and took off running, but before she had made it far, he was already by her side, had caught up with her and pulled her into his strong arms. She let go and cried on his shoulder. He just held her.

"I'm sorry," he whispered in her ear. "I'm sorry you're even thinking like that. Of course you can marry me. I want to marry you. No matter who you are."

Maria sobbed. "Really? You do?"

Aaron nodded. "Yeah, I do. And I get it. You want to find out more. And you have every right to go and see that guy. Even if he turns out not to be your father. But please let me help plan this. And please let me go with you."

Maria stopped sobbing and looked at him. "Okay. Yeah, I'd love for you to be there. I need you to stop me from doing or saying something stupid. My plan was to just slap him."

Aaron laughed. She smiled at him through her tears. Aaron just nodded and looked into her exotic hazel eyes, the golden-and-emerald-green flecks in the dark-brown iris sparkling in the sunlight, the blue rim shining brighter than the sky.

"We'll find out who you really are. I promise."

.

CHAPTER 11

"I promise, Drew. Yes, I'll go home soon."

"Okay, Cave Man. I'm heading out."

"You should. Go home to your family. Go home for dinner. I'll leave soon myself." Drew gave him a look.

"Really, I will. Go home, Mr. Markas. That's an order."

"You're crazy, Cave Man," Drew said, and closed the door to the general's office.

Brad laughed and fell back into his big, comfortable leather chair. He finished up a few more work items and then opened the top drawer of his desk. It held an unlabeled vanilla file folder inside, full of information about her. Elisabeth. His ex-wife. Everything he had collected over the years. He had her address and a phone number. A landline to the apartment she was living in. She must be one of the few people who still had a landline. He smirked, but his smile soon faded. He stared at the number.

Should I just call her? What would I even say? "I'm sorry?"

He shook himself and checked his watch. Evening.

She should be home tonight, right? Wait a minute. Time difference. There's a time difference. He had forgotten all about it. *It's way too late to call her. Midnight her time. Way too late.* He put the note with her number back into the vanilla folder and went back to his work emails.

But then he had an idea. *I can just email her. Perfect. Then I won't be at a loss for words.*

He shut down his work computer and took out his private laptop. He barely ever used it, barely ever checked his personal email. When he opened the inbox and scanned its contents, he lurched. He had to grab onto his desk to steady himself.

An email from Elisabeth? He looked at the date. *Yesterday. She wrote it yesterday.* And suddenly he knew why. *Important months ahead. So many important upcoming dates. Our little one's birthday. The anniversary of the disappearance. Our wedding anniversary. Oh my.*

His heart was beating as he opened the email titled with the simple subject line: *Hello.* And he started reading.

Tears were running down his face. Tears of joy, tears of shock, tears of sadness. So many emotions, he couldn't even explain them.

And then he just did it. He grabbed the note from the vanilla folder again, snatched his cell phone, and dialed her number. He didn't care about the time difference; he *had* to talk to her.

"Collins."

He recognized her voice immediately. She had answered after only a few rings. He smiled widely. *Still using my last name, I see. Our last name.* He knew answering the phone with your last name was common custom in Germany. Still, knowing that she hadn't changed her name warmed his heart.

"Isn't it a bit late to be sounding so chipper, Mrs. Collins?"

Silence on the other end.

He waited a bit, then his forehead wrinkled in worry. "Elisabeth? Are you still there?"

"Yes." Another pause. "Brad?"

"Yes. Hi. It's me."

"Brad?"

"Yes, still me." Silence. "Elisabeth, I got your email. I just read it."

"Oh, good. Good. Brad, I am . . . I'm . . ."

"I know, hun, I know. Me, too. I'm so sorry. So, so sorry. I should have taken that bereavement leave. I should've. I was a jerk. I just left you there, all alone. While I was flying high above the clouds, trying to take my mind off of—that—you were alone and . . . had no escape."

"Off of *that*? That's the best you can do?" He heard resentment in her voice.

"Elisabeth . . . No, I'm sorry. I said 'that' because I just can't stand to use her name. I haven't spoken it aloud in twenty years."

Tears were forming in his eyes, a knot deep inside his throat. His lip started quivering. "It's all my fault. I'm so sorry. All my fault. I let her down, I let you down. I'm just a big, dumb loser." He started sobbing into the phone.

"Oh Brad . . . no you're not. You're not a loser. You're just hurting. You're in pain. Still in pain. After all these years." Her words warmed his heart. He nodded. She continued, "So am I. I'm still in pain. Just an empty shell."

He sobbed again. "Me too. I'm so empty. So empty ever since I lost you both. My life has been in pieces. Ever since then." He grabbed his chest. His heart was aching.

"I know, Brad, I know. That's why I think Sarah is right, just like I said in my email. She's right. We need to find closure. We need to put the past behind us. It's been twenty years. We have to let go. Bury all that pain. Bury it right there on those white beaches."

He sniffed and used his hand to wipe away the snot. "You're right."

"So, can you meet me there? Meet me and maybe help me forget the past and fill our empty shells?"

His tears stopped flowing now, his hopes high. "You're saying I can fill your empty shell? Me?"

"I don't know. Maybe. Yeah, maybe you can fill the part of my heart that's been missing. Put the pieces of it together again."

He smiled widely. "Yes, Elisabeth, maybe I can. I want to try at least."

"Good. So, you'll come to Florida when I'm there?"

He glanced at his calendar hanging on the wall, filled with meetings for the next few weeks. Brad had no idea if he could go to Florida or not, but he knew he needed to go there. "Yes, I'll be there. Definitely. I promise."

"Good, Brad. That's good."

"Yeah. I can't wait to see you again."

She laughed. "I've changed. You know, it's been twenty years."

"Well, you were always beautiful. I bet you still are."

He heard a snort on the other end of the line. "Well, the most important thing is that we find closure. Put the past behind us. I'm thinking about bringing Enti. We can bury her there, on that beach."

He laughed. "You still have *Enti*? Oh my gosh. Her favorite cuddle toy . . . the weird security blanket with the three feet—a blue one, an orange one, and a tan one, right?"

Elisabeth laughed. "Yep, that's right."

"And the silly hat on a duck's face. Enti. The ugliest toy ever. What were your parents thinking?"

"I don't know. Guess they thought it was a cute gift? Or they liked the colors?"

"Bright orange, tan, and blue? Yeah, not my personal favorite."

She laughed a warm laugh. "Nope, not mine either. But *she* loved it from the start. I guess because of the duck head. Its stitched-on smile, those big black eyes. Is all that matters to her."

"Yep, she always took that thing everywhere. No matter how hard we encouraged her to choose something else. It was always Enti. Remember how we would even hide it in a pile of toys, and she'd still find it? She always gravitated to that one."

"For sure. It was the first thing she grabbed onto, the first thing she sucked on, on those three feet, the first thing she put over her belly."

He laughed, remembering it so very well. "Yeah, she always held on tight to Enti, even as a small baby. She had such a strong little grab and always curled her fingers around that ugly little thing, didn't she?"

"Yes, she loves Enti. Guess it shows she doesn't mind it looking different with those three silly feet, their funny coloring. All that matters to her is the face of that silly duck—the wide, friendly smile, those big black eyes looking at her."

"I remember. I still believe it showed she was kind-hearted, inclusive, not prejudiced—so very loving."

"*Was*? Oh. Yes. She *was* kind-hearted," Elisabeth whispered.

Brad nodded, still thinking about that old toy. "Man, can't believe you held on to Enti all those years."

"Yeah, I did. It looks pretty old now. The bright orange, tan, and blue are faded into pastel colors now; its white face is a little greyish, but the smile is still there. Yeah, Enti's smile. She loved it so much. *Loved.*" Her voice held a note of sadness, but then took on a determined tone. "I guess it's time. Time to move on. Like Sarah said. So I can bring Enti? And we'll bury her there on the beach? Together?"

Tears were welling up in his eyes. "Yes, Elisabeth, let's do it. Together. I'd like that."

"Me too."

He sighed. "Okay then, let's do it. I'll figure something out and make sure I can be there when you are."

"Sounds like a plan. Let's go back to Florida together."

"Yes, together. To Florida."

CHAPTER 12

In Florida, Maria and Aaron sat at the little round dining table in her college apartment. They were studying Google Maps on her phone and the Sullivan's Plumbing website on Aaron's laptop. Maria smiled and gave him a kiss on the cheek.

He looked at her. "What was that for?"

She shrugged. "Just for being you. For being so organized and such a good planner."

He smiled and his bright-blue eyes lit up in happiness. "Speaking of which, here's the plan: You'll try to talk with both your aunts this week to find out what they know about your mamá's divorce. You'll also try to think back on what you heard from your mom over the years and record everything in this." He pointed at a new little notebook on the table. "We'll do our best to piece everything together."

Maria nodded.

"Then, on Saturday, we'll go to Jacksonville. You and me. You'll bring your notes and we'll come up with a plan of what to say to the guy when we meet him."

Maria nodded. It all sounded great. Yet she felt uneasy about it. She didn't say anything about that to Aaron and instead called her mamá. They were finally talking again.

"Buenas noches, Mamá. Te amo," Maria said before hanging up.

Aaron looked up from his laptop. "How is she?"

"Fine. She has no idea what we're up to."

"I bet. How could she?" He focused on his laptop again.

Maria looked over his shoulder. "What are you doing now?"

"Just studying. Finals are coming up. Then graduation, my commission into the Air Force, then the move."

The move! Maria had been so busy figuring out her own life, she'd forgotten all about it.

"It's all coming up quickly," Aaron sighed, and looked at her.

Maria let out a big sigh as well. "Yeah, it is. I promise I'll let all this go after Jacksonville. We really gotta focus on that important stuff too—studying, finals, your graduation."

Aaron chuckled. "Really? You promise not to hatch any more crazy ideas after this trip?"

"I promise," she said, and gave him a kiss.

They smiled and both sank into their studies.

Aaron was fast asleep. Maria smirked.

Of course, fast asleep. He always falls asleep within seconds. But I can't. Never could, but especially not now. So much going on. Unknown future, unknown past. It's crazy. Our trip to Jacksonville. Seeing my father.

She frowned. *My mom's abuser. Hope we got the right guy. Must be him, though. I'm sure he's the guy who helped rebuild Mamá's shop. Her beloved tailor shop.*

Maria smiled. She had so many good memories of it. *Playing with the fabric. Having Mamá sew little dresses for my dolls. Trying to do so myself. Poked my little fingers with the needles.*

She fell asleep and dreamed.

She was surrounded by big piles of fabric. Colorful, fun fabric. Different kinds of fabric. They all felt different and looked different, and it was all so beautiful. She loved this store.

She looked around and stood up. She was next to a pile that was much bigger than her. She felt a bit tired and wanted her pacifier.

Where is it? Oh, found it.

She saw it on top of the pile of fabric. She tried to reach it but was too small and couldn't reach that high.

"Mamá?" she called out, but her mom was up front talking with a customer.

She knew she couldn't interrupt. Mamá got mad whenever she did that, scolded her many times and told her not to interrupt when she was talking to a customer. So, she decided to climb up the pile to reach her pacifier.

It was fun climbing it. She knew it was okay to do so with clean hands and clean feet. No shoes. She had just gone potty and washed her hands, so she was sure it was fine.

I need Schnulli.

That was the name of her pacifier. She wasn't sure where that word had come from or why she said it, but Mamá had also learned to call it that even though she'd told her it was a silly made-up word. Made up, but cute.

Ok, let's get Schnulli.

She looked around quickly to make sure the coast was clear, determined to climb the mountain of fabric. She started and pulled herself up, putting her feet gently on the ledges of fabric that stuck out. She pulled up and moved one foot, then the other—hand, foot, hand, foot, up we go.

I'm coming, Schnulli!

She giggled, but all of the sudden her hand slipped on a very smooth fabric, and she couldn't hold on any more. She fell, she screamed and fell, she'd hit the hardwood floor soon and was prepared for the pain. She called out for her mamá and fell, right into the water.

Water? I fell into water? What happened to the floor? But I'm definitely surrounded by water.

Deep water. So much water. She was sloshing around.

Schnulli? Mama?

She couldn't breathe. Someone was holding her tight. Holding her underwater. She gulped in mouthfuls of water. Disgusting water.

She couldn't breathe.

Schnulli? Mama? Where did this water come from? Did a pipe burst in the store? We need a plumber. Jonathan Sullivan is a plumber. So much water! Help, help, so much water, I can't breathe. Please let go, I want Schnulli. I want Mama! Can't breathe, let go. Help, water. Mama, help. . . .

"Maria, Maria," someone screamed and shook her.

She opened her eyes. She looked around and saw Aaron. He was shaking her, stroking her cheek as she lay on her pillow, which was soaked in sweat.

"Are you okay?" He stroked her head, gently.

She nodded and found she couldn't say anything just yet.

"Another strange dream?"

She nodded again. "I dreamed I was drowning."

He raised an eyebrow. "Drowning? Strange. Well, maybe you have so much going on right now that you feel like you're drowning?"

"Maybe," she whispered. "Yeah. A lot." She took a sip of water from the glass on her nightstand. She turned her pillow around to the dry side and cuddled up close to Aaron. "A lot going on."

He nodded and gave her a kiss before he quickly fell asleep again. She listened to his deep breathing, watched his chest rise and fall in the dark. She felt safe in his arms. But way deep down inside she had a nagging feeling that the drowning dreams had nothing to do with her workload.

CHAPTER 13

Work. Another long workday. But Brad had a plan and called in his exec.

"Yes, sir." The major saluted him. "What can I do for you?"

The general looked at some paperwork. "Major Starke. Lately I've been reviewing the F-35 program at Eglin AFB. I'd like to have an update on where we're at. Give me a quick top-level briefing on what you know."

"Yes, sir. Our office has been overseeing Eglin's F-35 program for years. It's going well. The jets are finally operational. They've been really ramping up their training pipeline recently with new pilots. In fact, Eglin's been requesting a senior member of the Air Staff to come down and see all the progress they've made. And that would be you, sir!"

The general nodded. "Yeah, I know. Maybe it's time to go down there and see the Lightning in action, huh?"

Major Starke stared at the general. "Sir? You mean for a TDY?"

"Yes. Major Starke, please plan a temporary duty trip there for me and Mr. Markas. I would like to go at the end of the month."

"Sir? A TDY to Eglin, sir?"

"Yes, Major. You seem surprised. You're usually on top of things and always do a great job putting together my TDYs."

"Thank you, sir. I know."

"So, get to work then."

"Okay, sir, as you wish." The major stared at him with his eyebrows raised, saluted, and turned around.

Brad sighed. "Major Starke, what is it? What's on your mind?"

The exec turned around again. "Sir, I can't help but remember what you told me when I first started working for you."

Brad looked at him. "And what did I tell you?"

"The ROAR, sir. *R*espectful. *O*n task. *A*ccountable. *R*esponsible for having a plan B—and a plan C, just in case."

"Very good, Major. I still don't see why you seem so confused."

"Well, sir . . . you also told me you would *never* go TDY to Eglin Air Force Base. Ever. I was to avoid planning a trip there at all costs, indefinitely, even though they're constantly asking you to come visit."

General Collins stared at him, then broke out into a smile. "You're right, I did tell you that. Well, I changed my mind."

The exec looked at the general—the tall man with the strong shoulders, brown hair with some grey streaks in it, and those exotic eyes, now smiling at him—and couldn't help but feel uncertain. "You were very adamant about never going, sir."

"Well, Major Starke, I understand now that scheduling a visit there is important. See, even old farts like me learn new things from time to time."

The major nodded. "Very well then, sir. I'll get to work."

"Fantastic. Just make sure it's at the exact time I told you. Please confirm dates with me prior to booking."

"Yes, sir!" The major saluted and left the room.

A knock at the door. Drew came in.

Brad looked up from behind all the stacked papers on his desk. "Hey, Drew, what's up?"

Drew sat down in one of the big chairs facing the general's desk. "Major Starke is planning a trip to Eglin AFB."

"I know."

Drew raised his eyebrows.

"They've been asking me to come visit and see the F-35 program's progress firsthand. You know that, Drew."

Drew tilted his head now. "Yeah, I know. They've been begging for you to visit for years. I've been there a few times already. Even Major Starke has been there."

"Right. Time for me to go, don't you think?"

Drew still gave him a funny look. "That would be fantastic."

"So, what's the issue then?"

Drew laughed. "You're funny, Cave Man, you're funny. The issue? It's *Eglin*, man. For years you avoided going. Years. You always got steaming mad when we even mentioned it. And now you're suddenly okay with going?"

"Yeah, I am."

"Really? You are?"

"Yeah. I told Major Starke to set it up."

"I heard. That's why I'm here."

"So?"

Another laugh. "Cave Man, why in the world did you change your mind? All of a sudden?"

"Yeah. Well, Drew, I realize now I was being silly."

Drew raised his eyebrows again. "I'm not buying that."

"You know I have to go. For the program. To represent the Pentagon. I can't put off my duty any longer. It's been great that you took on that role in my place, but now it's time for me to go."

"Yeah, you're not wrong. But I remember not too long ago—just last week, actually—you were saying yet again you weren't going to go. You told everyone you weren't going TDY to Eglin, now or ever."

"Told you, Drew, I changed my mind."

"And I'm asking you: *why?*"

Brad lost his patience. He slammed his fist on his desk so hard the papers briefly jumped up into the air. "It's none of your business, Mr. Markas. And I already told you why."

Drew jumped out of his seat. "Holy cow, Cave Man. What's gotten into you?"

"Nothing," Brad barked, his voice low. "We're going to Eglin at the end of the month, and either you come with me or I'm going alone."

Drew squinted at him. "Fine then. Don't tell me what changed your mind. Would just love to know."

The emerald-green flecks in the dark-brown iris of the general's unique hazel eyes seemed to explode and take over—his eyes turned completely green, the way they did when he was agitated. "None of your business."

"I've known you for years, I'm your best bud. But whatever." Drew threw his hands up in the air. "Don't tell me then. I'll go with you, though. I know it'll be hard for you."

"Don't you dare bring that up, Drew."

"Fine, Cave Man, fine. You play your role well. Everyone admires you. But you know what?" Drew paused then said, "You're really hard to get along with sometimes. But I've stuck with you 'cuz I know, deep down inside, you're a lonely, sad man hurting so much. And you're a good friend. My best bud, actually. But man you're stubborn."

Brad looked at Drew and sighed. "I know, Drew. I'm sorry. Yeah, please go with me. I'll need you there. You're right, it'll be hard, but you know what else you were right about? When you told me I have to let go. It's been twenty years, man."

Drew nodded. "You'll be fine. Sure, I'll go with you. Though I still get the feeling there's more you're not telling me."

Brad stared at his desk. "I just need a little closure."

Satisfied, Drew nodded and walked out. Little did he know that his best friend wasn't planning on finding closure—he was going there to meet Elisabeth, his ex-wife, and pick up the pieces of their past.

CHAPTER 14

Come on, pick up. Maria listened to the ringing of the phone. She was calling Tía Mariella, the older of her mom's sisters. As Aaron had instructed her, she had the notebook and a pencil in front of her. She waited. The phone rang and rang. She was ready to hang up when suddenly Tía Mariella picked up.

"¿Aló, Maria? How are you? It was so great to see you and Aaron the other day. What a handsome, polite young man."

"Yeah, he's a good guy. And I agree, it was great seeing you all," Maria said, and took a deep breath before continuing. "Listen, Tía Mariella, I just couldn't stop thinking about what you and Tía Monica mentioned on the balcony that night."

"What did we mention?"

"You said that my father really hurt Mamá. Do you know any more about that?"

There was a sigh on the other end of the line. "Maria, you have to leave that topic alone."

"I will, but I just need to know what you meant when you said that man hurt Mamá. I'm old enough now to understand, Tía Mariella. I'm about to get married and I need to know what Mamá's marriage was like to really understand what I'm getting into."

A snort on the other end. "You definitely don't want your mom's marriage."

"Exactly. He didn't only hurt her by leaving, did he? You said him leaving was good for Mamá?"

"Yes."

"Okay then. He also didn't just hurt her by having affairs, did he?"

"No."

"Tía Mariella, can you please give me more than just a few terse words?" Maria waited.

A sigh, snort. "Maria, I don't know if you'll want to hear this."

"I called you and asked specifically about it, so obviously I want to. I just want to know, want to understand. I have no urge to ever meet the guy." Maria bit her tongue. Her face flushed. *Good thing this is only a voice call.*

"I don't know much, but I do know he was very charming at first. A good-looking American. Your mom was so busy trying to make a life for herself, to provide for all of us so we could come join her in the United States. She didn't want to date around. And she didn't. You know her. She's a hard worker, determined, always making sure all of us are taken care of. She wasn't even looking for a guy knowing it would be a distraction. But then he showed up at the tailor shop after a pipe broke and ruined it. Your mamá's old boss hired him to take care of the faulty plumbing."

Aha, a plumber. Now I'm sure the guy in Jacksonville is my father.

"As I said, he was very charming, and once the plumbing was fixed he helped out with new flooring. Worked for free after hours at the store. Martina's old boss had already decided to sell the shop. And your mamá expressed interest in it, so she gave it to her. Well, no, not for free—she had to put some money down. Your father helped with that. In fact, *he* paid for it. And fixed it up for free. So your mamá felt like she was in debt to him. All he wanted was a date with her. The story seemed very romantic at first."

"Sure sounds nice," Maria agreed.

"They fell in love and got married. Him being an American helped your mom become a citizen, and then she was able to sponsor us coming to the United States. It seemed like a blessing. She couldn't have done it without him. And he seemed *so nice* when Martina spoke of him. She never told us otherwise until we came over. Only then did we learn she had already divorced."

"I see. Did she tell you when they got divorced?"

"Yeah. It was during her pregnancy with you."

Lie! That's definitely not true. Maria was determined to find out more. "So, how exactly did he abuse her?"

A sigh on the other end. "You already know about that?"

"I kind of figured it out. I just want to understand what kind of jerk my father was."

"Oh, Maria. It's okay, mija. You are nothing like him. You are your Mamá's treasure. Her everything."

Maria sighed. *I know. But how can Mamá love me so much after what happened back then?*

"Martina only told us she had no clue how much he drank until after they were married. Whenever he became drunk, he changed. He wasn't such a nice guy anymore. He got agitated easily. Angry. He would knock over things, throw things. . . ."

"Did he hit her?"

"It started a bit later. Not at first. He just threw things her way. Then his aim got better and she got hit a few times. When she started defending herself, he got real angry. He started hitting. Yes, that's what she told us. She had to call the police a few times to get him to stop."

Maria nodded. *The complaints in the database. Makes sense.* "Why didn't she leave him right away?"

"Please understand, she had no choice but to stay with him until she got her citizenship," Tía Mariella said. "And he told her she couldn't leave him until all her debts were paid. The money he had given her for the tailor shop."

What a jerk! Maria was furious. "How could Mamá stand sharing a bedroom with him when he was being abusive?"

She was agitated, her voice loud. Her aunt noticed. "Maria, calm down! And you know that's something we don't talk about."

Maria shook her head. *Of course not. Nobody likes to talk about it.* "Tía Mariella, did he *force himself* on her? After they got divorced?"

"What? No! It might not have been fun love-making, I assume, but no. And definitely not after the divorce. He was not much interested in her anymore when she had you. He left when her belly grew! Force himself on her, you said? Maria, what are you talking about?"

Maria was smart enough to understand she had to stop right there. *If Mamá told her sisters the same story about them getting divorced while she was pregnant with me, I can't tell Tía Mariella about my theory that he came back in anger a few years later and that the encounter resulted in my birth.*

She looked down at her notes and raised an eyebrow. She had almost forgotten about that odd comment Tía Mariella had made earlier. *Worth it to ask more.*

"Tía Mariella, you said Mamá didn't tell you about her divorce?"

"No, she didn't. You know, we were still in Venezuela at the time. Your mamá was working hard on the paperwork. We couldn't communicate as well in those days. We didn't really know of your existence either until we came over to the United States."

"What? But you came over when I was two years old already," Maria said.

"Yes, you were the sweetest little two-year-old. So very shy and not very good at language yet, but so clingy to your mamá. A special bond."

"So, she didn't tell you anything when she was expecting me?"

"No, she didn't. It shocked us when we first saw you at the airport."

Maria made sure to write that down. "Don't you think it's odd she didn't tell you about me during her pregnancy and for two years after I was born?"

"I don't know. Not really. It was hard to communicate back then. Hard to call between America and Venezuela. The few times we got to talk was all about immigration."

Guess that makes sense?

"Like I said, we didn't know she had divorced or that she'd had you until we arrived in the United States."

"When did you immigrate again?"

"All of us got here in October 2003."

Maria jotted that down. *October 2003. I would have just turned two years old that September.*

"Okay, thanks Tía Mariella. I'm just so sad Mamá went through a marriage like that."

"I know, mija, I know. It was hard, but it's over now. And your mom is so happy now. So happy to have you. You're her everything."

Maria smiled. "I know."

Maria also called Tía Monica. Turned out she knew the exact same story. It was the same information Maria's other aunt had told her an hour before.

"You didn't know I existed until you came over?"

"No, we had no idea. But when we arrived, there you were, in your mamá's arms. You were so shy. So clingy. We couldn't even hold you for quite a while. You didn't seem to trust any of us at first, especially not your Tío Eduardo. You were so shy, especially around men."

For some reason, Maria wrote that down. Her hand seemed to move automatically across the paper to write down that she was shy around men. *Wait. This has nothing to do with what I want to find out about my father and whether he raped Mamá.* She scolded herself and was about to erase the note when her aunt continued talking.

"When your cousin Stephanie was born that winter, you were very protective of her. Just like a big sister. Especially around men, so protective. But you soon learned that Tío Eduardo just adored his little daughter and began to trust him as well."

Again, Maria's hand moved across the paper to take notes, as if led by a ghostly hand.

"And you two were so cute. We couldn't take enough pictures of the both of you!"

Maria smiled. *True. We have lots of pictures of little baby Stephanie and me.*

"Your mamá was happy to finally have some pictures of you."

Wait. What?

"We don't have any pictures of you as a baby," her aunt went on. "Your mamá didn't take any. Too expensive, I suppose. She didn't own a camera until after we came over."

Maria thought about it and recalled searching for pictures back when her senior class in high school did a "Guess Who?" page for their yearbook. *The yearbook committee collected baby pictures of the senior class and scrambled them up, and people had to guess which baby had become which senior. But I couldn't find any baby pictures and ended up using a toddler picture. Never thought about it again. It's odd, though. If Mamá was so proud of me, why wouldn't she have taken a single picture of me in my first two years of life?* Again, Maria's hand jotted down a note in her notebook.

"Did pictures and cameras cost that much back then?"

"What, dear? Oh, no, not too much, but your mamá sure had to turn over every penny."

Maria stared at her notes. She hadn't uncovered any clues as to whether her abusive father had come back to take advantage of her mom. Her aunts' stories matched each other, but the official online database listed 1998 as the year of divorce. *Way before Mamá was even pregnant with me. I was born September 2001.*

She closed the notebook and titled it *My Past.*

Maria lay down in bed and texted her mamá to say goodnight, then called Aaron to tell him all about the conversations with her aunts.

"That's very interesting," he said and repeated all the information he had just been told. "You were afraid of men? And your mom didn't tell her sisters about you? And she doesn't have any pictures of you until after your aunts came over?"

"Yeah, not until I was about two years old."

"That's odd. Don't you think?"

Maria shrugged her shoulders. "I guess it makes sense they couldn't communicate much and that mamá couldn't afford a camera or pictures. Cameras were expensive and so was developing film."

Aaron snorted. "Well, maybe, but still, I think it's very odd. And we definitely know now that your mom lied—to everyone!"

"Unless the date of the divorce in the database really is incorrect?"

"Maria," Aaron interrupted her, "Come on, you know that's very unlikely. It's much more likely she lied."

Maria sighed. "Yeah, I know, you're probably right. But she probably had a good reason for it. I think she wanted to protect me, didn't want me or anyone to know that I am . . . you know . . . a product of . . ." She still couldn't even say it out loud.

"Maria, please, whatever happened back then—you are a good person and your mom loves you. And *I* love you."

"I know, thanks, Aaron. I love you too."

"Well, that's good, my love. 'Cuz we're engaged and will get married."

"Yeah."

"Well, Maria, get some sleep and try not to worry too much, okay? Goodnight, my love."

"Goodnight. Sleep tight."

She hung up and snuggled up close with her pillow. She missed Aaron and his strong, protective arms, the arms that kept her safe. Soon, she fell asleep.

She was at the airport, snuggled up tight in her mamá's arms. She sat on her mamá's hips and sucked on her pacifier. She closed her eyes to concentrate on the sucking motion.

The noise of all the people coming and going scared her. She didn't like loud noises or deep voices. Especially deep voices that belonged to strong-looking men. Those scared her badly. She wasn't sure why, they just did. And there were lots of men around tonight. Big ones, tall ones, strong ones, some running, some strolling around. She noticed it all, and it was too much, too much.

I don't like it. I need Schnulli.

She wiggled. "Shhh. . . . It's alright, mija," her mamá whispered. That calmed her down. She snuggled up and dozed off to sleep.

Suddenly, she was squeezed tightly, by strong arms—strong arms not her mamá's arms. She abruptly opened her little eyes and saw a big man hugging both her and her mamá. Her eyes widened and turned completely green, the color they always turned when she was agitated.

"No, no," she yelled, and lost her pacifier.

"Oh, pardon," said the big man and let go of her and her mamá. She snuggled up close to her mom and peeked over her mom's shoulder, only to see him standing there now, right behind her mom, just staring little her into the eyes.

"Hola, bonita," the man said with a smile.

She didn't know what to do. She looked at him and saw his strong arms and screamed. He would hold her tight, squeeze her again until she couldn't breathe, pull her under, and she'd lose her pacifier and wouldn't have anything.

Schnulli, where are you? Schnulli?

"No, no Schnulli!" she screamed.

Her mom rocked her gently, saying "Sssh."

"No, no man! No, no!"

She kept yelling, sensing she was in danger. She wiggled, wiggled so much that she fell, fell out of her mamá's arms and kept falling, deeper and deeper, deep into the water.

Water? Where does the water come from? Did the airport flood?

But there was nobody there anymore. Everyone had left. No strangers, no strange man, not even her mamá. No Schnulli. Only water.

The water surrounded her, swallowed her up as she was dragged deeper and deeper by those strong arms she disliked so much. Those strong arms held her tight, so tight under the water that she couldn't breathe, couldn't breathe, just swallowed water, one big gulp after the next, more and more, until everything around her went black, pitch-black. . . .

She opened her eyes and saw nothing but darkness. Maria felt around her. *Pillow. Blanket. Nightstand. Oh, nightstand. Phone on nightstand.* She picked it up to check the time. 3:34 a.m. The middle of the night. She was in her bed in her college apartment.

She touched her forehead. It was wet. Wet with sweat. Maria sat up and reached for a tissue to dab off the wetness. She turned her pillow over.

I gotta wash these covers soon. They keep getting drenched in my sweat. My sweat from those strange dreams. Why in the world do I keep dreaming of drowning? I don't even mind the water. I'm a good swimmer. Mamá had me learn super young. Like when I was a toddler.

Wait a minute. . . .Just a toddler? Like in my dreams? Did I fall into a pool somewhere and almost drown and that's why Mamá had me take lessons?

Suddenly, Maria was wide awake. She turned on her nightstand lamp and got up to retrieve her notebook titled *My Past*. She jotted down a note: *Ask Mamá how old I was at my first swim lesson.*

CHAPTER 15

Swimming. They were at the pool on campus. The boys were already in the water while the girls all lay on the lounge chairs. The air shimmered in the heat and little drops of water clung to the chairs. The heat and humidity were unbearable.

Brandy wiped the sweat off her forehead. "Y'all, it's so hot. I thought a Friday afternoon at the pool would help, but look at me, darlings: I'm in my bikini and still sweatin' like a pig on my daddy's farm."

Keisha and Maria laughed and went back to watching the boys. They were taking turns jumping off the diving board, trying to catch a thrown football in midair as they jumped. Their attempts were more or less successful.

It was Aaron's turn when Jim threw the ball. The timing was off and Aaron missed it—the ball hit him in the head instead and bounced back onto the concrete while Aaron splashed down into the pool.

Everyone laughed. Aaron came back up rubbing his head. "Terrible shot there, Jim. My turn now!"

Aaron pulled himself out of the water, but Jim was already running, trying to get to the ball before him. Aaron started chasing his friend.

"Guys, be careful, it's slippery," Keisha warned.

"Yeah, y'all, no running around here at the campus pool, walking feet only," Brandy said, reminding them of the pool rules.

"What, you're the lifeguard on duty now, Brandy?" Nick asked with a smirk and none of the boys listened to her. Soon enough, Jim slipped and landed on his butt.

"Aua!"

He rubbed his bottom while the others slapped their thighs in laughter.

"Hey, Keisha," Nick yelled over to them, "I think your boyfriend needs help. You better check out his sore bottom!" Aaron and Nick kept laughing while Jim rubbed his butt and whined.

Keisha rolled her eyes. "Tell you what, guys, you better stop that game of yours and figure out something else to do before you really hurt yourselves. Jim, you can use the cold pool water to heal your sore butt 'cuz I certainly will not be helping you. You gotta listen, boy."

The girls grinned as the boys slowly walked over, then stood at attention right before Keisha and her friends. They saluted and said "Yes, ma'am" in unison before jumping back into the pool with a big splash that got the girls wet.

They wiped off the water and laughed. Suddenly, Brandy's laugh faded. "Y'all, it's just so sad."

"What's sad? That we got wet?" Keisha looked at Brandy.

"Nah, not that. It's sad summer's coming. I'll miss y'all. We'll all be in different states soon: Texas, Georgia, and Florida." She sighed, then perked up. "I'll definitely be staying in Georgia all summer now that Nick will be stationed there. My family and Nick, together in the same state. Exciting!" She smiled her brightest smile, her blue eyes shining brighter than the afternoon sky.

"That's nice," Keisha mumbled. "I still have to figure out how I'm going to explain to my mom why I'm going to Texas. And find money for a ticket. And still go to Chicago to see my family there."

Maria nudged her gently. "You'll be fine. Just drive to Texas with Jim. He'll have to move by truck anyway, right? And then drive to

Chicago from there. Just tell them it's a road trip for school research or something."

Brandy's blue eyes widened. "Your momma still doesn't know about you and Jim?"

"She kind of knows. But she's not happy about me staying at his place."

"You'll be fine," Maria assured her. "Your momma just has to understand you're all grown up now and can make your own perfectly fine decisions. And Jim is a keeper. She'll like him once she gets to know him."

Keisha shrugged. "Yeah, I suppose so. Easier said than done, though, girl."

Brandy nodded. "True. Y'all, boys and families are so complicated. I'm a bit worried about my daddy and Nick."

The girls nodded, and each drifted off into their own thoughts until Brandy suddenly blurted out, "I'm jealous of you, Maria."

"Me?"

"Yeah! You know, being engaged makes everything easier. And having that fantastic, true relationship with your mamá you're always talking about helps. You talk about everything and have no secrets! That must be so nice."

Maria snorted. *Ha! No secrets, huh? That's what I thought. At least until last weekend. Mamá lied not only to me but to my aunts—basically my whole family.*

"Honey, Maria?" Brandy's voice interrupted her thoughts. "You alright?"

Maria sighed. Keisha looked at her suspiciously.

"Yeah, I'm fine. Just lost in thought. It'll be strange not to have the boys around next year."

They all nodded.

"Y'all, let's enjoy the time we have," Brandy said.

"You're right, girl," Keisha agreed. "Come on, let's go."

Keisha and Brandy got up and sat on the side of the pool, dangling their legs. "Come on, Maria," they called.

Maria got up from her lounge chair and joined them.

"Y'all, I'm still too hot," Brandy said, and pushed herself into the cold water.

"Wait for me!" Keisha jumped in as well.

Maria continued to sit there, dangling her legs in. The water was cold. She'd never liked cold water much, and it always took her a while to ease her way into a pool.

"Come on, Maria!" Her friends encouraged her to come in and splashed around. They were sure having fun.

Maria bent down to scoop up some water and splashed it on her belly. *So cold!* She bent down to scoop up water again when all of a sudden, she felt someone grab her hand and pull on it.

Surprised, Maria lost her balance and fell in headfirst. It was cold, so cold. Without warning, there was a flash in front of her eyes.

Suddenly, she felt small. Very small. Her hand was still being held—no, *she* was being held, her whole little body held by strong arms that pulled her down even further.

She involuntarily swallowed a mouthful of water and felt panic rise in her. She was surrounded by water, being dragged down into the mucky, deep water, being held down by big arms.

Help, help! Let me go! Let go off me! Please! I don't like this. Let go. I can't see. Such dark water. Wait, what?

With her eyes wide open, she stared through water that wasn't dark at all but clear, see-through. The sunrays lit it up. The pool's water was clear and clean, shining blue in the scorching sunshine. She realized she wasn't being held after all and quickly rose up to the surface, right in front of Aaron, who was treading in the pool's clear water right in front of her.

"Got you," he said and smiled, but his smile quickly faded when he saw Maria's face.

She just stared at him and, without saying a word, quickly swam to the side of the pool, pulled herself out, and walked away. She went over to her lounge chair and grabbed a towel to dry off. She felt goose bumps all over her body.

A gentle hand touched her shoulder. "Are you okay?"

It was Aaron. She turned around and saw his concerned ocean-blue eyes, his wet blonde hair dripping water all over his broad shoulders.

Her own exotic eyes had turned green, completely green.

"Don't *ever* do that again!"

"I'm sorry. I didn't mean to startle you. I was just trying to get you in the pool."

"Well, it was terrifying. Just sneaking up on me like that, seriously?"

He should know better. Know I'm scared of the water, scared of the pool. I can't even swim yet. I'm way too little. Why would Daddy do that? Wait, what? Daddy?

She shook her head. Her thoughts were going crazy. She looked down at her hands; her head was hurting. A splitting headache came on suddenly and she had to close her eyes.

When she opened them, she saw her hands again, but they were little hands, so little. Hands of a toddler. She still felt that strong hand on her shoulder, the strong, heavy hand.

"I was scared. So scared. You can't hold me underwater. I was swallowing water, more and more. More water. Don't even have Schnulli, I'm scared!"

Then those strong arms embraced her, hugged her. *No, wait, bad strong arms. Holding me down! Strong arms in a uniform, holding me, dragging me through water.*

Wait, what?

She shook her head, closed her eyes, and opened them again.

She realized she was out of the water, being hugged by strong arms—a guy in swim shorts, no uniform. She shook her head again and looked down at her hands, her slender, adult hands, and the ring on the left hand caught her eye. The beautiful engagement ring sparkled in the sunshine.

"I'm so sorry, Maria, I'm sorry. I was stupid," the soft, male voice said.

She shook her head again. Her head was pounding. *Aaron. Of course it's Aaron holding me, hugging me. We're at the pool. The pool on campus.*

She looked at him, confused. He gently touched her face, stroking it. "Are you okay?"

"I think so." She was still confused, so very confused by her own thoughts.

"I'm sorry. I just wanted you to come in and thought pulling you would be a fun time."

"You didn't . . . hold me underwater, did you?"

Aaron shook his head and gave her a funny look.

"You're not wearing a uniform."

Now it was Aaron's turn to be confused. "What? Why would I go swimming in my uniform? Maria, are you okay? What's going on?"

"I don't know. I think I just had a dream—the drowning dream."

He raised one eyebrow and looked at her. "But you're awake!"

"I know. It was weird. Almost like a flashback." She felt uncertain, not sure what to say or think. Aaron's arm was still around her, so she leaned into him. She felt safe in those strong, tan arms that hugged her. For a while, they just sat there on the lounge chair, holding each other.

"Are you okay, Maria?"

She nodded. "I think so. It was just weird."

Aaron's stare was intense. "For sure. You were acting kinda strange. Mumbling something about being held underwater and not having a 'Schnulli.'"

"Really? I said that? I talked about Schnulli?"

He nodded. "Yep, something like that. Don't even know what that is."

"It's my pacifier. The name I gave my pacifiers," Maria explained.

Aaron laughed out loud. "You were missing your pacifier? Well, your voice did kind of sound like a toddler's in that moment."

"Like a toddler," she mumbled. "That's it. That's it!"

Aaron looked confused. "What?"

"I felt like a toddler in that moment! It wasn't me talking, it was my toddler self."

Aaron raised an eyebrow. "Maria, what are you talking about? That sounds completely crazy."

He's right, it does sound crazy. But somehow I know it's right. I had a flashback to my toddler years. Is that even possible?

"Aaron, I need a minute to call Mamá and ask her something." Aaron's eyebrow was still raised. "Look, I had another weird dream last night. About drowning. I'm not sure why, but it must have something to do with my past."

His ocean-blue eyes were resting on her. Eyebrow hovering. "I don't understand, Maria. I thought we were looking for your father? We found a Freudian explanation for the drowning. Remember? So much going on that you feel like you're drowning."

She shook her head. "I know *you* came to that conclusion. I know you like your explanations and everything lining up nicely."

"What's that supposed to mean?"

"Nothing, sorry. I just have a feeling there's more to it than that."

"A *feeling*? Come on, Maria. You and your silly feelings!"

She stared at him. Her eyes sparked in anger. "My feelings are *silly*?"

"No, that's not what I meant, Maria, I was just—"

"What did you mean then?"

"I'm just saying that you're making too big a deal out of this. I don't think . . . It all just sounds completely insane."

She crossed her arms and looked at him. "Oh yeah? Insane? Well, Mister I-Need-An-Explanation-For-Everything. Maybe I *am* insane. Maybe I am a product of rape. And maybe then, you'll want this back."

She slipped off her engagement ring and pushed it into his hand, then stormed off.

CHAPTER 16

Aaron stared at the ring in his hand sparkling in the sunlight. His mouth was open; his heart was aching. He stared at the gate to the campus pool. It was still moving, swinging shut.

Maria was gone.

She'd left so fast he hadn't had time to react at all. He closed his hand and felt the ring in his palm. He flinched when someone touched his shoulder.

"You alright, man?" It was Nick, standing next to him. "What happened?"

Slowly, Aaron turned his head toward him, his blue eyes a dark blue, churning like a stormy ocean.

"Why did Maria jet off already?"

Aaron shrugged his shoulders and opened his palm again. The ring sparkled in the glimmer of the sun's heat.

Nick saw it. "Oh my gosh! You guys had a fight? No way, it was so bad she gave you back the engagement ring?"

Aaron nodded slightly, still staring at the ring.

Nick squeezed his shoulder. "Come on, man. Come. Sit down."

He did as he was told and sat on one of the lounge chairs by the pool. Nick plopped down next to him and cleared his throat, still awkwardly rubbing Aaron's shoulder in support. "It'll be alright, man. It'll be alright."

"What'll be alright?" Jim came over, toweling off the pool water, and Brandy and Keisha followed.

Brandy looked around the empty campus pool. "Where's Maria, y'all?"

"She left," Aaron mumbled.

"What? Why?" Jim looked confused.

"Without saying goodbye to any of us? What's up with that girl?" Keisha wondered.

Then she too saw the sparkling engagement ring lying in Aaron's hand. In a trance, he watched her towel slip out of her hand and fall to the concrete floor.

"Gosh, Aaron! Oh boy. She gave you back her ring?"

Without looking up, Aaron nodded.

"Y'all, what's going on?" Brandy looked from friend to friend, then plopped down onto the lounge chair opposite Aaron and Nick. Jim sat down on the other end. Keisha picked up her towel and plopped down next to Jim on the edge. Suddenly, the lounge chair seesawed and hoisted up the side Brandy sat on. She screamed, her legs dangling in the air, her bottom sliding into Jim.

"Keisha, move!" Jim yelled. She did as she was told and jumped back up. The lounge chair with Jim and Brandy on it crashed back down.

"Oof," they both exclaimed, and everyone, including Aaron, had a laugh.

"Oops," Keisha said.

Jim gave her a look. "Goodness, girlfriend, what were you thinking? You didn't see that coming?"

"Nope. I'm not an engineer."

Everyone laughed again. Keisha gestured for Jim and Brandy to scoot over and sat down next to Jim. "Sorry Brandy, sorry boy," she said. "But at least we got Aaron to laugh."

Everyone looked at him. His laughter had evaporated; he was staring at the ring again.

"So, Aaron," Keisha started, her voice soft, "Tell us what happened. We were just swimming and having a great time and here you are holding Maria's engagement ring. What the heck?"

Aaron shrugged his shoulders, still staring at his palm and the ring in it.

"Come on, Aaron. Tell us. We're your gang. Right, y'all?" Brandy said.

The friends all nodded. Nick squeezed Aaron's strong shoulder again in encouragement, but all Aaron could do was sigh and say, "I'm not sure."

Keisha looked at him and tilted her head. "As in 'you're not sure you want to tell us' or 'you're not sure what happened?'"

"Not sure what happened."

"Why'd she give you the ring back? You two have a fight?"

He looked at Keisha. "I guess so."

She raised her eyebrows. "You *guess so*? Boy, there's no guessing. Maria is obviously mad at you."

"That makes sense, y'all," Brandy said and nodded enthusiastically until Jim elbowed her to get her to stop.

Keisha held Aaron's gaze. "You and Maria never really fight. But you did earlier on campus. Now this. There must be a reason. Right, Aaron? She's been acting strange lately. Is there something going on between you two?"

He shook his head. "No, not between us."

"Okay, what is it then, boy? I know something's up. It's so obvious. My girl doesn't storm out without saying goodbye. That's not her. And she wouldn't give you that ring back if nothing was going down between the two of you. Spill it, boy."

Aaron stared at her, and everyone stared at Aaron. *I can't tell them about Maria's dad. I can't tell them about her dreams. She didn't even tell her best friend Keisha. She'd be even more mad if I did. I know she's hurting. Her mom betrayed her. Her past doesn't make any sense. She's hurting. This has nothing to do with me.*

Nothing to do with me?

His face lit up. He slipped the ring on his pinkie and got up. "I have to go."

The friends stared after him. "What?"

"I gotta go find her. Have a great night, guys. See you later." He packed up his things and ran off, leaving his friends baffled, just sitting on the lounge chairs by the pool.

I have to find her. We need to talk this through. She's right, I hate not understanding the big picture, but clearly there's something strange going on. Something strange about her dad, something strange about her mom.

He thought back to their conversation last night when Maria had told him about the phone calls with her aunts. *There are so many strange little pieces. Martina didn't tell her sisters about her daughter. There aren't any baby pictures of Maria. It doesn't make sense. Maria was right. There is something strange about her past. And I'm going to figure it out. Yes I will.*

Determined, Aaron got into his car and sped off toward Maria's apartment.

CHAPTER 17

Maria sat on her soft, blue carpet, still in her bikini, and dialed her mamá's number. The phone rang and rang.

Come on, pick up! I have to talk to you. Come on, Mamá.

Another ring, then an "¿Aló?" Maria smiled and greeted her mom.

"Mija. So good to hear your voice. I'm just finishing up at the store."

"Good business today, Mamá?"

"Always."

Maria could hear her content smile. "I'm proud of you, Mamá. I have so many good memories of your shop. Me playing there in the fabrics. Tea party with my dolls."

Laughter on the other end of the line. For a while, they just chatted about the good old days. Then Maria got quiet.

"Mija, what's going on? You seem upset."

She sighed, tears forming in her eyes. She stared at her left hand, at the imprint the engagement ring had left behind even though it'd only been there a week.

"Mija?"

Through her tears, Maria had to smile. Her mom knew her so well. "I had a fight with Aaron."

She heard a gasp. "Oh, no, mija. Why?"

"We were at the pool. Aaron pulled me underwater."

Even though they were only communicating by voice, she felt as though she could see her mom's confusion.

"I've been dreaming of drowning. Very strange drowning dreams. Aaron pulling me under reminded me of them."

"Oh, mija. I'm sorry. But it's not Aaron's fault, is it?"

Maria shrugged her shoulders. "I guess not. But I got really mad at him."

"It's okay, mija, it's okay. Just talk to him again. You two will be fine. You're a great couple. ¡Pareja maravillosa!"

Maria sighed. "Mamá, did I ever almost drown?"

"What? No!"

"But didn't I learn to swim early."

"Sí. You did. You had immense fear of water. Even during bath time. So I took you to the local pool for swim lessons. But you just screamed and screamed. The instructor didn't know what to do with you."

"And then?"

"There was this sweet teenage girl. She was an exchange student at the local high school who happened to be there during your swim lesson. Johanna was her name. She swam by and said something to you. And you suddenly stopped crying and just looked at her. You calmed down immediately."

"Interesting. What did she say to me?"

"I don't know, mija. She spoke German to you."

"German?"

"Yes, she was an exchange student from Germany. Speaking German calmed you down for some reason. Just like that, you lost your fear of the water and jumped in. She became your friend and taught you to swim. I offered her money for all that time she spent helping you, but she didn't want any. She enjoyed teaching you and was such a sweet girl. I liked her a lot. And you liked her. And now look at you, you're such a good swimmer."

"I know. I am a good swimmer. But *German* calmed me down?"

"Sí, mija."

"Strange." Maria suddenly got up and grabbed the notebook she'd been recording evidence in. "So, she only spoke German to me?"

"Sí, German. It helped you. Don't know why. She was very friendly and had a calming voice. She had just gotten to the U.S. that summer to start her exchange year, so she wasn't good at English yet."

Maria wrote this down in the notebook. "She had just arrived? From Germany?"

"Sí, Allemania. Deutschland."

"Deutschland," Maria repeated. She kept thinking about Germany. *Deutschland. That sounds so familiar.* Maria got lost in thought thinking about Germany, then rubbed her eyes and focused on the conversation again.

"—so you lost all of your fear and bath time was much better also."

"Bath time?"

"Yes, mija. Remember? I just told you. I started swim lesson because you were so afraid of baths."

"Really? I don't remember that at all."

Her mom laughed. "No, mija, you wouldn't. You were very little."

"How old was I?"

"It was the summer before my sisters immigrated. August, I think."

"So I was almost two years old?"

"Almost, yes. You turned two that fall. Still had all of your black hair."

"My black hair?"

"Yes, you had dark-black hair when you were little."

"Really?"

"Yes, mija, you don't remember?" Maria could almost see her mom's content smile.

"No, I don't. But I don't recall any pictures of me with black hair."

"No, not many pictures," her mom said. Maria could sense the moment the smile faded.

"Mamá, I don't think you have any pictures of me as a baby. Why not?"

Silence on the other end.

"Mamá? I asked you a question. Did you hear me?"

"Sí."

"So? Why aren't there any pictures of the time when I was a baby?"

"No pictures of that time."

"Mamá . . . you must have at least one of them."

"No."

"Why not?"

"It was tough times, Maria. Not much money."

"Mamá, pictures didn't cost that much."

"No. But the cameras."

"You really don't have a single picture of me as a baby?"

"No."

"Not a single picture?"

"No, Maria. I said no. ¡Basta!"

"Mamá, you tell me you love me. If you love me so much, why didn't you take a single picture of me as a baby?"

"I do love you lots, mija. Having pictures or not says nothing of my love for you."

"I know, Mamá, but it's odd. Is there a reason you don't have any pictures of me from that time?"

"No, no reason, just no money," her mom explained. Her voice was starting to sound shrill.

What's going on? "Mamá, what hospital was I born at?"

"Maria, *stop it*. What has gotten into you?"

But Maria was on a roll. Her tongue spit out everything that had occupied her mind the past week. "What hospital was I born at? What was my birth like? Why didn't you ever tell anyone about me until after Tía Monica and Tía Mariella came over?"

"Maria, Maria, please! Please stop the questions," her mom begged.

"Mamá? Are you hiding something from me? Something about my past? About my father?"

There was silence. A long silence.

"Mamá?"

"I'm here."

"Did you hear me?"

"Sí."

Maria started to get mad. "You did?"

"Sí."

"Then answer!"

"¡Naguará, Maria! Do not bring up your father again! Just you and me! It's just you and me! You hear me?"

Maria was mad. *Why in the world can't I even mention him?* She screamed into the phone, "Mamá, what are you hiding from me?"

She couldn't help it anymore. Her hands were shaking, her whole body was trembling. She jumped up and started pacing back and forth in her apartment.

I know there's something. Why won't she tell me? My mamá, my own mother who tells me everything. I love her, I trust her, but she betrays me. My father didn't leave when she was pregnant with me. She lied to me. What else is she not telling me? I know there's a piece to the puzzle missing, and I know Mamá is holding that missing part but is keeping it from me. She won't tell me. Won't tell me the truth on purpose.

She had no intention of hurting her mom, but she was out of control and the words came out without her having any power to stop them.

"You got divorced way before I was born. You lied about getting a divorce when you were pregnant with me!"

Maria heard a gasp on the other end.

"I know he abused you! I know. I'm sorry, Mamá. I'm sorry about that. I understand you don't want to talk about it, but you lied. Lied to *me.* Yet it doesn't add up. If you got divorced before you were pregnant with me, how did you get pregnant with me? How? With whom?"

Silence. Maria couldn't see her mom on the phone. If she could, she would have seen all color flush from the small, gentle woman's face, seen her turn ghostly white and her whole body start to tremble, her hands shaking and fluttering.

"Mamá, you got divorced way before I was born. Didn't you? *Didn't you?*" No answer. "I know it! What happened, Mamá? I need to know. How did you get me? Please. Tell me. How did you have me, get me?"

The woman on the other end of the line sunk to her knees, sobbing, incapable of answering. Silent tears streamed down her face. The phone slipped out of her sweaty palms and hit the ground of her tailor shop. *Thump.*

Miles away on the other end of the line, Maria heard the sound of the phone hitting the ground and stopped her interrogation-style questioning.

"Mamá? Mamá?"

She was suddenly afraid, afraid something had happened to her mom. To the woman she loved. She realized how much this conversation had gotten out of hand, how much her words must have hurt her mom.

But don't I have the right to know what happened? Don't I deserve to know about my own past? My gosh, Mamá. Are you okay?

"Mamá? Mamá? Please answer. Mamá, please. Mamá, are you alright?"

No answer came.

Maria didn't know that her mom was on her knees, staring at the phone on the floor, her tears dripping onto the screen. Maria couldn't know that her mom's thoughts were racing—she was far away, in a different world, a world and a past she had run away from the past two decades. She didn't hear her daughter's pleas; she had forgotten all about the phone call, such was the pain that haunted her, the pain of the past.

A sound made its way up to her ear. Her daughter, begging her to answer. Asking for her mamá. Her daughter was crying now, she could tell by her voice. That voice she knew so well. That little one she knew so well and loved more than anything. Her daughter.

"Mamá, please," the begging voice called from the tiny phone.

Still kneeling on the floor, Martina slowly picked up the phone and held it to her ear.

"Mamá, please, are you okay? Mamá, please answer. Please. . . ."

"I'm here," she whispered. "It's okay, mija. I'm here. Mamá is here."

Relief enveloped Maria. She stopped her frantic pacing and sank to her knees atop the soft, blue carpet. "Mamá, I was so worried. I'm glad you're okay. I'm sorry, Mamá. I'm so sorry."

"It's okay, mija, it's alright."

"Mamá, I didn't mean to hurt you, it's just. . . ."

"I know, mija, I know. But you have to let the past be the past. It's you and me now. You and me. Hear me?"

Martina Sullivan had found her voice again. Her voice was back, her mind clear. She had to protect her daughter, her treasure. Had to make sure her little one was okay. Just her and her daughter. They belonged together. Just the two of them.

She heard Maria's sobs on the other end. "It's okay, Maria. Please. Just me and you. I love you so, so much."

"Te amo también, Mamá," Maria said.

Click.

Maria stared down at her phone, knees on the floor, uncomprehending at first. Then she understood.

Her mom had hung up on her.

Her thoughts raced and confusion gripped her. She made a fist and hit the carpet.

Mamá didn't explain anything. Was she so hurt by her past that she can't even talk about it? So hurt by my dad? My biological father? By the monster that raped her and is responsible for my existence? That must be it. Monster! My father is a monster! I'll slap him! Tomorrow! Monster!

Her face turned red. She threw her phone on the floor and it bounced away. She stared after it through the tears in her eyes.

Her doorbell rang shrill and loud. She stared in surprise but otherwise didn't budge. Just stared out the window. The doorbell rang again and again.

What in the world? Who's this annoying person ringing the doorbell over and over?

Still in her bikini, her face red, eyes completely green, lips pressed together, she walked to the front door and swung it open at the eighth ring. She locked eyes with Aaron, who was standing on her welcome mat in his swim shorts.

"You forgot something," he said, and held up her engagement ring.

CHAPTER 18

Aaron gawked at Maria. She was so beautiful. Her purple bikini looked great on her sun-kissed skin, and her wavy, auburn hair fell loosely over her shoulders and elegant neck. Despite not wearing any makeup, she had the prettiest face he'd ever seen. A perfectly formed nose with freckles all over it, big kissable lips, the most unique exotic eyes. But as she stared at him, he noticed they were completely green. He knew that meant she was agitated.

"Maria, please take the ring back," he begged her, and held it out. She continued staring at him, tears dwelling in her eyes. "I'm sorry, Maria. Please forgive me. I didn't mean to suggest you're crazy or insane. I just don't like not having an explanation."

He saw a tear roll out of her freakishly green eyes. Her shoulders hung down. She suddenly looked small and broken.

"Maria, I love you, no matter what. I meant what I said at the ball. I choose *you* to be my wingwoman for life. That's all I want. You!"

She was still looking down. Aaron watched as the tear dripped onto the welcome mat, right next to his foot. It hurt to see her this sad.

He took her left hand in his and slipped the ring back on, then held it tight. Her whole body was shaken by deep sobs. He pulled her in for a long hug, right there on her apartment's welcome mat.

They were lying in the dark arm in arm in her bed. He held her close as she snuggled up more firmly against him. He smiled and gave her a kiss on the forehead. "I love you, Maria," he whispered.

"I love you, too. I'm glad you came over."

"Oh, yeah?"

"Yeah. Definitely. I need you."

He smirked. "Oh yeah? What for?"

She laughed. "For everything, silly."

"That's good, 'cuz I need you, too."

"Oh, yeah? For what?"

"For life. Forever!"

"That's good. 'Cuz I need you forever too. I'll never ever take this ring off again."

She lifted her arm and felt the ring on her finger. He lifted his hand and ran it over the ring and her hand, then cupped her face and gave her a kiss.

"Hi there, fiancée."

Her phone buzzed on her nightstand. Aaron sat up and glanced at it, then handed the phone to her. "Text from your mom. Oh, and an earlier one from Keisha. And Brandy. And Keisha again."

Maria sighed and read through the texts. She then answered her mom's. Aaron watched her intensely. She felt his stare. "What?"

"Are you two alright?"

She sent the message then turned off the phone, handed it back to Aaron, and shrugged her shoulders. "I guess so."

Aaron put the phone back on the nightstand and turned to her. "You and your mom have been fighting a lot lately. It's very unusual."

"I know. But she doesn't tell me anything anymore. You should've heard her today."

"I know, you told me earlier. Maybe she was hurt so badly that she feels too much shame to admit whatever it is that happened, happened?"

Maria nodded. "Yeah. That's probably it. Maybe we can find out more tomorrow, in Jacksonville."

"Yeah, exactly." Aaron thought for a bit. "But none of it makes sense. I'm confused by the new stuff you learned today."

Maria propped herself up on one elbow. "What do you mean?"

"Your fear of water as a toddler and the way you got over it. Think about it. Why would a scared little toddler that knows English and Spanish calm down hearing German, a language she can't speak and doesn't understand?"

Maria shrugged her shoulders. "Maybe it just sounded nice?"

Aaron laughed. "Have you heard German before? It doesn't exactly fall under the 'soothing-beautiful-languages' category. It's not like French, with all its romantic singsongy sounds. My high school in Montana offered German as a language, and many of my friends took it instead of French. So I know it has some pretty rough-sounding noises."

In the darkness, Maria heard him giggle and felt the warmth of his body. She sat up now. "Can you say something in German?"

"What? Why?"

"I don't know." She shook her head, realizing it was a strange request. But somehow she felt it was important.

Aaron thought for a while. "I really don't know much. Only a few things my friends would always say around me."

"Come on, Aaron. Try it."

He thought hard, then came up with something. "Mein Name ist Aaron. Wie heißt du?"

She stared at him. Her head started hurting, her thoughts spinning. *Ich heiße Maria.* She shook her head. *That doesn't sound right. No, it wasn't right. Hallo, du Kleine! Hallo, wie heißt du?* She closed her eyes. Her head hurt, hurt so much. She touched her temples and rubbed them.

Aaron noticed it. "Maria, are you okay?"

"I know that one," Maria mumbled.

"Well, it's pretty standard. A lot of people know that. From movies. German is often used in the World War II movies so many Americans love to watch. Common German things, like 'stopp' and 'halt' and 'schneller.'"

"Maybe," Maria mumbled, still rubbing her head, "maybe that's where I've heard it before."

Aaron nodded and pulled her in closer to him. "We'll find out more, Maria. Trust me, we will. Let's just go to sleep now. We need to be fresh for Jacksonville tomorrow. Okay?"

She gave a weak nod. Her head was still pounding from the bad headache. It was the strangest feeling.

She sighed and cuddled close into his well-trained shoulders. He was such a good-looking guy, nicely tanned, his six-pack impressive. She was a lucky girl and should be more thankful for her wonderful life. But something gnawed at her, right at her heart. She had a feeling something was missing in her life. Something important. She just didn't know what. She sighed again. The headache persisted.

"Good night, Aaron. I love you."

"Good night, my love," he whispered, and fell asleep within seconds. Maria closed her eyes and soon fell asleep also.

◇◇◆◇◇

She heard someone trying to wake her up. She tried to open her eyes. But they were heavy, so very heavy. Still so sleepy. She didn't want to wake up yet. She wanted to keep sleeping. Dreaming.

"Hallo, meine Süße! Guten Morgen." There it was again. The friendly, calming voice. She smiled and sucked at her pacifier.

Schnulli. I love my Schnulli. You taste so good, Schnulli. You feel so good, Schnulli. Her head was being stroked by gentle hands. The friendly, calming female voice kept talking to her while stroking her cheek. The hand wandered toward her ear and gently pulled on her ear lope.

"Dingeling!"

The hand pretended to ring a doorbell, right there on her earlobe. She giggled but held on firmly to her pacifier and made sure her eyes stayed closed.

"Hallo, dingeling."

The earlobe doorbell rang again. She giggled and kept listening to her mama's voice. She loved hearing her speak her native language. The mama-language. It was beautiful. She was learning both mama and daddy language. She loved them both. Both her mama and her daddy and both ways they spoke to her.

She kept giggling as the hand moved across her face, to the doorbell, then gave a knock on her forehead before gently squeezing her nose.

"Guten Tag, Herr Nasemann," her mama laughed.

She finally opened her eyes and looked up at her. But she was all blurry, she only saw outlines of her mama's figure. She seemed to disappear, disappear even as she was sitting there right there on her bed.

Wait, Mama!

"Meine Süße," she kept saying. Her voice faded, her beautiful mama-language went away.

She started to panic. *How could Mama fade away like that? Just sitting there on her bed, on her wet bed.*

What? Wet bed? No, no, no, what is happening?

She sucked at her pacifier to keep calm, to think, to feel safe. But it was wet all around. So very wet. The water ran all over and swallowed her up. A wave knocked away her pacifier, a wave of mucky water just washed it out and carried it away.

Far, far away.

"Nein, Schnulli!" she screamed, but gulped a big mouthful of mucky, yucky water. Then the strong arms were holding her, holding her down deeper in the water.

No, help, help me! Mama, Mama, please help me! I can't breathe, please help me! Mama, bitte, bitte, Mama, komm zu mir!

She kept begging for her Mama to come and help her, save her, be with her, she begged in the mama-language, and all of a sudden, she saw the faded picture of her mama in a bright-white blinding light saying, "Meine Süße, meine kleine Süße," before it all went pitch-black around her. . . .

"Maria, wake up."

She heard a loud, deep voice and threw her head from side to side to get out of those awful arms holding her down, but then she realized she wasn't being held at all.

A hand on her cheek. *Thank God, it's Mama.* She listened for her mama's voice, her native language, but all she heard was that deep voice. "Wake up, Maria, wake up! You're dreaming again!"

She quickly opened her eyes and saw Aaron sitting there, right there next to her in her bed. Aaron. Of course. It was Aaron.

"Are you okay? You were talking, mumbling something."

She shook her head. It was still hurting, the headache still there.

"Another weird dream? The drowning dream?"

She nodded. She had a splitting headache. She rubbed her head. Aaron turned on the nightstand light, got up, and returned with a glass of water. She took some deep gulps while he pushed the damp hair out of her face.

"I'm worried about you. These dreams are really disturbing you."

She nodded. "They're weird. So intense. So real. I'm always drowning."

He nodded. "I'm sorry, Maria. It's strange you're suddenly having them. Ever since the Air Force Ball. There must be some connection."

She snorted. "Drowning and the Air Force Ball? There's no connection."

"Except for the Freudian one. Seems you've been feeling overwhelmed. By our engagement?"

She leaned over to give him a kiss. "No, definitely not. I want to marry you. I love you."

"But why are you suddenly having these dreams? Why now?"

She thought for a bit, then her face lit up. "They started after the ball, you're right about that, but they seem to have more to do with my father. Ever since the ball, I've wanted to learn more about him."

"Maybe. But that doesn't make sense either. Drowning and your father? No connection there. Right?"

They both thought for a bit. Then Aaron said, "This time you actually talked in your sleep. Well, mumbled something. It was hard to make out. Something like 'meine Süße'" He struggled to pronounce the words.

Maria stared at him, then at the small round table where her laptop lay.

"Say that again."

"Um, meine Süße?"

Maria jumped up, turned on the lights, and went over to her dining table where her laptop was lying. She sat down in one of the chairs and opened up the computer to pull up Google Translate.

Aaron watched her, one eyebrow raised. "What are you up to?"

She typed in *sweetheart* and had it translate to German. *Schatz.* Maria stared at it. *I think I recognize that word, but it's not the one from my dream.*

"What are you googling?"

Maria sighed and explained what she was doing.

"You think that word from your dream is German for 'sweetheart' or 'darling?'"

She nodded.

"But why German? I don't get it."

Maria didn't answer and instead kept google-searching for a list of cute German names to call your loved ones. But none of them listed the one she had heard in her dream.

"Maybe it's nothing," she said, finally giving up. "It was just so odd that Mamá was speaking German in my dream."

"What? Your mom was?"

"Yeah. At least I think so. But she kind of looked different than normal. Well, it was a dream after all. My brain probably just mixed up her and that exchange student she told me about. Who knows? It's all just so confusing."

She put her head in her hands and felt it throb. She closed her eyes and felt the sensation again, echoing down the winding ways in her brain.

Meine Süße, mein Engel, kleine Maus.

She shook herself involuntarily, holding her head tight in her hands, as if trying to shake those strange words out of her head.

Aaron came over and stroked her hair. "Maria, what is it?"

"I don't know, don't know! These strange words are stuck in my head. I don't know what language they are or what they even mean. But somehow I've heard them before. I don't know why. But I can't find them online, don't even know how to spell them. I just don't know. It's not English, it's not Spanish. I thought it's German—but why would it be? I've never learned any German."

She looked up at Aaron and looked so lost and sad that his heart sank. He got up and sat next to her, pulled the laptop over, and started typing something in. "Okay. So, we're looking for sweet names you call your loved one, right?"

Maria looked at him, then nodded and watched. He typed *German words of endearment* into the Google search engine and hit enter.

Another list popped up. The words seemed to just jump off the screen at Maria—they were dancing all around her, forming sounds and triggering faint memories in her head.

Süße, Maus, Hase, Engel.

The words were haunting her, dancing around in her brain, and then she saw the silhouette of a young woman sitting by her bed, a young, tall woman with reddish-brown, wavy hair and freckles on her nose. The picture faded, replaced by German words—lovely, horrible German terms of endearment hurled around, echoing inside Maria's brain.

She screamed and before she knew it, she hit the floor.

CHAPTER 19

"**M**aria!" Aaron jumped out of his chair to help her. "Maria, oh my gosh, are you okay?" He kneeled next to her and the toppled chair she had fallen out of.

"I know those words," she whispered. "All of them. I know them all."

He looked at her, looked deep into her exotic eyes whose muted green flecks had turned bright-green and overwhelmed the other colors. Agitation.

"Are you sure? You're positive you know German?"

"I don't know. But I know these words. 'Sweet,' 'mouse,' 'bunny,' 'angel.' That's what they mean, right?

Aaron stared at her, then pulled himself up onto the chair. He knew she hadn't seen their translation—you had to click them first to see the English translation. Maria had fallen out of her chair before he was able to do that. He proceeded to translate the website that had come up in his Google search and there it was, black on white.

She was right. Every single word she'd said. She had correctly translated those German words. German terms of endearment.

How in the world does she know this? He stared at the screen, then at Maria. His heart was pounding. *It's scary. There's something in Maria's past that's scary, so unfathomable we can't understand it. It's jumbled up in pieces and just so odd. I don't understand. And there's nothing more I hate than not understanding.*

"There has to be a logical explanation," he roared, his voice deep.

Maria stared at him. She had never heard him speak that way.

"We'll find out. There must be an explanation. No excuse. We'll find it. We will succeed," Aaron barked.

He stared beyond the little round table into the dark room. Maria was so surprised by his way of speaking that her head had cleared. The headache was almost gone, replaced by a faint ache. She peered up at Aaron.

"Yes, sir," she said. "Sounds like you're giving an order here." They regarded each other and smirked for the first time that night. "So yes, sir, *we will succeed*," she said, repeating his words in a lowered voice.

Aaron stared at her, then got off his chair and sat next to her on the blue carpet. "I'm sorry, Maria, I didn't mean to bark orders."

She smiled at him. "Well, you are an airman after all. I suppose it's good you know how to give orders."

"I'm sorry. It's not how I should be talking off-duty with my loved ones, though. I just don't like all these unknowns we're facing. Guess the stress made me go into soldier-mode, like when I'm on a mission."

"With the way you shouted, sure sounds like you're ready to be a real airman, not a cadet any longer. You're ready to go out there and get to work. Guess you will be soon." She sighed.

"Yeah, but as a second lieutenant I won't be the one barking orders—I'll be on the receiving end." He laughed and smiled at her.

She smiled back. "Yes, sir, that's correct, sir! But one day, you'll give orders, sir!"

"Yes, ma'am!" Aaron saluted her, then gave her a kiss on the forehead.

In that split second, her headache came back on suddenly, so strong, forming a bright light in front of her eyes, so bright that she had to close them. An image formed in her mind.

She felt small. So small. Looking at a man in uniform saluting her. Smiling at her. Giving her a kiss on the forehead. "Yes, sir, Daddy."

The bright light disappeared along with the image in her mind, and she was looking straight at Aaron, her hand still hovering on her eyebrow in a salute. Aaron stared at her; his own one eyebrow raised. "What did you say, Maria? 'Daddy?'"

Confused, she lowered her salute and felt the headache throbbing again with such force that she couldn't help but rub her temples. "I need to lay down again." She crawled over to her bed.

"Okay, sure. I'm sorry, Maria."

As she pulled herself up into bed, she looked back and smiled at him. "What for? Don't be sorry. I'm sorry. I'm the basket case here." Suddenly, she looked so sad, tears dwelling in her eyes. "Are you sure you still want to marry me? Maybe I *am* going crazy."

Aaron looked at her. He came over and stroked her head. "Yeah, well, maybe you are, but I doubt it. There must be a logical explanation for all this. Don't worry, we'll figure it out. Maybe we'll know more tomorrow, after our trip to Jacksonville."

Maria nodded.

"Let's go back to sleep. You'll want to be alert tomorrow. Unless you think we shouldn't go anymore?"

Maria sat up in her bed. "No, let's definitely go. I need to meet that guy. That might help. And if not, at least I'll have seen my dad and confronted him. It'll make me feel better."

"Yeah, of course. Good plan."

"Aaron, can I ask you a favor? Come lay down with me. I need you to protect me."

"Protect you?"

"Yeah. From myself. From my dreams, I suppose."

"Of course, how can I resist?" He smiled, his ocean-blue eyes sparkling. "Let me power off the laptop. Be right there."

"Okay." She lay back down and closed her heavy eyes. She quickly fell into a deep sleep before Aaron could come over.

He listened to her breathing softly, her body still. No dreams yet. He found her notebook and wrote down the German words of endearment with a big question mark next to them. Then he joined her in bed and lay awake a while, deep in thought.

Why in the world does she know all these words? I'm sure it's something from her past, not just her mind playing tricks on her. We've gotten glimpses of her past. She's not crazy. No, she's smart, sane.

No matter what, I'll protect her. Just like she told me to. Protect her from everything, everyone, herself. I'll make sure she's safe. 'Cuz I love her.

The alarm clock shrilled bright and early. Aaron opened his eyes and realized he was all alone in bed. *Where is Maria?* His eyes scanned the apartment and found her sitting by the window, watching the sunrise with a steaming cup of coffee in hand. She was deep in thought.

"Good morning," he said, and sat up.

Maria turned around and smiled. "Good morning, sleepyhead. There's coffee and milk in the fridge."

Aaron got up, walked over to the little kitchenette, and poured himself half a cup of coffee, then filled the other half with milk. He walked over to Maria and plopped down on the soft, blue carpet next to her chair. For a while they both just looked out of the window at the palm trees glistening in the morning sun.

"Ready for today?"

"Yeah, I guess so." She looked at him. Her eyes were hazelnut brown, a sign that she was calm.

"How is your head?"

"Good. Headache's all gone."

He nodded. *That's good. I'm worried about her. And scared. Not sure what's going on.* He looked at the clock.

Maria saw his glance. "You're fine. You didn't actually sleep in that much. We still have lots of time to get ready and have breakfast. No worries."

He smiled, his ocean-blue eyes sparkling. *She knows me well, and I know her well. Can't wait to marry her, spend the rest of my life with her. We're meant to be together. We'll have a family together some day. She'll be an awesome mommy. Our kids will be so cute. Will they have her eyes? Those eyes that are one of a kind. Unusual, exotic.*

"Ready Maria?"

She looked at Aaron as she put on her shoes and grabbed her purse, then gave a slight nod. "A bit nervous."

He gave her a kiss. "It'll be alright. And here, don't forget this." He handed her the notebook labeled *My Past*. "Heads-up, I wrote a few new entries in it last night."

She looked at him, her eyebrows raised. "Okay, thanks, I guess. But I won't look at it now. It will just make me more nervous and confused."

Aaron smiled. "That's probably a good idea. I need you focused and sharp on this trip. Let's go learn more about your father and hopefully the truth about your past."

She smiled her brightest smile at him. "You're awesome, Aaron."

He winked at her. "I know." Then he gave her a kiss.

She put the notebook in her purse, and they walked out of her apartment to her car. "Here, you drive. I'm too nervous."

"Okay." Aaron opened the passenger door for Maria like a gentleman then got behind the wheel of her car, and off they went.

He turned onto the highway. They were both quiet and pensive as the car sped toward Jacksonville, on the road to unlocking the secrets of Maria's past—the truth about her father and her birth.

CHAPTER 20

They were parked in the lot of a little strip mall in the middle of Jacksonville and looked out the windshield at the storefront that read "Sullivan's Plumbing."

"Well, there it is. That's definitely your last name on that sign," Aaron said. "Are you ready?"

Maria nodded. *I'm not ready at all, but if we tried to wait until I am, we'd spend all day right here in this car, staring at the sign.*

"Come on, Maria. You got this. We got this. I have my plan. You'll see. It's all planned out." He showed her some scribbles on the notepad he always carried around and gave her a kiss. "Come on, let's go. It'll be fine. Trust me."

She took a deep breath and nodded.

Yes, I trust him. He's good at planning missions. A true leader in the making. My Aaron. I can see him sitting in the Pentagon one day, making sensible decisions about how to handle yet another international crisis. He'll be phenomenal.

She took another deep breath and got out of the car first. Her car. Her old blue Oldsmobile.

It's pretty shabby, but reliable. That's all I need. And I love blue. Blue like the carpet in my apartment. Blue like Aaron's eyes. Blue like the sundress I'm wearing, matching my light-blue purse. I'm blue—all blue. She couldn't help but grin.

By her side, Aaron whispered, "Did I mention you look stunning? I mean, you always do, but even more so today."

She smiled. *Well, I want to make a good impression on the man I'm about to meet. On Jonathan Eric Sullivan. My dad. My biological father.* She sighed.

"It'll be fine, Maria. Just stick to the plan."

She nodded.

"And no slapping," he reminded her with a wink.

She smirked. *He really does know me well.*

They walked hand in hand toward Sullivan's Plumbing. He squeezed her hand to give her encouragement. "We'll get some answers today. Don't worry, I'm with you."

Maria nodded. A big knot formed in her throat. Not only was she about to meet her biological father, she was about to face her mom's abuser. And she was totally going behind her mamá's back. She had always promised her mom that she wouldn't go looking for her dad. And now she had. And hadn't even told her about it.

My sweet, little Mamá. The one who raised me, loved me no matter what. Gave me everything she could and made sure I had a good life.

A little bell rang when Aaron opened the door to Sullivan's, snapping Maria out of her thoughts.

"Good morning," said a cheerful female voice from behind the counter. "How can I help you today?"

They looked around. The store was well kept. Neatly organized shelves stocked with plumbing material lined the walls of the store. There were many signs and awards on the counter, including a few that proclaimed *Plumber of the Year* and *Jacksonville's Best Plumbing Store.*

They sure have good credentials, thought Maria.

She felt the lady's eyes on them as she scanned the store for its owner. But he wasn't there—nobody was in there but the single solitary employee.

Maria noticed a door behind the counter. *Maybe he's in the back? He better be. I didn't come all this way only to meet his employee.*

"Good morning," Aaron said, and Maria felt him squeeze her hand.

"Good morning," she also said, greeting the lady as they approached the counter.

"We're here to see Mr. Sullivan," Aaron explained. "We have a few questions about a big project we have coming up."

"Oh, a big project? Well, if it involves plumbing, you've come to the right place." The lady smiled and opened up a book.

Aaron smiled his most charming smile. "Yes, it sure does. We're gonna redo all the plumbing in our new house."

"Oh, a new house? Y'all, that's just fantastic," the lady said.

Maria smiled and nodded. *Where's my father? The man I came to see?* She was getting impatient already. Another squeeze of her hand. *Aaron knows how I feel. He wants me to stay calm and patient.*

"Which house did you purchase? There are a bunch of nice houses on the market around here right now. Maybe we can start with an address to get something on the books for your project?"

Maria's smile faded. *An address? She must be joking!* Another squeeze. She took a deep breath and found her smile again. *Such a fake smile, but who cares? It only has to be convincing to that lady.*

"Please, sit." The front desk lady pointed to two chairs near the front of the counter.

"Thank you," Aaron said, "My fiancée and I just purchased a fixer-upper in Jacksonville Heights on Bellrose Avenue."

Maria stared at Aaron.

"Ah, it's a beautiful area. Y'all gonna love it there. I think I know the one you're talking about, saw it for sale the other day."

"Yeah, we found it online via the Zillow app. Gotta love that app."

The front desk clerk smiled and Maria glanced at Aaron. She was fascinated. She had underestimated him, and only now appreciated how important it was for him to be here with her. *If it had just been me,*

I would've failed already. Didn't realize we needed to have more than a plausible story to see the boss of the store. Of course Jonathan Sullivan isn't just sitting around working the front desk!

"Ah, Zillow. Yes, I love that service." The lady now looked at Maria. She started nodding. That was all she could think of.

"So, did you two just get married?"

Maria kept her fake smile plastered on, even though she wanted to frown and tell the lady to cut the small talk.

"No, not yet. Will be in August, in Miami, my fiancée's hometown. We'll be looking to move into our new house right after the wedding and were hoping the plumbing will be all done by then."

The lady looked at her books.

"Well, we are pretty busy . . . but August shouldn't be a problem," she said with a big smile.

"Wonderful. Thank you, Ms. Carmal."

Maria looked at Aaron. *How in the world does he know her first name?* She glanced at the middle-aged lady and noticed a small pin with her name on it. *Man, Aaron is good. Perceptive.*

"I'm Aaron, Aaron Heikinnen," he introduced himself, "and this is my fiancée, Maria!"

"Y'all, nice to meet you," Ms. Carmal said, and shook their hands. "And welcome to Sullivan's Plumbing. We're looking forward to working with you on your fixer-upper, Mr. and Mrs. Heikinnen."

Maria looked at her, confused. *Heikinnen is Aaron's last name, not mine. Unless I take his last name when we actually get married. Will I? This lady automatically assumed so. Typical. But I guess a girl is supposed to, huh?*

Maria got lost in thought. *Will we actually get married in Miami? I've have been so preoccupied with finding out more about my past that I haven't thought much about my own future. My marriage. When? Where? How? So much to plan.* She forced herself to listen to the awkward small talk again and tuned back in to hear crucial information.

"—so we would like to talk to Mr. Sullivan himself. We heard he's the best. You know, Ms. Carmal, I know a thing or two about plumbing myself, so I'd just like to make sure we're in the best of hands. I'd like to personally speak with the boss himself."

Ms. Carmal smiled. "I see, Mr. Aaron, I see. Let me check his calendar."

Aaron nodded, Maria as well.

"How does Monday at four p.m. sound? Mr. Sullivan should be in the office at that point."

Monday at four p.m.? That doesn't work at all. We're here today, today to speak to him and see him! Maria wanted to yell at this lady but felt a long squeeze of her hand.

"Ms. Carmal, you see, like I said, we're from Miami."

The lady nodded with a big smile. *Nicely done to tie that in, Aaron.* Maria kept listening.

"We were here to close on the house this week but have to go back tomorrow. Still gotta work to, you know, pay off that loan."

He smiled, his blue eyes sparkling. Ms. Carmal was affected the same way many women were and couldn't stop looking at this good-looking young man's ocean-blue eyes. Maria couldn't believe it.

"Ms. Carmal, my future mother-in-law offered to pay for the plumbing work if we got something on the books today. You know, she comes from a good family that made a name for themselves in Miami, and I don't want my future mother-in-law to turn into a *monster-in-law* if she doesn't get her way."

Maria wanted to scold Aaron for his portrayal of her sweet mamá, but knew better and kept smiling and nodding. *Stupid, this is stupid!* But she played along. She heard Ms. Carmal laugh.

"Oh no, darlin', we sure don't want handsome you getting in trouble." She sighed and batted her fake eyelashes at Aaron, who smiled widely, his eyes sparkling.

Seriously? Maria started to get mad, but kept up her own wide, fake smile.

"Mr. Aaron. Let me check again."

"Yes, please, Ms. Carmal. We'd really appreciate that. *I'd* really appreciate it. And I'll make sure to tell your boss you've been the most helpful clerk I've ever met. A wonderful face for the store." He smiled a wide smile.

This time, Maria squeezed his hand.

Ms. Carmal checked her books and pointed at an entry. "So, Mr. Sullivan is doing a big job this weekend. But he usually checks into the store around lunchtime. You know, he always eats his lunch here. And spends his break here."

Aaron and Maria nodded.

"How about y'all come back at one p.m., darlings? Would that work?"

Aaron stood up, held out his hand and took hers, and shook it firmly a few times before saying, "Wonderful. That sounds like a great plan. We can't wait to meet Mr. Sullivan at one p.m. Great talking to you and doing business with you, Ms. Carmal. We appreciate you very much."

"Aw, thank you. Mr. Aaron, thank you." She smiled and batted her eyes.

Maria stood up and quickly shook her hand also. "See you then, Ms. Carmal."

The clerk's smile faded. "Yes, see you then."

Maria bit her tongue to avoid saying anything she'd regret, and cautioned herself not to take Aaron's hand or arm as they walked out. *It's ridiculous to have a grown woman admiring a man twenty years her junior.*

They walked out and Aaron waved goodbye. "See you later, Ms. Carmal."

Once the little bell had rung again and the store's door closed behind them, Aaron took her hand and pulled her to the side.

"I think that went well," he said with a smile and gave her a kiss.

"Yes, Mr. Aaron, handsome Mr. Aaron, it went *very* well," Maria mocked and batted her eyes.

Aaron laughed. "Jealous, are we?" He smirked as they walked hand in hand down the sunny sidewalk toward a Starbucks to waste their time.

"No, not jealous. Just disgusted that a woman that age would behave like that. She could be your mom!"

He laughed out loud. "Could be, but isn't. Just gotta charm the ladies now and then to get my way. It worked."

Maria shook her head in disbelief. "Yeah, it did, Prince Charming. I guess I never considered we'd have to talk to someone else in order to see . . . to see, you know . . ."

". . . the boss," Aaron finished her sentence. "That's why you always need a plan. And must do your research. I knew they had a clerk and that it was most likely a woman. So, I concocted a plan, googled what houses recently sold in the area so we'd have a plausible story and—"

He was interrupted by the biggest kiss Maria could give him. He passionately kissed her back until she pulled away from him.

Catching her breath, she said, "I know, I know. By myself, I wouldn't have been able to get an appointment with the boss and probably would have ended up slapping Ms. Carmal instead."

He winked at her. "Exactly!"

"So, Prince Charming, how can I repay you?"

"Oh, I have an idea," he said, and pulled her in for another kiss.

CHAPTER 21

The little bell over the door of Sullivan's Plumbing rang as Maria and Aaron walked in. Ms. Carmal looked up and broke out into the biggest smile when she saw them.

"Mr. Aaron," she said, "so good to see you again, darlin'. Let me get the boss for you. He's in the back. Like I said, eating his lunch." She winked.

Aaron nodded. "Thank you, Ms. Carmal. Really appreciate it."

She got up and walked through the door behind the counter. Through it they heard her say, "Jonathan, that young man I told you about is here to talk about the plumbing job in Jacksonville Heights."

Someone mumbled something back at her.

"Okay, I'll let them know."

The clerk came back through the door. Aaron and Maria looked at each other, then at Ms. Carmal. "He'll be ready in five minutes. Please, sit," she said, and offered them the same chairs they'd sat in a few hours earlier.

After they'd made themselves comfortable, Ms. Carmal spoke up. "So, Mr. Aaron what do you do for work?" She leaned on the counter and looked at him, completely ignoring Maria. Maria was having a hard time keeping up her fake smile. Her cheeks were already hurting from all that forced smiling.

"Oh, I'm in the military," Aaron said casually.

"In the military! Ah, wonderful, wonderful. Thank you for your service, thank you, Mr. Aaron. We'll make sure to give you a military discount on your project. We're big supporters, you know."

"Thanks, Ms. Carmal. I appreciate that."

"Of course, of course, anything for our military. Our strong military. God bless the military. And the United States." Ms. Carmal went on and on, batting her eyelashes at Aaron.

Maria felt like that fake smile would soon be forever stapled onto her face. *Wonder if I'll be able to move my mouth again after this? That lady is ridiculous.*

She suddenly felt Ms. Carmal actually looking at her. It caught Maria off guard, as she'd completely ignored her up until now. But no doubt she was looking at Maria now, then actually started talking to her. "Darlin', you know what I like best about our military?"

Maria kept smiling and shook her head.

"The guys' physique. I mean, look at these men. So strong, so noble, so honorable."

Maria widened her smile further than she'd thought possible and nodded. *This is stupid.*

"So no wonder the divorce rate is so high in the military!" Her eyes widened at Maria. "Those good-looking boys are like rock stars. Dreamy."

Wait a minute. Did she honestly just suggest I'll end up divorced? How could she dare even say that? Maria's smile faded. *It's not right. Who in the world does she think she is? Telling me that Aaron will cheat on me. No way.*

Maria ripped her hand out of Aaron's, and before he could stop her, Maria was already going at it. "Listen up, Ms. Carmal, I understand that you are—"

"Hello there!"

A deep, cheerful voice interrupted Maria midsentence. She looked up at the man who had just emerged from the back door. He was middle-aged, perhaps in his fifties, and slowly going bald. You could tell his hair used to be lighter, but it was blondish grey now. He was of a compact stature, not much taller than Maria herself, but had wide, broad shoulders that clearly had once been well-trained and muscular. He had greyish-blue eyes, a grey mustache, and thin lips.

Maria stopped talking and stared at him.

"Mr. Sullivan," Aaron said. He got up from his chair, reached across the counter, and shook his hand.

"You must be the young man that just bought the fixer-upper on Bellrose Avenue in Jacksonville Heights?"

"Yes, sir."

Maria looked at her fiancé. *Sir? He doesn't deserve to be called "sir." You don't call an abuser "sir!"* She started getting mad, but before she could think about it any longer, Mr. Sullivan had reached out his hand to greet her.

"And this young lady must be your fiancée," he said, and smiled.

His teeth were crooked and yellowish. Maria didn't know what to say or do, so she let him take her hand. A shudder ran down her spine. His hands were rough—strong but rough. Not as smooth as Aaron's. He held her hand in his for a while and looked her up and down.

"This young man is in *the military*," Ms. Carmal told her boss, who kept looking at Maria as he held her hand.

"*Is* he?" He smiled. "I bet he is. The military guys always get the prettiest girls, don't they?"

Jerk! Maria ripped her hand out of his hold. It took everything she had to concentrate on the conversation.

"Yes, Mr. Sullivan, indeed," Aaron said. "We military guys sure get the best girls."

Seriously? Maria gave him a look.

Aaron quickly took her hand and squeezed it. *Play along*, his eyes told her, *just play along*.

She got the message and turned back to Mr. Sullivan again. Not much bigger than her. Stronger, but not taller. She eyed his strong shoulders—broad, strong shoulders. She shivered. He made her uncomfortable. No, more than uncomfortable.

"This is my fiancée," Aaron explained, and squeezed her hand long and tight.

That was the signal.

She looked at Jonathan Sullivan, looked him in the eye, her heart pounding, pounding so loud she thought the whole store could hear it.

"Mr. Sullivan, I am Maria."

He smiled at her.

"Maria *Sullivan*."

He now stared at her.

"The same last name. Oh my, what a coincidence," Ms. Carmal said. The man said nothing.

"I'm Maria Sullivan. And I'm your daughter."

He just stared at her.

"Say what?" Ms. Carmal exclaimed in surprise.

"My mother is Martina Sullivan. Martina Marie Sullivan." He still stared at her, not saying anything. Nobody did. Maria and Jonathan Sullivan just stared at each other.

"Does that ring a bell, Mr. Sullivan? Or should I say *Dad*?"

His stare changed. He took in a sharp breath, stroked his belly, and then, as if playing a role in the theater, his lips pursed up. He started to laugh, a loud, noisy laugh. "I'm sorry, Maria, but you must be mistaken. I do not have a daughter."

"Not that you *knew of*. Don't tell me the name Martina Marie Sullivan doesn't ring a bell."

"Of course it does. She's my ex-wife."

Ms. Carmal gasped.

"Exactly, your ex-wife. And my mother!"

He laughed again. "No way. She wasn't pregnant when we got divorced. How old are you anyway?"

"I'm twenty-one. Turn twenty-two this fall," Maria said.

She could see that he was thinking. Then he smiled at her. "I'm sorry you never knew your father. But it ain't me. Martina and I got divorced three years before you were born. Twenty-five years ago this fall. There's no way I'm your father."

Now it was Maria's turn to stare at him.

"Young lady, I'm sorry, but it sure ain't me. Just look at us! You look nothing like me!"

She did look at him then, really *looked* at him. He returned her gaze. Ms. Carmal's head darted back and forth between them, while Aaron glared at Mr. Sullivan, his expression intense.

He was right. He looked nothing like her at all.

"So, you're saying you haven't seen my mom since your divorce?"

He laughed. "No, definitely not. She didn't ever want to see me again, and neither did I. The last time I saw her was at the courthouse in 1998. Way before you came into this world, young lady. Whatever your mom told you, it ain't true. I'm not your father. No way. Not me."

"But why is your name on my birth certificate then? How do you explain that, Jonathan Eric Sullivan!" Maria was mad, her eyes flashing in anger.

He stared at her and almost appeared a bit uncomfortable. He seemed to think about what she had just said. "What?"

"Your name. On my birth certificate. It says it, black on white, that you're my father. Even lists your full name. Why?"

He shifted his weight from one leg to the other. "Listen, young lady, I've no idea how my name got on there. I haven't seen Martina since our divorce, and there's no freakin' way I'm your father!"

"Legally you are. My birth certificate proves it."

"That's no proof at all. You can put a suspected father on there without it being true. Your mom lied!" He stared at her, red-faced. "Martina lied to you. I'm not your father. I suspect you know where babies come from, yeah? Well, I *can't* be your father. You want me to go dig up my divorce certificate to prove it? It's not possible. Your mom lied to you and everyone else and just put my name on there."

Maria stared at him. *Did he just accuse Mamá of lying and faking my birth certificate? Falsifying his name on it? No way. What a jerk.*

"So, Jonathan Sullivan, you're telling me you didn't return to see my mom in, let's say, New Year's 2001?"

"What? No, I didn't. Why in the world would I celebrate New Year's with my ex? She hated my guts. Probably still does, and therefore put my name on that document to spite me after being fucked by someone else!"

Maria's head started spinning. *He didn't just say that about Mamá!* Her face turned completely red in anger, and her eyes turned green. "You're such an asshole. Such a jerk. She divorced you because she was afraid of you. You abused her, hit her! How could you? How could you hurt an innocent woman, the woman you said you loved? How could you? I'll make sure you go to jail and—"

Before she could finish, he'd stepped around the counter and was eye to eye with her, nose to nose. His grey eyes coldly regarded hers, he was angry, so very angry, but then Maria saw his eyes flash down, look down just for a split second, as if intimidated by her. But then he looked straight back at her, stared into her eyes.

Then Aaron was there pulling her away from him. He stood between them and opened his mouth to say something when suddenly Jonathan Sullivan roared, "Get the hell out of my store! Now! Out! Both of you! Before I call my lawyer! Everything was settled during the divorce and I have nothing more to say. Out. Now!"

Ms. Carmal watched on in shock. She hadn't moved from her chair behind the counter, didn't say a word.

Aaron took Maria's hand and pulled her along with him. As they fled, she stared over her shoulder at him. At Jonathan Sullivan. The man who was her mamá's ex. The man she'd thought was her dad.

But is he really my dad?

She wasn't so sure anymore. She knew for sure he was an abusive guy and hated him for it, for what he'd done to her mom, but she wasn't sure if he had gone further than that. Further than what the courts already knew. She was so confused as Aaron practically dragged her out of the store.

"You ain't my daughter," the man yelled through the doorway. "I'm not your freakin' father! Better ask your mom who really is. Let her tell you that story! It's not me, and if you ever come back, I'll call the police and have you arrested!"

The little bell rang and the door closed behind them. Aaron half-pushed, half-dragged Maria to the car. She didn't know what was happening as she was pushed into the passenger seat of her own car. Aaron jumped in beside her, and they buckled up then peeled out of the parking lot and sped down the highway.

CHAPTER 22

Jonathan Sullivan watched the young couple drive away. He started grinding his teeth. His eyes were clouded over, his eyebrows pulled in, his hands in fists.

Ms. Carmal knew better than to say anything, so she just started cleaning the counter that didn't need any cleaning. She knew her boss's outbursts well and was sure she'd soon be scolded for even letting the young couple come in.

She hadn't known. She hadn't known of his ex or his past but was certain the reasons for the divorce the young woman had stated were true. He always got angry easily, but luckily she was just an employee who could go home at the end of the day and get away from him whenever he was in a bad mood.

"Ms. Carmal," he said, "I'll be in the back making a phone call. Don't let anyone disturb me. Then I'm going back to that weekend job. I expect you to keep idiots like that away from me. You hear me? Keep them away."

She just nodded and was relieved when he disappeared through the back door and slammed it shut. She started looking through the shelves to make sure everything was in order. One more little thing could lead to her boss boiling over at this point, and she would do anything to avoid that.

Jonathan Sullivan sat at his desk and stared at the wall in front of him. The wall was mostly bare, with just a few pictures hung.

I want a drink now, but I can't do that. I can't relapse. I've been sober for quite a while now. Martina. She was a beautiful woman. Not sure what she looks like now, but she sure was pretty back then. Yeah, I drank too much when I was with her. I sure did. Not proud of it. Just can't control my anger when I drink. I know that. Tried to be sober, but it took me years to succeed. Started over from scratch, built this business, made a name for myself. I cannot allow anyone to destroy this. Destroy the hard work and dedication I've put into this. I cannot let anyone take it away from me. Nobody.

He knew the woman with the exotic eyes was a danger to his plan. He had never forgotten those eyes. Those beautiful hazel eyes with a mosaic of golden-and-emerald-green flecks in the dark-brown center encircled by a blue rim.

None like them, those beautiful, exotic eyes. Begging. Looking so scared, so little. He'd watched their color change, seen the fear, the blank fear in those unforgettable eyes. They'd always haunted him, but he'd never thought he'd ever look into them again.

But then that day had come. Today, just now. He hadn't recognized her until she'd said all those things. And once he got close to her, he knew who she was. Once he saw those eyes. Those unforgettable eyes.

Shit! What should I do now?

He slammed his fists on his desk. He went over to his punching bag. His therapist had told him to punch the bag whenever he was feeling frustrated.

Punch the bag. Don't drink. Punch the bag. Don't drink.

He punched and punched the bag.

I gave that young lady a good story. Don't think she'll ever come back again. But what if Martina breaks down and tells? No, she doesn't know enough to implicate me. Doesn't know the truth. I gave her a good story back then.

As he punched the bag, he was growing more and more confident that everything would be okay. The secret was safe. *But just in case, I should let* them *know. That's a good idea. Let them know, just in case. Do the right thing. They deserve to know. They can figure out a plan together in case there's unforeseen trouble. I'll tell them I'm confident the secret's safe, but having a plan is always a good thing.*

Yes, I should let them know. Just in case.

He stopped punching the bag and searched for the hidden key to the top drawer of his desk. The key was in its hiding place on the bottom of the pencil holder. He unlocked the top drawer of his desk and pulled out a cell phone, a prepaid cell phone. His old BlackBerry. He hadn't turned that thing on in years. Twenty years, to be precise.

Hope it still works. Much better to use this instead of my personal cell or office phone. It beeped as the screen lit up. *Good, still works.*

He pulled out a notebook that only had a few phone numbers in it. *Good thing I wrote them down back then. I'm smart. Yes, I sure am.* He smiled.

But will they still work after so long? After all these years? Don't know. But have to try.

He dialed the last number on the list with his old phone. It rang and rang and rang. *Shit! This is the only number I have for my contact. The only number I was told to dial if anything went wrong. I only saw the guy once. Is this still his fucking number?*

Jonathan Sullivan had almost given up when someone finally picked up.

"Hello?"

"Hi, Bill?"

The man on the other end was silent for a while. "Yes. Who's this?"

"It's Sully."

"Sully." The voice on the other end sounded surprised. "It's been a long time. What can I help you with?"

"We have a problem, sir."

"Hold on."

Jonathan Sullivan heard a faint, "Excuse me for a moment, please," on the other end of the line, then the strong, male voice was back. "How dare you call me? We had a deal."

"Yes, sir, I know. But there's a problem."

"A problem?"

"Yes, sir. That . . . *mission* . . . twenty years ago . . ."

"Mmmh, yes."

"Well, what you didn't know. . . ."

"*What* did I not know?"

"Well, the mission actually ended a bit differently than you thought."

"What the fuck you mean?"

"Well, it may still be walking around."

There was a sharp gasp on the other end, then silence.

"Saw it today. A big surprise."

Still silence.

"Sir?"

"Yes. How the fuck did this happen?"

"Well, it's a long story. Not on the phone. I think we should meet."

"Meet? Us? No. We will never meet again. How did you get this number anyway?"

"It's still the same, sir. And I did not forget. 'Call you if there's a problem,'" Jonathan Sullivan said proudly. "And I guess there is one now. I still believe it's best we meet. Just you and I this time. The situation is under control, but I think we should briefly meet and come up with a contingency plan. Just in case. Because we might have a slight problem after all."

"We might have a slight problem," the man on the other end repeated slowly. "Agreed. After what you just told me. But do we really have a problem?"

"Yes, sir, I suppose we do." Sullivan sighed and sank deeper into his desk chair.

Laughter erupted on the other end. "No, *we* don't have a problem. *You* do. And don't ever contact me again."

A beeping noise. The caller had hung up. Jonathan Sullivan stared at the screen of his beeping phone. *Shit. That's not good. Not good at all. Fuck. What should I do now?*

CHAPTER 23

Maria and Aaron were at a park beneath some palm trees sheltering a stone picnic table overlooking the beach. The trees were swaying in the slight wind. The sun shone brightly onto the beach, its light reflecting in the waves of the Atlantic Ocean.

Aaron sat on the stone bench and watched Maria pace back and forth, back and forth. She hadn't stopped pacing ever since they left the car. Nobody had said a word and Aaron was beginning to feel antsy. He spoke up. "Maria, you need to stop pacing and calm down. I know that wasn't a fun time, but let's put our heads together and see if there's anything we missed that might help us out."

Maria kept pacing and mumbled, "Not a nice guy, not a nice guy at all." She suddenly stopped. "I can't remember much of what he said. Oh no!"

Aaron waved her over, and she finally took a seat next to him on the stone bench. "It's okay. I've something to jog your memory," he said, smiling, and pulled out his phone. "I recorded the conversation on my phone!"

Maria stared at him. "You did? Wow, that's brilliant." She smiled, but it quickly faded. "Isn't that illegal?"

Aaron shrugged his shoulders. "I guess so, but we just need it to jog our memories. We'll write down the important parts of the conversation in your notebook, and then I'll delete it. Then it never happened, yeah?" Maria still stared at Aaron. "You heard me, right? I can rely on you to forget I ever recorded this? Right?"

Maria's stony face broke out into a grin. She winked. "Recorded what? I have no idea what you're talking about."

Aaron laughed. "Good. Let's start then, shall we?"

Maria pulled out her notebook and a pen and nodded. Her hands were shaking, she could barely hold the pen, but she knew she had to stay calm. "Ready," she said, and Aaron pressed play on his phone.

The recording was terrible quality since Aaron had recorded it through his pants pocket, but they could hear clearly enough. Maria took notes while they both stared at the black screen of his phone, listening to the crinkly voices coming from it.

The recording ended. They looked at each other.

Aaron was the first to find his words. "Well, this guy isn't a nice guy at all, but his story lines up. And he didn't deny any accusations about hitting your mom. He was adamant about not having seen her since the divorce." Maria nodded. "And he doesn't look like you at all. Not even a little bit."

Maria nodded again. *Yeah, have to admit that. He doesn't even have my strange freckles that nobody else in my family has.*

Both Maria and Aaron were deep in thought as they read through the notes again.

"He said it's easy to put a 'suspected' father on the birth certificate," Maria said, and looked at Aaron. "Is that true?"

Aaron shrugged his shoulders. "It's a possibility."

"So, you're saying he's telling the truth and Mamá just put his name on there?"

"Maybe. I don't know, Maria. The only one who does is your mom." Maria stared at him. "Anyways, did your mom collect alimony or child support from him?"

Maria shook her head and started turning the pen in her hand, absent-mindedly.

"Should we listen to it one more time before I delete it?"

Maria's eyes met Aaron's and she nodded. They both leaned over his phone, which Aaron had laid atop the stone picnic table, and listened to the recorded conversation again.

"Stop," Maria yelled suddenly. Aaron pressed the pause button. "This part of the conversation, right after I abruptly end my sentence telling him that I'll make sure he'll go to jail. There's a pause. Or am I imagining it?"

"No, you're right. There *is* a pause. What was going on right then?" Maria and Aaron thought back to the actual conversation. "I think that's when he came over and was nose to nose with you."

"Right, I remember it now. He was staring into my eyes."

But there was something else, something even more important about those few seconds. Maria closed her eyes to think back to that moment and suddenly remembered. "He looked down. He looked down at the floor as soon as he looked into my eyes."

"That's true. I saw that, too. He looked down, almost as if seeing your eyes shocked him. He seemed overwhelmed for a split second."

"That's strange," Maria mumbled, and wrote it down. "Why would he look away when he specifically came over to intimidate me by staring me down?"

Aaron smirked at his fiancée. "Well, you do have pretty intense eyes. Exotic and unique."

Maria laughed. "I know you love my eyes, but what does that have to do with anything?"

Aaron thought for a quick second before he spoke out loud. "Well, your eyes are one of a kind. I've never met anyone with those kinds of eyes before. They're extremely unique. People you meet are often so fascinated by your eyes that they're taken aback, stop and stare deeper into them."

"So, what are you getting at? Jonathan Sullivan wasn't fascinated at all. He looked away as soon as he saw them."

"Exactly!" Aaron got up and started pacing around the stone picnic bench. "It was more like he was shocked to see them, don't you think?"

She turned around and watched him pace, then shrugged. She wasn't sure. *He's making me nervous. Aaron never paces. I've never seen him pace before. That's my job, the way I react. He's the calm one. What's going on?*

"He was shocked to see your eyes," Aaron continued, "I'm positive he was. The pause in the recording explains it. Why? Why was he shocked?" He looked at Maria as he paced back and forth behind her.

"I don't know, Aaron. Why would he be shocked?"

Suddenly, he stopped pacing and looked at her. "Because he *recognized* your eyes. He's seen them before."

"What? That doesn't make any sense at all. Even if he did come back to . . . to . . . you know, to . . . Anyway, he never met me before today. Not as a baby either."

"I know. I believe that."

"Aaron, you're confusing me. What do you mean?"

"Think about it. Babies' eyes start off the same. True eye color doesn't come out until six months or so after birth."

"I don't get it, Aaron."

"Jonathan Sullivan hasn't met you before, but maybe he recognized your eyes because he knows someone else with the same eyes."

"You're saying Jonathan Sullivan isn't my father, but knows someone who is?"

"Maybe."

Maria was confused. "But how would that person know Jonathan Sullivan?"

"A mutual friend, maybe?"

Aaron and Maria looked at each other. Her eyebrows were raised. *Mutual friend?* She wrote that down, then looked back at Aaron, who had sat down again.

"Well, sounds like we both agree Jonathan Sullivan's not your dad. But maybe someone else who knows him is."

Maria sighed. "I don't understand why his name is on my birth certificate. It doesn't make sense."

Aaron put an arm around her. "I agree. I see only one way to finding out the truth."

Maria read through the notes they'd written again and sighed, then nodded. "You're right. Mamá is key to all this. I'll have to talk to her again. At least I have hope she wasn't abused at the time she conceived me."

Aaron gave her a kiss on the cheek. "See! That's good. Yeah, talk to her again."

Maria wrote down, *Ask Mamá about my exotic eyes*, and then closed the notebook. She leaned into Aaron's strong shoulders and thought for a while. Her eyes lit up. "Maybe I can go back and ask Jonathan Sullivan if he has a friend that looks like me?"

"Maria!" Aaron rolled his eyes. "I think he made it clear he'll never talk to you again. Didn't you hear his threats?"

"Yes, I know. I get it. I should talk to Mamá instead. Makes sense." She sighed the deepest sigh Aaron had ever heard out of her.

He felt sorry for her. "I know this is hard. But you can do this. I'm here for you."

"I know. Thanks Aaron." She gave him a warm kiss on the lips and smiled at him. "Nothing more we can do here today."

"Yep, I think our recap is done." Aaron picked up his phone and deleted the recorded conversation.

Maria rubbed her temples. She felt a headache coming on. "Well, we didn't find out too much, huh?"

"Well, at least now we know that guy's not your dad," Aaron pointed out, and put his phone in his pocket. "That's something like a new development."

"Yeah, I guess so," Maria said, and rubbed her head. Her headache now throbbed in full force. *I need to figure out a way to talk to Mamá about all of this. It's so confusing. I'm so confused.*

She took the notebook and the pen and dropped both items into her purse. Then she noticed her purple bikini was in there and suddenly had an idea about how to forget her troubles for a while. *I owe Aaron some fun.*

She looked at him. "Hope you brought your swimsuit. I've got mine right here." She took out her bikini and waved it in the air.

"I didn't bring one. Why?"

"You don't have a swimsuit with you? Oh dear, Aaron. You're normally the organized one." Maria laughed out loud. "I guess you'll have to go swimming in your boxer shorts, then."

"What? Swimming wasn't part of the plan."

Maria got up. "Well, it is now. Come on. Let's be spontaneous for once and have some fun. The beach is right there. The beautiful ocean. It'll be so fun."

Aaron got up as well not looking too excited, but then his face lit up. "Wait a sec, I think I have an extra pair of PT shorts stashed in your trunk."

"Perfect. I have towels in there also. Come on, let's go."

They jogged back to Maria's car, then found the closest beach-changing-rooms and disappeared inside. Within minutes, the two were dressed in their swimsuits, and ran down to the beach, towels over their shoulders. They dropped their towels onto the sand and ran straight into the shallow, cold ocean water. The water splashed up around them as they ran in laughing loudly.

Maria stopped abruptly as a wave of cold water enveloped her up to her belly button.

"Come on, Maria, it feels great! Just jump in!"

She shook her head. "It's so cold. And the waves look so big."

"You'll be fine, I'm here with you." He took her hand. "Come on."

Instead of diving in with him, she pulled him in for a kiss. "Thanks for everything. I love you."

He looked at her, his ocean-blue eyes sparkling. He gave her another long kiss, then twirled her around, the splashing water glittering in the air around them. They stood there in the cold water, warmed by their strong, pure love and the sun shining down upon them.

CHAPTER 24

The sun shone down on the young couple on the beach, the blue water reflecting and scattering the light. She stared at the picture, a picture of her ex-husband and herself. She sighed and took another sip of her wine.

Elisabeth was out on her balcony again this dark night, looking at a picture album of long-gone times. The decorative outdoor lights illuminated the pictures just enough for her to see.

There he was. Her ex-husband.

I'll see him soon. Her heart started beating faster. *I still love him. Wonder if he still loves me? I loved talking with him. It was great to hear his voice the other day. Can't wait to talk again.*

Should I call him? She shook her head. *No, he said he'll call when his trip is all set. I need to be patient.* She sipped her wine again. She made sure to take little gulps each time as she was determined to drink less. And she had, ever since he had called her.

She glanced at the picture again. Saw the sand. The water.

Water. *Wawa*, her little one had called it.

She smiled, but her smile faded quickly. *She's gone. Forever. Drowned in wawa. My poor, little one. I might get him back, but she's gone.*

Her heart started aching. She knew he could fill a part of her empty heart, but a big hole would always remain there. She sighed and took another small sip of her wine. Sadness washed over her face again. Quickly, she closed the picture album. A bunch of newspaper articles fell out.

"Shoot!"

She set down the photo album and her glass of wine, got out of her chair, and started picking up the scattered articles from the balcony floor. She couldn't help but glance at them, and all the memories came back, suddenly, violently. *Accidental Drowning*, the police had concluded. But no dead body was ever found. They had searched all over, all over Choctawhatchee Bay. No body, no little girl, nothing.

Vanished. Gone forever.

And no answers, absolutely no answers. That was the worst. *It's still the worst. Having no answers. It ate me up, it ate him up, it made us fall apart. We accused each other, were so confused that by the end we could barely remember those few minutes leading up to the event and the painful hours and days after.*

She sighed and stared into the darkness. *Darkness. It's been darkness ever since then.* The newspapers had bashed them, made them look like terrible parents that had abandoned their little one. Parents who deserved to have lost their daughter. She had read every article ever written about it. And she'd kept all of the articles. The faded newspaper articles were still with her, right here, right now, scattered all over her balcony.

My baby girl. My sweet little baby girl. What happened to you?

A tear ran down her stern face. As she knelt down to pick them up, she kept looking through the scattered articles. Her eyes rested on a big picture of her daughter on one of the faded articles. Her little one's hazel eyes with their mosaic of golden-and-emerald-green flecks in a dark brown center and a blue rim on the outside. Her unique eyes stared back at Elisabeth.

She started sobbing uncontrollably.

Unbelievable. Still able to cry about this so many years later. Nobody understands me, nobody can understand the feeling of complete despair, the feeling of having your heart ripped out, the trauma of cycling through hope and fear over and over, up and down, waiting to hear something, to hear if the police have finally found her. But maybe he does? She looked up at the stars. *Yes, he understands me. Brad does understand me. He knows what it feels like. He understands that the fact they never found her still makes me feel like my heart is being stabbed by a knife, constantly and violently.*

She put a hand on her chest and pushed down on it, as if that might help heal her heart.

I wish they'd at least found her body. A terrible thought, but it would've given both Brad and I some sort of closure. Maybe then we wouldn't have fallen apart. Maybe then we could've been there for each other, comforting the loss of our only child. Maybe then we would have had another child together. But not getting that closure drove us apart. It tore us apart. He became convinced our daughter was dead while I was convinced she was still alive.

Is that still the case? No. I think Brad's right. And Sarah's right. I need closure. We both need closure.

Elisabeth grabbed all the scattered articles off the balcony's floor, then walked inside. She took them over to her little storage room, dropped them in front of the door, and sat down on the floor to organize them into a neat pile. When she was done, she picked up the pile and turned the knob of the door—it swung open with a squeak. She turned on the little lamp.

There it was. Her big black suitcase.

She touched it and a puff of dust rose into the air. She wiped away the remaining dust and zipped open the front pocket of her suitcase. She put the pile of articles inside.

All those things will fly back to Florida with me. Enti, too, of course. Yes, I'll take it all with me to Florida. I'll go back and find closure, bury the past once and for all. Yes, right there on the beach, on the sandy Florida beach.

CHAPTER 25

They were lying on their towels on the sandy Florida beach. Aaron had noticed that Maria had fallen asleep and was watching her. She was so beautiful, sleeping on her belly right there on the beach.

Sand was all around her. Lots of sand, more sand, sand everywhere. Sand as far as the eye could see. So much sand. Fun! She happily sat in the middle of the sand, deep down. She had built a big wall of sand all around her and could barely see over the top.

"My castle," she said, and smiled widely.

She reached for the big pink shovel and tried to dig deeper. But she hadn't quite figured out how to hold the shovel to get the sand where it needed to be, on top of the sandy wall. She tried again and pushed on the shovel with all her might, her little hands gripping the shovel's stick tight. She scooped it out of the ground and found it had a big pile of sand on it.

Finally, sand on it. She had done it. She was so proud of herself! The shovel wasn't stuck in the ground anymore, she had managed to pull it out, and had even kept the sand on it this time. She slowly and proudly tried to lift it up onto the wall around her but swung the shovel too quickly, and before she knew it the sand had slid off the shovel and sprinkled down all over her.

No, no, no. Not fair. And aua, it hurts.

"Sand in eyes," she screamed, "Sand in eyes."

She had swallowed a few grains of sand and tried to spit them out, then started crying. Upset about the sand all over her. Upset about failing to pile sand on the wall around her and make it taller.

She was sobbing and crying when big, strong arms lifted her up and wiped her face, first with a towel, then a wet wipe.

"Aw, my poor baby girl," she heard a calm, soft, deep voice say. "Poor baby girl. That was a good try, my sweet pea. Sorry that happened. But no worries, I got you. We'll clean this up in no time and try again."

Her eyes felt better and she slowly opened them, looking straight into her daddy's friendly, handsome face. "Hi there, sweetie. There you are! All clean. No worries, I got you. Daddy is here."

Daddy?

She looked up into the laughing, charming, likable face. A tan face, clean-shaven, with short, spiky brown hair and sparkling eyes. Big brown eyes with a mosaic of golden-and-green flecks in the dark brown center, a blue rim around it. They smiled at her, sparkling in the sunlight.

Exotic! Exotic eyes! What? Wait!

She felt the world spin around her as she was suddenly ripped out of her daddy's arms by someone else, someone with strong arms and a uniform on. This guy was in a hurry; he quickly jumped over her sandy wall into the hole that was her castle and went deeper and deeper into it, deeper and deeper into the sandcastle until she was surrounded by water, water all around her. It swallowed her up and she couldn't breathe.

Help, water, water, help me!

With a scream, Maria woke up and saw nothing but sand. Her heart beat faster. *Where am I?* She jumped up quickly and stood face-to-face with Aaron.

"Holy cow, Maria! Are you okay?"

She stared at him, her eyes wild and green. She looked around, her breathing heavy.

"It's okay, Maria. You fell asleep sunbathing. We're at the beach. In Jacksonville."

She focused on Aaron. Looked at him. His eyes were calming her down. He gave her a hug. She felt his warm, sun-kissed skin on hers, his warm breath whispering in her ear.

"You're okay. I think you just had another dream. Another nightmare."

She nodded and whispered, "It was just so weird, so strange. I saw a man with my eyes. He was playing with me in the sand."

Aaron held her tighter. "I'm sorry, my love. I'm sorry. Sooner than later, I think you need to call your mom and ask her all those unanswered questions."

Maria had calmed down and nodded. "I know, I know. But not yet. Let's enjoy our day, okay?"

He gave her a kiss and they sat down on their beach towels. Her phone blinked. Incoming text. She looked at it. "It's Keisha, wondering if everything's okay. What should I tell her?"

"What do you mean?"

"Well, I haven't touched base with her or Brandy since I left the pool. And I'm not sure what to tell them. I don't want any of my friends to know about our investigation into my past. It's too complicated."

Aaron raised an eyebrow. "Why? Just tell them the truth. You're a bad liar, and Keisha in particular would know right away you're lying to her and just get mad at you. You don't need that drama before finals."

"I know. But I don't want her to think I'm the product of rape. Or that my mom faked my birth certificate."

"Well, just tell her what I told Nick and Jim."

"You already told your friends? Gosh, Aaron, you need to talk with me before you go blabbing on about me to our friends!"

"I need to tell you what I text with the guys?"

"No, not that. You know what I mean. If it involves my personal life, ask permission first. Not to mention our stories need to line up."

Aaron still had his one eyebrow raised. "See, Maria, that's where things can get complicated fast. Just tell them the truth so you won't get caught lying because our stories don't line up."

"I know, but I'm. . . ."

Before she could go on, Aaron showed her the text he'd written to Nick and Jim. Maria couldn't help but smile and shook her head. "Wow. Guys really are less complicated."

Aaron grinned. "Told ya. Just text Keisha the same. We fought, made up, and went to Jacksonville together today."

Maria laughed and laid back down on her towel, then started texting Keisha and Brandy.

Maria's phone rang just as they arrived at her apartment. It was her mom. She stared at the screen and the incoming FaceTime call.

"Aren't you going to pick up?" Aaron asked her as the phone kept ringing and ringing. Maria shrugged her shoulders and thought for a moment longer, then closed the front door and picked up. Her mom's face appeared on screen.

"Aló, mija. ¿Cómo estás?" Her mom noticed Aaron standing there behind Maria. "Oh, hi Aaron!"

"Hi, Martina. ¿Cómo estás?"

"¡Muy bien!" Martina smiled. "You will learn Spanish in no time."

The three of them laughed. They were just starting to talk when Maria pointed out she had to use the bathroom; it had been a long trip home with no stops. She darted away, and Aaron kept talking to Martina.

"So, what did you guys do today? Looks like you just got back? Where did you go?"

"Ahem." Aaron thought a bit before answering. "Jacksonville. We went to Jacksonville today."

"Ah, nice. Why there? You already have a beach where you guys are at."

Aaron's face turned red and he smiled awkwardly. *When will Maria finally be done?* He knew it had only been a minute, but he had no idea what to tell her mom.

"Well, we decided to go there because . . . because . . . we . . . wanted . . ."

Aaron watched as Martina's face grew curious. And suspicious. *Maria! Come back!*

He heard her washing her hands and wanted nothing more than to get off the phone, but it was too late.

"Aaron, I can see it in your face. What are you hiding?"

Oh dear, these damn FaceTime calls.

When Maria stepped out of her bathroom, she stopped dead at the words coming out of her fiancé's mouth. "We went to a plumbing store in Jacksonville. A store called Sullivan's Plumbing."

Maria quickly ran over to where Aaron was sitting and grabbed the phone out of his hands. "Mamá, I'm back. So, what have you been up to today?"

Her mom stared at her through the screen. "*Maria?*"

"¿Sí, Mamá?"

"A *plumbing store* in *Jacksonville, Maria?*" Martina's face was red with anger.

"Nada, Mamá. It was nothing, not important."

"Give me Aaron back," Martina said, her voice stern, her face red. "I want to speak to Aaron again!"

"Mamá. . . ."

"No! Aaron!"

Aaron looked over Maria's shoulder and said in a small voice, "I'm here."

"¡Muy bien! Now, what's this all about?"

Maria looked at him, and he looked at her. They had a special bond, a way of communicating without actually saying anything. His eyes flashed. *I had to tell her. Now is the time to ask her about the truth.*

"Maria? What is this all about? What are you two hiding?"

Maria took a deep breath. "Well, funny you should ask, Mamá . . . I have the same question for you. What are *you* hiding?"

Her mom gawked at her through the screen.

"We went to Sullivan's Plumbing, Mamá. Found the store online and realized it was in Jacksonville. Put two and two together, figured it must be my dad's store. So we went to see him."

Martina's face passed beyond angry red and was now ghostly white. She couldn't speak. She just stared at her daughter through the phone, stared and said nothing. Not knowing what to say, she was forced to listen.

"I wanted to meet him. I did my research, Mamá. After yesterday, you probably figured out I know you got divorced three years before I was born. I also know you divorced him because he was abusive. I saw the entries about domestic abuse."

Martina's head was spinning. *She's not supposed to know that, not supposed to know any of that.* But she couldn't say anything and just kept listening, had no other choice but to listen.

"We saw him, Mamá. Not a nice guy. Not nice at all. I don't understand how you could have ever fallen in love with him. Mamá, what were you thinking?"

No answer, of course. No answer, just the long stare.

She looks scared, Aaron thought. *Martina looks scared.* He kept listening to Maria.

"Anyway, this guy sure was Jonathan Eric Sullivan. Your ex. And the guy on *my* birth certificate. But he said he doesn't have a daughter.

He also brought up that you got divorced three years before I was born. He said he couldn't be my father. He said he hasn't seen you since the divorce and that you both never wanted to see each other again."

Whoa, she nodded. Maria's mom nodded. Aaron quickly grabbed Maria's purse, pulled out the notebook and a pen, and started writing things down. Maria barely noticed what he was up to, so engrossed she was in telling her story.

"He insisted he never saw you again and then said you probably don't know who my real dad is and just used *his* name on the birth certificate. He said it's impossible for him to be my dad. He said it must be someone else."

Martina didn't move. Her mind was racing. Her face had meandered back to its usual color—still slightly white, but more or less normal. She was thinking, had to think quickly, but wasn't quick enough and heard her daughter ask the question again.

"Mamá, is Jonathan Sullivan my father or not? Is it another guy? Or . . . or . . . did he . . . did he come back and rape you?"

Martina gasped. *Oh my gosh, did Maria just ask me that? She did, didn't she? Yesterday, she hinted about it, but now she actually went and said it out loud. Loud and clear.* Martina stared at her daughter through the screen and couldn't say anything. She saw Maria's face, saw her feisty personality, saw her hazel eyes shift bright green.

"Mamá, did he come back and rape you? Did he hurt you bad? Am I a product of rape?"

Through the screen, Martina saw a tear run out of her daughter's now green eyes. She saw the tear drip down, saw more forming, saw the pain in her beautiful eyes, her beautiful face. Tears started streaming down now. "Mamá, did he *hurt* you?"

Through the phone, Martina stared at Maria. Her heart sank.

Poor mija. I know you would hate yourself more than anything if you were a product of rape. You're such a sensible, empathetic child. And you love me! I know you would never forgive yourself if you had caused me so much pain, such unthinkable pain. I can't let you believe the rape story. I have to stop this. Even though the rape story would be the perfect story to hide my secret from you.

But I can't do that to you. I can't.

CHAPTER 26

"Mamá, please, I need to know." Martina heard Maria begging, saw her crying, watched Aaron wrap his arms around her.

In that moment, she decided to go along with Jonathan's story after all. It was the only thing that could make Maria stop searching, the only story that might hide the big secret.

Can't tell her the truth, I just can't tell her. I need her to be my daughter, my special daughter. Forever mine. Mine. Can't lose my special bond with Maria.

So, she decided to speak. She knew she had to look and sound convincing. Her mind was racing, but she knew now what she had to say. "Maria, mija, please don't cry. Please don't. Yes, Jonathan did hurt me."

Maria's tears stopped flowing. She looked horrified as she stared at her mom through the phone.

"He did hurt me—throughout our marriage. He was nice at first. Charming. Helped out at the store. Even lent me money to buy the store, helped renovate it. He seemed like a good guy, funny, sweet, supportive—until he drank. He was a completely different person when he drank. Mean, angry, talking down to me. But the next day, when he was sober again, he apologized. Every single time he apologized. Told me it won't happen again. And I believed him at first. It went well for a few weeks, until he drank again. And it happened—again. But he apologized, swore to change, and was a sweet, loving husband for a while. But the next time he had too much to drink, it started getting worse. Every time, it got worse. He yelled, he shouted, he shoved, he started throwing things. He couldn't control himself. The more he drank, the more he was out of control. He started pushing me, choking me, then hitting me."

Maria stared in horror. "Mamá, oh Mamá, why didn't you call the police? Why didn't you leave him?"

Martina sighed. "I did. After a while. I called the police a few times. As you saw in the official entries. And when it got bad and I finally knew he couldn't change or control himself, I decided to get a divorce. And then we did divorce. That day was a good day. I knew he could never hurt me again. And that day was the last time I ever saw him."

Martina saw Maria raise her eyebrows, then saw how her expression changed to a look of soft, gentle concern. "Mamá, you can tell me. You can tell me. Tell me what happened. Tell me everything. Please don't protect him. It's just you and me, remember? I'm here to help you."

Martina sighed. *I love that girl so much, so very much. Nothing can ever come between us. My daughter. Yes, my daughter. I need Maria to be just my daughter!*

"Maria, he told you the truth today. He did not come back. He did not come back and hurt me ever again. Don't worry, mija. He didn't hurt me any anymore, and when I found out I was pregnant with you, it was the happiest day of my life. You're not a product of hate or pain—you're a product of love."

Maria looked at her mom, baffled but relieved. Martina felt her relief as if it were her own and smiled. *Jonathan had a good idea for once. Thank you, Jonathan.* She went on with her story.

"I met this guy a few years later. I'd already sworn to myself to never marry again, seeing how the last Mr. Nice Guy had turned out to be a disaster. I was focused on the store and on getting my sisters into the United States. I didn't need any distractions. But one night, I decided to go out to my favorite tapas bar. And there was this guy. Good-looking, so handsome, so gentle-mannered."

Martina watched Maria's face light up. *Aw, my baby girl. Love seeing her smile, seeing her happy. Took a while to get that from her. . . . I can't bear seeing her sad again. Have to make sure this story is a happy one.* "He was kind, so kind. And funny. Wonderful humor."

"Did he look like me?" Maria's tears were all dry, her hopes alive.

Martina knew Maria was digging her story, and she was eager to please her daughter. "Sí, mija, he did. He had very similar features, had your—"

"Eyes?" Maria interrupted, and Martina heard the excitement in her daughter's voice. *What else can I say to make her happy?* "Yes, yes! Your eyes. Your exotic eyes!"

She saw Maria smile widely. "I knew they had to be from my dad."

"*And* your freckles," Martina went on. "He was such a kind guy."

"Mamá, why didn't you stay with him?"

Martina was taken aback. She had to think quickly to make sure the story made sense. Had to come up with something that would explain why she wouldn't have stayed with such a nice guy.

What can I say?

She took in Maria's hopeful face on the screen, then noticed Aaron's face in the background, his arm around Maria.

Aaron. Military. Yes, that's it! That's good.

"Well, he was only in town for a few days. We met every night before he went off. He was in the military and ended up being sent on a deployment."

Maria couldn't believe it. *A guy in the military? Like Aaron?* She smiled, but then Aaron interrupted the moment by saying, "Deployment? Deployed where?"

Martina had to think quickly. *What wars was the US military involved in back then?* She couldn't remember, but knew she had to come up with an answer quickly.

"Africa," she blurted out. "To Africa. He went to Africa on some sort of secret mission. But he couldn't tell me about it." She sighed a convincing sigh. "I don't know what happened to him after that. I never saw him again. By the time I found out I was pregnant, he was gone. Like I said, he was only in Miami for a few days."

Maria looked at her mom. *That's so sad.* She wanted to give her a hug. Instead, she gave her phone screen a kiss.

"Thank you, Maria!" Martina smiled. She knew it had been a good story. Made sense, made Maria happy, and, most importantly, would make her stop searching.

"What was his name?" Maria asked suddenly. "And why didn't you put his name on my birth certificate?"

"Well," Maria's mom said, trying to buy herself some time, "eh, I can't tell you."

Maria's smile faded. Her eyes changed again, and the hard stare came back.

Martina didn't know what to do and found she was left with only one option: she ended the call and quickly turned off her phone.

Martina was pacing in circles around her living room. Finally, she stopped and took out a piece of paper and wrote down a name, then scratched out and rewrote the last name a few times until she'd found a nice-sounding name.

Back at Embry-Riddle, Maria and Aaron stared at her phone. "What just happened?" he said.

"I don't know. I'll call her back." But whenever Maria called back, it went straight to voicemail.

"That's odd," Aaron said.

Maria tried again. Same thing. They were both looking at each other when the phone came to life. An incoming FaceTime call from her mom.

Maria quickly picked up. "Mamá, what happened?"

"I ran out of battery," she explained. "So sorry, mija. Had to find my charger and plug it in. We're good now."

Aaron and Maria glanced at each other. Just the batteries. Sure. That could happen to anyone, they knew. Made sense.

"Anyway, Maria, your father's name is Jonathan Smith," she said. "Same first name as my ex-husband. Ironic, huh?"

Aaron raised an eyebrow, Maria's face showed astonishment. That was quite the coincidence. He wrote the name down in Maria's notebook followed by *military deployment to Africa*.

"But why didn't you put his name on the birth certificate?"

"Well, mija, because he . . . he . . . was married to someone else!"

Maria gasped.

"Look, we just had a quick fling. I promised him I would not tell anyone. So, I never did. He was such a nice guy. He said he loved me and would have to think about what to tell his wife. He said he would contact me when he returned from his deployment. But he never did. I don't know if he returned from the mission.. . . ."

Maria stared at her mom. *I finally learn the truth about my real dad . . . but he was killed in action?* Aaron scribbled something in the notebook.

"Since I promised to not tell anyone about us and to wait until he contacted me again, I put my ex on the certificate. At the very least, their shared first name honored your actual dad. Nobody questioned me at the hospital when I told them the father was my ex-husband and that I didn't want him to know."

Maria sighed. *Another Jonathan. Wow. Crazy story. So relieved I'm a product of love. Still, my dad cheated on his wife. Cheated with Mamá. Maybe he isn't a nice guy after all? And did he not contact Mamá because he is a coward and didn't want his marriage to end, or did he actually die in Africa? Either way, not good.*

"Well, Maria, now you know. Nobody knows of this. Not even my sisters. Please keep it that way. This is between us. I want to remember Jonathan Smith the way he was. The nice guy that I fell head over heels with. Please promise me you will not do any more research on your dad. You know now."

Maria nodded. It was a lot to take in. "Sí, Mamá, no more research. I promise. Thanks for telling me about my dad. And I'm so happy I'm not a product of hate."

Martina laughed. "No, mija, you are made of love, pure love. And I love you so, so much."

"I love you too, Mamá."

Martina said good night to Maria and Aaron, then hung up. She smiled and stared at her phone for a while. *Yes, it's a good story. I could tell by Maria's gestures and looks that she will keep her promise. She will stop researching her past.*

She sighed. *Good girl. My mija, my daughter. A wonderful human being. And she trusts me. Me, her mamá. Yes, I'm her mom and will always be her mom. That's the way it is, must be, always will be.*

CHAPTER 27

Aaron looked at Maria and could tell that she was completely satisfied by what she had just heard. She believed every word her mom had told her.

"Aaron, isn't that wonderful." She sighed contentedly and leaned her head onto his shoulder. "I'm so glad no rape happened. That weird guy isn't my dad. I'm so glad. And isn't it ironic that my real dad has the same first name? And was also in the military?"

He nodded with a weak smile. "Ironic. Yes. What a coincidence."

She looked up at him. "It sounds like you don't believe it." Her eyes narrowed.

"No, Maria, it's fine. Your mom's story makes sense. And I'm so happy the guy we met today is not your dad. And your mom is right. You *are* perfect and have so much love in you—that kind that can only exist when someone's conceived with lots of love."

Maria smiled at him now. She was happy. Aaron closed the notebook and quickly pushed it under the bed. He didn't want her to see his notes. Not yet. She started kissing him and he got lost in her soft kisses, her exotic eyes. All thought left him.

They were cuddled up closely in bed, Maria in a deep sleep next to him. But tonight, it was Aaron who struggled to sleep. He stared instead at the ceiling.

He had a feeling that Maria's mom was hiding something else. Something much bigger than an everyday cheater who had cheated on his wife. He'd have to look up that guy later in the military database.

But he couldn't tell Maria about it. She had finally found peace, was sleeping quietly and contently next to him. No more nightmares. No more questions. He couldn't tell her he wasn't convinced by her mom's story.

Why not? Not sure. But I feel like Martina's still hiding something.

Suddenly, he had goosebumps all over his body. *Something isn't right. Something is scary. Don't know why. But I'll find the missing pieces. It's my mission to uncover the truth behind my fiancée's past, and I won't rest until the job's done. Nothing but the actual truth.*

CHAPTER 28

"**O**kay, mija, have fun tonight. But be careful when you guys are out. Remember, mija, fight back if anyone ever hurts you!"

Maria laughed. "I know, Mamá. You've always told me that. But please don't worry, Aaron will be there and protect me. And we're going out as a whole group to celebrate the end of finals."

Martina nodded. "Sí, I know, I know. That's good. And you guys all deserve it. I'm so glad finals are over for all of you." She winked an eye. "And I bet *you* did very good."

"I hope so," Maria said.

"I'm sure you did good, mija. But no matter what, te amo."

"¡Yo también te amo, Mamá! Well, I gotta go. See you soon. We're excited for your visit."

"Me too. Have fun today. Text me when you're home."

Martina hung up the phone and started closing up the store. She was humming her favorite song in glee.

I'm so excited I was invited to Aaron's commission and graduation. Get to meet Aaron's parents for the first time. I know he's a nice guy and a good match for my Maria. But I need to protect her. Always have. Maria was so scared at first. So scared. Poor little thing. Yes, still need to protect her, make sure she's in good hands. Meeting Aaron's parents will help.

179

Martina smiled as she turned off the lights and locked up her tailor store. She started whistling as she walked home and began to think about plans for next week. She had invited Aaron's family to visit for a day in Miami.

I'll make those fun pastries again for our Sunday brunch. And really get to know Aaron's family. It's important to get to know them. The way they interact with each other, the way they talk to each other, the way they look at each other. The way parents talk and act often says something about the love for their children and hints to the child's genetics. She frowned. *Well, usually. Maybe not in Maria's case.* She scolded herself. *Don't think of that. I am Maria's family. Yes I am. Just me. Great to hear Maria is doing well again. Good to know she's not digging into the past anymore.*

Martina was so happy her daughter was focused on the future again. As she opened her apartment door and walked inside, she saw the framed high school graduation picture of Maria. She looked so beautiful in her cap and gown.

Martina shut the door and walked over to study it more closely. She still remembered how proud she had been that day watching Maria walk across that stage to receive her diploma. Hearing her speech as the valedictorian of her class.

Such a smart girl. Always has been. She definitely must have gotten her smarts from her mom. For sure not from me. She sighed. *Maria always tells me I'm smart and need to be proud of myself. I suppose I do run a tailor shop all by myself. I've built it up and made a good life for myself, for all of us. Yes, I need to be proud. And yes, I am smart. I guess.*

She looked at the picture and sighed. *But my intellect is not even comparable to Maria's. Her intelligence must come from her mom. Her biological mom.*

Martina shook her head. *Stop it! Stop thinking of that! Maria can never find out. I'm her mom and always will be her mom!*

She turned around and sat on the couch. She sighed again, a deep sigh. *I feel so bad about lying to my little girl, but it had to be done. I decided long ago to keep the truth hidden to protect the two of us, both myself and Maria. Who knows what really happened to Maria's mom? I never got the full story, only pieces of it. It was so confusing. Maybe I should've acted differently? Maybe I mishandled the situation years ago. But it's too late now. No going back. I was thrown into this and didn't know what to do. Just followed directions.*

It's too late now. The truth needs to stay hidden. The story I came up with makes sense and will keep everything the way it is. Maria must be my daughter! Nobody else's. Just mine!

CHAPTER 29

"Mine?" Elisabeth laughed. "No, these eyes of mine aren't sleepy yet. I know it's late here, but I don't need much sleep." She sighed. "Or maybe I do. But I can't find peace enough to sleep."

"Me neither. Well, anyway, it's been good talking with you again, Elisabeth." Brad Collins pushed the phone even closer to his ear to better hear her voice. He could almost hear her smile.

"Yeah. I'm starting to like these late-night calls," Elisabeth said, and grinned. "Gives me something to do, something to look forward to."

"It does, huh? Well, that's good. And I've got even better news."

"Oh, yes? And what could that be, General?"

He laughed. He loved it when she teased him. *Nobody else can keep up with my wit. Nobody but her. And nobody but her can render me speechless like she does. She's always gotten in the last word. Still does. I miss her. Can't wait to see her in person.*

"General? You still there?" She lowered her voice and giggled. "This is unacceptable! You better focus on the mission, sir. Talk to me. Give me the plan."

He smiled. "Yes ma'am!"

"Well then, go on, Brad. Don't keep me in suspense. Did your request to travel to Eglin work out?"

"Yeah, it did. My exec did a great job planning the TDY. Busy days on base, though. But it'll be good. And exactly the time you're there. Well, I arrive on Sunday. Couldn't convince the Air Force to pay for a whole weekend before the meetings."

"Ah, too bad. Always busy with work."

"Elisabeth, I'm sorry—"

"I'm *joking* Brad. This time I'm joking. Don't worry, it's okay. Completely fine. I might be jet-lagged at first anyway."

He let out a sigh of relief.

"But we can meet on Monday right away, can't we?"

"Of course. For lunch and dinner?"

She smiled—he could hear it through the phone, could picture her grin. His heart skipped a beat faster.

"It's a date then," she said.

"Yes it is. A date."

"Looking forward to it, Brad."

"Me, too."

"Okay, keep me posted then, alright?"

"Yeah I will. Of course I will." He smiled his biggest smile in years.

"Call me again before your trip?" Elisabeth said.

"Of course. And before yours."

"Yeah, definitely. Nighttime is good for me."

"It's a phone date then." He grinned. "I'm glad to hear you're available at night."

She laughed. "Don't tell me you're jealous of a possible nighttime acquaintance?"

"Well, I mean. . . ." He searched for words. "I know we're divorced and all, but—"

"Brad, don't worry. Sarah really tried to set me up, but I have no room in my heart for anyone."

"For *anyone?*" he asked, his heart suddenly heavy.

"No one . . . but you," she whispered.

He jumped up from behind his desk, his eyes sparkling brightly. "Well, that's good, that's really good."

"Is it?"

"Yeah, it is. Because there's nobody else that understands me the way you do. Even now. I know it. I feel it. You're still my soul mate. My best friend."

Elisabeth laughed a lighthearted laugh. "Good. But don't tell Drew you said I'm your best friend."

Brad smirked. "Nah, I won't tell him. And you better not either."

"Me? I don't usually hang out with him."

He laughed. "Not yet. But you might soon. He's coming to Florida too. I still work with him."

"What? I thought he retired?"

"He did. From active duty. But he can't imagine a better boss than me, so he's continued working for me, as a civilian."

"Ah, I see. Sure. Can't pass up a great boss like you, huh, General?"

"Nope, you can't." He grinned. "No one can pass me up." He heard her laugh. He loved talking with her and couldn't wait to see her.

CHAPTER 30

Maria was doing her makeup when the doorbell rang. She was so surprised that she missed her lips entirely and smeared lipstick all over her cheek. *Argh, silly me!* She quickly wiped it off and went to the door. It was Aaron. She let him in and gave him a kiss.

"You're early," she said. "I'm not ready yet. Wait, wasn't Nick supposed to be with you?"

"No, not yet. There's still time before we go out and he wasn't ready to go yet."

She looked at the clock on the wall before heading back into the bathroom to finish her makeup. "No wonder, it's still super early," she called back to Aaron, who was in the living room taking off his shoes.

"I know, just wanted to come over to talk to you—alone," Aaron said. He now stood in the doorframe to her small bathroom.

Maria stopped mid-mascara and looked at him. In a serious tone she said, "What's up? Everything alright?"

"Yeah, I guess so." He looked down at his feet, avoiding eye contact with her.

"Aaron, what's going on?"

"Well, I just got a call," he said, and kept looking down. "Eglin Air Force Base wants me to come in right away. On June first."

Maria stared at him. "June first?"

"Yeah."

The hand holding her mascara brush dropped down further. "Aaron, that's the Monday after graduation weekend."

"I know."

"Which means next week is your last week here."

"Yeah."

"You're moving away in just one week?"

He nodded and looked up at her. She was so beautiful. Even with just one eye of makeup on. It hurt him just thinking about having to leave her behind. He'd live hours away and no longer see her every day. He sighed.

"How can they just tell you what to do? It's not fair," Maria said, her voice raised.

"Maria . . . it's my job. My first job. These are my superiors we're talking about. It's an order—they need me to be there June first, so I'll be there June first."

"But you're not even commissioned or graduated yet."

"No, but I will be by June first."

"What makes them so sure you will be?"

He now smirked. "You're saying you think I didn't pass my exams and won't graduate or be commissioned?"

She realized how ridiculous that sounded. *Duh, of course he's gonna graduate. Probably even with honors. Aaron is super smart. Just so strange to think he'll soon graduate and no longer be in college anymore. Starting work at his new job as a second lieutenant in the Air Force. I just thought we'd have more time to hang out and relax before he got started.*

She set down her mascara and walked over to where he was standing in the bathroom door frame and gave him a hug. "I can't believe the next chapter of your life will start in about a week."

"I know. Me neither. I'll hate to leave you behind."

They just stood there in a long hug, not saying anything.

"Wherever you go, whatever you do, I'll be right here waiting for you," Maria said and started humming the famous eighties song.

Aaron smiled and looked at her. "Well, I was hoping you wouldn't just stay here, you know. Maybe go with me, help me move?"

She smiled her brightest smile at him. "Of course I will. You'll need some serious help decorating your new place!"

He laughed. "Yeah, you're right. I'm not very talented at that."

She shook her head and thought back to the time they first met, when Aaron and Nick had just moved off campus into their apartment. "I want you to get a real table to eat at."

"Hey, come on, the ironing board was genius, you have to admit. Took care of two things at once. I call that innovation. We'd iron our uniforms and then eat our meals off it. Kept the food nice and warm. Genius!"

They laughed together and Maria rolled her eyes. "Well, Mr. Genius, with the move coming up, you better get to planning."

"I know, that's why I came over so early. Wanted to talk to you about that. Thought my dad could help out with driving the truck and lifting all the heavy stuff."

"Sounds great. Your family will be here for graduation anyhow. Your mom and sister can help too."

"Maybe, though I doubt it. Emma and my mom still have school. Summer break is a few weeks away. Doubt my mom can take off from teaching or will let my sis miss days of school. But my dad can take off to stick around. Don't think he's in court right now. I'll call them to ask about it and make a plan."

"Sounds good, but that shouldn't take too long. You're still way too early for our night out."

"I know. After the call, I figured you could help me look at apartments in the area around base? Research online together a bit. And book the moving truck. The TLF—"

"The what?"

"Oh. That stands for 'temporary lodging facility.' Basically like a little hotel on base."

A little hotel?

"Eglin Air Force Base has their TLFs right by the water, I heard."

TLF? Right by the water? Maria stared into space.

"Everything okay?"

She looked at him. "Yeah. TLF. Just sounds so strange."

He laughed. "You better get used to all the acronyms. The Air Force loves their acronyms."

She nodded. *TLF. Strange acronym. But why does this particular acronym send chills down my spine?*

She shook it off and quickly gave Aaron a kiss. "How about you call your family and make plans with them while I get my other eye ready?"

He laughed a warm, loud laugh that made his blue eyes sparkle. "You're beautiful no matter what. But having your eyes match one another is probably for the best."

He winked at her, turned around and sat down in a chair by the table, took his phone out of his pocket, and dialed his parents' number.

Maria went back to the bathroom mirror and picked up her makeup. As she was brushing the black mascara onto her long eyelashes, it seemed as if her own eyes, with their mosaic of golden-and-emerald-green flecks in the brown center encircled by the blue rim, were staring her down. Her own eyes looked back at her, overwhelming her, and she helplessly watched them change color. They turned a bright green that clashed with her golden eyeshadow.

She closed her eyes for a split second, breaking eye contact, only for a bright white light to appear behind her eyelids. When she opened her eyes again, another vision of the past played out before her.

She saw herself in the mirror—except she was little, a little toddler now, looking into the bathroom mirror in a small, foreign bathroom, white towels neatly folded all around her. White towels and a sign, like the kind a hotel uses to remind their guests to please reuse their towels to help save the environment.

Just then she noticed she was being held by a tall, slender woman with freckles around her nose that matched her own.

"Welcome to Eglin's TLF," she heard the woman say.

TLF? TLF? Eglin's TLF?

The eyes reflected in the mirror widened in horror. She felt chills running down her spine. The TLF at Eglin Air Force Base. She stared in the mirror and saw her toddler self laugh in the arms of the slender freckled woman, who smiled and repeated "TLF!" over and over again.

"TLF!"

"TLF!"

"TLF at Eglin Air Force Base!"

It all went black.

"Maria? Are you okay?" she heard a voice call.

It was Aaron. Aaron's voice. He had been talking on the phone but was now talking to her from the other room. She sat up and looked around. She was in her bathroom on the floor. She pressed her back to the wall to steady herself. Above her was the little sink with its mirror, and here she was on her bottom, just sitting there. *What the heck?* She noticed the opened mascara had rolled across the floor behind the toilet.

"Maria?"

She shook her head, unsure of what had just happened. "Yeah. I'm fine."

"Okay," she heard him say and then continue his phone conversation.

She picked up the mascara and stood up. She looked in the mirror and saw she had mascara smeared all over her face below her left eye.

Oh my gosh, what just happened? My mind must be playing tricks on me.

She grabbed one of the makeup-remover towels and wiped off the excess mascara. She felt a bit dizzy but was otherwise okay. She looked into the mirror; her image peered back nice and clear at her.

It's just me. There's nobody else here. Well, except Aaron, in the living room on his phone.

"Excellent," she heard him say. "Sure, I'll check with her to see if she's ready."

Maria quickly finished up, trying to avoid the mirror as much as possible. For some reason it scared her now. *Scared of a mirror? That's so silly!* She shook her head and joined Aaron.

"Hi," she said, and waved at Aaron's family via FaceTime.

"Maria, you look stunning," said Grace Heikinnen, Aaron's mom. "I heard you guys are going out tonight?"

"Yes, we are. Just celebrating the end of finals," she explained, and they started talking about tonight, their plans for next week, and the news of Aaron's quick move to his first assignment.

"We're looking forward to seeing you both next week," said Jack Heikinnen, Aaron's dad. Emma and Grace nodded.

"And looking forward to finally meeting your mom, Maria," Grace added. "I'm just sorry we won't have time to visit Miami and see where you grew up. I know your mom was looking forward to that as well. Unfortunately, there's no time for that anymore with Aaron's quick turnaround. I'm so sorry. Would have been nice to at least see her for a brunch before our flight home on Sunday."

"I know. I'll admit, I think my mom will be upset. She had planned to cook you some very special Venezuelan pastries."

Aaron's mom and sister sighed. "Ah, too bad."

"Maybe your mom can bring some to Daytona for us to try?"

"Emma, don't make demands of Maria's mother. That's rude!"

Aaron and Maria laughed. "I bet she wouldn't mind baking. She'll just be upset there won't be time for you to visit in Miami. Suppose you'll just have to come back another time."

The Heikinnen family nodded. They said goodbye. Maria watched Aaron take notes. *He's written out the timing for everything. Always prepared. Impressive.*

They switched to researching rental moving trucks online. "I think Penske is most affordable. I just need a small one, don't you think?"

Maria nodded. "Yeah. What about your car? I'll need to bring mine so I can return home. Does that mean your dad will drive yours?"

"Nope. I think we should get a trailer and tow it behind the truck. Then my dad and I can take turns driving. It's a long six-hour drive and will be tiring driving an unwieldy vehicle at night. What do you think?"

She grinned at him. "Perfect. Genius."

"Told you I was a genius." Aaron winked at her and booked everything. "Alright, apartments next." He was on a roll and eager to continue their research. "Let's find our future home together."

Maria looked at the clock. "Aaron, I don't mean to dampen the mood, but there's not too much time left before we have to go and meet up with our friends."

He looked up and sighed. "You're right. We can research apartments later then. We'll have plenty of time to think things over." Maria nodded. "But I do think we have time to at least book the TLF now. It's moving season. I don't want them to get booked out. It's much cheaper on base, and those units have a living room, kitchen, and two bedrooms."

Maria smiled. "Sounds good. Let's look it up then."

As Aaron typed in *TLF at Eglin AFB*, Maria's smile faded. The words seemed to jump out at her, jump out and slap her across the face. She kept staring at the computer as an image appeared on-screen.

"'Air Force Inn,'" Aaron read out. "No, that's not right. We don't want a hotel room, we want the actual lodging on base with the little kitchenette and two bedrooms. Who knows how long we'll have to stay there."

In a trance, Maria watched quietly as Aaron eagerly researched where they would be staying.

"That's it," he called out, pointing at the photo of a collection of old-looking one-story buildings. There was a half-sandy, half-grassy area in the middle of the buildings. He clicked on pictures of the inside. There was a tan-and-greenish-looking couch, a little half-table facing a kitchenette with old-looking white cabinets, then two bedrooms—one with a king-sized bed and one with bunk beds—and a hallway that led to a small bathroom with tan tiles.

Maria gasped.

"I know, I know, they're pretty old and shabby-looking. I think they're like twenty or thirty years old, but they're in a nice location right by the marina and a little beach strip. And they're cheap."

Maria kept staring at the photos. All the little hairs on her arms stood up and she started shaking, breathing heavily. She stared at the pictures, the words on the page: *TLF at Eglin AFB.* They jumped out at her—the words left the page and jumped out and swirled all around her.

TLF. White-sand beaches. Marina next door. A marina with boats. Speed boats. Pontoon boats. Boats to fall off of. Splash. Water to swallow you up. Mucky, murky water.

Sweat dripped down her face now, her hands bunched up.

TLF at Eglin AFB.

Her head was spinning. She stared at the web page. That half-sandy, half-grassy area in the middle of the one-story building that led down to the water. She saw herself running down there, to the water.

Into the water.

Splashing.

Drowning.

No! Not again! Don't drown!

She screamed, a shrill scream that escaped her throat before she broke into sobs, tears streaming down her face.

She stared at the pictures and barely noticed Aaron staring at her, one eyebrow raised. "Holy cow. Maria, are you okay? What is it?"

"I've been there. I know that place!"

"What?"

"I know that place. That TLF at Eglin AFB."

Someone is playing with me.

She felt like a puppet, a lifeless puppet. Her thoughts were indifferent, she was indifferent. She didn't know what she was thinking, doing, saying. All jumbled up, thoughts all jumbled up.

CHAPTER 31

She was being shaken, shaken gently.

"Maria, listen to me," she heard a deep and gentle but concerned voice. "You have to stop this. Snap out of this funk!"

Someone now took her head and gently turned it toward them. She was now staring into ocean-blue eyes. Ocean-blue eyes she could sink into. *Drown in. I'm drowning. Again.*

"Maria!"

Her face now got kissed, a kiss on the forehead, and she closed her eyes. She let her head sink into the gentle, strong hands that gripped her, sank right into them with her eyes closed.

"Maria?"

I know that voice. That gentle, low voice. Aaron. It's Aaron.

She quickly opened her eyes and looked at him. Suddenly, all the brain fog was gone. "Aaron? What's going on?"

He looked concerned, looked deep into her eyes, then glanced over at his computer. He reached over and suddenly closed the laptop. Maria looked at it. "What are you doing?"

"We were booking a place on base, remember?"

"Oh, yeah. Did you find something?"

Aaron looked at her with a funny look on his face. She smiled at him, her head clear. "What? Why are you looking at me like that? I thought you were going to book something with two rooms."

"Yes."

Why is he acting so strange? We just booked the truck and need to get a place to stay at.

He looked at her with that funny look. "You don't mind me booking the TLF?"

Maria ignored him and got up and touched her face. It was wet. "Why is my face wet?"

Aaron gave her an intense look. "You don't remember?"

She shook her head.

He thought for a while. His face was ghostly white. He kept staring at her, his one eyebrow raised.

"Aaron, what is it?"

"We looked at the TLFs on base and you suddenly freaked out. You were screaming and everything. Crying. Frantic."

She started laughing and waved him off. "Don't be silly!" Then, she realized he was serious. "Oh my, I don't remember that at all."

Aaron seemed confused. Maria was, too. "Oh my gosh, I'm a basket case!" She jumped up. "You think I'm crazy, right? *Am* I crazy?" She was now pacing, pacing back and forth, thinking about her state of mind. *Is it possible? Am I a psycho?*

Aaron watched her for a while, his eyebrow still raised. Suddenly, he stood up and came over. "Maria, stop. Stop it. We'll figure this out. I have a plan. Can I try something?"

Maria stopped pacing and faced him. "Sure?"

"Let's sit back down. Come over here."

She did as she was told. Aaron opened his laptop, and the pictures of the TLF at Eglin Air Force Base appeared on screen. Maria stared at it. Her arm hairs started poking up again. She started shaking, sweat breaking out all over. *Oh my gosh. I know this place.* She stared at the pictures until, suddenly, Aaron closed the laptop again and she was staring at her blank wall.

"Maria, what is it?" she heard Aaron ask from far away.

Her brain fog lifted. "I don't know. That place scares me. I feel like I know it."

Aaron said nothing.

Maria's brain felt clear again. "That's silly, isn't it?"

Aaron kept thinking and didn't say anything.

"Aaron? Am I crazy? Am I a basket case?"

Aaron still didn't say anything, just stared at the floor, completely ignoring her.

"Aaron? Do you still love me?"

Aaron looked up and saw her exotic eyes filled with sadness. Sadness and fear. He hugged her. "Maria. I do still love you, and always will. I'll always love you."

"What if I turn into a crazy person? I've been acting so strange lately."

He looked at her and thought for a bit. "Well, you don't act strange that often. Usually only at night, with those nightmares now and then."

Maria grimaced. "That still seems like a lot."

"It's okay, Maria. I really don't think you're crazy," he assured her, and gave her a kiss. "I think you have PTSD."

Maria stared at him. "What?"

"PTSD—post-traumatic stress disorder."

"I know what PTSD is. I just don't understand why you think I have it. I haven't had a traumatic experience in my life."

Aaron nodded. "Yeah, not that you know of."

"What? Come on, Aaron, that's ridiculous." Her face turned red, her eyebrows crunched in. She stood up.

Aaron stayed calm and opened his laptop again. He turned it toward her. Maria looked at the picture of the TLF at Eglin AFB. She started feeling chills run down her spine. The hairs on her arms stood up. She started sweating, breathing hard, her head hurting.

He closed the laptop lid again. "So, tell me this: did you have chills looking at that picture?"

She looked down at him where he sat in front of the closed laptop. Her eyes green, her face red, mascara smeared all over her face from her tears, she nodded.

"Did your arm hairs stand up?"

She nodded again.

"Did you start sweating, breathing hard, feeling dizzy?"

Slowly, she nodded again. *How does he know all that?*

"Everything you just experienced is classic PTSD. All us cadets learn about it. So we can be aware of the signs in case we ever experience it."

Maria looked at him. *Okay, he's starting to make sense.*

"So, you're not crazy . . . you just have PTSD." He smiled at her.

She looked at him, her face still red. "So you think this makes me feel better than thinking I'm crazy? Aaron, what the heck?" She pouted and stared at him with smeared mascara all over her face.

"I'm sorry, Maria, but you asked me if you were crazy, and my answer is no. But there is something going on and you can't deny it. You just can't deny it. Think of those dreams. Those nightmares. There's something going on that you don't understand. Something in your past that resulted in PTSD."

She stared at him. *He's making sense, the explanation's logical. But why? What's happening to me?*

"I don't know what caused this, Maria, but let me help you find out. Please."

She nodded with a dry mouth. "But how?"

"I don't know. Let me ask you this: have you ever been to Eglin Air Force Base?"

She shook her head.

"Did you *feel* something when I said that?"

"Said what?"

"Eglin. Eglin Air Force Base. Eglin AFB."

Her head started spinning, pounding, a headache coming on. She touched her temples.

"Headache?"

She nodded, rubbing her temples. *Wait. What?* "So, you're saying I'm not just upset over you leaving to go there?"

"Exactly."

"But I've never been there before."

"I know. At least *that's what you think*."

"Aaron, this is crazy. This is freaky!"

"I agree, I agree."

"Stop it," she yelled at him, "you're being mean!" Tears dwelled in her eyes.

He went over to where she was standing and hugged her, held her tight. "Maria, I love you. But you have to admit, there's something strange missing here. A big piece of your past we don't seem to know. I understand it scares you. It scares me too. It doesn't make sense. You know I hate it when I don't understand something because there's no logical explanation."

Maria had to smirk. *Yes, I know that.*

"So please, let me help you. But I can only help you if you'll admit there's something weird going on. If it turns out there's nothing, it's nothing. But if there *is* something strange, please let me help. I'm still not convinced your mom's story about your 'new dad' is true.. . . ."

Maria looked up. "What?"

"I don't know, Maria. There's something here that's connected to your dad. The drowning dreams, the German, Eglin AFB. It doesn't make sense at all, but something is there. Something we're missing. Unless you really are just a basket case.. . . ." He teased her with his brightest smile. "But you know yourself that's not true! You're smart, beautiful, and amazing."

She sighed. *Flattery aside, he's right. Something strange is going on. It isn't just all in my head. There has to be an explanation. But what?*

"Maria, I'm not sure where to start, but please let me write something in your notebook. The one—"

"—labeled *My Past.* I know."

She went to look for it. Her mind was clear now, sharp as usual. She found it and handed it to Aaron. "I'll let you write this strange moment down. Once you're done, book that housing. We gotta go there. In the meantime, I won't look at those pictures again. I promise. I'm going to clean myself up while you do all of that. Okay?"

"Okay. I love you."

"I love you too." She lingered long enough to give his soft lips a nice, long kiss.

"And then we'll go out and dance," she called back as she walked to the bathroom.

"Deal."

CHAPTER 32

*E*glin's TLF. She stared into the darkness of her room and tried not to let the fear take over this time. *Temporary Lodging Facility at Eglin Air Force Base.* She could feel sweat forming on her forehead. She felt sick to her stomach. *Maybe I had too much to drink?*

But Maria knew that it wasn't that evening's drinks. It was the fear inside her that made her nauseous. Fear of Eglin's TLF. *No idea why, but I know deep down that Aaron's right. There's some sort of secret that I need to uncover. It somehow involves this place. Why? No idea. When would I have stepped foot on an Air Force base? I never have. Ever. Maybe it's something else, maybe the TLF apartments we saw online just looked like some other homes I've been at before?*

She sighed and decided to focus on other things. Her time out tonight had been fun. The yummy Mai Tai drinks at the beach bar. The awesome time she'd had dancing the night away in the nightclub with all her friends. *It was amazing. We sure did celebrate the end of finals week in style.*

And Aaron was so sweet. She looked over at him. He was deep asleep next to her. She watched him breathe, in and out, heard his slow, steady breath. She sighed. *In just eight days, we'll pack up and move him to his new job. His first duty station.*

At Eglin Air Force Base.

The chills came back. She took a deep breath and thought back to the fun time at the nightclub Razzles. The dancing, the disco lights, the music, the drinks, the cheers. With a smile she fell asleep.

She was dancing. Happily dancing in circles, moving her feet quickly to the beat, laughing, having fun, enjoying the time. She watched her little feet move, didn't have to think about where to put them as they easily moved and shuffled across the floor, one little foot after the other.

Wait. What? Little feet? I'm average size, which is more than annoying because that size is always sold out.

But she certainly had little feet as she looked down. She realized she wasn't in the nightclub anymore; she was dancing on an ugly tan carpet. She was dancing in a room, a small room with a tan-and-greenish-looking couch and a little half-table that faced the kitchenette's white cabinets. She knew there was a hallway that connected to a small bathroom and two bedrooms, one with a king-sized bed, the other with bunk beds.

That's my room, the one with the bunk beds.

She laughed and started dancing across the room and down the hallway into her room. A tall, slender woman followed her, also shuffling her feet over the ugly carpet, dancing along. Laughter filled the spaces. She giggled and turned back to her mom, but somehow could only see her silhouette.

"Mama," she called, laughing, and tried to make out her face, but it suddenly got all blurry, all strange, and the face seemed to disappear, disappear into the distance, into a bright-white light.

"Mama," she screamed, and tried to reach for her mom, but she couldn't. A strong man was holding her little arms tightly, and her screams were muffled by the water, the dark, mucky, murky water that rushed in and engulfed her. She swallowed a mouthful of water, then another, again and again until everything went black.

"Maria! Maria! Wake up!"

She was being shaken, shaken hard. She slowly opened her eyes. Darkness all around her.

"Maria, it's me, Aaron."

Slowly, her head cleared, and she realized she was in her own bed in her college apartment next to Aaron, her fiancé.

I'm safe. I'm not drowning. I'm not little. I'm a grown woman who had a nightmare. Again.

"Maria, was it another nightmare?"

She nodded, her throat dry.

"The drowning one?"

She nodded again, unable to speak.

"This is the first one you've had since your mom told you that story about Jonathan Smith, right?"

She perked up and was wide awake now. She thought about it for a while, then nodded.

"Can you tell me about your dream?"

She nodded again and tried to remember the dream, then told him everything, every odd little detail she could recall.

"Interesting," Aaron mumbled. Maria looked at him. She didn't understand. "It's interesting that you encountering those photos of the TLF at Eglin Air Force Base brought back the same drowning dream you were having while looking for your father."

She sat up straight. "So, what does that mean?" Both thought for a while. She added, "It doesn't make sense to me at all."

"No, it doesn't." He put an arm around her. "We'll figure it out, Maria. Something's not right. Maybe talk to your mom again?"

She shook her head. He saw it through the gloom. "Well, let me come up with a plan. I'll think of something. Okay?"

Maria nodded.

"Let's try to sleep now, okay?"

She nodded again and cuddled close to Aaron. But she felt scared. Really scared.

"Please, protect me," she whispered, and was thankful when Aaron just nodded without asking any more questions.

He's so sweet. I love him so much and can't wait to marry him. I need to keep focusing on that part of my life. Just that. Determined to think only about her wedding, that exciting time in her life, she fell into a deep, dreamless sleep.

CHAPTER 33

"**I** can't believe you're going to Eglin next week," Maria sighed. They were scouring the internet for apartments in all the towns surrounding Eglin AFB. They looked in Valparaiso and Niceville, in Shalimar and Fort Walton Beach.

Every time they looked up a city and saw pictures of it online, Aaron closely watched Maria. However, she seemed fine and happily helped him do his research. She didn't show any signs of stress when looking or reading about each new city.

It's so strange. Her PTSD is somehow only connected to the Air Force base. Only with Eglin. I have no idea why.

He had been secretly jotting down notes in her notebook to preserve every little detail that might eventually help them solve the strange puzzle about Maria's past. Aaron almost seemed more worried about the situation than Maria. For some reason, she had recently fixated on planning fun things to do with Aaron's family and her mamá during their upcoming stay at Daytona for Aaron's graduation and commission. And she'd thrown herself into planning Aaron's move.

She's sure good at packing. Granted, I don't have much to pack, but the few things I do have, Maria takes care of. I love how she organizes them into boxes, labels them according their contents, and stacks them by room. Who says she's not a planner in her own right?

He smirked and returned his focus to their online search.

"Okay, Aaron, I think we have a good list of apartments to tour. Now come on, back to packing."

He sighed. "Already?"

"Yep. ¡Vamos!" She closed his laptop and got to work. They heard Nick rustling around inside his own room. "See, even Nick is packing."

Aaron got up and started pouting. "Yeah, I know. But he and Jim have so much more time than me. They even get to go on a post-graduation trip. Not fair."

"Aw, poor Aaron." Maria moved closer to him and gave him a big kiss. "Does that make you feel better?"

He smiled. "A little."

"Good. Just remember that I'm proud of you. Sad you have to leave so soon, but I bet it's a good sign the base needs you there so quickly."

"I guess."

"It'll be fun. And I'll be there with you. All summer!"

He looked up from his packing and grinned. "Yeah, that's a huge bonus!"

"Exactly. We'll have fun exploring the area, going to the beach, decorating your apartment. I really think the apartments we're gonna see have huge potential!"

"You're right. Yeah, it'll be fun. It's exciting . . . but also kinda sad, huh?"

Maria's smile faltered. "Agreed. What am I going to do here without you next year?"

"Study, of course." Aaron grinned.

"Ha, ha, very funny. Yes, study *and* party. Without you then, fine!"

"Nah, you're gonna party with me first. At my new duty station. First job." He elbowed her, then gave her a kiss on the cheek.

"Yeah, I know. I'm looking forward to it."

He gave her a funny look. "Really?"

"Of course. Why wouldn't I look forward to it?"

"Remember where we're going? You're looking forward to Eglin Air Force Base?"

They both watched Maria's arm hairs stand up. Aaron saw her close her eyes. She started breathing in and out, in and out.

"You okay? What are you doing?"

She opened her eyes again. "Mindful breathing exercises. I gotta stay sane, right?"

Aaron laughed, but deep down inside he didn't feel like laughing. *What in the world is going on? Why the heck is Maria so scared of Eglin Air Force Base?*

CHAPTER 34

Eglin Air Force Base. He had to mentally prepare himself for his visit and was packing already. He liked being prepared and knew he had to take extra care this time. He needed to be on top of things so his feelings wouldn't take over.

He needed a good plan. The best plan. A plan that carefully laid out every step on base, so he could avoid the one area he couldn't stand looking at. The one place that had led to all this fear, all this numbness. The one moment that had taken everything from him, broken his heart. Broken it into such tiny pieces that it never healed again.

The Temporary Lodging Facility at Eglin Air Force Base—the TLFs. Where he had lost it all. His little girl. His family.

Just thinking about it made him start sweating. A drop of sweat fell onto his military duffel bag, which lay open across the wooden floor of his house. His big, empty house. His life had been empty ever since that fateful night at Eglin's TLF. *So empty, so lonely.*

He sighed and wiped off the sweat. *Focus. Just focus on packing. And on the one good thing coming up. Seeing Elisabeth. I'll finally get to see Elisabeth again. Together we can face this. We can do this. Find closure. Maybe I should sponsor her on base, so we can go back to Eglin's TLFs? Look at our old home together. Find closure there. Bury everything there, the whole past. Yeah, maybe.*

He pulled open a drawer full of tan military shirts. He grabbed a few and threw them into the empty duffel bag, then bent down to count them and realized he'd only put two shirts inside. *That's not enough. Two.*

That's so young. Two years old. She hadn't even turned two years old yet.

He stared at the shirts and the duffel bag. Suddenly, a bright-white light shone out of it, and he had to close his eyes for a second. When he opened them, he saw her, a picture so clear, forever burned into his mind.

She was laughing, giggling. Her innocent giggles filled the empty rooms with laughter and made him laugh as well.

"What are you doing, pumpkin?" He looked down at his little girl, just a small toddler who had crawled into his military duffel bag. More giggles and the wide, innocent, bright smile. Her hazel eyes with their mosaic of golden-and-emerald-green flecks in the dark brown center encircled by a blue rim were sparkling.

"Help pack. Help Daddy pack." She grabbed a black military shirt out of his hand and threw it into the duffel bag.

He laughed a laugh so happy and loud that it filled up the half-empty rooms around them. "You're ready to help Daddy pack?" She nodded with a wide smile. "Pack for Daddy's new assignment?" Another happy nod. "Are you excited to move? Move down to the beach by the water?"

She nodded again. "Yes. Wawa."

He smiled widely. He loved it when she tried to say "water" and only "wawa" came out. It was the cutest thing he had ever heard.

"Are you ready to swim in that nice warm ocean water?"

"Yes. Swim in wawa. Enti, too," she said, and pretended to swim inside the duffel bag, her favorite stuffed toy next to her.

He laughed, his eyes sparkling from the joy of this precious moment. "That's not water, little pumpkin! Come on out and we'll pack so we're ready for the real water, okay?"

She squeaked in excitement and sat up in the bag. "Pack. More!"

"Okay, ma'am, let's do it!" He pulled out more black undershirts, but before he could neatly lay them inside, his little daughter had already grabbed the pile out of his hand. Most of them fell into the bag in a jumble, but she held on to one of them, unfolded it and held it up to her face, hiding behind it.

"Oh no, where did she go? Where did my little girl go? Where could she be?" A little giggle. "Mmh. . . . Let's check *here*!" He lifted the unfolded shirt to look straight into her excited little eyes.

"Peekaboo," they said at the same time, and laughed together.

She let the shirt fall into the duffel bag and picked up another one and held it up to his own face to play peekaboo. He kept playing the same game over and over again with her. Every time he lowered his shirt, there she was, sitting in the duffel bag, giggling, laughing, smiling back at him.

Then he lowered his shirt and found she was gone. His little daughter was gone, leaving him holding the tan shirt in his hands. He stared at the duffel bag that only held the two tan shirts he'd put in earlier, the duffel bag that sat on the wooden floor of his big empty house, the duffel bag he would bring with him on his TDY to Eglin Air Force Base.

He scrunched up the shirt he was holding and scolded himself. *Stupid, you're so stupid! Playing peekaboo with a ghost, with nobody. She's not here. Hasn't been here a long, long time. Haven't seen her in twenty years. No trace of her. My little girl is gone. Gone! Vanished! Gone, never to be seen again.*

And I'm still *going crazy over it. Playing peekaboo with a memory. Sheesh. Good thing nobody saw me just now. What would they say if they saw me, a general, playing peekaboo with nobody? They'd be stunned and definitely send me to a psychiatrist.*

He started laughing. A loud coarse laugh escaped his throat as he stared into the military duffel bag he was packing for his temporary-duty trip to Eglin AFB. So he could go back to the place where his little girl had vanished. Under his care. Just vanished. Disappeared.

His laugh turned into a sob, a loud sob. Tears now dripped down into the duffel bag, onto his clean, washed military shirts.

I miss you so much. So much. My little baby girl. Where are you? The general kneeled in front of his bag, sobbing, crying, his pain so deep he could barely stand it. *I'll never forget you. My precious little girl. How could you have just vanished? Gone in just eight minutes. The police said you drowned. Walked out into the water and just drowned. But why didn't they find your cold little body? Did it really wash out to the ocean, far from Choctawhatchee Bay into the Gulf of Mexico and then the Atlantic Ocean? The police thought so, and I believed them.*

My little girl, drowned. In deep water. Wawa. Drowned in wawa.

Brad Collins got up and walked through his big house in search of a Kleenex. He finally found a box on his kitchen counter, still thinking back to long-gone times. *Elisabeth didn't believe them though. She was convinced someone kidnapped our little one. But why would someone just kidnap another person's child? Who* does *that? Back then, we couldn't think of a single person who would've wanted to hurt our family by taking our only child. Neither of us had any enemies. We thought through other scenarios, like someone who wanted a child and couldn't have one. Stole her out of jealousy.*

But we didn't know anyone who fit that description. For goodness' sake, we had just moved to Eglin AFB, we didn't even know anyone there yet. Who in the world kidnaps a child from a family that just moved into the neighborhood? It didn't make sense back then, doesn't make sense now.

It does make sense that we neglected our little one. Left her alone long enough for her to wake up, walk out to the water, and drown. That not only makes sense, it's a fact. We did leave her alone. Thought she was sleeping. Thought she'd be safe. Safe while we did our laundry.

It's my fault. All my fault. It was my idea. Those stupid, dirty uniforms that needed cleaning. I should've worn that damn dirty uniform! Should've. But instead, I insisted on going to the laundromat. With my wife. So stupid! And Elisabeth just came along, to keep me company. It was stupid. It ruined my life. Ruined it by losing my only daughter, my precious little daughter. Damn it, stupid uniforms!

And then I lost her: my rock, my wife, the love of my life. I just couldn't stand seeing her broken, knowing it was my fault. She had given up everything for me. And I ruined it all. That night at Eglin Air Force Base. He loudly blew his nose, used another Kleenex to wipe away his tears, and filled a glass of water. He poured it down his dry throat. Filled it up again and drank it all up.

He cleared his throat, took a deep breath, and walked back to his duffel bag to keep packing. *I'm so glad I get to see Elisabeth again. Get a new start with her. Heal my heart. Well, part of it. The other part will stay empty forever.*

I was a fool. I should've stayed with her, been with her, helped her grieve. Together, we might have found closure. But we had different beliefs, different hopes. So we fell apart. But next week, we get a chance to fall back together. To finally find closure. He smiled and went back to packing.

As he put more shirts in his military duffel bag, he suddenly remembered something. That day he had played peekaboo with their little daughter. It wasn't just her who'd climbed into the duffel bag—she had brought her favorite toy with her, that ugly, silly security blanket she was so attached to.

Enti.

He remembered that Enti had been with her that day as they played peekaboo. She had needed Enti whenever she felt insecure, like the day they packed up to move to Florida.

Then it dawned on him. All color flushed out of his face. *Damn. Elisabeth was right! She always insisted our little daughter would've brought Enti with her if she just walked out of the TLF looking for us. Damn it! She was right all along. Neither the police nor I believed her. We missed the significance of this detail at the time.*

He stood up and started pacing. *She was kidnapped. Elisabeth, you were right. I understand that now. I'm convinced. But are you? Oh my gosh, Elisabeth! Why didn't I believe you?*

Brad Collins paced back and forth in his big, empty house, thinking hard. *But who in the world would have done such a thing? The police questioned everyone there, everyone that could possibly have had access to the TLF at the time. They talked to the guy who was at the laundromat with us, the three other families who were living in our building, the single military captain and his dad, the cleaning staff, and. . . .*

Wait! The cleaning staff?

Brad started pacing faster. Suddenly, he remembered the conversation he'd had with his wife just hours before their little one disappeared. The conversation was crystal clear in his mind; it echoed down into the depths of his brain, the conversation he and his wife had had just an hour before their little one had disappeared:

"Remember a few nights ago at the laundry facility when Moana noticed the TV show the cleaning lady was watching? She picked up the Spanish words right away. Even the cleaning lady was amazed," he remembered himself saying.

His wife had agreed and told him, "Moana still knows that lady's name. She has great memory."

Oh my Gosh. The cleaning lady. Did they look into her? Did the police even look into her? Or had they already concluded an accidental drowning had occurred?

Elisabeth, you're right! Moana would've never left Enti behind. Never! Why am I just now realizing that, twenty years later?

He paced so fast that he tripped over the duffel bag on the floor and fell down onto his knees. With shaking hands, he pulled his cell phone out of his pocket and dialed his ex-wife's number.

Their plans at Eglin AFB were about to change.

CHAPTER 35

Maria was packing another box that was bound for Eglin AFB. She shook her head to rid herself of that strange feeling she got whenever she thought of that place. *Still doesn't make any sense why that name brings on goosebumps. The name of a place I've never been to. Well, not that I know of.*

She sighed deeply and focused on the packing bin before her. Maria was happy Aaron had agreed to buy plastic bins for his move instead of cardboard boxes. These they could reuse every time they'd ever have to move for the Air Force.

Every three years, apparently. Sounds fun, but also exhausting. Fun to explore new places, exhausting to start from scratch again and again, having to find new friends, a new home, a new place to fit in. But that's the military lifestyle, I suppose.

And I can't say I wasn't warned. I know exactly what I'm getting into marrying Aaron. He's just too good a guy to let go of over a little challenge like that. The love of my life. I'll follow him wherever he goes. I knew that long before he proposed to me. She looked at her sparkling engagement ring glistening in the light of the setting sun shining through the window. The diamond threw little sparkles over the half-packed bin. Maria was so fascinated by it that she didn't notice Aaron walk into the room.

"Hi there," he said. Maria jumped a little, then looked up at him. His arms were full of military camouflage stuff. "Oh, my gosh, Aaron. I didn't hear you come in."

He laughed. "Yeah, I noticed."

"What's all that stuff you've got?" She pointed at his arm full of military stuff.

"Well, since I'll soon no longer be a cadet, I need to get my uniforms ready for work. I just met with a tailor. They're gonna stitch on my new rank and get my name tags made."

She stared at him. "Can they get all of that done that fast? There's so little time."

"Yep. The rank isn't a problem, and the name tags will be ready tomorrow."

"How can they sew your name on your uniforms if they're right there in your arms? Did you forget to hand them over?"

He laughed. "No, silly, the name is on a Velcro strip that goes right here." He pointed to the strip above his chest pocket. "Same for the rank. They can sew the rank and name on the jacket and hat, but most people have both on a Velcro strip."

"Smart," Maria said, and got up to look at all the stuff. "What are all these tan and white shirts for?"

"Well, the white ones go under our blue uniform, which is all ready to go since I need it for Friday's commissioning ceremony, and the greenish-tan shirts are for the camouflage uniform. That's the one I'll wear to work every day."

"Guess you won't need much other stuff to wear then, huh?"

He laughed again. "I guess not. You'll be seeing me in green a lot from now on."

This time it was her turn to laugh. "Good thing green goes well with your blue eyes!"

He smirked. "I guess so. Lucky me." He gave her a kiss. "Would you mind cutting off the tags on these shirts while I get the rest of the stuff out of the car? Then we can pack them."

She nodded and watched him walk out before picking up the greenish-tan undershirts. She searched for scissors and found them in between some of the boxes that were already packed. She started cutting off the tags. *That's strange. I remember these shirts being black.*

She kept cutting. *Wait! What?* Her hand froze. *I remember them being black? What the heck am I talking about?* She shook her head. *Aaron always had shirts just like this, even for the ROTC uniform. Greenish-tan shirts. So why in the world would I even think of these undershirts being in a different color?*

She scolded herself quietly and kept cutting the tags off the shirts, staring at them, wondering about them. She finally picked one up, unfolded it, and held it up to the window. Rays of light shone through the cotton material. She bent her head left, then right, then left again to inspect it. *Just a greenish-tan military shirt. Nothing more. Just a shirt.* Kneeling on the floor, she held it up high again in the bright sunlight coming through the window. As she slowly lowered the shirt she was holding, a crystal-clear image formed in her mind.

She saw him.

"Peekaboo," he said. He wore a wide smile, and his hazel eyes—a mosaic of golden-and-emerald-green flecks in a dark brown center encircled by a blue rim—sparkled as he laughed.

Shocked, she held up the shirt again, the *black* shirt, saw the bright light shine through the dark cotton, then quickly lowered it again, only to find ocean-blue eyes looking at her, irritated. Aaron. It was only Aaron.

"Are you alright?"

"Yeah, yeah, I'm alright," she mumbled, and folded up the shirt she was holding. The shirt that was greenish-tan. She shook her head, almost imperceptibly, but it was enough for Aaron to notice.

"What is it, Maria?"

"Don't know. I thought these undershirts . . . looked different. . . ."

"Different? What do you mean?"

"I thought they were black, I guess."

"Are your eyes working okay? They're clearly a dark tan. Oh wait, I see. You're talking AF history. Yeah, they used to be black. Back in the early 2000s they were black, to match the other camouflage uniforms they wore back then. Then, in 2007, they changed the undershirts to a light-tan color that was more suited for the desert deployments of that time. They actually just recently changed over to this darker undershirt and uniform." He held up his new uniform beside a greenish-tan undershirt. "But not too long ago, and for quite a while, the Air Force had black undershirts to match their old camo."

The shirt slipped out of Maria's hand as soon as Aaron finished his explanation. "Black undershirts?" She looked at the pile of shirts that surrounded her, then looked over at the pile next to Aaron.

No way! A military duffel bag!

She closed her eyes in disbelief, but when she opened them, the bag was still there.

So fun! Yeah!

She grabbed a shirt and crawled right into the brand-new military duffel bag *he* had just brought in and thrown on the floor.

That's my favorite game!

She made herself so small that he couldn't see her. She put the shirt over herself and completely covered herself with it. She was small enough to fit under his big military shirts, especially when she made herself so small. She giggled and waited. Waited for her daddy to ask where she was and then lift up the shirt to say "peekaboo."

She giggled and could barely contain her excitement when she felt the shirt being lifted, but she just heard, "Maria, what the heck are you doing?"

She was disappointed. *Who is Maria? That's not my name!* She started pouting, closing her eyes.

She felt herself being shaken and opened her eyes again and looked straight into Aaron's.

"Maria?" He looked concerned.

Maria grabbed her forehead. She had a headache now, a bad headache. She took a few deep breaths and then focused on Aaron again. Suddenly, she realized she was sitting in his new bag, a camouflaged duffel bag. There was a shirt draped halfway over her.

She was confused. "Why did you throw your shirt over me?"

Aaron stared at her, one eyebrow raised. "I *didn't*."

"What? How else would this get on me? And why am I sitting in your bag, or whatever this thing is?"

Aaron just looked at her, his one eyebrow still raised.

"Oh, oh . . . I did that, huh?"

He nodded.

Maria took the shirt and folded it up. Her headache was still there, though not as intense as a few moments ago. She sighed a deep sigh. "I don't know, Aaron. This is freaky. It was like I'd seen all this before. Military undershirts, a duffel bag. When I was little. Just a toddler. And then, I somehow *felt* like a toddler. It was so strange. I just can't explain it."

He looked at her, his eyebrow still raised, his mouth hanging open. Maria started sobbing. "I'm so weird, I'm just *so weird*. Losing my mind. I'm a psycho!" She covered her face with both hands.

Aaron came over and knelt down to hug her. Gently, he stroked her back. "You're not, you know that. You know that, don't you, Maria? I love you, Maria!"

She sobbed.

"*Maria*! Do you hear me?"

She nodded. "If that's even my real name," she whispered through her tears.

"What? What did you say?"

She stopped sobbing, her tears suddenly dried up. "I said *if that's even my real name*."

"I heard that. I just don't understand what you mean by that."

"I don't know. I just had the sudden idea that I'm someone else. At least my toddler self thinks 'Maria' isn't correct."

Aaron let go of her and stared at her.

"Oh my gosh, listen to me. That's absolutely absurd! Ridiculous! I'm absolutely crazy!" She stood up, so did Aaron.

"No, stop it, Maria! You're not crazy. This situation is. Just the situation, not you." Aaron did his best to convince her, but Maria just shook her head and kept pacing. "So, you said you remember black military undershirts?"

"I think so. I used to play with them. Yes, I played with them."

"You *played* with them?"

"Yes. Peekaboo."

"*Peekaboo*? You played peekaboo with a black military undershirt?" She nodded as she paced the room.

"With whom? Who would play that child's game with you?"

She shrugged her shoulders.

"Maria, think! Who did you play that game with? Think, Maria, who did you play with?"

"I don't know!" She stared at him, rubbing her head, her head throbbing in pain, deep, deep pain. "I *don't know!*"

She looked down as she paced, and when she finally looked back up she was staring straight into a greenish-tan shirt that was being held up in front of her. She stopped pacing and stared at it. The shirt was held high, the sunlight from the window shining through it. Strong arms held it up so that it covered the person's face—then suddenly the shirt fell and the person behind it said, "Peekaboo!"

Maria's face lit up. "Peekaboo!" she giggled. "Peekaboo, Daddy!"

The next thing she knew was a piercing pain in her head, and everything went black around her.

When Maria opened her eyes, she was stretched out on the floor, her legs up on a packed bin, her head resting on a pile of shirts. Aaron stroked her hair. "Maria? Are you alright?"

"I think so. What happened?"

"You fainted. You just fainted all of the sudden."

She pulled her legs down from the bin and cautiously stood up. She was surrounded by packed and half-packed bins and a bunch of military undershirts, camouflage uniforms, and a military-issued duffel bag.

Of course. We're in the middle of packing. I just fainted while packing? That's so strange. I've never fainted before. Weird.

Oh.

Oh no.

Suddenly, Maria remembered. All color left her face, and a concerned Aaron moved in closer, ready to catch her.

She smiled a weak smile. "It's okay, Aaron. Don't worry. I won't faint again. I just remembered why I did in the first place."

CHAPTER 36

Aaron came over to give her a big hug. His mouth was dry, his hands shaky, his breath quick. *Something scary must have happened to Maria in the past. I have to assume this is only the beginning, just a few small bits of a secret so immense even she has no idea how far it reaches.*

Who does? Her mom? Yeah, her mom. I bet she's the only one who could answer what's causing all these strange occurrences.

Can't tell Maria yet how extremely disturbing this is. All of this. The dreams. These flashbacks. Flashbacks to a guy in the military? Her dad? Doesn't make sense. I need to know more.

I need to be the strong one, the one who can help her find and face the secrets buried deep in her past. Back when she was a toddler. He had no idea what to say or do, but as he embraced her in a warm hug and felt tears on his shoulder, he knew he had to encourage her.

"Don't worry, Maria. We'll figure out what all this means. We'll piece it together. Somehow."

She stayed silent, but he felt a slight nod on his shoulder.

"Let's eat something, shall we?"

She nodded again, got out of his hug, and wiped away the silent tears she had been crying.

It was dark when they returned to Maria's notebook to see if they could make more sense of everything. Aaron just needed to have an answer.

"If your mom's Jonathan Smith story is true, maybe he's the guy in your flashbacks? Maybe you met him sometime after you were born?"

"Maybe," Maria mumbled, then pointed to an entry in the notebook. "But why did Jonathan Sullivan look down when his eyes met mine? Think he knew the other Jonathan?"

Both Maria and Aaron were confused and pondered over the notebook, deep in thought.

"What about the German words? The German terms of endearment you somehow know."

Maria shrugged. "I thought we concluded I must have learned those from the exchange student that taught me how to swim?"

He nodded. *Yep, that's what we came up with. But that seems so strange. Though maybe it isn't? Just don't know anymore.* He let out a deep sigh.

"It's okay, Aaron. Like you said, we'll find the truth." Maria just had to believe that. "I'll ask Mamá about Jonathan Smith again, the military guy who is my dad, and a possible connection to Eglin AFB. Maybe he was stationed there after he returned from deployment?"

Aaron looked up straight at her and smiled. "That would make sense, Maria. That must be it! Maybe your mom decided to drive up there with little you and see him, whether he was divorced or not."

Maria nodded and wrote down the theory in the notebook.

Aaron looked at her. *Yes, we need to talk to Martina. We just have to.* He almost couldn't wait and wanted to tell Maria to call her mom now, but he knew she was tired. And it was never a good idea to bring up the past shortly before bedtime.

And bedtime it was. Both of them decided to head to bed. Well, to the mattress that now lay on the floor surrounded by bins filled with

Aaron's belongings. They looked around. Sadness washed over Maria's face.

Aaron seemed to read her mind. "No worries, my love, this might be the end of college for me, but it's *our* new beginning." He pointed to the engagement ring on her finger. "See, there it is. Always a reminder of our beginning. We'll be husband and wife and have a family one day."

She smiled at him, then her smile faded. "Yeah, but I have another year of college ahead."

"I know, I know. But it'll be a fun senior year for you. And you'll have so much fun planning the wedding. It's all up to you. Whatever you want to do, I'm cool with it."

"Really?"

He nodded.

Her eyes lit up. "Let's get married next spring. I love the spring, the blooming trees, the flowers. What do you say?"

The room was dark, but Maria saw Aaron smile. "That sounds wonderful, Maria. A spring wedding."

"Yeah. Just imagine all the fun colors we'll use for the decorations, the flowers, the centerpieces . . . the bridesmaids' dresses! I definitely want Keisha to be a bridesmaid, and Brandy, and your sister of course."

Aaron nodded.

"Who should be the maid of honor? I always thought it would be Keisha, but would that upset Brandy? And what about your sister? Maybe Emma should be maid of honor? I assume you want Nick and Jim as your groomsmen. But what about the best man? Who should be best man? Oh, and can they get time off in the spring? Now that you guys are working, I guess that's uncertain. Maybe if it's around Easter? What do you think?"

As Maria went on and on with her happy thoughts about their wedding, Aaron fell asleep. She didn't notice until he started snoring loudly. She grinned.

Men! As soon as you start talking wedding plans, they're out. Literally.

With all the wonderful thoughts of wedding plans flitting through her head, she soon joined him.

She was looking at flowers, all kinds of beautiful spring flowers.

Exactly what I want for my wedding. It'll be beautiful.

She smiled and bent down to smell a dark-purple flower and then a dark-pink flower that looked just as beautiful.

These are exquisite. Wonder what kind they are.

She closed her eyes and took in a deep breath, and when she opened her eyes again she realized she was surrounded by beautiful flowers, some purple, some dark pink. She stood in a whole field of these flowers, these beautiful, lush flowers that were almost as tall as her.

What? As tall as me?

She suddenly realized that she was small again, just a small, little child in a field of flowers. She looked up and saw mountains. Tall mountains.

"Isn't it beautiful, pumpkin?" she heard a male voice ask.

She smiled widely and nodded.

"These are Wasatch wildflowers," the man explained. "They grow in the spring right here."

"Here?" she asked, her voice small.

"Yes, they grow only here, on the Wasatch Range, right here in Utah."

"Utah?" she asked with that small voice.

"That's right, pumpkin. Utah. Daddy is stationed here in Utah, so that's our home right now."

"Utah. Home," she repeated, and looked up at the tall man who almost blended into the grass of the field. Only the pink and purple flowers stood out in contrast to his green flight suit.

"Daddy peekaboo," she heard herself say in that annoying, tiny voice that made her feel so helpless.

Then she heard him laugh, a loud, warm laugh. "You're so smart, little minno," he said, and bend down by her side. "Daddy's almost blending in, huh? It's called camouflage. And that's exactly what uniforms are for, even flight suits. Smarty pants."

He started tickling her and she started laughing and laughing. "No Daddy! No Daddy!"

He stopped tickling her. "No more tickles?"

"Tickles? No. Peekaboo? No. Daddy no peekaboo in flawas," she said with a smirk, and pointed to his uniform then at the colorful flowers around them.

He laughed a loud laugh. "You're one impressive little child. You're right, Daddy only blends in with the grass, but not the flowers, does he?"

She shook her head and laughed. "No, Daddy!"

They both laughed together, and he held her hand as they walked through the field of wildflowers on the Wasatch mountain range in the warm spring sun. The colors were beautiful, and she was so content walking next to her dad that she couldn't imagine anything better. She loved her daddy so much.

"Alright, pumpkin, let's go home." He led her out of the field of flowers.

"No, no," she said, "Stay. Flawas. Peety flawas."

"I know they're pretty. You're so right. But it's getting late. I bet Mama's ready for us to come home. I bet she's all done with the packing by now. But how about we take one of these beautiful flowers back with us? Back to Mama, to remember Utah before our move?"

"Yes, flawas for Mama," she said in her small, happy voice.

"Pink or purple?"

"Pink and pupo. Pleeeese."

He laughed and picked one of each, then picked her up in his strong arms and walked out of the field. "Yes, these beautiful flowers are for Mama, to remind her of our home here in Utah. I bet there won't be flowers like this in Florida."

As if she was all-knowing, she shook her head. "No, no flawas in Florida!"

"But you know what? There'll be lots of palm trees at Eglin," he said, and smiled at her.

What? At Eglin? Mama packing for Eglin? No, no, not Eglin. Eglin AFB.

"Lots of palm trees and sand and water."

"Wawa? No wawa. No wawa! Flawas! No wawa!"

But it was too late. The field of flowers, the mountains, the grass all disappeared, turning into water—deep, dark, mucky, murky water that surrounded her, submerging her deeper and deeper until it was all around her and she couldn't breathe. It swallowed her up completely.

"No, wawa! Flawas! No, Daddy, Daddy help," she screamed, but there was no one to hear her and it got all dark around her, pitch-black and dark.. . . .

"Maria," she heard a male voice in her ear. "Maria! Wake up!"

She opened her eyes and looked around. She saw strange things all over. *Am I back in the mountains? Tall, strange things around me, ahead of me, behind me.*

She squinted and her eyes got used to the darkness. She realized she was in Aaron's room, on the mattress on the floor in between all those packed bins. *Just bins. No mountains. No flowers. No water. Aaron!*

She looked at him, realizing he was watching her intensely. "I'm okay, Aaron. I'm okay. Just another dream."

"Just another dream? The drowning one?"

She nodded and thought back. "But not at first. I think we were in the mountains. In the mountains in a field full of flowers. Beautiful flowers."

Aaron looked at her. "'We?'"

She nodded. "Yes, Daddy and me. We picked flowers for Mamá. Pretty pink and purple flowers." Maria started telling Aaron about her dream; the words just tumbled out of her, full of happiness, full of love.

He sat up and looked at her. "Maria? Do you hear yourself?"

"What? Yes, of course I do. I'm telling you about my dream."

He nodded. "You sure are. Yet you're telling it to me as if it just happened yesterday. As if it makes sense that your dad was in uniform and you were picking flowers for your mom at home. A home somewhere in the mountains. I thought it's just been you and your mamá this whole time. *In Miami.* Always Miami. No mountains, no mountain flowers. No dad."

Maria didn't know what to say. She felt stupid. "I just don't know, Aaron. It felt so real."

"So, when did the drowning part start? In the mountains?"

She shook her head. "No, not there. There was no water. It just kind of went to that part, I think. Not sure how the dream got there."

"Think about it. Just think."

She took his advice and closed her eyes and went back to her dream.

She could immediately see those beautiful flowers again. Then a guy in uniform talked to her and said, "Yes, these beautiful Utah flowers for Mama, to remind her of our home here in Utah. I bet there won't be flowers like this in Florida. But you know what? There'll be lots of palm trees at Eglin. Lots of palm trees and sand and water."

Her heart started beating so fast that she had to breathe faster to keep up, to keep the oxygen flowing to her racing heart. She felt her hands and forehead grow damp. "Oh my gosh!" She grabbed Aaron's hand so forcefully that he shifted uncomfortably under her strong grip.

"We were about to move, just like you. Moving to Eglin AFB. It was shortly before we moved away from Utah." Her voice was clear, crystal clear, cutting through the darkness.

Aaron was confused. "What? Utah? 'We?' Maria, what are you talking about?"

Before she could answer, her grip on his hand loosened and everything went black around her.

When she opened her eyes, she found herself in a similar position to how she'd awoken earlier. Her legs were propped up on a bin, her head placed on a soft pillow. Except this time, it was dark and she was on a mattress, Aaron next to her. "Oh my gosh, Maria, you just fainted again. *Again.* That's the second time today. Are you okay?"

She nodded. "I'm fine. Really, Aaron, I'm fine. Just tired. I'm just tired. Can we sleep now?"

"Okay. Sure. If you think you're alright."

"Yeah, I am. I'm fine. Just tired."

"Okay, then. Get comfortable."

That's exactly what she did, and within minutes she fell into a deep, dreamless sleep. Only this time, Aaron was wide awake. Wide awake and completely disturbed.

CHAPTER 37

Once he was sure that Maria was asleep, Aaron got up, found his phone, opened up the Notes app, and wrote: *Utah. Look up AFB in Utah.*

He wondered, *Is there an AFB in Utah? Pretty sure there is one. Wait. Why not look it up now?* So, he searched on Google and, sure enough, there it was. A base called Hill Air Force Base. It was close to the Wasatch mountain range.

A mountain range? He was sure Maria had mentioned mountains. *Yes, definitely. Mountains and flowers. Flowers?*

He kept researching and almost dropped his phone. There they were. Pink and purple flowers, called Wasatch flowers, which only grew in the mountains of Utah in the spring. He gasped. *No way. Her dream had it all right. How could she know that? Why would anyone know that without having lived there before? Can dreams be that specific?* Aaron shook his head. *Definitely not.*

He thought about it even longer and concluded it must have been a memory, not a dream. *A memory? From Utah? Maria also mentioned Eglin AFB. A move to Eglin AFB. A move to Eglin AFB when she was little. Maria's mom and dad were stationed together. Moved together.*

In the dark, he stared at the notes, illuminated in the backdrop of the phone's light. *If Maria's dreams are true and actually happened, then Martina has a lot of explaining to do! Without a military ID, she couldn't have lived on an Air Force Base. Unless, of course, she never did but someone else had. Someone else with access to Maria.*

If "Maria" is even her real name.

Now he was sweating. Sweating so hard that his phone slipped out of his hand. He recalled when Maria had said, *"If Maria is even my real name. My toddler self doesn't think so."*

He wiped the sweat from his forehead and looked for his phone in between the sheets. He heard Maria's soft, even breathing; she was in a deep sleep.

Oh my gosh. I can't tell anyone about this. Not yet. Not yet. First, I need to put more pieces together to find out the dark secret that lies in her past. His mouth was dry, so dry. He swallowed hard, then saved the notes on his phone and turned it off.

He sat still until his eyes adjusted to the darkness. He looked over to where Maria was lying next to him, her breathing steady, even, her eyelids fluttering. *You're so beautiful, Maria. And so smart. I'm a lucky guy.*

Aaron smiled, but his smile quickly turned into a frown. *But your past scares me.* He gently pushed a lock of her hair off her face. *What happened to you, my love? My beautiful fiancée. Don't worry. I'll find out. I promise to find the truth, to make sure you're safe and happy.*

Maria woke up groggy and tired after the restless night. She stretched and looked over to Aaron, who was still in a deep sleep despite his alarm clock going off loudly.

"Come on, Aaron, wake up." She shook him gently. He moaned. "Come on, sleepyhead. Your parents and Emma are getting in today. We have to go pick them up from the airport in Orlando this afternoon."

"This afternoon. Still time to sleep," he groaned without opening his eyes.

"No, no, no, don't think you can sleep more. Lots to do still. And such an exciting weekend ahead. Tomorrow is your Air Force commissioning ceremony. Then your graduation."

He moaned again.

Maria walked out and brewed some coffee, then came back in with a big cup for the both of them. The amazing coffee smell finally made Aaron get up. While sipping their coffees, they strode quietly into the apartment's kitchen. They didn't want to wake up Nick as he had come home late last night. Aaron made breakfast, a simple meal of toast, jelly, and peanut butter.

Maria rolled her eyes. "Typical. Two guys in an apartment and that's all you have?"

He smirked, but his smirk wasn't as convincing as usual. He was tired, super tired. Exhausted, actually. And he couldn't stop thinking of that dream last night.

Utah. The move to Eglin AFB. Then that one disturbing sentence: "If Maria is even my real name." He played it over and over in his head. *What does that mean? What in the world could that even mean?*

He looked at Maria, who was calmly eating her piece of toast and sipping her black coffee. *How come she's so calm? Doesn't she remember last night?* Aaron was so tired he could barely hold his own toast. *Military base in Utah. Pink and purple flowers in the mountain range next to the base. I have to show Maria those flowers. Maybe she'll recognize them from her dream. Well, memory. The flowers. Yes, have to show her.*

He quickly got up to look for his cell phone and disappeared into the bedroom.

"What are you doing?" Maria called softly after him.

"Looking for my phone."

All the blinds in the bedroom were still closed and keeping out the bright morning sun. He was working the shades open to better see when a shrill, loud cell phone ring started. He was so startled that he jumped, stumbled over one of the packed bins, crashed into another, and fell into the stacked pots and pans that Maria hadn't boxed up yet. The loud booms and bangs that followed had Maria jumping up from her stool in the kitchen.

"What the heck is going on in here?" Nick was standing in the doorframe of his bedroom with only his boxers on. His hair was wild.

Both he and Maria rushed into Aaron's bedroom to find a comical sight: he'd finally reached his phone and answered it while still lying in the mound of pots and pans. Nick and Maria looked at each other and burst out laughing.

"Sorry we woke you up," Maria said, but Nick just kept on laughing.

"Yes, sir, that's me," they heard Aaron say. He looked at Maria and gestured for her to close the door, which she did, granting him privacy.

"Well, guess it's something important," Nick said. "Glad he got to the phone call with a bang."

Maria laughed. "Yeah, no kidding. He answered it *and* acted as your alarm clock at the same time. Who knew he could multitask so well?"

"Yeah, who knew. Well, I'm up now. Better get some breakfast also."

"Sure. What do you want? Toast and peanut butter, or peanut butter and toast?"

Nick smirked. "Come on, Maria, those are great choices!"

Nick and Maria ate their toasts together at the kitchen island, chitchatting loudly.

A few minutes later, the door to Aaron's bedroom slowly opened and he came out, looking a bit stunned. He still had his phone in his hand

and was staring at it, until he finally realized Nick was there. "Oh, good morning, Nick. Sorry I woke you."

"That's okay, man. Guess we can blame your phone."

Maria nodded and wondered, "Who was that, Aaron?"

"That was Special Agent William Barrett," Aaron said and both Nick and Maria looked at him in surprise. The room fell silent.

"A special agent? Why would they call you?" Maria asked.

"It's about my security clearance. About the interview for the TS."

"Oh, I see. That makes sense. You had me worried there for a minute, man," Nick said, before stuffing the last piece of toast in his mouth.

"'TS?'" Maria said. "What's TS?"

Nick laughed. "Better get used to all the acronyms, Maria, because—"

"—the Air Force loves to use them, I know! But what does TS stand for?"

"Top secret," Nick and Aaron said in unison.

"Very funny, guys, I'm asking what it stands for and you're joking around?" Maria started getting mad when it dawned on her. "Oh. Oh, I see. TS means top secret."

"Yes, ma'am."

"That's a good thing, right?"

"Oh yes, very good," Nick said, and gave Aaron a pat on the shoulder. "This guy here is gonna be a hotshot soon. Good to get that clearance. They must really want you for that new job, huh? When's the interview?"

"Monday," Aaron said, "Monday at fourteen-hundred."

"Wow, man, fast. That's Monday at two p.m." Maria was thankful Nick translated the time from Air Force jargon for her. He went on, "You should be proud. You'll get that clearance in no time."

"Maybe," Aaron mumbled.

Maria looked up. She knew that look and that voice. He was worried. "What's going on, Aaron?"

"Well, Special Agent Barrett also said that we need to go over my paperwork in person. They need to show me something."

"'Show you something?' What does that mean?"

He shrugged his shoulders. "Not sure. But he sounded pretty serious about it."

Nick looked up from his third piece of toast. "Don't worry, man, it'll be fine. Probably a silly spelling mistake or so. They always sound serious about every tiny little thing. Don't let them intimidate you. Go in full force on Monday, all nice in your new uniform and rank, and you'll be fine, Second Lieutenant Heikinnen."

"Nick is right, you'll be fine! I'm proud of you." Maria got up and gave Aaron a kiss. "And now, finish your breakfast and let's get ready for the day."

"Okay." Aaron sat down at the kitchen island.

Nick looked him up and down. "Man, you look tired. Thought you wanted to go to bed early last night while we were out? Guess you guys didn't get much sleep, huh?" He winked at the young couple.

Maria rolled her eyes.

Aaron just stared ahead. He wasn't in the mood for jokes. Besides having Maria's strange dreams to worry about and lose sleep over, he now had this phone call to worry about. What he hadn't told Maria and Nick was that they needed him to come in quickly to question him over something specific they'd found in the paperwork he'd handed in.

Something incorrect.

He was one hundred percent positive he hadn't made a mistake filling it out. He had gone slowly and looked it over again and again, then had both Nick and Jim look at it, and even his ROTC teacher. They had all said it looked perfect. Perfectly correct.

The only thing he hadn't done himself, and nobody had really questioned, was the one piece of paper he had gotten from Martina Sullivan. Maria's birth certificate.

He replayed the conversation with the special agent in his head. *"Something in your paperwork is incorrect, possibly fraudulent, Lieutenant.*

You need to come in as soon as possible for your interview. We'll talk then, Lieutenant."

Fraudulent? What the heck does that mean? Maybe Nick's right and they're just trying to scare me. Or did they really find something? A fraudulent piece of paper? Maria's birth certificate. Could it be?

He shivered. *"If Maria is even my real name."* That strange sentence popped back into his head. Suddenly, his toast slipped out of his hand and landed upside down, peanut butter smearing the floor.

"Aaron! Look at that mess. Can't you hold on to your toast?"

But Aaron just stared ahead. *Oh my gosh. Her birth certificate. Fraudulent. A fake? Maybe Maria isn't her real name? And maybe Martina was never on those bases in Utah or Florida. Only Maria was. Little toddler Maria, without Martina. Without her mom. Without the only mom she's ever known.. . . .*

I must be going crazy. I'm exhausted. Having a hard time keeping Maria's dreams and the facts straight. I just don't know what to believe anymore, what to do. His thoughts were tumbling all over each other, his head a mess of thoughts, strange thoughts, thoughts that didn't make sense at all. *No baby pictures. Not her real name. Fraudulent paperwork. Oh my gosh, what's going on? Who is Maria? And who is Martina Sullivan? Moved from Utah to Eglin. . . .*

His thoughts so preoccupied him that he didn't even notice Maria picking up the bread from the floor and cleaning up the mess while yelling at him. He only reacted when she was face-to-face with him.

"Aaron Philip Heikinnen! What in the world is going on with you?"

He shook his head and tried to shake off these strange thoughts. He was tempted to tell Maria, but he couldn't just yet. *I need to do more research. Can't bother her with my assumptions. She wouldn't believe me.*

But I know. Don't need to show her the flowers in the mountain range anymore. I already know they match her dream. Her memory? Chills ran down his spine. *I need to find out more. How? From Martina!*

He was tempted to call Martina and ask her about everything. But he knew he couldn't. *I have to wait. Until Monday. Until I confirm the "incorrect paperwork" is actually Maria's birth certificate. And if it is, I'll have the proof to confront Martina over her lies.*

Yes, have to wait. Just can't bear to tell Maria anything yet. It would break her. Martina and her are so close. They've a perfect mom-and-daughter relationship. I can't break that based on an assumption. Maybe I'm freaking out over nothing—a spelling mistake in my paperwork?

"Aaron!" Maria physically shook him this time. "What's going on?"

He looked up and saw her worried face. "I'm sorry, Maria. No worries. I'm just a bit confused. Confused and nervous about that call. And it was a rough night with your dreams.. . . ."

With a guilty conscience, Maria looked into his worried ocean-blue eyes and his long, dark-brown eyelashes. She gave him a kiss, then hugged him. "I'm sorry, Aaron. I'm such a basket case. I'm sorry you're worrying about that during the middle of what should be an amazing, once-in-a-lifetime experience, a happy day. You'll be commissioned into the Air Force tomorrow; you're graduating from college on Saturday! It's amazing, and I'm so proud of you!"

"Thanks. It's okay. It's not your fault, Maria. Let's stick to the plan: pack some more this morning, get Nick's room ready for your mom, and then we go get my family this afternoon."

She smiled at him. "Sounds good."

They just stood there and hugged each other for a long time, then cleaned up the kitchen and started packing the pots and pans Aaron had stumbled over.

"I do want to call my mom today before picking up your family, though. I need to ask her if I was ever on an Air Force base before," Maria said while packing.

Aaron looked up, shocked by her determination. "Sure. That would help, I guess. Let's see what she has to say."

He tried to sound as casual as he could. He was more than interested to hear what Martina had to say. *Martina. Maria's mamá. If that's even true.* But he kept that thought to himself for now and kept on packing the last few items, then helped Nick and Maria prepare the apartment for the woman they were just talking about—Maria's mom.

Or whoever she was.

CHAPTER 38

The sun was shining bright on her way to work. It was a beautiful day and she was in a good mood. Today would be her last day at the store this week. Martina had decided to close her shop on Friday and Saturday to spend time with Maria, Aaron, and his family.

She was so excited to finally get to meet his family and see Aaron graduate. She was excited about the graduation and the Air Force commissioning ceremony—whatever that might be like.

She smiled. *Very exciting times! And soon, I'll have a wedding to plan. Maria's wedding. Mija.* She sighed. *Hope you let me sew your wedding dress. I bet you won't turn down that offer. No, not you, my daughter. A wedding dress handmade by your mamá will bring the uniqueness you're looking for—and deserve.*

She happily whistled a little tune as she let herself through the front door of "Love It Again – Martina's Tailor Shop." She stepped inside and prepared to open for the morning.

Once the time came, she unlocked the door, turned the door sign over to *OPEN*, and waited for customers to arrive. After half an hour, nobody had come in yet, so Martina decided to work on a few projects in the back, by the sewing machine.

If anyone comes in, I'll hear the little bell ring at the front.

She was happily working on one of her customer's dresses, widening the back around the zipper, when she heard the little bell chime. She quickly dropped the dress she was working on and stepped through the colorful curtains toward her front desk with a big smile on her face, ready to greet her first customer of the day.

As she stepped through the curtains, her smile quickly faded. Her heart started beating, pounding against her chest, as she saw *him* standing there.

"Hello, Martina," he said in a low voice, a big, fat, fake smile playing at his thin lips. He looked as big and strong as he had twenty years ago. She remembered how strong he was, remembered all those times he had squeezed her arms, hands, and neck, those times that he had pinned her to the floor and sat on her with all his heavy weight, knowing she was having a hard time breathing.

She stared at him and had to steady herself on the front desk so she wouldn't faint or fall over. *What is he doing here?* Instinctively, she looked over her shoulder to formulate an escape plan. Find a hiding place or something to defend herself with. Sweat broke out on her forehead, and her heart pounded against her chest in fear.

"Don't you want to say hello to your husband, Martina?" he said, his voice raised, that fake smile on his lips.

"*Ex*-husband," she whispered, and wondered where she had left her cell phone. At least the store's landline was right next to her. She would probably have enough time to dial 911.

"What was that, Martina? Did you say something?"

"N-no. No, I didn't."

He came closer and closer and now leaned against the counter and leaned over until he was eye to eye with her. "What did you say, Martina?" he whispered. He was still smiling.

She just stared at him, stared him into his greyish-blue eyes and shuddered.

"Did you say *no*? Did you say you didn't say anything?" He now put his arm on the counter and flexed his still-strong-looking bicep.

Martina shook her head. He had done it again, intimidated her, and she felt so small, so useless, like nothing. And so afraid.

"I heard you say 'ex-husband.' Is that right? Did you say that or did you not?"

She nodded slightly.

"Martina, did you say it or not? Answer me!"

She nodded again.

"Stop that stupid nodding. Stop that nodding! Or are you stupid? You hear me, stop that nodding."

She nodded, and he started laughing. "You nodded yes to being stupid. Ha, I thought so. You stupid woman."

She didn't know what to do; she was paralyzed by fear. She wanted to tell him to get out of here, to leave her alone—wanted to threaten to call the police and get him locked up for going against the restraining order—but not a word escaped her mouth. It was as if her mouth had been sewn shut, sewn shut by the same needles she did her work with. She tried, she really tried to open her mouth, to say something, to stand up for herself, but even now, over twenty years later, she couldn't.

She felt paralyzed, her whole body felt paralyzed.

There he goes again. Jonathan Sullivan, my ex-husband, making me feel so helpless, so afraid.

He had now reached over the counter with both hands and grabbed her arms, was squeezing them so tight it hurt her. Hurt her badly.

"Martina, do you want to know why I'm here?"

He looked deep into her beautiful brown eyes. She nodded slightly.

"Is that a nod? Are you nodding again, stupid?"

Another faint nod.

He laughed a laugh that rang like a loud drum in her ears. He shook her. "*I won't tell you until you say something.*"

Martina just looked at him. *What does he want? What should I say?* She knew, remembered from back then that anything she said would be wrong. Anything. Any words that left her lips would piss him off even more, would lead to more pain for her. He tightened his squeeze on her upper arms, so tight that she felt her veins pulsing beneath his squeeze.

"Say something! Come on, woman, say something!"

She just stared at him. She had so much to say. She wanted to scream, "*Leave me alone! Let go of me! I will call the police! Get the heck out of here! Just go, leave me alone!*" But the words wouldn't come. Only a slight whisper that didn't make any sense escaped her lips in fear.

He stared at her and saw her eyes watering, either from fear or because he really was squeezing her arms tight. Or both.

He didn't care. He had to take care of business here, and this was what always got the job done, what he did best. Suddenly, he let go of her and gave her a push to help her along. He saw her hands lose their hold on the counter, saw her stumble backward, trip over the legs of the stool that stood behind the counter, and fall backward to the ground, right on her bottom. She caught herself with her arms and narrowly avoided hitting her head on the concrete floor.

Before she could get up, he walked behind the counter and stood there, towering over her. The small guy now looked as tall as a skyscraper and as wide as a department store. Like a concrete building that was about to crush her.

"*What have I done to deserve this?*" she wanted to ask, but couldn't. Her lips wouldn't move. She couldn't make them move. He leaned down to look at her and laughed his cruel laugh. The laugh she remembered so well.

"Poor Martina. Did you hurt yourself?" he pouted. Before she knew it, he had grabbed her under her armpits and violently pulled her up onto her feet so they were eye to eye once more. "Since you don't ask, *I* will tell you why I am here."

He squeezed her armpits tight, so tight that the wire of her bra painfully cut into her chest. She wrinkled her forehead in pain but withstood his stare.

"It's about your daughter." He spat out the words in disgust.

Martina stared at him. *About my daughter? Oh my gosh. He's here for Maria. No, he can't have her. He can't hurt her. He needs to stay away from her. What does he want from her? No, not Maria.*

"Yes, about your daughter. And I tell you what, Martina. You will keep her in line. You hear me?"

He now grabbed her by the back of her head to push her nose to nose with him. She could feel the warmth of his breath, could smell the pungent alcohol there. *Of course he's drunk. He's always at his worst when he's drunk.* She remembered that all too well.

"If you don't keep your daughter in line, you'll regret it," he roared at her with his deep, stinky breath. "You will, and she will!"

What? Maria? He will hurt Maria? Come after her and hurt her? No, I can't let that happen. Not my Maria. Mija!

With the power of a mom's will and the instinct to protect her little one, she suddenly grabbed his arm and pushed it down with all her might so that her head came free. She twirled around to get out of his grip and was free. Free of her ex-husband's painful squeeze, free of her numbness.

"Stop it, Jonathan, just stop it," she said, her voice strong, determined. "You will not *touch* that girl! You will not *hurt* that girl! You will never. I will not let it happen! Do you hear me?"

Jonathan Sullivan looked at her in surprise. He had not seen this coming. *Since when does Martina dare stand up to me? Dare yell at me? That little woman. Who does she think she is?*

Martina saw his face turn red in anger. She saw it, but was prepared. He stepped closer and followed her, tried to push her into the corner, but she sidestepped him and was by the colorful curtain. Not a door, just a curtain. A curtain hiding a whole room behind it. An escape. When he got close again, she suddenly lifted her hand that held scissors—sharp, shiny tailor's scissors. Surprised, he stopped his approach.

"Enough, Jonathan, enough! You will not get close to my daughter! You will leave her alone! I will call the police and tell them you are threatening my family. I'm sure they would love to look at your record and punish you for breaking the restraining order—breaking it twice, for both myself and my daughter!"

She stared at him, scissors raised. Stared him down, making sure he would not hurt her little girl. The strength of a mother gave her the power she needed to stand up to him, the bully and abuser.

Suddenly, Jonathan Sullivan began to laugh and laugh—not his cruel laugh, but as though he were laughing at a joke someone had just told. Martina grew irritated. She kept the scissors raised and stared at him.

"Oh, Martina. Look at you. How silly. How silly you are. I was only here to let you know that you need to leave me alone."

What? What is he talking about? She was so perplexed that she lowered her scissors for a second—long enough for him to move in quickly and disarm her. He threw the scissors through the curtain.

He had a hold on her again and stared at her. "I'll tell you what, Martina, you gotta keep that girl under control. Don't ever let her come to my store again, you hear me?"

Martina stared at him.

"Do you hear me? Do you understand?"

She nodded.

"Good! Fine woman you are. Listening is a good thing. You need to keep your daughter under control. She's never to approach me again. Quit her digging, you hear me?"

"Yes."

"Good. Good then. If either you or your daughter dig any deeper into what happened back then, I *will* find you. And I will punish you for breaking your word. Punish you both. Do you understand, Martina?"

She nodded.

"You will make sure to stick to this new story: She is your daughter. You gave birth to her. You don't know who her dad is but used my name on the birth certificate. You will *always* tell that story, or I will take her from you. You hear me?"

No, don't take Maria. Martina nodded.

"You will lose her if you tell any other story! Understood?"

Martina nodded.

"Say it out loud! Repeat after me: She is my daughter. I gave birth to her. I put my ex-husband's name on the birth certificate. I don't know who her dad is. I slept around too much to remember who her dad is."

Martina stared at him. *I didn't sleep around at all. What is he talking about?*

"Repeat it. Now!"

"She is my daughter. I gave birth to her. I put my ex-husband's name on the birth certificate. I don't know who her dad is."

"Good, good girl, Martina," he praised her, but quickly fell into yelling again. "But *you forgot a part*. Say it."

Martina shook her head.

"Are you disobeying me?"

Before she could say anything else, he spat on her, right into her face. Her eyes burned from the hot, angry spit tinged with alcohol.

"Say it, woman. Say it now: 'I don't know who her dad is. I slept around too much to remember.'"

Martina was in shock and close to tears, but she managed to whisper and repeat his words.

He beamed as he smiled and held her close. "That's a good girl. Yes, that's what it was like. That's the story. Always will be the truth. Get your daughter in line or she'll have to get to know this part of me. You don't want that, do you?"

Martina shook her head in fear.

"I know, honey, I know. You don't. You'll do as I say. You will. You like being submissive. I know."

Martina nodded. She was numb again, couldn't move or say anything. And before she knew it, he started kissing her, forcefully. She tried to push him away but couldn't, had to endure him kissing her, more and more.

There was a chime.

There! She'd heard it. *The little bell. The little bell above the front door to the store! Thank goodness, the bell. Someone is coming.*

"Hello?" she heard a female voice say, and Jonathan Sullivan suddenly stopped and turned around, surprised. There stood a middle-aged woman at the counter, a bunch of slacks in hand.

"Oh, there you are. It's dark behind that counter. But your colorful curtain is beautiful. Brightens everything up nicely."

Martina found her words again and straightened herself out. "Yes, thank you. I like it, too. My daughter picked it out when she was young," she said with a smile.

"Beautiful," the woman said, then noticed the man behind the counter. "Oh, I didn't know there's two of you."

Martina looked at Jonathan Sullivan. "No, there isn't. This gentleman was just leaving."

Her ex-husband stared at her, then looked over to the woman. "Yes, yes I was. Just leaving. Just dropped off a bunch of clothes and helped carry them back here," he said, and smiled.

The woman tilted her head and looked a bit suspicious. "Well, that was nice of you."

He nodded and stepped into the warm welcoming area of the tailor shop. "Goodbye, Martina. Thank you for *complying* with my requests." He waved and smiled before he left the store.

Martina exhaled deeply as the little bell above the door rang his departure.

"Are you alright?"

Martina looked at the friendly woman for a while and nodded.

"Are you sure?" The woman came closer. "Do you need any help?"

Martina looked at her. "No, it's okay. That man was my ex-husband. It's never fun to see him, but he still likes to use my tailor shop, and obviously his money helps me out."

"Argh, ex-husbands. Tell me about it."

Martina smiled at her. *This lady has no idea how much of a saving grace she was. Thank you, thank you, thank you.* She started discussing lengthening the lady's slacks. *I'll give her a big discount for saving me from Jonathan Sullivan.*

Working on dresses, pants, and slacks helped take her mind off the scary encounter that morning. Sewing calmed her. She was so glad that woman had arrived just in the nick of time. After she had left, Martina had stepped outside to make sure Jonathan Sullivan was really gone. And he was. No truck in sight.

His visit had really shaken her and she wished she could talk to someone about it. But she couldn't. She couldn't tell her sisters or brothers-in-law; she couldn't tell her friends or daughter.

Especially not her daughter.

No, not Maria, my Maria. I can't bear the thought of losing her. Definitely won't let anything happen to her. Especially not at the hands of Jonathan Sullivan. Turns out I already told her the perfect story, the perfect cover-up story. It's a good story.

She laughed a sad laugh. *I know that even my ex would approve of that story. Why did he even come back to make sure I wouldn't say anything else? It's been a few weeks since Maria visited his plumbing store. Maria hasn't returned there. Or has she?*

Suddenly, Martina didn't know what to think. *Did she go back even after I told her about Jonathan Smith? Oh my, I hope not. I trust Maria. She promised not to do anymore research. Did she break her promise?*

Her sewing needle hovered as she thought, and she almost poked herself with it when her cell phone rang. After the turbulent morning it had been very quiet in the store, so the loud ringing startled her. She looked at her phone. Incoming FaceTime call from Maria. She had to smirk just a little.

Maria's nose must have been itching knowing I was just thinking of her. She made sure she looked okay and wiped off her puzzled look before picking up the phone.

CHAPTER 39

"¡Aló, mija!"

"Mamá! What are you up to?"

Martina held up the dress she had been sewing. "Just working on a few projects for my customers. Look at this dress. Isn't it beautiful?"

"Sí, Mamá, hermoso vestido."

They talked a little bit about Martina's work, her projects, her store.

"I will close up tonight and not open again until Monday. So excited to come to Aaron's commission and graduation. And to meet his family. Ah, tu familia."

Maria nodded. "Yes, they're so nice. In just a bit we'll pick them up from the airport. They're landing soon. We have my apartment all set for them. And we just finished setting up *your* room."

"Ah, gracias. Are you sure that Nick is okay with me staying there?"

"Sí, Mamá, he'll be staying with his parents in their hotel suite. It's totally fine. And he confirmed you can stay until Sunday."

"No, just one night is fine. I will leave after graduation."

"Mamá, you can stay. Spend more time with me and Aaron and his family."

"I don't know. I can't sleep in Nick's room that long. Poor guy."

"Mamá, I just said he doesn't mind. He'll stay in a hotel with his parents."

"I know, I know. What does he like? What can I bring as a thank-you?"

"Nothing, Mamá. He really doesn't need anything."

"Maria! You *always* bring a little gift as a thank-you for the host," Martina scolded her daughter.

Maria smirked. "Mamá, you're so sweet. Sure, bring something. You can bring whatever you like. Actually, Aaron's sister wanted some Venezuelan pastries since we won't make it to Miami. Maybe you can bring those? They would be perfect for Nick as well. He loves to eat."

"Sí, I will bake and bring some. ¡Muy bien! Wonderful idea!"

"Too bad we can't visit you in Miami, Mamá."

"I know, I know, mija. But Aaron's new work is more important. So proud of him that they want him to start so early. They must really need him."

Maria smiled and turned the phone to show Aaron. "Thank you, Martina," he said and smiled, then tapped on the notebook, urging Maria to get to the point.

She inhaled deeply. "It'll be very interesting to be on an Air Force base, right, Mamá?"

"Yes, very exciting."

"Have we ever visited one before?"

Martina laughed. "What? Why would we have been on one before? We don't know anyone in the military. And as far as I know, you need an ID to be allowed in."

"I know, Mamá. Or you need someone who can sponsor your visit."

"¡Exactamente! Maybe I can go on base sometime if Aaron sponsors me? Would be fun to see."

"So, you've never been on a military base?"

Martina laughed. "No. Never!"

"Not even with my dad?"

The smile on Martina's face faded quickly and her expression turned stern. "With your dad?" She stared at Maria through the phone. *¡Naguará! Why is she bringing up this topic again? Did she actually go back to see Jonathan a second time after all? Is that the reason he came by this morning? ¡Naguará, I need her to stop! Stop the questions, the seeking, the everything. Need her to stop to stay safe. To not get hurt. He'll hurt her. Hurt us both.*

"Mamá, were you ever on a military base with my dad?"

"Maria! Why would you even ask that? You promised me to not research anymore! You promised to not go back and see him!"

"What?" Maria was confused.

"You said you would not go back. ¡Naguará! I trusted you. You shouldn't have gone back to see him."

"Who? See who?"

Martina got even more uneasy and didn't know what to do. *Why is she being so difficult? Acting like a naughty teenager? I need to protect her, need her to be safe.* "Jonathan Sullivan! You promised to never go back and see him. He is not nice; it is not safe. My goodness, Maria!"

Maria's forehead crinkled. Aaron raised one eyebrow. They looked at each other, irritated, then back at Martina. "Mamá, I *didn't* go back. Why would I see Jonathan Sullivan again? You said he wasn't even my dad."

Martina closed her eyes for a second and let out a sigh of relief. *Thank goodness, she didn't go back. It must have just taken Jonathan a while to show up and threaten me, the lazy man. Good. What a relief.*

"Right, Mamá? Jonathan Sullivan isn't my dad, is he?"

Martina realized her mistake. *¡Naguará! Silly me. Of course she believed my Jonathan Smith story. I should've known. That's good. That means she will never go back to see Jonathan again.* She let out a sigh of relief, then noticed her daughter's expression. She saw she was suspicious.

I need to quickly fix my silly mistake. Need to be convincing.

"No, no, he's not. He's not your dad. I told you, I put his name on the birth certificate because I couldn't put Jonathan Smith's name. He was married and I didn't know what happened to him after his deployment." Maria looked at her, studying her face. "Remember, mija. I told you already."

Maria nodded. "So. . . ." she started, and Martina knew her hesitation meant nothing good was coming. "You never saw Jonathan Smith again?"

Martina shook her head.

"He didn't know me?"

Martina again shook her head.

"So, you and I never visited a military base to see him?"

"No, mija, we were never at a military base. Why?"

Maria seemed to be having trouble finding her words. "Because . . . Because . . . I keep dreaming of a guy in uniform playing with me when I was little. Playing with me in the mountains. And at a beach. Playing peekaboo with him and his military shirts."

Aaron was curious what her mom would say. He moved closer to Maria so he could see Martina more clearly and study her face. But all he saw was genuine surprise. She looked surprised and innocent.

"You're dreaming of a guy in a military uniform playing with you? And you think it's your dad?"

Maria nodded. Aaron quietly wrote down Martina's reaction in the notebook.

"I don't know about that, mija. I never saw your dad again. You never met him. Maybe your brain is just making up these dreams to come to terms with the new information. I know you're a deep thinker. But it's just a dream, mija!"

Maria thought a bit, then nodded. Suddenly, Aaron interrupted the mother-daughter conversation. "Martina, what military branch was Jonathan Smith in again?"

Martina stared at Aaron. *Is this some sort of trick? I'm not even sure anymore what I've told them. What military branch? Don't even know the names of all the branches.* She had to think quickly.

"Army," she said. "Some sort of special forces."

Maria nodded. "You did mention that he went on a special mission to Africa. So Special Forces make sense. Right, Aaron?"

He looked up from his notes and stared at Maria, then at Martina through the phone. He nodded a weak smile. "Yeah," was all he said.

Maria sighed. "You're probably right, Mamá. I must be trying to process all this new information in my head when I'm asleep. And with Aaron leaving soon. . . ."

"I know, mija, it's a lot. A lot to take in and think about." Mother and daughter in agreement, they carried on their conversation.

Aaron didn't bother to listen any longer. He stared at his notes, then got up and walked away to sit elsewhere and think. He took out his phone and opened up the Notes app. *Special Forces might be right, but Army doesn't make any sense. The mountain range in Utah that Maria dreamed about was close to a specific military base. Close to Hill, an Air Force base. Just like Eglin is an Air Force Base. Maria is specifically dreaming about a guy in the Air Force, not the Army.*

Something isn't right. Her dreams are too specific, like memories. Her reaction to Eglin isn't normal. There's something there, something dark hidden deep inside her.

He sighed and looked over at Maria, who was happily chatting away in Spanish with her beloved mom. He shut down his phone and kept looking at his fiancée. *She's beautiful. I love her so much. But I know I didn't make a mistake on my security clearance paperwork. If that fraudulent paperwork really is Maria's birth certificate, then something here isn't right at all.* He looked down at the floor. *I just don't know what.*

All I know is that Martina is hiding something. Something big. Something unthinkable.

CHAPTER 40

*I*s *it that unthinkable? Or is it possible?*

Elisabeth was in the middle of packing and had stopped to stare at Enti. She thought back to the conversation she'd had with her ex-husband a few nights ago. She kept replaying it in her head. "*You were right, Elisabeth. You were right. She's been kidnapped.*"

She folded another one of the t-shirts on her bed, then put it into the suitcase that was lying on the ground, opened up and half-full. She looked back at Enti. It was on her bed in between all the clothes she wanted to pack.

Am I ready to go back? Back to the Gulf of Mexico? She closed her eyes for a second. She could almost hear the ocean's waves, almost feel the ocean breeze and taste the humid, salty air. *It's beautiful. I remember. I remember it too well.*

Sadness washed over her, as it usually did when she thought of her lost daughter, her broken marriage, her broken family. Deep sadness. But this time, she felt something else as well. Something she hadn't felt since that fateful night at Eglin.

Anger.

But not anger toward her ex-husband. Not anger over him insisting on going with her to that silly laundromat. No, anger toward the police. *I'm angry, so angry. Brad's right. The police didn't believe me, they had labeled me a hysteric. Well, I might have been at the time, but who wouldn't be?* She sighed and exhaled deeply. *But Brad's right. I did bring up good points. Three reasons why the "accidental drowning" theory couldn't possibly be correct. Three reasons: the locked door, Enti, and no body found. There was no dead body! Wouldn't it have washed on shore somewhere? A little body like that?*

A shudder ran down her spine. Her heart ached. *I can't think like that. It hurts too much, thinking of her being dead.*

She closed her eyes and the anger took over again. Anger at the police. *I know someone took her. Someone somehow stole my little girl right out of her bed. In just eight minutes. Why? Who? No idea.* She let out another deep sigh. *But Brad does. He has a new suspect. And he's right. It could have been that Hispanic cleaning lady.*

She folded another shirt, neatly, orderly, determined. *This time the police will believe my reasoning. They'll take us seriously. Yes, this time, the police will believe and take action. They will because now Brad's a general, and he'll present the kidnapping theory. They won't dare dismiss him. Yes, Brad's right, they'll listen to him. We need to open up the case again. We have to. Because now Brad believes me. We both believe it happened that way.*

Elisabeth peered down at Enti and started talking to her. "We'll find out what happened, Enti, we will! You know as well as I do that Moana would have never walked out all by herself. Not without you."

The faded, stitched-on smile was almost not visible anymore, but Elisabeth knew it was there all the same. It felt as though this little stuffy friend had just nodded, wisely.

Yes, Enti knew. She did not just walk out.

CHAPTER 41

*S*he did not just walk out! Brad was still thinking about the last conversation he'd had with his ex-wife. *The truth dawned on me a bit too late. Twenty years too late. Still, I'm so relieved Elisabeth isn't mad at me. At least not anymore. Together, we'll find out what happened. Yes we will. And the police will help us. We'll unseal the case and get to the bottom of it.* Lost in thought, he smiled.

"What are you smiling at?" Drew asked.

Perplexed, Brad looked at his friend.

"Don't tell me you're happy to see Senator Clifford?"

Brad groaned and grimaced. "Certainly not. He's a waste of our time. You know that. The senator is a pain in everyone's behind."

Drew couldn't help but laugh. "Yep, he sure is. A rich, power-hungry man who pretends to have his constituents in mind but is really just in it for himself."

Brad nodded. "Yeah, he sure is. And he'll be here any minute."

Both Brad and Drew looked at the clock over the door of the general's office. Drew sighed. "Man, I just don't know what happened. We used to have lots of fun with him at the Academy."

Brad, who sat behind his giant mahogany desk surrounded by paperwork and a few of his awards, gazed back at his friend. "Yeah, we did. But that was a lifetime ago. Before he ditched the Air Force."

Drew had to chuckle. "Before he *got* ditched, more like?"

Brad looked at him. "Yeah. Unfortunate."

They both nodded, and before Brad could say anything else, they heard a knock at the door. They looked at each other and sighed.

"Come on in, please," Brad said, and immediately fell back into his professional speaking-voice. He only ever let his guard down around Drew. The door opened, and Major Starke led the man behind him inside. Dressed in a navy-blue suit, fancy light-blue shirt, and dark-blue tie, the senator could've been mistaken for an Air Force officer dressed in his official blues uniform.

Still trying to look the part, Collins thought before he said, "Hello, Senator Clifford. How are you today?"

"Well, sir, that depends on how our little conversation goes today." The senator plopped himself down in one of the big chairs facing the general's desk.

"Well, Senator, sounds like you won't waste any time," Brad said, and waved his exec out. "Thank you, Major Starke, for bringing in the Senator. Please close the door so we can get started."

"Yes, sir," Major Starke said, saluted, and left the office.

"Please sit, Mr. Markas." He offered Drew the other seat in front of his desk, right next to the senator.

"Hello, Senator Clifford," Drew greeted their guest, who didn't reply.

Brad's face turned red. "Senator Clifford, I'm sure you remember retired Lieutenant Colonel Markas. He just said hello to you, by the way."

"I'd rather get to the point! My time is precious, I came all the way out here, and the last thing I need is to be lectured on who is who and who said what, General."

Drew looked at his friend and urged him to stay calm and ignore the senator's words, but Brad couldn't do that. Not with this guy. "Well, Senator, you should consider your manners sometimes and take the time to greet people. Just a suggestion."

"Nobody asked you for your opinion, General. Or is greeting people an order you throw around here?"

"It's just part of being respectful, as the military strives to be. But we sure know you had issues with that in the past, don't we, Senator?"

Drew gave his friend a look that told him he had gone too far. Brad sighed and looked down. *It's the truth, but often people don't want to hear the truth.*

The senator was nonplussed. "Well, the military is also about integrity and responsibility. Shocking you made it this far, General, as you certainly lack a sense of responsibility."

"Excuse me, Senator, but I doubt I lack that. I wouldn't be here if I did."

"Not lacking responsibility, you say? I see. Well, if we could put the question to your little daughter, I assume she might think differently."

Drew turned in surprise to look at the senator beside him. Not even five minutes had passed and the conversation had already grown tense. Brad glowered at the senator, his face red, his eyebrows crunched in, as though he were ready to punch him in the face. *How dare he bring my daughter into this. My missing daughter. My sweet little pumpkin. Snatched away from me in only eight minutes. Yet he's right. I was irresponsible. Irresponsible that night. It's all my fault. My sweet little daughter. Gone. Forever.*

His thoughts were racing, his heart was aching in pain. His hands formed fists and his eyes had turned completely green.

Drew knew that color pointed to his friend's agitation. He jumped in. "Senator, let's be civilized and get to the point. We heard you're here because of our upcoming trip to Florida, your home state. You have something to tell us about the program we're working on?"

The senator took his eyes off the general and looked at Drew now, then nodded.

"Very good, sir. Let's look at the paperwork and talk about the program briefly," Drew said. He got up and walked around the desk to grab a folder. As he went, he quickly squeezed his friend's arm to ask him to come back, come back to the present, to this meeting. He knew that Brad's thoughts were on that fateful night twenty years ago. He had to snap out of it if this meeting was to go anywhere.

The squeeze helped. Brad looked down at his arm, then saw the folder containing the briefing on the F-35 program. He stared at the picture of a jet. *Beautifully crafted jet. Fast, efficient.* He was back and focused on their work.

He picked up the folder and leaned back in his chair. "So, Senator, what would you like to talk about?"

"Your F-35 program. My good Floridians up there by Eglin AFB are disturbed by it."

"Disturbed?"

"Yes, disturbed. Literally. The jets are too loud!"

Brad and Drew exchanged glances. *Seriously?* Brad thought. *They're fighter jets. Of course they're loud. What do people expect, living next to an Air Force base that trains fighter pilots and tests fighter jets? It's like complaining about the cars being too loud after moving into a house built right next to a highway!*

Brad and Drew said nothing, opting instead to hear the senator out. They had known it would be a ridiculous meeting and had come in expecting it, but not quite like this. They had no other choice than to listen to the senator.

"The good people of Florida deserve better. If you can't dial back the noise, you could at least offer them compensation to help them endure their suffering. A part of every penny the program makes. Otherwise, we might have to suspend flying over the civilian area that surrounds the base."

"You know you can't do that, right? The jets have to start and land somewhere."

"I understand, General. That's why I'm looking for other ways to help those poor civilians that I'm responsible for."

Drew tried to hide a grin and looked at Brad, who just rolled his eyes. *Unbelievable, this guy. Who votes for an idiot like him? Well, guess all those people he charmed. Guess it helps that he's a charismatic, good-looking guy. Can't argue there. Fit, well-trained, always with a golden Florida tan. Wavy beach-blonde hair, a perfectly formed straight nose, blue eyes. Everyone's darling, and especially well-liked by the retirement communities in Florida. Those southern ladies.*

But that doesn't change the fact that he's an idiot. I can play his little game.

Brad focused on the senator again and the three men continued to discuss the issue in a somewhat heated debate. After about half an hour, the senator was ready to leave. "Thank you both for this constructive meeting. And enjoy your visit to my home state next week."

"Thank you, Senator."

"Especially you, Cave Man. Enjoy! It must be like twenty years since you've been there. Wonder why. Oh, yeah, probably didn't want to go back, huh? Must be hard to stomach your failure. Well, safe travels, gentlemen."

Brad couldn't believe his ears. *He mentioned it again. Guess trying to bring me down helps him cope with his short stint in the Air Force. Even used my call sign and then threw another gut punch about my family. Despicable.*

But the senator is right. I did fail. I did. Failed in the worst way possible. Failed by not protecting my little daughter. Definitely avoided going back there all these years. It's been twenty years. My baby girl would be an adult now.

My beautiful baby girl. I didn't give her a chance to grow up. It's all my fault. I didn't protect her.

In a trance, he watched the senator leave and then plopped down into the big chair behind his desk. He buried his head in his hands and sighed a deep sigh. *Failure. I'm such a failure.* He could feel the tears forming in his eyes and buried his head deeper into his hands.

Drew came over and patted his back. "It'll be okay, Brad. We'll go to Florida together. I'll be there with you every step of the way. You can do it."

Brad nodded. "Thanks, Drew, appreciate it."

"You're welcome." Drew gave him a last pat on the back, then walked toward the door and, with a nod, left the general's office.

Brad watched Drew walk out. *Gotta love Drew. He's a great guy. So supportive. Always there for me. My best friend.*

He leaned back into his chair, picked up a pen and started playing with it. *I feel terrible lying to him. I just know he wouldn't approve. Wouldn't approve meeting Elisabeth and picking up the case.*

He sighed. *But I have to. I'll have to face my failure. I'll face it with Elisabeth by my side once more, and together we'll somehow figure out what happened the night our little one disappeared. We'll uncover the truth. Find out what happened to our baby girl. Yes we will. Next week at Eglin AFB.*

CHAPTER 42

"**I** still can't believe you're starting your very first job next week," Maria said to Aaron while sitting in his car on the way to the airport in Orlando.

"Yeah, pretty cool, huh? First job. First new home at Eglin AFB," Aaron said as he hit the blinker and turned left toward the *Arrivals* sign.

There it is again. That strange feeling. Maria watched her tiny arm hairs stand up in response to Aaron mentioning the base. *So strange. Why do they even do that? I've no control over my body at this point. No idea why I react this way.*

Before she could ponder it further, Aaron's phone lit up in its car holder. "Kinda busy here. Can you check on that for me?"

"Sure." Maria swiped through and read the messages. "They landed. They're exiting the plane right now."

"Okay, tell them we're almost there."

She started typing, and within seconds received a reply. "They don't want us to park. Just pick them up curbside. Letter D area."

"Okay," Aaron said, and signaled again to change lanes. It wasn't too busy, but cars were constantly pulling up. They turned into the curbside-pickup area and searched for the Letter D area.

"There." Maria pointed at a sign.

Aaron saw it and swiftly weaved in and out of the lanes of cars pulling up to park and load passengers before departing. Aaron found a good spot by the curb. Both of them craned their necks about, looking for his family. Nowhere to be seen.

"That's strange. Where are they?" Aaron took the phone from Maria. It beeped. "Of course. Emma had to use the bathroom. They're on their way out now."

Maria smirked. *Why not let the poor girl take her time and use the restroom in peace? Well, I know Aaron. He likes everyone to be on time. Good thing I've always been punctual. It's somehow ingrained in me, deep down inside. Sure different than the rest of my family. They all run on "Venezuelan time," as I like to call it.* She smiled.

"Hmm. I guess we have time for a quick kiss?" Aaron grinned with the most charming smile before leaning over to kiss her, but Maria pushed him away.

"Aaron, your family! Come on now. They'll be here any minute."

"Knowing Emma, she'll have to stop at a store and buy a piece of gum real quick, then get distracted looking at the souvenirs, and then—"

"There they are!" Maria got out of the car without letting Aaron finish. Her mom had taught her it was important to greet people and make sure they knew you were excited to see them. She started waving frantically. Aaron got out of the driver's side, closed the door, and stood next to her, waving as well. His family noticed them and waved back as they beelined toward them.

"Hi there, big bro," Emma said, a big grin on her face as she hugged Aaron. "And hi to you as well, Maria. My soon-to-be sister!"

Maria smiled and gave Emma a warm hug. Aaron was next hugged by his mom, who didn't seem to want to let go of him. Maria stood face-to-face with Jack Heikinnen, Aaron's dad, a reserved man, a lawyer. She wasn't sure if she should hug him or not. Her Venezuelan heritage told her to just hug him, but thinking of his manners and profession, Maria held herself back and instead awkwardly put out her hand for a handshake. "Hello, Mr. Heikinnen."

He smiled a warm smile, took her hand, and ended up pulling her in for a quick hug. "Hello, Maria. Please, call me Jack. I thought we agreed to that when you came to visit in Montana?" He winked at her and she nodded with a big smile before Grace Heikinnen, Aaron's mom, scooped her into a big hug, swaying her from side to side.

"Maria, it's so *good* to see you again." Grace Heikinnen kept swaying Maria in the hug, and she noticed that Grace was crying when she felt something wet on her shoulder.

"Mom, you can let go of her now," Aaron said.

Emma laughed. "Yes, mom, Aaron's right. Maria is gonna get seasick if you keep swaying her back and forth like that." The siblings laughed and Jack smiled.

"Oh. Oh okay. I'm sorry," Grace said, and let go of Maria. "I'm just so happy to be here. And so excited to see you again, Maria. Oh, Maria. We're all so happy you're going to be a part of our family. Actually, I take that back—you already are!" Then she stepped forward again to give Maria another big hug.

"Thank you," Maria said, "I'm very excited, too." She was relieved that Grace was crying out of happiness.

Once she let go of Maria, she went fishing inside her purse for something. "Do you need a tissue?" Maria said. She felt inside her own purse, found a to-go box of Kleenex, and handed them to Grace.

"Aw, Maria, thank you. You're so sweet."

Maria smiled at her future mother-in-law. "My mom always cries out of happiness, too, and I take after her, so I always carry those around in my purse."

Grace dabbed her moist eyes and blew into the Kleenex after handing the box of tissues back to Maria. "I have a feeling your mom and I will get along great. I can't wait to meet her tomorrow."

"Me neither," Emma shouted, and jumped into the backseat of the car. "Maria, will you sit next to me?"

"Emma, Maria is going to sit next to Aaron in the front," Jack scolded his daughter while he and Aaron loaded the last of their luggage into the trunk of the car.

"It's okay, Jack" Maria said. "I think you should be with your son this ride. All us women can cozy up together in the backseat."

"Oh, Maria, I don't want you to get squished between Emma and me," Grace protested, but Maria had already taken her place in the middle backseat of Aaron's small car.

"It's no problem at all." So, Grace and Emma climbed in next to her while Jack and Aaron sat up front.

Off they went, back to Daytona Beach. As usual, Aaron and Jack discussed topics none of the girls were interested in, while they held their own conversation about wedding plans. Maria had to show off her engagement ring repeatedly. Emma wanted to know all about the color theme Maria had in mind, the bridesmaid dresses, and plenty of other details Maria hadn't even thought of. Emma started a list to remind Maria what she needed to think about, and the three had a great time together dreaming up the wedding of a lifetime.

Then Emma asked, "Who will walk you down the aisle?" and Maria's smile faded.

"Emma!" Grace gave her daughter the evil eye.

"Well, I don't know. One of my uncles could do it. Or maybe I should just walk by myself?"

"Or my dad can take you," Emma blurted out. "He's gonna be your new dad anyway!"

"Emma!" Grace was outraged by her young teenage daughter's insensitivity, but Maria just smiled.

"You know what, Emma? That sounds like a great idea. I like it!"

"See, mom? Don't have to be mad at me!"

"I'm sorry, Maria, about Emma's behavior," Grace said, ignoring her daughter.

"It's alright. I've thought about this already. You know, Mamá and I have been talking a lot about my birth father lately, so it naturally came to my mind."

"Really? Who's your dad? What was he like? Did you ever get to know him?"

"Emma!" Grace said again, more forcefully this time.

"What? Maria brought it up."

Maria laughed, but her laugh faded quickly. *Emma has a point. I did bring it up. What should I say? That my mom had a fling? That her ex-husband was an abuser? Oh dear, what did I get myself into? And it's only been the first half-hour of Aaron's family's visit.*

She took a deep breath. "Um, no, I've never met him. But my mom assured me he was a nice man. Unlike her ex-husband." Emma and Grace both looked at Maria, surprised. "Actually, he was also in the military, like Aaron. He left on a deployment. A secret mission. He never returned."

Emma's eyes grew wide and Grace looked at her feet, neither saying anything for a moment. "I'm sure it must have been very hard for your mom," Grace finally said. "I can't imagine what she's been through."

"Yeah, it wasn't easy, raising me all by herself. But she managed."

"Heck yeah, she *did* manage. Very well, actually. 'Cuz you're very cool, Maria," Emma said.

Both Grace and Maria had to laugh at the teenager's compliment, then they moved on to a different topic. *Guess that went well enough. I successfully left out the juicy details. There's still so much I need to figure out myself.*

CHAPTER 43

"That was a fun night with your family," Maria said as they walked into Aaron's messy room, full of boxes. "Hope they sleep well in my apartment."

"I'm sure they will. They were tired after the trip. And after all that food." Aaron rubbed his belly. "I think I ate too much. Hope I can fit my pants tomorrow."

Maria laughed. "No worries. You can digest in your sleep. Come on, let's get ready." Aaron nodded.

Once they were all set for bed, Maria texted her mom while Aaron laid out his new blue uniform to wear at the Air Force commissioning tomorrow. He inspected it to make sure it was all set. He also put out the shiny black shoes that went with the uniform and inspected those as well.

"Oh no. There's a stain on my shoes."

Maria walked over to look at them. They seemed perfectly clean to her until Aaron pointed out a tiny stain on his left shoe.

"Looks like a drop of water landed there," Maria said. "Nothing bad. We can quickly fix it."

"No, not quickly. I'll have to shine every square inch of the shoes again!"

"Oh. The way you do it, that'll take a while."

He sighed. "Yeah, I know. But it's protocol. The only way to shine them."

She smirked. "Only one way to do it, huh?"

"Yes, the Air Force taught us how."

"Oh, Aaron, I'm sure they did. I know they did. But guess what?" His eyes followed her as she walked away, then returned with one wet paper towel and one dry one. "There's always more than one way to do it. Watch and learn."

"Maria, what are you doing? We have to use black shoeshine and need to rub it in—"

"That's what they teach you to keep you busy for hours. Watch this!" With one quick wipe of the wet paper towel followed by a quick wipe with the dry one, the shoe was once again as shiny as a shoe can be.

"Wow, Maria, that's amazing! It actually worked!"

"Of course it did, Brad," she said as she balled up the paper towels.

Aaron stared at her, his jaw open.

"What? You're giving me too much credit. It was a neat trick, but not *that* impressive." Maria got up to throw the paper towels into the trash.

Aaron swallowed hard. *Brad?* When Maria came back into the room, he was still staring at the shoes.

"Aaron, seriously, they're all clean and set for tomorrow. Look at them. They look great. *You* will look great. Believe me."

She came over to hug him. Deep in thought, he continued to stare at the shoes. She laughed and gave him a kiss on the cheek.

"I do believe you," he mumbled. "But what was that you said?"

Puzzled, Maria looked at him. "What's up with you? I just said it obviously worked."

"And then?"

"Then . . . nothing?" She studied his face. "I don't understand what you mean."

He took her hands, and looked at her. "Do you know a guy named Brad?"

"What? Why would you even ask me that?" Maria started to get angry.

Doesn't matter. I heard her say it loud and clear. "Do you *know* someone named *Brad*?"

"What do you want from me, Aaron? Are you jealous all of a sudden of some random made-up guy named Brad? What the heck?" She ripped her hands out of his and crossed her arms across her chest.

"Maria, just tell me, do you know a guy named Brad?"

She stared at him, anger in her eyes. Aaron already knew the answer, but he was curious how she'd act. *Why did she say that name? Is the idea of him somehow connected to the shiny black shoes that go with Air Force uniforms?*

"No, I don't know a guy named Brad. Come on, Aaron, you're being ridiculous."

"So, if you don't know a guy named Brad, why did you tell me, 'Of course it did, Brad?'"

"What? I never even said that. You must have misheard. Aaron, that's so silly. I don't know a guy with that name. Except Brad Pitt. Fine, be jealous of him then."

"Maybe I should be.. . . ."

He laughed and looked at Maria, looked into her exotic eyes, her unique eyes green with anger. He could see that she was still mad at him and had no idea what he was talking about.

Aaron thankfully had learned enough about PTSD in his ROTC classes to put one and one together. He was convinced Maria had just had a Freudian slip. *Maybe she suddenly remembered her real dad's name? The guy from her dreams or memories. If she just recalled specific details about shined black shoes, uniquely shined like they have to be in the Air Force, it might be another piece to the puzzle.*

Maria continued to stare at him with a defiant look. She wasn't sure what had gotten into him to inquire about silly things like that, but she sure couldn't stay mad at him for long. Especially not when she saw his long brown eyelashes and his beautiful ocean-blue eyes looking into hers, a concerned look in them. She leaned over to give him a kiss.

"Let's get some sleep! You have your commissioning tomorrow. It'll be a big day."

He nodded.

She cuddled up close to him on the mattress on the floor, in between all the plastic bins. Those bins would soon be on their way to Eglin AFB. That name still scared her so much.

Aaron felt her uneasiness. "It's okay. Just think of all the fun things to come. Commissioning, graduation. The parties after. Our wedding. Don't forget that."

"How could I?" In the dark she held up her left hand. "When I have this constant reminder. It's a beautiful ring, Aaron. I love it."

"And I love you." He gave her a kiss. But secretly, he couldn't wait for her to fall asleep. He certainly didn't plan on getting much rest or sleeping now. *How can I?* His mind was all over the place as he tried to sort his thoughts about his fiancée's dark past.

He stared at the wall opposite them through the gloom. The wall with his uniform and shiny black shoes. Those shiny black Air Force shoes had brought out a Freudian slip in Maria.

She must have seen shoes like these before. Not just someone random wearing similar shoes, but ones exactly like these, sporting a stain. She must have seen someone wipe them off using that trick of hers. A person talking to a guy named Brad.

Brad . . . a guy in uniform? The same guy in uniform she dreamed about all those other times? Her dad?

He listened to Maria's even breathing and was sure she was asleep now. Quietly, he got up from the mattress on the floor, grabbed his phone and Maria's purse, and snuck out into the living room. He pulled the notebook labeled *My Past* out of her purse and looked over the notes. *Where should I even start?*

Nothing really made sense. He tried to find common factors in the wildly scribbled notes. *Air Force. It all comes back to the Air Force.* He grabbed a pen and wrote it in capitalized letters. "AIR FORCE." He kept searching. Maria's weird drowning dreams had started with researching her dad. "FATHER," he wrote down. What else was a common theme? "DROWNING." Yes, for sure—he wrote it down.

He looked at these three capitalized words. Then he scribbled names next to "FATHER": "Jonathan Sullivan, Jonathan Smith, Brad." Next, he wrote down the bases she had dreamed of: "Eglin AFB and Hill AFB." He stared at the word "DROWNING." He wasn't sure what to make of it. Nothing to add to that. He sighed.

Am I forgetting anything else? Oh yeah, Maria said she was always little in her dreams. A small child. "TODDLER," he wrote down in capitalized letters. He kept thinking, but had no idea what to make of that. *Anything else?* He looked through the notebook again. *Yes. Forgot about that.* "GERMAN," he wrote down. Adding that made things even more confusing.

After staring at the notebook for a while, he got up and made himself a peanut-butter-and-jelly sandwich. He brought it back to the couch and ate it while his eyes bored into the words he had written down. He knew there was something dark in her past, so dark and unfathomable that it was buried deep down in her memory. So deep. Like PTSD.

She definitely has PTSD. And her post-traumatic stress is triggered by Air Force uniforms? Yes, it's somehow connected to the Air Force. But what's the source? Where did she experience her trauma? He finished his sandwich and kept thinking. *Eglin AFB. My new home. The TLF. Maria must have been there. For sure. If so, she must have been a little toddler, perhaps two years old at the time. It would have happened about twenty years ago. Sounds right.*

He took his phone and typed in "Eglin AFB 20 years ago." He got all kinds of hits showing what the base had looked like, what they had improved, which new programs they had added, what other military branches had been included, and so on.

Nothing informative. Nothing he needed to know.

He thought again as he scrolled through the pictures of the base. Beautiful. Just a beautiful place. He looked at pictures of the TLF again, then the Fam Camp—the camping area on base—and at advertisements for the outdoor rec center, where you could rent boats and stuff. All of it was close to the marina, close to the TLF.

Looks beautiful. Pretty view of the water. The whole area is surrounded by water. Wait! Surrounded by water? He ruffled through the notebook until he found what he was looking for. *Drowning dreams.* He gasped. *Could it be? Is Maria afraid of Eglin because she almost drowned there?*

He jumped up and started pacing. *How can I find that out?* Phone in hand, he paced back and forth across the living room. Then he had an idea. He typed in "drowning accident at Eglin AFB 20 years ago."

To his astonishment, his search pulled up over two hundred hits. "Toddler Drowns at Eglin Air Force Base" was the first article he read. When he scrolled down to the picture of the missing toddler, the phone slipped out of his sweaty hand and crashed onto the floor.

For the first time in his life, Aaron felt dizzy. So dizzy that he had to hold on to something. He grabbed the bar stool by the kitchen island and closed his eyes for a second to make the spinning stop.

Could it be? Is it really her?

Slowly, he opened his eyes then walked into the kitchen to get a glass of water. He gulped it down, then went over to the living room and picked up the phone again. The picture stared back at him. A picture of a cute little girl with reddish-brown hair, two little pigtails, and a smirk on her face. A cute little girl with hazel eyes, a mosaic of golden-and-emerald-green flecks in the dark-brown center encircled by a blue rim.

I would recognize these unique eyes anywhere. I've gazed into them for three years, seen them laugh and cry and change color when agitated. The eyes alone convinced him this cute little baby-girl was Maria.

Shocked, he plopped down onto the couch and skimmed through one of the articles. *Her parents had just moved to Eglin AFB. Stayed in the TLF. Toddler drowned accidentally.. . . .*

Aaron stared at his phone. *What? That's not right! If that girl in the picture is Maria, she's obviously alive and didn't drown. What happened to her parents? Did they drown?* He skimmed the article to find something on the parents. *Parents left for eight minutes to do laundry at the laundromat. Left sleeping daughter alone in TLF.* He stared at the article on his phone. *Holy cow! Who does that? Who just leaves their toddler alone?*

He kept reading. The press had asked that very question. "We were on a secure military installation," they quoted the dad as saying. "Brad and Elisabeth Collins are devastated by the disappearance of their daughter." Aaron gasped. *Wait? What? Brad Collins? Brad.*

Right away, the sentence Maria had mumbled earlier that night came to mind. "*Of course it did, Brad.*"

For the second time that night, his phone slipped out of his sweaty hands, and he was hit by a wave of dizziness. *Oh my gosh. Brad. Brad Collins.* His thoughts were all jumbled up. The hair stood up on his body. He wasn't sure whether he was having a panic attack or was simply scared.

No, he was definitely afraid. Afraid for Maria.

Stop! Just breathe. Just think. Have to focus. He looked back at the article. "Captain Brad Collins." *Brad Collins. That name sounds familiar. Where have I heard that before?* And then it dawned on him. *Twenty years have passed, so that guy is definitely not* Captain *Collins anymore. He's* General *Collins now! And I just saw him. At the Air Force Ball. The guest speaker. General Brad Collins. Could he actually be Maria's dad?*

Abruptly, he stood up and started pacing again. *If General Brad Collins is Maria's true dad, then the lady mentioned in the article, Elisabeth, was her mom. Right? But who is Martina Sullivan then? How did Maria come to her? And why do the articles all say she drowned? What in the world is that all about?* He grabbed his phone. He needed to read more about this case. He needed to make sure the general was actually Maria's dad. He needed to verify Maria was actually the little girl in the picture. *But how? How can I find out for sure?* He was deep in thought and didn't notice Maria standing in the bedroom doorframe.

"Aaron?"

Surprised, he jumped and dropped his phone for the third time that night. "Maria? What are you doing here?"

Maria looked at him, her arms crossed in front of her. He could tell she wasn't amused. "I was about to ask you the same. Why aren't you sleeping?"

"I . . . I . . . was just . . . you know . . . looking at my phone," he said, and picked it up off the ground, quickly closing the browser with a nimble swipe of his fingers.

"Aha."

He looked at her. She was clearly unconvinced and gazing at him suspiciously. He knew he couldn't tell what he'd learned just yet. It would be too much. He cleared his throat, his mind working quickly. "I just couldn't sleep. So much going on, you know. I was looking over my speech. Making sure it's all set."

Maria uncrossed her arms and came over to him. She gave him a big hug. "Oh, Aaron, your speech will be awesome. You'll be great. Don't be nervous."

"I know, I know," he said, and walked back into the bedroom arm in arm with her.

He *was* nervous, though. Not about his speech. No, nervous for her. About her past. A shudder ran down his spine. *I know Maria isn't who she thinks she is. And Martina Sullivan isn't who she pretends to be. But then, who in the world is she?*

CHAPTER 44

Martina Sullivan had the biggest grin on her face as she drove her small Toyota toward Daytona Beach. She was so excited to finally meet Aaron's family, soon to be Maria's family as well. And so excited for Aaron to start his first job.

He'll make good money, provide for my Maria and her family. Their family! ¡Dios mio! How exciting to think about grandkids. I know Maria doesn't want to have kids right away and needs to finish college, but she loves little kids and is good with them. She's good with everyone. A real people person. So kind, so outgoing. So proud of her! That little shy toddler has turned into an amazing young lady.

Her mom must have been fabulous.

She quickly pushed that thought away. *I'm her mom. It has to be that way. It's the only safe thing to say, to think, to stick to. Jonathan will not like it if I ever talk about what really happened. He wouldn't like it, and if he doesn't like something, it's not safe for anyone. Not for me, and especially not for Maria now that he knows what she looks like, all grown up.*

Why in the world did she go see him? A big knot formed in Martina's throat just thinking about it. *So dangerous! It was so dangerous to see him.* Her navigation suddenly talked to her, disrupting her thoughts. Thank goodness for navigation devices, now conveniently found on the phone. She had almost missed her turn. The last thing she wanted was to be late for Aaron's commissioning ceremony. She was so happy to have been invited.

She glanced over to the passenger seat to make sure everything was still there. Her purse was on the passenger seat, next to the gift for Aaron, nicely wrapped. Her overnight duffel bag was in the trunk. In front of the passenger seat in the footwell was a big container full of Venezuelan goodies. She had stayed up late to bake everything fresh. Her gift to Nick for letting her stay in his room, and her welcome gift to Aaron's family. *I hope they like it. And hope they like me. Hope they don't think I'm too simple, not smart enough. They're a very educated family. Aaron's dad is a lawyer, his mom a teacher. Will they look down on me 'cuz I don't have a college education?*

No, they won't. I'm sure Aaron's family is just as outgoing, warm, and caring as he is. If he turned out like that then his family must be just as lovely. She came up on the exit ramp. *There it is. The exit sign for Daytona Beach. Soon I'll be at Embry-Riddle Aeronautical University.*

She reached the university campus and looked around in awe. It sure was beautiful. Breathtaking, even. *So proud of Maria for getting a scholarship to this beautiful, well-known-and-liked university. Sure, it's a smaller campus, but that just makes it feel even more wonderful. More like a home.* She saw all the beautifully planted palm trees lining the street and looked around for the parking lot that Maria had told her to park in.

There it is! She saw the sign for it and a row of cars forming a line to park there. *That must be the right place. Where there are people, there's something going on.*

And so it was: a bustle of people, the women all dressed up in elegant dresses and a few in ballroom gowns, the guys in suits, and then the occasional casual dresser. Martina had to smile. *America. The Land of the Free. Here you can even wear jeans to exciting once-in-a-lifetime events. Only Americans can get away with that.*

She found a parking space, turned off her car, and logged out of the navigation app that had kindly told her she had just arrived at her destination. She texted Maria, and her phone blinked in reply immediately. *Meet us at the entrance*, it said in perfect Spanish.

Aw, mija. So smart and bilingual. And about to see her fiancé graduate and commission into the U.S. Air Force. Wow.

Martina grinned, got out of the car, smoothed over her flowery dress, and swapped out of her simple, comfortable ballerina shoes into her dressy white high heels. Those perfectly matched her white dress with the flowers on it. Flowers in different shades of red.

She walked around the car to open the passenger seat and got out her light-red purse, the same shade as the flowers on her dress. She put the four small bags of homemade Venezuelan pastries in it as well as the small, beautifully wrapped gift for Aaron. She quickly checked herself out in the rearview mirror, making sure that her lipstick hadn't smeared and her curly hair looked fresh, then locked the car.

On her way toward the entrance, she kept an eye out for Maria and her soon-to-be family in-law. She nervously followed the crowd of people, all taller than her—but then, she was used to that. As the crowd moved on, she spotted Maria, Aaron, and the Heikinnens standing right there by the entrance. She took a deep breath, hoping they would like her, and walked toward them.

Maria, Aaron, Emma, Grace, and Jack were all standing in front of the entrance to the huge auditorium. It was early and not yet time to go in, but Grace Heikinnen sure was nervous. She wanted to get a good seat for her son's commissioning ceremony. She hoped that Maria's mom would finally arrive so that they could walk in and grab their seats.

"There she is," Maria suddenly exclaimed, and started waving frantically.

"Where?" Emma scanned the crowd of people that were walking in.

"There," Maria said, and pointed at a small woman with a round frame, beautiful bouncy, curly brown hair, and dark-brown eyes, who started waving back.

"That woman in the white dress with the red flowers on it is my mamá!"

"I see her now," Jack Heikinnen said and raised his hand in a wave.

Emma had started waving frantically herself. "You weren't kidding when you said you and your mom don't really look alike. You look nothing alike at all!"

Aaron grunted. Emma was right. *They look nothing alike at all.* He had noticed that before, of course, years ago, but knowing what he knew now, the fact that there was no resemblance to speak of was actually kind of shocking. *Who is Martina Sullivan?* He looked at the woman walking toward them, then at Maria. *No resemblance. Sure, Maria is nicely tan from the summer sun, but her mom has naturally tan skin.* Regardless, Maria ran over to hug her mother and spoke perfect Spanish to her.

"Aw, I wish my Spanish was that good. I'd get an A-plus all the time then," Emma said.

The little friendly-looking woman hugged Aaron and gave him a kiss on each cheek. He stiffened up, but nobody noticed. Maria was back with the rest of the Heikinnens and officially introduced her mom to them.

"This is my mamá, Martina Sullivan. Mamá, ella es Grace, mamá de Aaron, e este es Jack, el papá de Aaron, e ella es Emma, hermana de Aaron."

"Hello, it's very nice to finally meet you all," Martina said, smiling, and shook Jack's hand.

"Pleasure's all mine," he said before Grace came over to give Martina a big hug. She happily hugged her back before giving Emma a hug as well.

"I love your flowery dress," Emma said. "Can I feel the fabric?"

"Emma, please." Grace scolded her daughter while Martina just laughed.

"Sí, of course you can touch my dress. Anyone that likes fabric is my soulmate," she said with a smile. And before they all knew it, Emma and Martina were talking fabrics and dresses. Emma was very interested in hearing all about her tailor shop.

Grace finally interjected. "Shall we go inside?"

"Relax, mom," Aaron smiled, "the doors aren't even open yet. But I have to go soon."

"Where do you need to go, young man?"

Aaron looked at Martina. He wanted to scream at her, yell at her, ask her who the heck she was, but knew he had to be quiet for now. He tried to stay as calm as possible. "We cadets have to line up and walk in together."

"More like *march in* together, ya think?" Emma smirked, and gave him a friendly elbow bump. They all laughed.

"Before you go, Aaron, I need to get a picture of my daughter's handsome fiancé!" Aaron and Maria stood next to each other and smiled for the camera.

"¡Bello! Aren't they just stunning together?" Martina almost broke out in tears.

"Yes indeed," Grace agreed, and pulled out a to-go box of tissues from her purse. She dabbed at her own eyes before offering them to Maria's mom.

"Oh dear, it's not even your wedding day yet and both moms are already crying," Emma commented, and Jack smirked the same smirk Maria saw on Aaron's face every day.

The two women looked at the couple. Aaron's blue dress uniform matched his ocean-blue eyes, and his shiny black shoes gave him a sleek look, while Maria's gold-and-blue dress matched not only her own eyes but also her fiancé's uniform and eyes. The dress fabric's thick golden streaks brought out the golden brown in her eyes, while the blue streaks perfectly highlighted the blue rim encircling them. Her simple makeup brought out her beauty; her freckles underlined her fun-loving nature. Her hair was up in a bun, tied together with an Air-Force-blue ribbon, and showed off her elegant neck. They sure looked stunning together.

The whole party was dressed elegantly. Aaron's mom was wearing a red dress that unintentionally matched the flowers on Martina's dress. Jack wore a grey suit with red shirt and grey tie to match Grace's dress. Emma's green dress with the blue polka dots stood out, yet still managed to match the blue of Aaron's uniform.

While the families stood together and took pictures, Jim and his family came over with Keisha accompanying. Aaron introduced everyone before he and Jim had to run off to line up for their walk-in.

Maria gave him a long, big hug. "Good luck, Aaron. You'll do great. You know I'm proud of you, and I'm sure your parents will love it too. And my mamá. Go get 'em. Love you." He smiled and gave her a quick kiss, then walked in to line up.

Keisha was next to Maria now. "How's it going, Keisha?"

"Pretty good, girl. They seem to like me so far."

"I told you so."

Maria smiled and gave her a hug before the girls were interrupted by Emma. "What are you girls talking about?"

Keisha and Maria looked at each other and smiled. "Better get used to having a nosy little sis, girl." The two friends laughed together.

"Well, Emma," Maria said, "we were just wondering if us young *girls* should all sit together during the ceremony."

"Yes, yes, please."

Emma linked arms with Maria. Maria in the middle, Keisha on one side, and Emma on the other, they announced, "The doors are now open!"

Jack and Grace, Martina, and Jim's parents all looked up.

Grace linked arms with Martina and started walking them forward. "Gosh, what are we waiting for? Let's go in!"

CHAPTER 45

Jonathan Sullivan watched them go in. He was leaning on the door of his truck chewing his gum, his jaws tight, his hands making fists. *Can I trust her? Can I trust that woman?* He still wasn't sure.

His phone beeped with a text. He pulled it out of his pocket and looked at it. A bunch of missed calls from the store. And now a text from his employee. He opened it and read.

Boss, where you at? The crew is waiting for you. Everything okay?

He stared at the text and kept chewing his gum. *Not sure if everything is alright. Hope so. Hope Martina won't talk. But have to make sure she won't, so I've got to keep an eye on her. Followed her all the way to Daytona Beach.* Of course, he knew he couldn't tell his employee any of that.

He sighed, spit out his gum, and sat down in the truck. He was sure the group he was watching would be in that big building for a while, so he had time to call her now. As if he were an actor in a theater readying himself to perform, he took a deep breath, cleared his throat, and dialed his store's number.

"Boss, you okay? We were worried sick when you didn't show up for work today again. Everything alright, darlin'?"

He coughed and whispered. "Oh, I'm sorry I worried everyone. I'm just not feeling well."

"Oh no, darlin'. I'm so sorry to hear that boss."

He coughed again. "Thank you, Carmal" he said, his voice convincingly coarse. "I think I got hit with a bad summer cold. I'm sorry I didn't even call." Another cough, then a breath in, wheezing. "I've just been so weak and sleeping nonstop. Slept in until just now."

He heard a gasp on the other end. "Oh no, boss. That's terrible, so terrible. You just sound so sick. Are you sure it's just a cold?"

He took a deep breath in again and made a whistling sound that carried through the phone when he exhaled. "I assume so."

"Could it be COVID?"

He was silent for a bit. Then his face lit up. *That's actually a great idea.* "I don't know. Maybe it is. I just feel very sick, so weak."

"Oh boss, do you need anything? Can I help with anything? I can bring you some soup?"

Another convincing wheeze. "No, no. If it's COVID, I might get you sick too." He coughed again. "I'll just stay home and rest. I'll have to take off the whole weekend, but I hope"—he fell into a coughing spree that slowly petered out before finishing—"to be back on Monday."

"Oh boss. Poor thing. Please don't worry. We've got your back. I'll run the store for you. Your crew is doing fine also. They're on site at that job right now. No worries, we got this. You stay home and rest, darlin'. Just get better."

He smiled, then coughed again. "Thank you, sweetheart, thank you. I'll be in touch."

"Okay, boss. Take care."

He coughed one last time, then hung up. *Yeah, I will take care. I'll take care of things real good.*

He looked at the fancy university building and got out of his truck again. He leaned against the driver's door and lit himself a cigarette. With the first puff, he broke out into a laugh. *COVID. Ha! Well, perfect excuse. Perfect. Damn I'm a good actor.* He puffed on his cigarette and reminisced. *Juilliard really missed out.*

He frowned and waited, just leaning there on his truck's door.

CHAPTER 46

"The doors will close in half an hour. Please take your seat now." She heard the announcement and nervously clutched her purse as they sat down in their seats. Her eyes were wide open, looking around, constantly wondering if she had done the right thing. *What in the world was I thinking? Well, this wasn't my idea. I never wanted to go back, never. Not back to the land that destroyed my life. Destroyed my family, broke my heart.* She clutched the purse more tightly as her thoughts raced.

Suddenly, a touch on her arm. She jerked to the side—it was Sarah. Only her friend Sarah. "Elisabeth, relax. It'll be okay. I'm right here, next to you. It'll be fine."

Elisabeth looked at her friend and gave a very slight, quick nod. The plane was still being loaded, and while most people in their area at the back of the plane were already seated, there were still a few open seats left around them. The four seats in the middle row in front of the wall facing the bathrooms. The two friends thankfully sat in the two-seat side of the plane, which had plenty of leg room given the bathrooms were literally right next to them.

She started relaxing a bit as Sarah pointed out all the things that were being loaded onto the plane. Their window had a good view. It was a beautiful day and predicted to be a smooth flight over to the United States.

Back to the United States. Back to Florida.

They had to land in Atlanta first and switch planes there before heading to Fort Walton Beach. To VPS. Valparaiso Airport. The place Elisabeth had vowed to never see again. And now, twenty years later, she was sitting on the plane that would take her back there, back to her past and all the painful memories.

Sarah and Elisabeth watched the luggage being loaded onto the plane and didn't notice as a family walked in and took the four remaining seats next to them in the middle row, until they heard a baby cry. Elisabeth looked over and saw them. A family of five, a beautiful family. Two little toddlers around two or three years of age that looked like twin boys, and a small, little baby in the arms of its mother. The toddlers were seated in the middle in between their parents while their mom and the baby sat on the seat closest to Elisabeth.

She stared at the baby. It had calmed down immediately and was sucking on its pacifier. It barely had any hair, but it did have big, beautiful, light-brown eyes that were intensely looking around. The baby seemed to be only a few months old and kept sucking on the pink pacifier. Its eyes fixed upon Elisabeth, who stared back at the baby.

Must be a baby girl. Pink pacifier and matching pink flowery onesie sure points to that. Then the baby's little hand reached out toward Elisabeth, and her heart melted. *What a beautiful little baby girl.*

Before she knew it, she was playing peekaboo with the little one, who giggled happily, until their play was interrupted by an unfamiliar voice. "Oh, entschuldigen Sie. I'm sorry. I hope she isn't bothering you too much."

Elisabeth looked over at the mom, who looked more than stressed and tired. She assured her that she wasn't bothered at all. "Nein, alles gut. Es stört mich gar nicht."

The young woman smiled a warm smile and tried to sit the baby down on her lap. But the baby girl was too engaged in her play with

Elisabeth and squirmed around. The mom spoke to her in soft German until the baby sat back into her mom's lap. The two toddlers in the middle were jumping up and down on their seats while the dad tried to make them sit down, speaking English to them.

A mixed family. Elisabeth sighed. *Beautiful, mixed family. With wonderful, smart, bilingual kids. That should've been me.*

Her thoughts were interrupted as the young woman this time apologized for her toddlers' behavior. Both Sarah and Elisabeth started a conversation with her. They were interrupted several times by the baby girl, who was wanting to move around and kept squirming.

"I assume you ordered a baby bassinet for the flight?"

The young mom looked at Elisabeth, surprised. "A baby bassinet?"

"Yes, since you're sitting right in front of the wall, you can have one. It's a little cot, or bassinet, for a baby younger than one year old that the flight attendants can attach to the wall. Then you can be hands-free as your little one lies down to sleep there."

The mom's eyes flickered with hope. "That sounds fantastic. I had no idea that was an option."

"Usually, you have to reserve it in advance, but since it only works with seats in front of a wall, which you're already sitting in front of, and you do have a baby, I doubt they've given it to someone else. It should be free."

Elisabeth helped wave over one of the flight attendants, who was very helpful and brought over the attachable cot. After it was installed, the little baby girl was happily lying in it, playing with a bunch of toys. The mom stored away all her family's luggage and was now able to help take care of her two boys. She was visibly relieved and smiled at Elisabeth and Sarah. "Thank you for letting me know of this. This is genius. I had no idea. Can't believe we didn't know about this until now. We just didn't travel much with the twins—I barely left the house after they were born. It was just too much. This bassinet is amazing. Thanks again."

Elisabeth smiled. She loved helping others. It helped her forget her own life, a life full of pain and sorrow. "For takeoff and landing, you cannot have your little one in it. She needs to sit on your lap then."

"Okay, good to know. You must have kids yourself to know so much?" Elisabeth's smile faded. "I assume you've traveled a lot with your little one or little ones to be aware of the bassinet and its rules."

Elisabeth stared at the young mom, then at the little baby girl in the bassinet. The baby looked up and caught Elisabeth's eyes, fixated those light-brown eyes of hers on Elisabeth and grinned a wide, toothless grin. Elisabeth's stare faded and her face softened as she waved to the little baby in the bassinet. For a moment she felt like she was there again, at that time twenty years ago. "Hallo, Süße. Hallo, meine Süße! Hallo, Moana!"

"Moana? No, her name is Ella."

Elisabeth looked at the mom again, shocked. She hadn't even noticed that she'd been talking to the baby out loud. *Oh my gosh!* She felt Sarah's hand touch her arm gently, but Elisabeth had already panicked. *I remember all those long flights back to Germany with Moana. The first time we went, she was about four months old, just like little Ella over there. I traveled with her so often to see family and friends back in Germany. My baby girl, my beautiful baby girl.*

"Moana? Is that your daughter?"

Elisabeth stared at the mom. A complete stranger had just used the name of her dead daughter! She couldn't bear it, couldn't stand that woman using her name.

"Very pretty name. How old is Moana now?"

Elisabeth could feel the tears forming in her eyes.

"I see she's not flying with you today, so I assume she must be grown up?"

What an annoying woman! Asking about my daughter. She has no right to use her name, no right to know anything. She needs to stop.

She felt Sarah's grip on her arm again, then heard her say, "Yes, she's all grown up."

The mom smiled at the two middle-aged ladies. "Wonderful. How old is she, if you don't mind me asking? And what does she do? I love hearing about kids growing up. It's so much work raising them and great to hear how they turn out."

How they turn out when they grow up? Elisabeth gasped and couldn't believe her ears. *They turn out missing. Dead, probably. They turn out to be gone or dead! No, no, my baby girl! Were you kidnapped? Are you still out there somewhere? Mama and Daddy are coming to look for you, mein Engel.*

She put her hand in the purse on her lap and felt it. The softness of the toy. The softness of the cuddle blanket. Enti. Her missing daughter's favorite toy. *Enti always calmed her down, always traveled with her on these long overseas flights.* Elisabeth had automatically put Enti into her purse without having to think about it. *Accessible. Accessible at all times. As if at any moment I expect to hear a little voice asking for her on this overseas flight.*

But there is no little voice. At least not for me. That little voice was silenced a long time ago. A very long time ago in the very place I'm flying to now. Oh my gosh! How could I have thought this was a good idea? It's not a good idea at all. I can't do it. I can't bear it.

"I would love to hear about your daughter Moana," the young woman next to Elisabeth said again.

All of a sudden, Elisabeth started yelling and screaming. "No! no! You have no right to hear about her! No, nein, nein, nein!"

The young woman looked up, shocked, as did the toddlers, the dad, and the rest of the passengers in the rows around them.

"Stop asking about her! Stop it!" Elisabeth pushed away Sarah's arm, grabbed Enti out of her purse, got up, and ran into the restroom. She locked the door and sank down onto the floor, holding Enti tight in her hands, looking at the old, faded toy with the wide stitched-on smile.

"Oh Enti. Oh Enti. What was I thinking? Everything reminds me of Moana. Everything. The plane, the bassinet, the airport. And now

I'm going back to the place where she was taken from me. I don't think I can handle it."

She sobbed and hugged Enti tight. She heard soft voices through the wall. *Probably Sarah, trying to save face for me yet again. I know I acted ridiculously. I did. It's not that young woman's fault at all. Yet I yelled at her. Yelled at her like a crazy lady, screamed at her even though she did nothing wrong. No mistake made. The only true mistake happened twenty years ago, when I left my daughter alone. Alone long enough to be kidnapped. That mistake ruined my life, back then and even now.*

Can I ever go back to normal, back to being a sane, happy person? Will it help if I see Brad and open up the case again? I'm not sure. The pain runs so deep, so deep in my chest. She had to clutch her chest to push the pain away. Enti helped her along.

A big red sign suddenly appeared over the lavatory door. *Return to your seat,* it read. The plane was ready to taxi away from the gate and take off. Take off into the unknown.

Can I handle it? Going back? Can I do it? She laughed a sad laugh. *Well, I assume I won't do it well. Just consider the embarrassing moment I just had. I can't even bear to hear my missing daughter's name. My dead daughter's name.*

Sitting there under the blinking red sign on the airplane's bathroom floor, she stared at Enti. *No! She's not dead! I know I was trying to convince myself of it to find closure, but now that Brad finally believes me, believes that she was kidnapped. . . .*

Maybe she's still alive?

Elisabeth stared at the old, soft, faded toy with its stitched-on smile. It seemed to encourage her. "We'll find out what happened, Enti. We will. On this trip, this time."

CHAPTER 47

"It's time, it's starting! Let's sit down. Get your cameras ready," Grace told the group, and they all took their seats in the black folding chairs that had been set up for visitors on this side of the auditorium. The rows in the middle were reserved for the cadets, while the stage occupied the far end.

The Heikinnens, Maria and her mom, Keisha, and Jim's parents had all found great seats close to the stage as well as the area where the cadets and soon-to-be second lieutenants would sit. Everyone chatted with one another to pass the time, and Maria was pleased her mamá and Grace were getting along great. They sat next to each other, with Emma on Martina's other side, followed by Maria. Keisha sat between Maria and Jim's mom. They leaned forward in their seats anxiously as the ceremony began.

The ceremony's speaker greeted the guests and asked them to stand. They all rose and watched as the cadets marched in with military music playing in the background.

"Oh my, they all look so alike," Keisha whispered to Maria as rows of cadets, all dressed in the same blues uniform, marched in.

"They sure do."

"I can't even make out Aaron. They're all wearing the same thing," Emma blurted out, and was shushed by her mom.

"Welcome to the military and their uniforms," Maria whispered to Emma. "You know, they are all *u-n-i-form*."

Emma grinned. "As long as you don't accidentally kiss the wrong guy in uniform, I could get used to this." The girls all giggled, then quickly quieted down when the national anthem started playing. They stood at attention, hands on their hearts, until the last soaring notes ended.

"Please take your seats," the speaker of the ceremony announced, and then introduced the detachment commander, a friendly-looking officer.

He took over the mic and started talking about the cadets' wonderful achievements, their hard work, and their dedication. Then, he honored the distinguished graduates, among them Nick, Jim, and Aaron. Their families clapped loudly and proudly. Then the commander announced the various commissioned group and had them stand in recognition: the fighter pilots, the navigators, the acquisition guys, the maintenance officers. Each group received a loud round of applause.

After his speech, the detachment commander asked the whole group to stand and take their official oaths. The sea of blue stood as one and each raised their right hand. The commander had them repeat after him: "I—state your name—do solemnly swear that I will support and defend the Constitution of the United States against all enemies, foreign and domestic. . . ."

And on they went. Hearing these young men and women in their blue uniform take their oaths made both Maria's and Aaron's moms cry. Maria herself felt uneasy. She wasn't sure why, but for some reason, a big knot formed in her throat. *It sounds so serious. Wars. Deployments. I don't want Aaron to go abroad to fight wars and face danger. I want him with me at all times. I suppose that's selfish of me.* She scolded herself quietly and glanced over at Keisha, who must have had similar thoughts. Maria could tell by the way her friend looked.

Suddenly, Keisha squeezed her hand. "It'll be okay. Those boys will be fine."

Maria looked at her friend and nodded. *At least I won't be alone if Aaron ever has to deploy somewhere overseas. There'll be other military spouses dealing with the same thing. That's comforting to know.*

After the oath, the cadets came up on the stage according to the groups they were being commissioned into. The pilots were first to go, so Jim was in that group. Navigators next. Keisha and Maria watched Nick go up and clapped for him as he pinned on his new rank of second lieutenant. It was distinguished by a single gold metal bar that went on both his hat and on each shoulder of his uniform. He then got to pick up his official commission certificate.

It took a while for each of the many cadets to come up, pin on their new ranks, and pick up their commission certificates, so Maria passed the time by scanning the room for their friend Brandy, but couldn't find her in all the rows of chairs set up.

Finally, it was the maintenance guys and Aaron's turn. They all got out their cell phones and took pictures of him as he pinned on his new rank, got his commissioning ceremony paper, and walked offstage. They cheered loudly the entire time.

After every single cadet had walked across the stage, the commander announced, "Ladies and gentleman, please stand and give a big round of applause to all of our second lieutenants!"

The crowd cheered and clapped. Aaron's parents hugged each other, then Grace hugged Martina while Emma and Maria did the same. They watched all the proud second lieutenants high-five each other and clap along.

"Now, please join us in reciting the poem, 'High Flight,'" the ceremony speaker, who had taken over the mic again, announced. A big screen came down and had the words projected onto it so everyone could join in the reading. The crowd recited the poem in unison.

"Thank you, ladies and gentlemen. Now please, keep looking at the screen for a little video commemorating our graduating officers."

It was the same video that Maria and Keisha had seen at the Air Force Ball weeks ago. It gave good insight into not only their hard work, training, and early mornings, but also the fun they all shared together as a team. The video reminded Maria and Keisha of that surprising moment when Aaron had proposed to Maria at the ball.

"Already seems like long ago, huh, girl?"

Maria looked at her friend and nodded. She glanced at her sparkling ring, then back to the video.

It ended with a photo of a group of young men smiling into the camera after a PT session. Among them were Aaron, Nick, and Jim. That photo froze on screen and the speaker announced, "Ladies and gentlemen, please welcome your fellow cadet commander who has a few words to share with his fellow Airmen. Please give us a round of applause for Second Lieutenant Aaron Heikinnen!"

Emma's mouth fell open and Aaron's parents looked confused. Martina threw her hands up in surprise. Keisha and Maria both clapped and cheered loudly as Aaron strode on stage.

"I'd be so nervous," Keisha whispered.

"I think he is, too. His walk is a bit timid."

Keisha giggled. "Nobody but his fiancée can see that. He looks pretty confident to me."

"It's all about the way it looks, isn't it?" Maria and Keisha grinned at each other and giggled.

Emma grabbed Maria's arm on the other side. "Did you know he was going to speak today? He didn't say a word to Mom, Dad, or me!"

"He wanted to surprise you." Maria grinned as Emma passed on the message right before Aaron started his speech.

"Ladies and Gentlemen, fellow classmates. Well, fellow Airmen and second lieutenants, I should say!" Cheers rose from the sea of blue. "We did it, guys, we did it!" More cheers. "After all those early mornings getting up to go run in the dark, do PT on the beach—and yes, do those sixty-seven push-ups in one minute while still being a bit hung over from the party the night before—we all managed to work hard enough to get to where we're at this moment. We just pinned on our first rank. The first bar. And this first bar is something to be proud of. It's like jumping your first hurdle. We all know the first hurdle always seems the highest and feels the hardest to overcome, but once you're past it, you've got momentum, you're moving along smoothly. All of us here today have jumped that first hurdle and are ready to start our careers!"

Applause. Maria glanced over at Aaron's parents. Jack Heikinnen seemed so very proud and his mom was holding a tissue to catch her tears. Her mamá was also dabbing her eyes, and Emma listened, fascinated.

"Over the last four years here at Embry-Riddle, we've gotten to know each other well, helped each other out in various trainings, worked together to reach the finish line—and I tell you, today, we have reached it. We are the newest addition to the Air Force! And though we may go our separate ways from here, we will all carry the same ideals wherever we go: new ideas, innovative ways of thinking, a passion to lead. We are the new generation, ready to make the world a better place!"

Cheers from the crowd. *Aaron is an amazingly good speaker. Humorous and sensitive. I'm so proud of him.* Maria kept listening.

"The world is waiting for us. Our new duty will take us to the four corners of the earth, but don't ever forget who gave us our wings— literally, of course—the wings to fly. It was our families, our guardians, our support system. Our friends and partners. Our detachment commanders and senior enlisted advisors. Please, second lieutenants, stand and give a round of applause to all those who gave us the wings to fly. To the moms and dads out there, to our brothers and sisters, our girlfriends and boyfriends, our fiancés and fian*cées*, our detachment here at Embry-Riddle—this applause is for you. It's our thank-you for having always supported us, for being there for us in good times and bad."

Big rounds of applause thundered from the sea of blue, the brand-new second lieutenants. Many turned to wave at their families encircling the stage. Even Maria was crying now, and Emma needed a tissue as well.

"Wow, girl, he's good," Keisha said as she dabbed at a tear in the corner of her eye. "You're a lucky girl." Maria could only nod.

"To our support system out there, please know that this is not the end, but the beginning. As we head out to explore the world and make it a better place, we still need that lift from you to keep us flying. That means you're not done yet! Keep the love and support coming to the Class of 2023, your new U.S. Air Force second lieutenants! Thank you, ladies and gentleman, and all the best to you, my fellow Airmen. Let's fly out into the wild blue yonder and show them what we can do."

Roaring applause greeted his closing words, and as Aaron walked offstage, the ceremonial speaker took the mic from him and said, "Ladies and Gentlemen, you heard Second Lieutenant Heikinnen! Let's send our men and women off in style. Please stand and join us in singing 'Into the Wild Blue Yonder.'"

Music swelled and the official Air Force song started playing. Most of the guests looked at each other in surprise, then Keisha pointed up at the words to the song, which were projected onto the giant screen for everyone to sing along. The brand-new second lieutenants were proudly and loudly singing the song, most of them in deep, out-of-tune voices, but they sure were having fun while the families tried to follow along.

Maria was singing as best as she could, watching the words on the screen intensely. The background showed an airplane zooming through the air. Maria's voice cracked. *Is that airplane in the background moving? Is it?*

She stared at it more closely as she sang along. *Don't think there's actually a video of a fighter jet playing. It's just words on a projector screen, right?* Suddenly, a white light appeared before her eyes. She closed them briefly, and when she opened them, she saw the fighter jet moving, the toy fighter jet.

CHAPTER 48

The little toy jet moved up and over her head, then came down again and zoomed around. Up and down, up and down. A man in a flight suit was singing, "Off we go, into the wild blue yonder, climbing high into the sun!" He kept singing as the toy jet flew around her. She giggled and reached for the jet, jumped as high as she could to get it.

Why is it so high up? And why is there a toy fighter jet flying around behind the words to the Air Force song? She tried to reach for it again and watched her little hand extend up high as the man in the flight suit turned around.

Who's that man?

"Daddy," she answered her own question, and giggled in a childish voice as he finished singing the Air Force song.

"Hey! Nothing will stop the U.S. Air Force!"

Daddy? It's my Daddy? In the Air Force? The toy airplane flew over her head and suddenly landed atop her tiny hand.

"Here you go, little pumpkin, a gift from Daddy." She wasn't sure what was happening. "To always think of me," she heard the man say, "even when I go off into the wild blue yonder." He started singing again.

No, no, it can't be! Daddy in the Air Force? In a flight suit? Singing the Air Force song? She was so confused, but before she could make sense of it, she heard the drums of the song stop, and everything went black around her.

"Maria? Maria? Are you okay?"

Her head was being held. *Where am I?*

"Mija," she heard a quiet, concerned voice say. She quickly opened her eyes and realized her head was in her mom's lap. Her mom was sitting on the dark floor. She looked around and saw Keisha, Emma, Grace, and Jack all looking down on her. She realized she was lying in front of a row of black folding chairs. *Oh my. Aaron's Air Force commission.*

Keisha bent down to help Maria sit up. "Are you okay, girl?"

"Yeah. Yeah, I think so. What happened?"

"You just went *boom, crash, down,* in the middle of the Air Force song," Emma explained with wild hand gestures.

"Luckily, Emma caught your head before you hit the ground," Martina said.

"Thank you, Emma. Thanks for catching me."

"Sure, sis! You're heavier than you look, though." Emma grinned then got elbowed by her mom, who looked at Maria.

"Are you sure you're okay?" Grace said, a worried look on her face.

Maria nodded, then got up, and felt fine. Her elbow hurt a bit, but she figured it was probably just a bruise. She must have hit it on a chair or the floor as she fell. She gently rubbed it but didn't say anything— the last thing she wanted right now was to worry anyone. She looked around. Strangers were gathered around the group, curiously watching the scene, some asking her if she was okay. After Maria assured the onlookers she was, they followed the rest of the crowd and left. Maria noticed the empty auditorium. "Oh my gosh! We missed the end of the ceremony? Because of me? Oh no!"

Jack stepped in. "No, Maria, we didn't miss anything. Please don't worry. You fainted right at the end of the Air Force song and then everyone was dismissed. They just marched out."

"I missed the march out?"

"There wasn't much to see," Emma said. "Just a bunch of blue uniforms lining up and marching out. You couldn't tell who was who in that sea of blue anyway." They all had to laugh at her comment.

"Well, let's go see our second lieutenants," Maria said, and grabbed her purse from under the chair.

Jack looked at her. "Are you sure you're okay?"

"Sí, yes, I'm fine. Definitely. Let's go see Aaron and Jim and the others."

Confidently, she led the charge, leading the group out so they couldn't see the fear on her face. She was confused, her thoughts troubled. *I fainted. Again. I never used to faint before. What's wrong with me? It all started with those strange dreams. Or are they memories?*

She turned and glanced at the screen. It still showed the final lyrics to the Air Force song as well as pictures of some fighter jets and other airplanes.

The planes were not flying, not in motion. It was a still picture.

The moving jet had been a toy. She had just had a waking dream. *A dream in the middle of the day while I'm awake? No way. It wasn't a dream, couldn't have been. It was too real. Something felt too real about it. Was it a memory, like Aaron thinks? I know he has a theory, know he's hiding something from me. Not sure what, but something. I need to talk to him. If he thinks these weird moments are memories, where did they come from? Memories of what?*

She shook her head, trying to shake off the troubling thoughts. The little hairs on her arms stood up as a big shudder ran down her spine.

CHAPTER 49

"**A**aron! Wow! Congratulations! We're so proud of you," Grace said as she fell around her son's neck and started crying.

Oh, they found him in the crowd, Maria just noticed. She had been too deep in thought, but seeing Aaron made her snap out of it. His parents and sister were busy congratulating him, oooing and aahing over the shiny golden bar on his shoulders and hat that were symbolic of the rank of second lieutenant. Maria's mom also hugged Aaron and had to stand on tippy-toes to reach his shoulders. Then it was Maria's turn to congratulate him, and she hugged him tightly and whispered, "I loved your speech and so did everyone else. And I promise to be there for you to make you fly."

"Thanks," Aaron whispered back, and smiled the biggest smile. He gave her a kiss and was looking into her wonderful exotic eyes when he saw it. *Something's wrong. Her eyes are a lot more greenish than normal, definitely more so than when I last saw them before the ceremony.* "Are you okay, Maria?"

"Yeah, I'm fine. Why?"

"I know something's up. I can tell by your eyes," he said.

She smiled a weak smile. "Guess you can see right into my soul, huh?"

He nodded. "So, what is it?"

She hesitated to tell him, but then Emma, who was eavesdropping on their conversation, said, "Oh, she just *fainted.*"

"You *what?*" Aaron looked at Maria, then at his family members.

"She suddenly fainted, but seems to be okay now," his mom explained.

"We made sure to check everything," Jack said. "No injury. She's good."

"When did you faint?" Aaron said.

"In the middle of the Air Force song," Emma answered for Maria. "She just crashed down next to me, but I half-caught her. Couldn't totally catch her. Too heavy."

"Did you hurt yourself?"

"No, Aaron, I'm fine. Please don't worry. I'm totally fine."

He looked around and everyone nodded, including Maria's mom. "She never fainted before," Martina said. "Maybe just too much going on, not enough to drink or eat?"

"No kidding. I'm hungry," Emma said.

"Oh, that reminds me." Martina searched her purse. "I brought these Venezuelan goodies for all of you. Freshly baked."

She handed each of them a small bag, and then a beautifully wrapped gift to Aaron. "Here, Aaron. This is for you. Also handmade. Congratulations, and I hope you like it!" She smiled.

Aaron looked at her and mumbled, "Thank you." He was still worried about Maria. *I know better. She's fainted before. Twice. After reliving those strange memories. Memories of her early childhood. Her very early childhood, without Martina. Did she just have another one of those strange memories? I have to talk to her in private, but there's no way to do that right now.*

People were bustling and hustling around them, congratulating each other. People coming and going, exchanging gifts. Before Aaron could even get to opening Martina's gift, a bunch of the other newly commissioned second lieutenants came over to congratulate him and introduce him to their families, who all told him how much they had enjoyed his speech.

Maria stepped aside, took her mom's gift, and put it in her purse so Aaron could enjoy all the attention he was getting. She stood next to her mamá, who put an arm around her and leaned in, whispering to her in their native language that she had made a great catch with Aaron. They enjoyed the scene playing out before them and just stood there, arm in arm, content to be together.

Someone tapped Maria on the shoulder. "Hey y'all, how ya doing?"

Maria knew who it was before she even turned around. "Hey Brandy, there you are. I've been looking all over for you. Couldn't even see you in the crowd."

"Ha, you missed this fabulous belle? Unbelievable."

Maria had to grin. Brandy sure did look fabulous, though. Her baby-blue dress brought out her blue eyes and stood in perfect contrast to her tan skin and blonde hair. Nick was right next to her along with his parents. They all introduced one another.

Maria's mom handed Nick his bag of goodies, and he was so excited that both he and Brandy tried the pastries right away. "Mmmh. . . . This is delicious," they both told Martina. Their enjoyment made her glow with happiness. So of course Emma had to try hers also, and agreed with them on how good it tasted.

"How come you got one, Emma? I thought I got this gift because Mrs. Sullivan is using my room," Nick pouted.

"I got a bag because I'm going to be Maria's sister—that's even more important than a *room*. I'll be her roommate for life!"

They all laughed, but Martina felt bad and took Nick aside. "I have more in the car. Big bag. I'll give you more, if you want."

"Sounds great," he whispered back.

They kept talking and talking until Jack interrupted them and said, "Sorry, everyone, but it's time to go. Aaron has a lunch date with his family and soon-to-be mother-in-law."

The friends said their goodbyes, congratulated each other again while taking a few last photos, then went their separate ways.

Aaron was walking hand in hand with Maria when he whispered in her ear, "You know I haven't forgotten about the fainting episode. I still want to hear all about it."

She leaned her head on his shoulder. She could feel the cool metal of his new rank against her skin. "I know. I'll tell you later. Not now."

"Was it what I think it was? Another strange occurrence, a dream, a memory—whatever you want to call it?"

Maria nodded. "I think so. But you know how it is—I'm not sure what any of this means."

As soon as she said that, she had that strange feeling again. The little hairs on her arms stood up, and a cold shudder ran down her spine.

Aaron noticed. "Okay, fine. Let's talk later. We should focus on celebrating. And eating. I'm starving!"

Maria grinned. "Me, too. Let me drive with Mamá, okay?"

"Okay. But you know you're my passenger now, right? For life!"

She smiled her biggest smile at him. "You're good with words, Second Lieutenant Heikinnen!"

Aaron smirked. *Yeah, I am. I'm pretty clever, but not clever enough to figure out what lies in Maria's past. I have pieces, but not the big picture. It's all so confusing.* His smirk disappeared from his lips as his face took on a determined look. *But I'm going to find out.*

Aaron was quiet as they sat at a big round table by a window overlooking the ocean at the Hyde Park Prime Steakhouse. They ordered their food and then Jack stood up and gave a little speech. Aaron looked up just in time to listen. "This toast goes to our son Aaron, who worked so hard to get to where he is now. Aaron, we are so proud of you, and wish you all the best for your career in the military."

"Cheers to that," everyone said, and raised their champagne glasses.

"In addition," Jack continued, "I would also like to thank Maria for her support. We've not just heard all about her support, we've seen it with our own eyes. She was there to help Aaron get ready for PT every morning, help quiz him for his exams, lifted him up whenever he needed a helping hand to do so. Every Airman needs a wingman, and Aaron has chosen his—a wing*woman*, as he has called it. Maria, thank you for everything you've done for our son, and for being willing to stick with him for life as his wife-to-be. Cheers to Aaron and Maria!"

"Cheers!" everyone cried.

Aaron looked at Maria. She was stunned. With the clinging of glasses, a tear ran down her face. He looked over to Martina, whose face was covered in tears, then at Grace, who also had watery eyes. Their glasses were clinking and they finally took a sip. Aaron gave Maria a kiss, and Emma happily gloated next to the young couple.

"To my soon-to-be sis-in-law," Emma said, and lifted up her glass of Sprite.

"Cheers," they all said again, clanging glasses, and took another sip.

Maria's mom took the next word and encouraged Aaron to open his gift from her. "It will fit the toast we are enjoying perfectly." She smiled and winked at him.

Maria searched for the gift inside her purse, took it out, and handed it to Aaron. He looked at the beautifully wrapped gift in Air Force blue with a golden ribbon.

"Open it!" Emma encouraged her brother.

He carefully started to open the fancy wrapping paper and kept everyone in suspense. A golden picture frame emerged. Both Aaron and Maria looked at it in amazement.

"Martina, this is beautiful," Aaron said, "Thank you. What a special gift." He passed it to his parents.

"Wow," Jack said. "This is real art. Made with love for sure."

"I love it!" Grace started dabbing her eyes again.

Martina smiled as they passed the golden picture frame to Emma.

"Wow," she exclaimed. "You made that? How?"

"I *stitched* it," Maria's mom said.

The picture frame held a blue cloth with the words "Air Force Commission to Second Lieutenant" and the date stitched in gold, and a golden bar signifying his rank on the left-hand side. To the right was a perfectly stitched portrait of Maria and Aaron, and the words, *Maria and Aaron, flying together for life.*

"How can you stitch like that?" Emma asked in amazement. "It looks like a real-life picture."

"Well, I used an actual picture of the two of them as a template," Martina explained as Emma handed the frame back to Aaron and Maria.

They looked at it more closely. It was full of details, made perfectly out of Air Force colors and the golden color of Aaron's new rank.

It must have taken hours. I have to thank her. Aaron got up and walked around the table to give Martina a hug.

"Take good care of my Maria," she whispered in his ear.

Aaron nodded and smiled. Then his smile faded. "I will, no worries," he said, and it came out rather coldly. He turned around and walked back to the table.

I just know she's hiding something. Something big. If my assumption is right, she's not really a loving mom who raised Maria all by herself. She isn't just protective of Maria, she's protecting something else. Her secret. If I'm right, she's a criminal, not a loving mom.

"Gracias, Mamá, me encanta," he heard Maria say, and saw tears dripping down her face.

Oh, Maria, what's your mom's secret? Your secret? He sat down, deep in thought.

"Yes, gracias, Martina," Grace now said in broken Spanish, and raised her glass. "To our two families. Wing families for life. Cheers."

Aaron almost choked on his champagne as everyone happily clinked glasses together. The women used tissues to wipe away their tears of happiness. Aaron couldn't help but frown. He quietly sipped on his champagne. *Who is Martina Sullivan? Do we want her in our lives?*

"How do I look? Is it bad?" Maria asked Aaron, ripping him away from his brooding thoughts. She pointed at her face.

He looked her over and forgot his worries for a second. He smirked. "Well, you probably should've worn waterproof mascara. You're beautiful regardless, though."

Maria just rolled her eyes. "Thanks. But I better go fix my face. To look even better for my second lieutenant." Aaron laughed as Maria asked to be excused.

She got up and left the table to look for the restroom.

"¡Maria, espérame!" Martina called after her. Maria turned around and waited for her mom. The two of them walked to the ladies' room together, chattering away in Spanish.

CHAPTER 50

I wish I knew Spanish. Jonathan Sullivan watched them walk away and got up from the small table in the corner where he had been sitting, watching the group. They were so wrapped up in their own chitchat that nobody had noticed him. Surprising, given he didn't really fit in. He wasn't dressed in a fancy suit, but the restaurant had let him in anyway.

This fancy restaurant. Probably embarrassed by a customer like me. No wonder they stuck me in the corner behind the plant. I fucking hate stuck-up people.

He frowned, then smiled. *But it worked out perfectly. A perfect hiding spot to watch the group at the big round table overlooking the water. So carefree.* He grinned as he carefully followed Martina and her problem child. He slipped into the men's room before they opened the door to the ladies' room. Nobody was inside using the men's facilities, so he just stood by the door, listening. Luckily, both mom and daughter talked loudly. But then his luck ran dry.

Fuck! All Spanish. I don't understand a single word. You better not tell her anything or you'll be in big trouble, Martina.

CHAPTER 51

Martina and Maria stood in front of the giant mirror in the restroom, touching up their makeup and chatting away in their native language.

"¿Estás seguro que estás bien? I'm worried about you, mija. You've never fainted before in your life. Not even as a child or teenager. It's very out of character." Martina looked at her daughter, who kept assuring her she was fine. "I just don't understand why you fainted. You've never done that before, mija."

"Mamá, I'm fine. Let's not talk about it now, okay?"

"Just tell me, mija. I'm worried about you and that fainting."

Maria's face turned red. "Enough, Mamá. I said let's not talk about it anymore. But fine, if you want to keep talking about it, fine then. Then you should know this has actually happened before, Mamá."

"It has? You fainted before? When?"

"I don't know. A few days ago, and then again another time before that," Maria told her, looking at her mom through the mirror, her face flushed.

"¡Naguará! ¿Estás embarazada?"

Maria turned away from the mirror and now stared at her directly. "No, Mamá, I'm not pregnant! Why would you even think that?"

"The fainting, sometimes your blood pressure changes when you're pregnant. So, you can faint if you are not careful. Oh, but Maria, it would be fine. You know I'd be excited."

Maria rolled her eyes. "I know, Mamá. But I'm definitely not pregnant. And don't get your hopes up, I'm not planning on having kids anytime soon. I want to enjoy life with only Aaron at first. Work, travel with him wherever the military takes him, and then—"

"But why do you keep *fainting* then? Are you sure you're not pregnant?"

"Yes, I am sure, Mamá! The fainting has nothing to do with that."

"With what then?"

"I don't know, Mamá. Please, let's just forget about it."

"But I *am* worried, mija. So worried for you. I just need to know you're okay. What do you think causes the fainting?"

"Please, Mamá. Let's not talk about that now."

"Maria, you can tell me. You can always tell your mamá everything. What is it, mija?"

"Mamá, for the last time, I don't want to talk about it right now—"

"Maria, *please*! You can tell me everything. And we will figure it out together."

"Oh, we will?" Maria stared at her mom, her eyes changing to a bright green.

Martina realized her daughter was getting upset and agitated for some reason. "I'm just trying to find out if you're okay and why you are fainting so much all of the sudden."

"Geez, Mamá, maybe because I keep having these strange dreams about my father, and now they're even happening in broad daylight, and it confuses me, hurts my head so much that I faint."

Martina stared at Maria. Her opened lipstick dropped onto the marble counter. *What did she just say? Strange dreams about her dad? She has to bring that up now? Here? Seriously? Thought she stopped researching.*

Stopped looking for her dad. Had bought into the Jonathan Smith story. But now she blames her fainting on this? No way! That's ridiculous!

Martina's eyes got smaller, her cheeks red. "Maria, why are you doing this now? Why would you bring up your father now, on this special day?"

Maria stared back at her mom. "Because you *asked me* for the reason why I'm fainting. You wouldn't let go! So I'm telling you, it has something to do with my father. I'm sure. I keep seeing things in broad daylight, and it's always about a man in uniform that I think is my dad."

"'A man in uniform?'" Martina repeated, her voice shrill. *How can this be? I know that can't be true. Has my fake story about Jonathan Smith confused Maria so much? Has it convinced her of something that isn't even true? That couldn't be true?* Her hands now started shaking. *I can't take back what I have told her. It's too dangerous, too dangerous for both of us. I have to protect her. And myself. I have to stick to that story.*

"So, Mamá, it's my turn to ask now: what aren't you telling me?" Maria took two steps toward her, was right in front of her now, staring at her.

Martina tried to withstand that stare, tried to be strong, tried to hold on. "Maria, I *told you* about your biological dad."

"But that's not all of it, is it? I can see it in your face, Mamá!"

Martina didn't know what to say. She wanted to hug her daughter and tell her she couldn't tell her and that she needed her to stop because it was too dangerous, but she knew that wouldn't help. *Maria will just keep asking about the danger. And he'll come back and hurt her, hurt us both. I know what he's capable of. I can't tell her the truth. It would shatter Maria's innocence, shatter her whole world. Can't do that. She needs to be my daughter. Only mine.*

She stared at the beautiful young woman before her in the golden dress with the wavy reddish-brown hair, wonderful curved lips, straight freckled nose, exotic eyes, and tall, slender figure.

She looks nothing like me at all, even more so than when she was a child. The child that showed up in my life so suddenly, so unexpectedly, so afraid. So broken and afraid. I gave her all my love. I built her up. Saw that scared little toddler grow into this confident, beautiful young woman who calls me Mamá.

I need it to stay that way! It's too late now to ask questions. I didn't ask any questions back twenty years ago, and I can't do it now. It's too late. Too late to know what happened to Maria's real mom. She shuddered at the thought of that. *I should've gone to the police. Should've been less selfish. But it's too late now. Definitely too late to undo the genuine mistake I made twenty years ago. Too late to undo the lie that everyone knows as Maria's life.*

CHAPTER 52

"Fine, don't talk then. Just keep watching me faint!" Maria packed up her purse and left her mom standing there in front of the mirror in the fancy restroom. She stormed out the door and almost ran into Grace Heikinnen.

"Oh, excuse me, Maria," Grace said and smiled at her. Maria looked at her with her wild green eyes. Grace was taken aback. "Are you okay?"

"Yeah, I'm fine." Maria maneuvered around her to walk back to the table.

Grace watched her walk away then pushed open the door to the restroom. There she found Martina standing in front of the bathroom mirror, her hands clearly shaking.

"Martina, are you okay?" Grace looked at the small, round, sweet little lady with the bouncy brown curls. She was white as a ghost. Grace took the woman's hands in support. "Is it about Maria?"

Martina looked straight back into the tall woman's eyes. *Grace Heikinnen. She definitely looks Swedish. Fair skin, blue eyes, long blonde hair.* Martina knew that the Heikinnens had Swedish ancestors on both sides of the family. *Another tall woman. I'm not tall. Maria is. Average height, but too tall for a Latina. Maria's brown hair and beautiful tan has always let me get away with the Latina heritage lie. But her real mom must be of European descent. Definitely not Hispanic.*

Maria's real mom. It's here again. The doubt. The feeling of being second best. I raised that girl. I made her what she is today.

"Did you have a fight?" Martina heard Grace and realized she had to snap out of it. It was bad enough that Maria had confronted her then stormed out of the restroom. The last thing she wanted was for Grace Heikinnen to storm out as well.

She needed a good, logical explanation. A quick one.

She nodded to buy herself some time.

"What happened?"

"Well, I guess she got mad at me for asking about her fainting spells again," Martina said, hoping Grace would be easily fooled by her story. "Well, I might have overstepped her boundaries."

"What do you mean?"

"When she told me she had fainted a few times lately, I told her there must be a specific reason. And I may have hinted at something that made her pretty upset with me."

"What was that?"

"I asked if she was pregnant," Martina said, and looked directly at Aaron's mom.

Grace let go of Martina's hand and brought both hands up to her mouth. "Oh my," she just said, shocked. "*That* wouldn't be good. Out of wedlock. No, that wouldn't be good at all." Now Grace started pacing back in forth in front of the large mirror with its beautiful, fancy marble countertop.

Martina watched the tall lady pace for a bit, then stopped her by gently grabbing her arm. "Grace, no worries. I raised her, so she knows I would never disown her if she got pregnant that way. She knows she can approach me with the truth. But she also knows that it's not fun to raise a child by yourself, not have a stable family. She knows because that's what she grew up with. A single mom, no dad."

Grace nodded. The color had left her face. "I don't think she needs to worry about that. We taught Aaron he would always be responsible for his own actions and needed to know that a child is binding for life."

Martina nodded. "They are engaged, about to be married. They're responsible kids. Well, don't worry, though—she's not pregnant!"

Grace exhaled deeply and looked relieved. "Oh, good, good." She smiled at Martina. "But then why did she storm out?"

"Because she got mad at me for even suggesting she was pregnant. She's always told me she'd finish college first and get married before having any kids. She thought I didn't trust her and got mad at me. You know, the mother-daughter fights. . . . They are exhausting."

Grace nodded. "Yeah, tell me about it. I thought Aaron was a tough teenager—until his sister hit her teens! Oh my, that Emma drives me nuts sometimes. But Maria seems so responsible. A real fine young woman."

"Thank you." Martina smiled. "But she's still my stubborn daughter, that much won't change."

The two moms laughed together and finished reapplying their makeup while chatting happily about the ups and downs of having a daughter. Martina smiled. *This conversation sure went well.*

CHAPTER 53

Her face flushed, Maria returned to the table, picked up a menu, and started studying it, hiding behind the tall slice of cardstock. Neither Jack nor Emma noticed her strange behavior, but Aaron did.

"You okay?"

"Let's just order," was Maria's short reply.

"Well, we can't until our moms get back. So, why don't you tell me why you're so mad?"

She took her eyes off the menu and looked at him. There they were again, those agitated green eyes he knew so well. He just couldn't put off talking to her any longer, he knew that.

"Hey Emma and Dad, can I steal Maria away for a minute? I just want to show her the ocean view for a second." He didn't wait for their consent. He got up and took Maria by the hand.

Emma looked confused. "We're right *by* a window. Wow, there's the ocean. What other view do you need?"

Jack smiled. "Let them go."

"Don't take too long! I'm hungry," Emma called after Aaron and Maria, who were walking toward the sunny patio right next to the ocean.

Once they were outside on the patio with the glass sliding doors closed behind them, Aaron urged her to tell him about everything that had happened. Words just tumbled out of Maria as she stood there in the sun by the beach, her golden dress billowing in the breeze. Aaron kept his hand on his head so his Air Force hat wouldn't blow off. He had to wear it with the uniform when outside of a building regardless of the weather. Air Force rules.

Once Maria finally paused for breath, he said, "It's nothing new that your mom doesn't want to talk about your biological dad. We knew that already, Maria."

She nodded. "But why not? I don't get it. If Jonathan Smith came back to visit when I was little, why wouldn't she want me to know about it? He must be the guy in uniform that I keep seeing in my dreams."

Aaron looked at her. *That's what you think then. Guess I'll keep it at that for now. The truth would be too unbearable. My theory would rock your boat, your life, your whole existence. I have to wait, have to do more research. Need proof. I'll get official proof on Monday, I bet. Special Agent Barrett will give me proof. Then we can confront Martina.*

But not now.

"Aaron?"

"What?" He hadn't been paying attention.

"I really think my dad was in the Air Force, Aaron. Same blue uniform as you, the flight suit, the toy plane he gave me. Or was he in the Special Forces, like Mamá said?"

Aaron looked at her. "Special Forces wear a different uniform. They do fly jets, though."

"Am I mixing up your uniform with the one in my dreams, then?"

He shrugged. *No, you aren't. You're just mixing up who's your real dad. And real mom.*

"Or do you think this Jonathan Smith guy fooled Mamá and lied about the real military branch he was in? Did he just lie to her?" She started pacing back and forth. "He just used her, didn't he? Lied to her. Don't you think so? I know you have a theory, don't you? What do you think? Tell me!"

He shrugged again, suppressing the urge to scream that he thought Jonathan Smith didn't even exist. Had never existed. Wanted to tell her that her mom was the one lying to her, that she had fabricated the whole story to hide something else. *To hide your family. Your real family, your real mom and dad. How can I tell you that? It would shatter you. Shatter you like a mirror, break you into a thousand pieces.*

"Aaron, come on, talk to me. I know you have a theory. Please, tell me."

He looked at her, his heart heavy. "Maria. . . ." he said, looking for words. "Yeah . . . I concluded that your real dad must have been in the Air Force. Not sure if your mom knows about it." *At least that's not a lie. Martina seemed genuinely shocked to hear Maria's claim that her dad was in the Air Force. But why? What is she hiding?*

He saw Maria looking at him suspiciously. "Yes, I think your mom might be hiding something more. Not sure what. But please, let's just wait to confront her later. Not this weekend. This weekend is about commission and graduation. Having fun with family and friends. Having fun before I start my new job. Let's wait until after we're at Eglin, okay?"

Eglin. Eglin Air Force Base. Just mentioning that word made Maria shudder. The little hairs on her arms were standing up again. Aaron noticed and looked at her as she stared into the distance at the ocean, the waves rolling in, the sandy beach. The ocean breeze felt nice, the air smelled salty. It was beautiful here.

She sighed. "I know, you're right, Aaron. We need to enjoy this. Let's just go back in." She took his hand.

Suddenly, a big gust of wind blew over them, accompanied by the thundering of waves crashing behind them. "Oh no, my hat."

Aaron let go of Maria's hand to run past her after his Air Force hat that had been blown away in the ocean breeze. She turned around and saw the hat flying through the air.

"Oh no," she heard again. The sun was so bright that she had to close her eyes for a second, and when she opened them again, she found herself in a long-lost time.

"Oh no, we need to catch the hat," she heard a woman say.

She looked up and saw the hat hanging up there in the sky, a man in a blue uniform running after it down the beach. The sand seemed whiter than before. It wasn't golden-yellow but almost snow-white.

Strange.

"Come on, let's help him catch the hat," she heard the woman say, and it seemed as if she was talking to her.

Who is that woman? She looked down at her feet and saw her pink plaid dress. *Wait, what? Pink dress? My dress is golden. Like Aaron's rank.*

She ran with the woman but didn't make it far. She looked at the man running after the hat. *Is that Aaron?* She tried to run faster.

"Wait for me, wait for me," she yelled into the wind. It was actually stormy now. *Where did this storm come from?*

"Let's go, let's catch Daddy's hat," she heard the woman say.

Whose hat? Daddy's? No, no, it's Aaron's, not Daddy's. Not Daddy's!

She looked down and saw her little feet running, looked at her small hands and saw them reaching up into the air. *Little hands and feet?* Yes, sure enough, she was little again. So small. Running after an Air Force hat flying in the wind.

"Got it," she heard the man say as he jumped and caught it out of the air. Then he came running over to her. "Got it, Daddy got it! Here's Daddy's hat. Naughty hat!"

She giggled as he put the hat on her head. It was way too big and slipped over her eyes, making the world go dark, and she felt so alone, so alone drowning in that big hat, gulping down water again, more and more until it all faded away.. . . .

"Maria," a strong male voice said.

She opened her eyes and found herself in Aaron's arms, who was having a hard time holding her up while keeping his balance. They were standing awkwardly on the sunny patio by the beach. Well, Aaron was standing, desperately trying to hold her up—she was half-standing, half-laying in his arms, her legs solid as Jell-O.

Aaron looked at her. Her eyelids fluttered, then she opened her eyes once more and returned his gaze, confused.

"What happened?" she said.

Aaron examined her eyes. They were now calm, back to brown, though with a sad look to them.

"Did I faint again?"

Aaron only nodded, his throat dry. *Twice in one day. What in the world is going on? What is she remembering?* "I was running after my hat when. . . ." He started his explanation, then immediately stopped when he saw her panicked eyes change to a bright green.

"Maria, look at me."

She did as she was told and noticed his Air Force hat was back on his head where it belonged. She looked into his calm, ocean-blue eyes.

"What did you see?"

She thought for a bit, then told him about the strange moment she'd had a minute ago. She remembered it all very clearly. Her mouth felt so dry. "Aaron, I keep having these weird dreams. Daydreams or something. . . ."

"Memories," he mumbled. "You said there was a woman chasing the hat. Did you see the woman's face? Did you see her face? Who was it?"

Maria shrugged her shoulders.

"Your mom?"

Maria looked at him and thought for a moment, then shook her head. "I don't think so. She was taller, much taller than Mamá. But I couldn't see her face. I don't think I know that woman."

Aaron just nodded. *You don't. You don't know her because you were taken from her somehow. But you remember her. You remember them both. Your family.*

His thoughts kept swirling round and round in his head. *I have to stay calm. Have to look over those articles again. The articles that mention the couple at Eglin whose daughter drowned. The Collins.*

Brad Collins. General Brad Collins. He deserves to know his daughter didn't drown. She's right here. At least I think she's right here. He looked at Maria, his blue eyes anything but calm.

"Aaron, are you okay? You look pale. Shocked. What's going on?"

He cleared his throat. "I'm just worried about you," he whispered, and then hugged her.

"I'm so sorry, Aaron. I am. I feel stupid, I feel like I'm ruining your life."

He shook his head, his eyes resting on her. "No, you're not. You're the love of my life. You've always been there for me, and now it's my turn to be there for you. To find out what all of this means. We'll find out what happened."

She looked at him, silent tears running down her face. Aaron took her chin and pulled her in for a nice, long kiss. It made both of them forget their sorrow, their worries, the world around them. Within that kiss, it was only the two of them, right here, right now, on the sunny patio on the beach.

Until they felt a tug on their arms. It was Emma. "Come on guys. You can make out later. We're all hungry. Let's order some chow!"

Aaron and Maria looked at Emma and smiled. Annoying younger sister to both of them soon. They followed her inside together, hand in hand, ready to take on anything that was thrown their way.

CHAPTER 54

"Aaron?" He looked up. Everyone had already gotten up from the table and was ready to leave the restaurant.

"You've been unusually quiet today."

Aaron looked at his dad and just nodded.

"Well, I understand. It's a lot to take in. Graduating, commissioning into the Air Force, starting your first job. Just know I'm proud of you, son."

"Yeah," Aaron just said and got up as well. "I appreciate that. And thanks for the wonderful lunch, Dad!"

"You're welcome, my pleasure."

Everyone else thanked Jack for lunch and then they left the restaurant. It was a beautiful, warm, sunny Florida day out.

"Let's go swimming," Emma blurted out. "It's so hot today!"

"It sure is warmer here than in Montana," Grace said, fanning her face. "And so humid!"

Martina grinned. "Always humid in Florida."

"Exactly, so let's go swimming," Emma said again.

They all looked at each other. "Okay, sure, why not take a dip in the ocean since we're here in Florida." Jack said. "Is that okay with our new second lieutenant?"

Aaron looked at his dad, then at the others. Emma nodded with a big grin on her face. "Come on, big bro, gotta enjoy the waves before work washes you away, right?"

He had to laugh. "Sure, sis, let's do it."

"Yay!" Emma gave him a big hug.

"Well, I suggest going back to get changed and ready, then meeting back on the beach for a little dip in the ocean—for those who want to. For those who don't want to get wet, just lounging around on the beach might be fun. How does that sound?"

Everyone nodded. "Sí, sounds great," Martina said. "Who's riding with whom?"

"I suggest we split up by apartment," Jack said. "Aaron, you can drive with Maria and her mom back to your place, and I'll drive Emma and Grace back to Maria's apartment. Okay?"

Everyone nodded.

"Okay, vamos," Martina said, and led the way to her car. She got in behind the wheel, with Maria up front and Aaron in the back. They started driving.

"That was wonderful. It was so nice to finally meet your family, Aaron!"

Aaron just nodded.

"Your mom and I had a great time talking to each other. She's great. I can see where your kindness and caring comes from."

Another nod.

Strange. He's being very quiet. "And your dad is wonderful, too. You look a lot like him."

Another nod.

Why doesn't Aaron say anything? He's usually a very friendly, chatty person. "You have a lot of your mom in you too, though. Her beautiful blue eyes for sure. You can definitely see that you guys are family," Martina said.

She gushed on and on as she drove, but Aaron only nodded and stared out the window. She watched him through the rearview mirror.

Why is he acting so strange? Why won't he talk to me? "*Right*, Aaron?" She now spoke to him directly, demanding an acknowledgment. But nothing. He said nothing.

"I bet people tell you guys all the time how lovely a family you look. And all so alike," she went on. "Don't people say that, Aaron?"

He pointedly ignored her. *I don't want to talk to her right now. Don't know what to say. Have to hold back, not be mean or say something rude—not yet. Can't even look her in the eyes anymore. What has she done? What is she hiding? Is she actually a criminal?* He stared out the window and heard Martina say "right, Aaron?" for the hundredth time and finally realized she needed confirmation, more than a nod.

"Yeah," he just said, and kept staring outside.

"Incredible how much alike you and your dad look."

Aaron was getting annoyed. *Yes, I know that. She's made that point the last five minutes straight. I need her to stop. Stop! Why doesn't Maria say anything?*

He looked over to the passenger seat. Maria was also staring out of her window, deep in thought herself. What an awkward drive! Martina went on and on about Aaron's wonderful family and how much they had in common and looked alike.

Finally, he couldn't take it anymore. "Yes, incredible how DNA works and how certain traits are passed down to the biological child. How funny! Of course, that's why children look *so much like their parents*," he blurted out in a deep voice that made Martina shudder.

What in the world is wrong with him? Martina had not seen Aaron this moody before. "Yes, funny, the DNA.. . . ." she said, her voice faltering. Maria didn't say a word. Martina glanced over at her and caught her daughter just staring out of the window.

"And funny how you and Maria look *nothing* alike," she suddenly heard Aaron roar in that dark voice. "Wonder what DNA has to do with that?"

What? Martina's hands slipped a little from the steering wheel.

Suddenly, Maria turned around and stared at Aaron in the back seat. Her eyes were green again, the blue ring around them shiny. In that instant he knew he'd gone too far. Maria was not happy, and her mom just stared straight ahead now in silence. Aaron became very interested in the passing landscape, wishing they would finally arrive.

"Just give me a sec to change out of my uniform," Aaron mumbled, and disappeared.

Maria ignored him. "Come on in, Mamá! Let me show you Nick's room. Bed is all made for you. And like I said, you can stay *two* nights, for sure."

Martina followed her daughter inside, her big duffel bag slung over her shoulder. She shook her head. *Nope, not after the way the two of them have just acted in the car, I'll only stay one night. Definitely not two. Not with them behaving like that! What in the world is wrong with them? Maria is always quiet and fainting, Aaron hostile and now shouting at me? What did I do to make him feel that way?*

Martina quietly unpacked her bag in Nick's room. She changed into shorts and a t-shirt to go to the beach with them. *I won't go swimming. Didn't even bring a suit. But this will do. And I can't wait to see Aaron's family again. Who knew they'd be the ones welcoming me so warmly, talking to me, spending time with me?* Martina let out a quick laugh. *I was afraid conversation with the Heikinnens would be awkward, but instead, it's Aaron I have trouble with.*

She had no idea why this was and kept thinking about it, until it dawned on her. *Maria's conversation with me in the restroom. Maria talked about seeing—no, daydreaming of her dad. A guy in uniform. I know Maria told Aaron about it. And Aaron is very suspicious of my Jonathan Smith story, even more so than Maria. Oh dear! What am I supposed to do? Definitely can't give them any more reason to be suspicious.*

Feeling determined, she grabbed her beach sun hat and walked out of Nick's room. "I'm ready, you guys," she called out to Maria and Aaron, who were in his room. "Let's go to the beach. ¡Vamos!"

Maria and Aaron stepped out in their swimsuits. Maria wore a cover-up dress over her bikini while Aaron was still looking for a beach shirt to put on. He was a good-looking, well-trained guy for sure. And Maria was just beautiful.

Martina smiled. *What a good-looking couple. They'll have beautiful children. Niños pequeños. Nietos. My grandchildren. And those grandchildren will be mine, legitimately. I won't mind sharing the grandbabies with Grace at all. Definitely want to be there when they're born. Finally get to hold a newborn, a baby. See that baby grow into a toddler. To see those first two years of life I missed with Maria. Won't miss it with my grandkids!*

I just need to leave a good impression on Aaron's family and ignore Maria and Aaron's cold shoulders.

"Vamos, guys," she said again, and headed out the door, determined.

CHAPTER 55

Jonathan Sullivan was sitting behind a palm tree in the park overlooking the beach, watching them. By now, he had figured out the situation, had recognized the young guy. *Her boyfriend or fiancé—or whatever he is. Doesn't matter so long as Martina doesn't say anything.*

When the group left the beach to head over to a little restaurant, he followed them again. *Perfect, I'm hungry again, too. And they don't even notice me at all.* He sat in a little booth in the back, close enough to overhear their conversation.

"No, Emma, you can't come with us to the Sky Rooftop Bar or the nightclub. You're fourteen. They wouldn't even let you in," the Aaron guy said.

The pretty little girl with the long blonde hair pouted.

"Aw, poor Emma. How about we make our fun together, niña pequiña?"

He saw the girl looking at Martina, still pouting. "Fun. Like what?"

"How about we go to the movies. There must be something good playing at the movie theater?" he heard Martina say.

Always the nice one, always the sweet one, that Martina. He kept listening to the conversation, then decided he knew what he had to do.

He sat in his truck in front of the Sky Rooftop Bar and waited for them to arrive. He saw the Aaron guy and "Problem Child," as he preferred to call her, arrive. Then Martina and that little girl with the blonde hair said goodbye to them. Probably to head off to the movies.

No need to go there. No, need to stay here and make sure Problem Child is kept in line. A bar is much more fun than the movies, anyway. Even though it would be best if I just watched a movie. He sighed, his heart heavy. *I was doing so well. Hadn't touched a drink in years. Now it's bad again. All because of Problem Child. Fuck! I had such a good life going on. Made a life for myself. Then* she *showed up at my store.* He sighed again and walked up the bar's stairs to find a good seat on top of the roof.

The whole night, he watched them partying, the boys downing one drink after the next. He kept himself in line and only drank a little. *Have to control myself. Somehow. Can't mess it up this time.* He sipped his beer, hiding behind another huge palm tree on the rooftop, sitting close to the group of three. *Problem Child, a pretty blonde, and a gorgeous black girl. Such pretty girls.* He tried not to think of how pretty they all were and listened closely. Luckily for him, they had to shout over the music to be heard.

"Don't they all look super handsome in the shirts we made for them?" he heard Problem Child ask.

"Yeah, girl, those boys look great in their matching '*We finally took off!*' t-shirts."

"To our handsome second lieutenants, y'all," the pretty blonde said, starting up a cheer as they clanged glasses.

"Unbelievable they're not gonna be at the same school as us next year," the gorgeous black woman said, and sighed. "They'll be so far away, huh, girls?" They all sighed in unison.

"And Aaron is leaving on Sunday already. Can you believe it, y'all?" the blonde said, and took a big gulp from her cocktail. The other two nodded.

Where is that Aaron guy going? he wondered, and kept listening closely.

The pretty young girls sat there on the bench overlooking the city; their talk regarding the boys seemed to have dampened the mood.

"Hey girls." One of the boyfriends came over and sat next to them in one of the cushiony chairs. "Don't we look fabulous in our new t-shirts?" The three pretty girls just nodded.

Now the Aaron guy came over with another friend. "Hey, what's going on here?"

"Not sure. I just told them how handsome we look in our shirts, but they all seem mopey." The boys all looked at each other.

"Oh dear, we gotta change that. Come on girls, it's time to party," one of them yelled, and raised his beer. They all said cheers, but the girls did not look much happier.

"What's going on? Why so sad?"

"'Cuz you're all leaving soon," the three girls said in unison.

"Come on, girls. We still have time. One more day. And don't forget: carpe diem. Enjoy every moment, here and now." The one pulled up the pretty blonde girl.

"Yeah, come on, Maria," the Aaron guy said, and pulled her up as well. "Let's enjoy the night. I know we're leaving for Eglin on Sunday, but you and your friends have to cheer up. And we know you love to dance.. . . ."

"Sooo. . . ." another of the boys continued, "Let's go to Razzles!"

As he watched the three boys leave with the three pretty girls, he had to hold on to his beer so it wouldn't slip out of his hand.

What the fuck did that Aaron guy say? Did he say Eglin? Does he mean Eglin AFB? He downed his beer in one big gulp. *Oh, fuck! I cannot let that happen! Will Problem Child remember anything when she's there? Will she? Nah, she was too young. Way too young. Or was she?*

He started sweating. *Fuck! Eglin AFB? You gotta be kidding me.*

He crushed the empty beer can with his bare hands and stood up. From the rooftop he saw the group had made it down the stairs and was walking down the street now, each one of the pretty girls in the arms of a boy. They walked across the street to a nightclub called Razzles.

He recalled his phone call with Bill. "*No, we don't have a problem. You do.*"

He grabbed onto the railing of the balcony until his knuckles turned white. *I have to make sure it turns out okay. Have to make sure I won't have a problem. I've built a good life for myself. Can't let anyone take it from me. Not now, after all these years.* He sighed. *Fuck! I should've just listened to them and finished it. Now the problem is back, haunting me.*

He let go of the railing and knew what he had to do. *Forget Martina. She's not an issue. I need to tail Problem Child.*

Silence her if I have to.

CHAPTER 56

Maria and Aaron returned late that night. Aaron had fallen asleep in the passenger seat—a sign he'd had a bit too much to drink. Maria smiled. *He deserves it. My brand-new second lieutenant.* Once the Uber brought them to Aaron's apartment, she shook him awake. "Come on, sleepyhead, we're home now."

Aaron opened his eyes. "Oh, okay. I'll be right in." He dozed back off.

Maria walked around the car to the passenger side and opened his door. "Nope. You're coming with me. Can't sleep in here, the driver's gotta go."

He sighed as Maria tugged on his sluggish form until he got out of the car. He made it into the apartment, managed to brush his teeth and put on his pajamas, then toppled onto the mattress on the floor in between all the packed boxes and passed out.

Maria was still using her makeup remover cloth in the bathroom when she peeked in on him. She shook her head. *He needs to hydrate, else he'll really suffer when he wakes in the morning.* She walked over to the kitchen to fill up two glasses of water. While she was filling up Aaron's glass, she heard a voice.

"Maria, mija?"

It startled her, but then she realized it was her mamá calling from Nick's room. Maria walked over to the door and poked her head in and smiled. "¿Sí, Mamá?" She couldn't see her, but she knew she was sitting up in her bed, looking at her. *Mamá has always done that whenever I've been out. And if she isn't there in person, she always texts or calls to make sure I'm home safely. Always there for me.* "Yes, Mamá, we're home safe and sound."

"¡Muy bien! Buenas noches," she heard her mom say. "Te amo."

"Te amo. Buenas noches, Mamá."

The moment the words left her mouth, her thinking went all fuzzy.

Buenas noches? I've said those words all my life. As long as I can remember. Why do they feel all wrong? Like not what I'm supposed to say.

She shook her head as if to shake off those weird thoughts and used her elbow to slowly shut her mom's bedroom door, then walked over to Aaron's room with the two water glasses in her hand. She managed to avoid bumping into the packed bins as she made her way toward the mattress on the floor. She found the bin they were using as their nightstand and put the glasses down. Her hands were all clammy and sweaty.

Maria laid down next to Aaron, who was snoring slightly. *Guys and their snoring. Not used to that. Didn't grow up with a guy snoring in my mom's apartment.* She let out a little laugh and gave Aaron a soft kiss on the cheek. He was in such a deep sleep that he didn't even notice.

"Buenas noches," she whispered, then winced. *Sounds so wrong, all wrong. As if it's not the right language for me.* She didn't want to think about it anymore and closed her eyes, ready to fall asleep, cuddled up closely with Aaron, who continued to snore slightly.

She opened her eyes and didn't know how long she had been asleep. She could still hear the slight snore, but it was bright out, the sun was shining.

She lifted her head off the broad shoulders she was cuddled up into, off the strong chest that moved up and down with every little snore. She smiled a big smile. She loved being cuddled up in his strong embrace, enjoyed hearing the slight snore of that big man.

Big man?

She looked up and realized it wasn't Aaron; it was an older man in a flight suit. Big black boots still on his feet.

"Daddy?" she heard her little voice whisper, as if she was asking herself the question. But instead, someone else answered.

"Shh . . . Daddy is asleep," a female voice called.

She turned her head to look in the direction the voice had come from, but the sun was shining too brightly and she could only see the silhouette of a tall, slender woman standing there. "You both were asleep on the couch," the woman said.

"Daddy?"

"Yes, you and Daddy." The woman came closer. "Come on, let Daddy sleep a bit longer. He had an early morning today. Let him nap some more."

She felt herself nod and put her little hands on his big chest. "Buenas noches."

No! That's not right at all.

"Good night, Daddy," she said instead. Yes, that sounds correct. Good night.

"Are you saying good night to Daddy?" she heard the woman say, and she nodded, smiling.

The woman laughed a soft laugh and as she came closer, and told her, "That's right, meine Süße, sag 'gute Nacht,' Daddy!"

Gute Nacht? Yes, that's right! It's "gute Nacht," not "buenas noches." It's "gute Nacht!"

The woman reached for her, but before she could get to her, the floor opened up and swallowed her. Her tiny body was swallowed in darkness. She tried to reach the woman in the bright sunlight, but her silhouette retreated further and further away as she kept saying "gute Nacht," and it got darker and darker around her. The snoring man on the couch disappeared.

No, wait, wait! Don't go! I just said "gute Nacht," not "goodbye." Good night, not goodbye!

But the dark hole in the ground did not relent, and her little body fell deeper and deeper until she was all wet again, wet and swallowing the muddy, murky water that surrounded her. Her parents were gone and she was swallowed up in darkness.

Good night, then, good night then.

Her eyes were getting heavy as her lungs stopped pumping oxygen into her little body. All she could feel was the wetness, the water. The water seeping into her lungs, swallowing her up. With her last strength, she whispered, "gute Nacht!" before the darkness took her.

CHAPTER 57

A loud scream woke him, followed by the squeaking of a door. Aaron sat up, completely sober. *Maria.* She was screaming next to him, screaming in her dreams. He started shaking her. "Maria, wake up!"

He looked up to see the silhouette of a small, round woman standing in the doorframe, talking rapidly a mix of Spanish and English. "Maria, are you okay? ¿Estás bien? Maria!"

Martina's hand fumbled along the wall and the overhead light turned on, blinding everyone. Maria opened her eyes. She squinted and mumbled, "So bright."

"Aaron, what is going on? Why is Maria screaming?"

"I don't know!"

Martina came over to the mattress to look at Maria. "¿Estás bien, Maria? Mija, fight back if anyone ever hurts you! ¿Entiendes eso?"

Maria nodded, then Martina looked at Aaron, her face stern. "Aaron, I truly hope you are not hurting Maria. I've never heard her scream like this before. What's going on?"

Aaron stared at Martina. *Did she just tell Maria to fight back if someone's hurting her? Me? Is she accusing me of hurting Maria? No way! I can't believe it.*

He jumped up, quickly, and stood face-to-face with Maria's mom. He bent over to look her in the face, straight into her eyes. His voice rumbled deeply as he said, "I would *never* hurt Maria. You know that. You're being unfair. What we should really be asking is, what have *you* done to *her*?"

"*Me*? What *I* have done to her? What are you talking about, Aaron? Who is the unfair one now?"

For a few minutes, they argued without even noticing Maria.

She was dumbfounded and watched her mamá and Aaron fighting, right there in front of the mattress on the floor. It finally became too much.

"Stop! Stop! Both of you," she yelled, and both Aaron and Martina stopped immediately and looked at her. "I just had a weird dream, a bad dream."

"Ha! I told you!" Aaron scolded Martina. "Told you that's what it was, and—"

"Another *nightmare*. The drowning dream."

Aaron and Martina looked at Maria. They both sat down, Aaron by her side, Martina at the end of the mattress. Martina found Maria's foot under the blanket and rubbed it, full of worries. "Mija. You screamed so loudly."

Aaron nodded. "Yeah, you did. But I couldn't understand what you were saying."

"Neither could I," Martina said, and looked at Aaron.

"I thought it was Spanish? But if you couldn't understand her . . . what was it then?"

Martina shrugged her shoulders. "It wasn't Spanish, this I know." She kept rubbing Maria's feet.

Maria looked at them, back and forth. "I don't know what language it was. I just remember saying good night or goodbye as I drowned. Not sure which," Maria whispered.

Martina looked at her. "Goodbye? To whom?"

"My daddy," Maria whispered in the tiniest voice.

"You dreamed of your dad again?" Aaron wasn't surprised, and watched Martina closely.

"Your daddy?" Martina's voice was shaky.

Maria nodded and then broke out in Spanish, explaining something to her mamá.

Aaron didn't understand a word but continued to watch Martina. *I see worry on her face, legitimate worry. She doesn't seem to understand the drowning dreams either.* Then he recognized her fear. Real fear. *What exactly is she afraid of? The police? That doesn't make sense. It's the drowning that scares Maria, but Martina doesn't seem to have a clue about it. Don't get it.*

Maria finished her story and looked to both Martina and Aaron. Without knowing what she had told her mom, Aaron said, "Maria has been having these dreams about drowning and her dad for a while now. Do you have any idea why, Martina?"

He looked at her. His blue eyes rested on her.

CHAPTER 58

Martina peered back at Aaron. She felt as if she was drowning herself. Right there in his ocean-blue eyes. *Have to keep it together.*

"Me? No, don't know. Maria never met her father. A guy in uniform, like she just told me? No. I don't understand it at all. Maybe it's all too much. Too much going on right now? Drowning as a symbol? Don't know. Maybe the new information about her dad? Just don't know."

She turned away from Aaron and scooted closer to Maria to give her a big hug. "I'm sorry, mija, I'm sorry. I'm worried about you. Can I help with anything? Do you need anything, mija?"

"No, Mamá, I'm fine. Let's just forget about it and all go back to sleep now. I'm pretty tired."

Martina got up. "Okay. Buenas noches." She got up, switched off the light, and left the room. Her hands were shaking as she returned to her own bed. She was concerned. Deeply concerned.

Martina lay awake in the dark room. The mattress beneath her wasn't the most comfortable. It was hard and seemed cheap. *Guess that's what*

a college boy has. But the hard mattress didn't help her calm down. Maria's dream was all she could think about.

How in the world is Maria now convinced that dream guy in uniform is her dad? How did this happen? Was my Jonathan Smith story that convincing? Guess that's a good sign, but it doesn't make any sense. If these dreams are memories, like Maria mentioned, she has the wrong guy in her memory. Or is there something I don't understand myself?

Deep down inside, she knew she should have asked more questions when Maria suddenly appeared on her doorstep. *What did he do to her? When Maria came to me as a little toddler, she was deeply distressed. Why in the world didn't I ask any questions? What was I thinking? Why didn't I go to the police?*

But she knew the answer. *Because I was threatened, afraid for my own life. Not just my own, but also that of the little, vulnerable toddler that was handed to me. The little, vulnerable toddler that so desperately needed someone to love and hug her, to help and cuddle her. The toddler who has stolen my heart from the very first minute I saw her. The one I've given everything to, given all my love and raised as my own. The one I've taken care of all my life. Fed and clothed her, sent her to school, given her an excellent education, and now a college degree. The little girl that was so silent, so quiet at first has become this amazing, confident young woman.*

She smiled into the darkness, her heart filled with warmth and pride. *I managed to build her up, gave that quiet, traumatized little girl a loving home, managed to bring out her smart, confident, loving personality. It took a long time. I sat with her many nights, cuddled with her many hours, taught her everything. Everything she is today and has become, I helped create. This confident, smart, beautiful, loving human being.* She didn't want to look back, think of what might have been. Of what had happened to that little girl before she entered her life.

It doesn't matter anymore. Our lives are intertwined now, forever. And for both our sakes, our safety, we need to forget the past.

CHAPTER 59

What lies in Maria's past? Aaron lay awake in the room opposite Martina's, deep in thought as well. Maria had finally fallen into a deep, dreamless sleep after telling Aaron all about her latest dream— or at least the parts she remembered. He was still trying to figure out what Maria had been screaming.

A goodbye to her father? Sounded more like "gut e nak" or something like that. But he had no idea what that meant, or if it even meant anything.

Maybe it's just scrambled-up words. Those sounds were definitely not English. More like deep, guttural sounds. Sounds that aren't part of the English language. Not part of the Spanish language either, as far as I know.

He kept thinking and thinking and suddenly it dawned on him. *Guttural sounds. Not very pretty sounds.* He remembered some of his classmates back in Montana making fun of the deep, guttural sounds of the language they all studied. A language he himself hadn't taken in high school. German. *German? Maria screamed something in German? Could that be? I need proof.* He sat up again in the dark and looked for his phone.

He found it on the packed bin next to him serving as a makeshift nightstand. The light from his phone was bright, but it didn't seem to bother Maria, who kept sleeping undisturbed.

He pulled up Google Translate and asked for "goodbye" in German. *Auf Wiedersehen,* his phone told him.

No, that's not it. Totally different than what Maria uttered before. He kept thinking. *Wait a minute. She mentioned saying "good night," didn't she? It's worth a try.*

He put the English words into Google Translate. It spat out *Gute Nacht.*

He stared at the foreign words. *That sounds right. But need to be sure.* He clicked on the little loudspeaker beneath the word, and the phone pronounced it aloud. "Gute Nacht," the computerized female voice said.

Yes! That's it. He was pretty sure this was the word that Maria had been screaming. He clicked on the button again, and his phone repeated the pronunciation.

Maria started twitching next to him in her sleep. *Did she just move her lips?* He looked at her, sleeping so soundly and peacefully. No movement. Then he had an idea. He played the German words again, close to her ear. The light from his phone's screen illuminated her beautiful face just enough for him to see her break into a smile.

"Gute Nacht, Mama," Maria whispered in her sleep, the smile broadening across her face, her eyelids fluttering.

Oh my gosh! She answered those words. In German. To her mom.

The phone slipped out of Aaron's hand and tumbled to the floor beside the bed. "Shoot," he said, and went looking for the illuminated screen before it went dark. He found it and logged out of the app, put the phone back on the temporary nightstand, then took big gulps of water from a glass that Maria must have put there while he was asleep.

He was definitely wide awake now and didn't feel tipsy anymore. His mind was sharp and ready to go. He just wasn't sure where to go with it.

Maria knows German! Why in the world does she know German? She never learned German. And yet she knows all these terms of endearment in German.

What about the word for her pacifier. Schnulli? Could be German. I need to know! He picked up his phone again and googled "pacifier" in German. *Schnuller*, his phone spat out.

Almost. It's almost German. He kept looking at the entries. *There it is. Schnulli, a cutesie name for a pacifier, comparable to the English "binky."* He gasped. *No way. No freaking way.* Aaron's mouth went dry again, his mind racing.

German has something to do with her past. It must! She knows this language subconsciously. In her sleep! A human must be exposed to a language early on to anchor knowledge of the language deep down in the brain. And German is definitely part of Maria's subconscious. Just like those dreams. Well, memories, I suppose. All buried deep down in her brain. Memories from very early childhood years. Faint memories. Memories of a mom that spoke German with her?

A mom other than Martina!

Aaron thought back to his earlier research. He got up, quietly, phone in hand, and found a spot on a bin further away from Maria. He didn't want to wake her. Then he started googling the drowning at Eglin Air Force Base twenty years ago.

Aaron was very focused on his research. He read more and more articles. They were all the same story, that a missing toddler called Moana Marie Collins had accidentally drowned. Had walked out of the TLF and just drowned. He looked at the picture again. The exotic eyes of the toddler stared back at him.

Sure looks like Maria. But she's alive! Hasn't drowned! How in the world did she get to Martina's in Miami? What happened? And are Brad and Elisabeth Collins really her parents? Need to learn more about them. He found a close-up picture of them.

Oh my gosh! The eyes in that picture. The picture of Brad Collins stared back at him. *Maria's eyes. They look just like hers! She really must be his daughter. And if she is, then the wife, Elisabeth, must be her mom.*

He took a closer look at the small, grainy picture on his phone. And then he saw it. *Those freckles. She has the exact same freckles. The same hair. The same elegant nose. Oh my gosh!* He had to hold his breath to make sure he didn't let out a scream.

Who is Martina Sullivan? How did the daughter of that couple end up at her place? And how is Maria alive, if that couple's daughter supposedly drowned? He looked through more and more articles. And then he found it:

"Moana Marie Collins – Kidnapped or Drowned? German-born Mother of Toddler Convinced Her Daughter Was Kidnapped"

Sweat formed on his forehead. His hand got slippery but he held on tight to his phone this time. *German-born mother? Elisabeth Collins is from Germany?* His throat went dry. He thought back to just minutes ago. "Gute Nacht, Mama," Maria had whispered. As if she had learned to say good night in German to her mom since the day she was born.

He kept reading. *"Elisabeth Collins is convinced her daughter has been kidnapped, but the police and FBI found this to be implausible, especially since they are on a secure military installation."*

He kept having a hard time swallowing, breathing. *Oh my gosh! Kidnapped? Martina actually kidnapped her? Must be. It's the only explanation. But how did she get onto Eglin AFB? And how did she get that fake birth certificate that lists her as Maria's mom? And what about the drowning? Why were the police convinced Maria drowned? If it is Maria, she's very much alive. There must be more to the story.*

He stared into the darkness, deep in thought. *There's definitely something that Martina knows and doesn't want to tell us. She seems afraid, afraid of something. Of what? The police? Well, if she kidnapped Maria, she should be afraid of the police. But wouldn't she then be aware that Maria's dad was an Air Force officer? She seemed so surprised by Maria's*

339

memories of her dad in uniform. He sighed, and a shudder ran down his spine.

It's unthinkable. This whole story is. Literally unbelievable. Nobody would believe me even if I told them it in painstaking detail. Neither Maria nor her mom. No, I need proof. Real proof. More than just an old, faded picture from some ancient newspaper articles. More than a hunch that Maria knows German. I need more, something real.

Suddenly, he couldn't wait to talk to the investigator on Monday. *Fraudulent paperwork.* Aaron was convinced he hadn't made a mistake in all that paperwork. *I'm a perfectionist. I checked it a thousand times. It really must be Maria's birth certificate. A fake?*

His mouth was so dry, his chest hurting. He felt as if he couldn't breathe anymore. Quietly, he picked up his phone off the floor and walked back over to the mattress where Maria was sleeping so peacefully. He drank the entire second cup of water on the makeshift nightstand.

He knew he couldn't do anything else but wait for now. Wait for Monday. *Or should I contact Brad Collins? General Brad Collins? Ask him about his daughter? Tell him she's alive? Maybe that's not a good idea. Maybe we just need to go to the police? But would they believe me? All I have is pieces of a story.*

He knew he had to think about it, think up a plan, next steps. He looked over at Maria, who was sleeping so calmly next to him. *Poor Maria. What happened to you?*

He leaned over to give her a kiss on the cheek. He needed to go back to sleep and wait. Wait for now, wait for their arrival at Eglin Air Force Base.

Little did he know that their arrival at Eglin would turn disastrous.

CHAPTER 60

Eglin AFB. Elisabeth was dreaming of Eglin AFB. White beaches. Emerald-green water.

She woke abruptly. It was still dark. Very dark. Pitch-black, actually. She couldn't see anything and was a little disoriented for a while. *Why does the outline of the room look so unfamiliar? And what's with that constant, low buzzing sound?* She felt chilled and pulled the covers over her. They seemed so different. She looked around again and could just make out the bed next to hers. *Another bed?*

Then she suddenly realized she wasn't at home anymore. She was in a hotel room at the Silver Shells Beach Resort in Destin, Florida. That was her friend Sarah sleeping right next to her. Elisabeth now realized that the air conditioning was on and had made the room very chilly.

Of course that's the buzzing sound I keep hearing. The A/C. Very American. And very typically set so low that I'm freezing. We were too tired last night to set it higher. But I need it to be in the seventies, not at sixty-five degrees. That's way too cold.

Elisabeth couldn't help but think back to all of the times she had argued with her husband over the A/C setting. She smiled just thinking of him. *I'll see him soon. I will.* She thought of him, thought of their family, their family living nearby here on the white sandy beaches. She shivered again—this time she wasn't sure if it was because she really did feel chilly or because of all the memories.

She looked over to her friend Sarah, who was sleeping calmly. *It's like a vacation to her. Here on the white sandy beaches in a wonderful beachside resort. Sounds great, right? But not to me. Brings back all these memories of long-gone times.*

Before she got too deep into her own thoughts, she got up and searched for the air-conditioning control panel. She found it hanging on the wall and immediately turned up the temperature. The buzzing stopped. Suddenly she felt wide-awake. She sighed. *Jet lag. Nighttime here, but already morning in Germany. Still on German time. That's okay, though. Gives me time to come up with a plan.*

She found her carry-on purse and took out Enti. With her daughter's best, most loved stuffy friend, she slipped behind the curtains and quietly opened the sliding door, just enough to step out onto the balcony. There she sat in the moonlight, looking out across the ocean.

The Gulf of Mexico. She heard the ocean waves but couldn't really see them. It was still too dark. She felt the ocean breeze and tasted the humid, salty air. She saw the shadows of the palm trees that were planted around the resort, waving to and fro close to their balcony.

It was beautiful. She knew it was and sighed.

I never wanted to return to this country. The country that shattered my dreams. The Land of Shattered Dreams, the Land of Nightmares. The Land of Thieves. Child-stealers. She sighed. *At least Brad believes me now. She was taken from us. Stolen from us. Yes, we will open up the case. She might be dead now, but we will find out what happened.* The waves crashed onto the beach. Elisabeth could hear them. She felt the breeze, the salty ocean breeze, and it almost whispered to her, told her that her little one hadn't drowned like everyone had said.

As she sat there on the dark, pitch-black balcony of the beautiful Silver Shells Beach Resort, she listened to the wind and was more convinced than ever before that her daughter had not died. *She didn't drown. She's alive and well, a wonderful, grown-up woman of twenty-two years. Somewhere out there still. Because she was kidnapped.* And right there on the balcony, she vowed, "We will find her, Enti. We will find her! Somehow, we'll find her."

CHAPTER 61

Brad couldn't sleep. That wasn't too unusual for him, but this night seemed different. He was sweating. Not because it was warm in his room. The A/C was set at seventy-two. It was comfortable, still early summer. July and August were the humid, muggy months in DC, and it wasn't even the end of May yet.

The A/C didn't even need to be on right now, but he'd set it to his preferred temperature anyway. Maybe because he always thought of Elisabeth when he turned the A/C to a setting that most of his guests found too uncomfortable, too hot. *But she was right. Setting the A/C below seventy degrees is much too cool, too expensive, too unnatural.*

She always crafted three reasons whenever she made an argument. Three reasons. A great way of arguing. I lost most of our arguments. He smiled. *Though I've won many arguments at work, thanks to her method of reasoning. Most people can't keep up with two arguments, let alone three.*

Elisabeth. I miss you. I've never found another woman like you. There's no second Elisabeth. You're special. Not just special to me, but special in every way. He broke out into a big grin. *And soon, I'll see you again. Glad you already landed safely. Glad to have gotten that text. Bet you're still dreaming, hopefully of me. Can't wait to see you again. So soon now.*

He rolled over in bed with every intention of sleeping some more, but then heard his phone buzz. He raised his eyebrows. *Who's texting me in the middle of the night?*

He grabbed his phone off the nightstand and looked at it. A text from Elisabeth. He smiled as he opened it. *Her nose must have been itchy.* He read her text and knew there was no going back to sleep anymore. He instead sat up in bed and dialed her number.

He heard her whisper on the other end. "Hey there."

"Hey. Why are you whispering?"

"Sarah's still asleep and I'm outside on the balcony. Don't want to wake her or any other neighbors. It's still the middle of the night."

"Sure is."

"Why are you awake then?"

"Well, because I was thinking of you."

He heard her smirk, could tell by her amused voice. "Did you?"

"Yeah, I did."

"Well, soon you won't have to think of me. Soon, you'll *see* me."

He sat up even taller. "I know. I can't wait. I'll fly out tomorrow."

"Yeah. I studied your itinerary."

"I see. How was your trip?"

"Oh, well, you know. Strange. Very strange, coming back here." She sighed.

"I understand, hun, I know. It'll be the first time for me also."

"First time back here? Really? You didn't have to come here for work the past twenty years?"

"Well, I should've. But I didn't. Couldn't stand it. Couldn't bear being there on base. You know, the same base that we . . . you know, that we . . ."

"Lost her?"

He sighed. "Yeah. Lost her."

"Brad?" He heard excitement in her voice.

"Yes?"

"You still believe me, that she was kidnapped, right?"

He smiled. "I already told you I do. Yes, of course. Told you I have a new suspect and am already planning to open the case again. Remember?"

She laughed. "I know, I know. Of course I remember, silly. But what do you think happened . . . after?"

He was confused. "What do you mean, *after*?"

She searched for words. "You know . . . after the kidnapping."

"I'm not sure I understand."

She sighed. "Brad, it's been twenty years. Do you think she's alive?"

His hands were suddenly sweaty, his voice hoarse. "Alive?"

"Yeah. You know. If she was kidnapped. You don't kidnap a child if you don't want the child to live."

Brad swallowed hard. He knew that wasn't true. There were unfortunately plenty of children out there who get kidnapped and then killed. "Alive?" He had to ask again to wrap his own head around it. *Could it be?* "Why do you think that?"

"Well, if your theory is right and the Hispanic lady kidnapped her, she probably wanted our child for herself."

"Maybe," he squawked, his voice raspy.

"Think about it, Brad. I've read all about kidnapping cases. There's the sick ones who kidnap a child to . . . you know . . . to sexually . . ."— her voice broke as she couldn't say it out loud—"but mostly it's men in those cases. If you think—and I agree—a woman took our daughter, the Hispanic lady, our child is probably still alive. Women kidnap children mostly because they can't have a child of their own. And they usually intend no harm to the child. They often compensate the kidnapping for their own emotional deprivation. They want love, the love of a child who adores them, so they take good care of the child to receive that love. And think about it! There was no ransom for her safe release, but it was a bold, very well-planned kidnapping. So it can only fall under the "maternity category". A women wanted a child, took our daughter, cared well for her. So she's still alive because that lady loved her, and raised her happily as her own."

"You're saying wanting a child of her own means you think her kidnapper cared well for our daughter? Loved her and raised her to be a successful young adult?"

"Correct, Brad. That's what I think. No ransom note, but a well-planned kidnapping by a woman who desperately wanted a child of her own to raise as her own daughter. Makes sense, right? Good reasons, don't you think?"

Reasons? Brad cleared his throat. *She had three reasons again: no ransom note, a well-planned kidnapping, a women desperate to have a daughter to love.*

"So, what do you think, Brad? Do you think that's plausible and she's alive?"

He knew there was no arguing with three reasons. As he thought about it even more, he broke out into a broad smile. "Yes, Elisabeth, I think it's possible. And if our daughter's alive, we'll leave no stone unturned. We'll search every grain of sand on that beach to find her."

CHAPTER 62

"Mom, you can let go now, okay? Please."

"Of course, son, of course," Grace Heikinnen said. "I'm just so proud of you. My college graduate! Such an amazing ceremony. We loved it. And achieving magna cum laude is impressive."

Aaron grinned at that. He looked stunning in his navy-blue gown and cap with the tassels on it, his eyes sparkling. Grace gave him a quick kiss on his cheek that left a red lipstick mark.

"Mom.. . . ." he scolded, and tried to wipe the wet spot on his left cheek away.

Emma laughed and handed him a tissue. "Might need to make it wet to get Mom's lipstick off. Congrats, big bro, proud of you!"

After a quick hug and wipe of his cheek, Aaron turned to his dad, who gave him a hug and a big pat on the shoulder.

"Proud of you, my son. Magna cum laude is definitely impressive!"

"Sure is," Maria said, smiling, and flew into Aaron's arms in a big hug.

"No kiss from you for your newly minted graduate?"

"Other cheek maybe? To match the lipstick smear on the left?" She laughed and looked at him, her exotic eyes sparkling in the sunlight.

"I don't deserve a real kiss?" Before he could complain any further, he got exactly what he wished for.

Now it was Martina's turn to congratulate him. She gave him a big hug as well, but to her it felt as if he stiffened up in her hug. *What's wrong with him? He's been acting strange all day. Trying to avoid me.* She was used to hugs being warmly returned, but this time, what she got felt more like a pat on the shoulder at best.

Before Martina could think about it too much, she was surrounded by Maria's friends and went to congratulate both Jim and Nick, then was swept up in conversation with all the happy graduates and their families. Everyone was taking pictures, laughing, chatting—the whole campus was bustling with joy and happiness. The graduates' college experience had just ended, yet it was the start of something new, the beginning of their next chapter in life.

After a time, families began to leave the university's graduation venue, and Jack told his son it was time for them to depart as well.

Aaron went with Jim and Nick to return their cap and gowns, and when they walked back out into the middle of the university's campus and saw their girlfriends standing there, it hit them.

"Man, I can't believe it. We'll never walk out of a university building again to meet the girls for lunch or dinner," Jim said, and sighed.

Aaron and Nick looked at him. Suddenly, they all had a heavy heart.

"We'll never walk out and just hang or play card games on a picnic blanket in the grassy campus field," Nick said.

"Yeah, you're right, guys. Guess we'll be in the work force from now on," Aaron agreed.

"Man, this sucks, guys. No more studying, no more parties. Just lots of responsibility."

Aaron tried to cheer up his friends before they reached their girlfriends. "Yeah, but we'll be good second lieutenants, right guys?"

His friends nodded but otherwise kept silent as they joined the girls. Everyone had a sad look in their eyes. For a while, they just stood there, staring at each other. They all sighed at the same time.

"At least we've got tonight, y'all," Brandy exclaimed as cheerfully as she could.

Everyone just nodded.

"Yeah. No need to say goodbye to Aaron just yet," Jim said. "We'll see you tonight, right?"

"Yep, definitely. Maria and I will be there. Meet you all at the Mai Tai Bar?"

"Yeah, at eight p.m.," Nick confirmed.

The friends then parted ways to celebrate with their families. Aaron was happy when Emma insisted on driving with Martina and Maria. After yesterday's strange car ride and then last night, he wasn't in the mood to engage in small talk with Martina again. He gratefully took a seat with his parents in his own car. Off they went to another restaurant in downtown Daytona Beach, and had such a good time together that he forgot all about what he'd read online last night.

"Martina, you really don't want to stay another night?" Grace asked. "We'd love to share another breakfast with you tomorrow morning!"

"Yes, nobody else makes brunch as well as you," Emma pouted.

Martina smiled. "Thank you, mi niña pequeña. But I want you and your family to spend time with Aaron before he goes off to his first job."

"But we've already been around Aaron for *so long*. He's been there for as long as I can remember." Everyone chuckled at that. "We'd rather see you, Martina, and enjoy your food."

"Ah, mi niña pequeña. I'm so happy you like my food. I will send you baked Venezuelan goodies in the mail. ¿Sí?"

"¡Sí! Please. That would be awesome. But I thought we could go to the movies again tonight while Maria and Aaron are out?"

"Ah, mi niña pequeña, such a sweetheart! I'm sorry. I need to get back to Miami. It's a long drive, and I need to get ready to reopen my store on Monday."

Aaron's family sure seemed disappointed, but Martina had made up her mind. She wouldn't dare stay another night with Aaron giving her the cold shoulder. And she couldn't stay another night because she was afraid. Afraid that Maria would have another one of those strange dreams that scared not only her daughter but Martina herself. It opened up old wounds, made her question her own behavior, the way she had handled that situation twenty years ago.

Martina gave Emma a big hug. "Goodbye, sweetheart. So nice meeting you. And no worries, mi niña pequeña, we will see each other again soon."

"Maybe we can visit for Christmas? We could see Aaron at his new home then drive down to see you in Miami. Maybe even stop by Disney World along the way."

They all had a laugh, and had to admit that might not be such a bad idea.

"We'll see, Emma," Jack said, and gave Martina a warm hug goodbye.

Grace had tears in her eyes. "So great meeting you, Martina. Please don't be a stranger. You have my number now. Please call to chat anytime."

Martina nodded and gave her a long hug. After the tearful goodbye, they split up in two cars again. The Heikinnens took Aaron's car and returned to Maria's apartment, while Aaron and Maria drove Martina back to Aaron's place.

Back at the apartment, Martina quickly changed out of her fancy dress, packed her belongings, and was ready to say her final goodbyes to Maria and Aaron. She knocked on the door to Aaron's room and peeked in.

Maria looked up at her from the bed on the ground. "Mamá, you sure you want to go now?"

Martina only nodded and put a nicely wrapped gift on one of the packed bins. "For you, Aaron! Congrats on your graduation!"

He was sitting in between all the bins packing a few items, but now looked up at her, his blue eyes sparkling in surprise. "For me?"

"¡Podía! You just graduated. Successfully. Of course it is for you!"

For a moment, she saw the old, gentle, kind Aaron again. He got up and walked over to her, eyeing the wrapped gift. "Do you want me to open it now?"

"Sí."

Maria came over as well, curious. Aaron picked up the gift and started feeling it. "So soft." Martina nodded with a wink. He opened the gift. Inside the wrapping were beautiful dark-blue bed sheets with a matching pillow set. Each corner contained a stitched-on graduation cap with *2023* embroidered underneath in golden thread.

"Wow!" Aaron was genuinely moved by the gift. Maria smiled. "This is beautiful, Martina. Where did you find it?"

"I made it. Just for you. For your new place. A unique bedding set for a special young man!"

Aaron looked up at her. "Thank you! Gracias, Martina." He walked over and gave her a hug—a long, loving, genuine hug.

She smiled. *That's the young man I've gotten to know, the young man my daughter will marry. A gentle, kind, smart, special young man.* The hostility she had felt earlier was gone.

Aaron was obviously moved. Martina looked at Maria, who stood there with tears in her eyes. Martina smiled. *I knew Maria would love this gift as well. She always loves the things I make for her.*

"This is really special, Martina. A very thoughtful gift honoring the graduation, the school, the school colors, this whole chapter of my life. Thank you," he said, and gave her one last squeeze. "You're a very talented tailor. A loving mom and future mother-in-law. Thank you so much."

"De nada," she said. "¡Mi hijo! You're welcome, very welcome, Aaron. Enjoy the new place, and all the best to you at Eglin."

He let go of her and suddenly stared at her. He slowly nodded. "Thanks again," he said, his voice cold. "Sure hope you can visit me— or us—there soon."

Martina was unnerved. "Yes, I'd like that. Eglin sounds like a nice place . . . right, Maria?"

But Maria's happiness had fled. Aaron looked at Maria and knew at once. Eglin. That single word had the power to send chills down her spine.

Martina noticed the abrupt change in both their moods, especially Aaron's. His gentle demeanor was gone, his ocean-blue eyes frozen over into a cold, dark blue. *What just happened?* Martina did not understand.

"Yes, Eglin sounds very nice," Aaron said, and sounded almost taunting. "Hey, any chance you've ever been there, Martina?"

She looked at him. *What a silly question!* "No, I haven't. How could I have been there? I've already told you that before. I couldn't even get onto a military base!"

Aaron stared at her, his blue eyes icy cold. Martina was confused. *What's he getting at?* She now looked at her daughter. *What's wrong with Maria now? Just standing there, staring into the distance, breathing heavily.*

"Has *Maria* ever been there?" Aaron demanded.

Martina stared at him. *What's going on?* In a flash, they'd gone from having a wonderful moment to an interrogation, all without Martina even knowing what she was being accused of. "Of course not. Why . . . How would Maria have been there? Ask her. Of course she hasn't been to Eglin Air Force Base!"

Maria's breathing got louder, and now both Aaron and Martina were looking at her. "¿Maria, mija, estás bien?"

353

Maria just nodded, kept staring at the wall and breathing heavily.

"Are you sure that Maria has never been there? As a *child* maybe? A small toddler?"

"No! No, she's never been there. Why would a small child go anywhere without her mother?" Martina looked at Aaron. His eyes could have frozen her to the spot.

"Exactly my question. Why would a little toddler go anywhere *without her mother?*"

Martina stared at him. She started feeling dizzy. *What is he trying to say?* But she didn't dare to ask. She just needed to get out of here. Out of this situation, this interrogation, this weird moment. *Is he hinting at something? The way he said "mother." What does he know?* She closed her eyes for a second. *It's impossible. Nobody knows. Well, except for my ex. But nobody else knows our secret.*

She was determined to keep it that way.

"Aaron, I wish you all the best. Enjoy the special bedding. Good luck at your first job and new home. Can't wait to hear all about it. Take care, and take good care of my Maria. Please." He looked at her. "You're everything to her and need to protect her. Please. Take good care of her. I love you both."

Despite his strange behavior, she gave him a quick hug, then walked over to Maria to give her a big hug and whisper something in Spanish. Maria immediately relaxed in her mamá's arms. Then, without hesitation, she turned around, grabbed her bag, and walked out of the apartment.

"Mamá, wait!" Maria ran after her. She stood at the open door to the apartment and waved goodbye to her mom. Aaron came over and joined her.

"Drive safely and *thanks for coming,*" he yelled after her.

Martina turned around and looked at the handsome couple in the doorway. "Thanks for having me. Take care and all the best." She waved and got into her car.

CHAPTER 63

He watched Martina wave goodbye. His Dodge Ram pickup truck was parked on the street across from the apartment. *Glad I have a pickup truck with recliner seats. Nobody can see me, and I got a pretty good night's rest.* He rubbed his bottom. *I mean, it's still pretty fucking uncomfortable, but I managed. Have to manage. Have to make sure there'll be no problem.*

He looked over again and heard Martina start the engine of her car. The Aaron guy and Problem Child waved one last time, then walked back into the building. He knew they were going out to party again tonight, but there was no need to follow them for now. *I've heard enough last night.* He frowned thinking back to the shocking news of the Aaron guy and Problem Child going to Eglin. He sighed and watched Martina drive away. *At least she's gone now. From what I can tell, Martina didn't say anything.* He smiled. *Good girl. Fine woman. I knew you wouldn't. I knew you wouldn't dare risk losing your precious daughter.*

He broke out into loud laughter. *Your daughter. As if.*

Once the door to the apartment had closed, he started his truck and drove away to find someplace to eat. Something cheap. Something good. He was tempted to check into a hotel tonight but decided against it. He'd just sleep in his truck again right outside of the apartment.

Have to make sure I don't miss them leaving. Need to tail them. Keep an eye on them at Eglin AFB.

As he was driving, he thought of that beautiful area. *It's so pretty there. So pretty in Destin and Fort Walton Beach.* He laughed out loud. *Well, not that I really have seen much of it. I didn't even get to set foot on land there.* He frowned thinking back of that time. *Wasn't cool, but had to stick to my orders.* He sighed. *All I really ended up seeing, for days and days, were the beautiful emerald waters of the Choctawhatchee Bay.*

CHAPTER 64

Choctawhatchee Bay. There it is. Don't think about it. She focused on the road again, changed lanes quickly, and passed the truck hogging the left lane. Her friend was frantically holding onto the doorhandle. "Elisabeth!"

She briefly took her eyes off the road to glance at Sarah. She couldn't help but smile. She knew her friend was uneasy about passing other cars on the right-hand side. It was illegal in Germany and so drilled into every German driver that it had taken a younger Elisabeth quite a while to adjust to the different driving rules in the United States. Passing on the right was something she hadn't done in decades, yet upon their arrival in Florida she discovered she actually enjoyed being able to do it again. She swiftly passed cars both left and right and was on the bridge now, the bridge that connected Destin to Fort Walton Beach. Okaloosa county. She slowed down.

"Wow, the view from up here is beautiful," Sarah said, and relaxed a little. "Look at the emerald-green water!"

"Ja, pretty," Elisabeth whispered. *Still can't believe I'm back here. Back where my child was taken from me.*

Sarah looked at her friend. "You alright?"

Elisabeth nodded. "Ja, sure."

"I know it's hard for you, Elisabeth. But I think it's good you're back here. Back here so you can let go and forget about them."

"Ja, sure, it's great," Elisabeth said sarcastically. She suddenly felt bad that she was lying to her. *All I want to do is see Brad and go talk to the police. But I can't tell her that. She seems so happy that I'm doing well.*

"I had such a fun time during our lazy day at the beach. That dinner at the fish restaurant was delicious too. I feel like you had fun, too, didn't you, Elisabeth?"

She nodded and focused on the road again. They were driving back to the hotel in their rental car.

"That's good, Elisabeth, that's good. See, told you it was a good idea to come here." Sarah smiled contentedly.

"Ja, Sarah, it was. You were right."

"I know, I'm a genius!" Sarah grinned at her friend.

"Well, maybe not a genius, but a very, very good friend. My best friend."

Sarah laughed. "I know. And guess what your best friend thinks?" Elisabeth quickly glanced over at her before she focused on the road again. "I think you're slowly turning back into being your old, happy self again. It took twenty years, but it seems like you've suddenly found peace again. I'm so glad. Not sure why, but it's wonderful, and I'm so glad for you."

"Ja," Elisabeth said quickly, and drove into the dark night.

The sun had just set and he was now staring into the darkness of the night from his front porch. His bags were packed and he would fly out tomorrow morning.

Back to Florida. Back to Eglin.

He studied his schedule. It was filled up with meetings. He'd first meet everyone in the test wing who had been working so hard on the new F-35 jets. Honestly, he was curious to see the planes again. The fast planes. The *loud* planes. He thought of the senator complaining that his constituents were bothered by the noise. He snorted.

Well, fighter jets are noisy. So what? Don't move to a base or live near one then. And people get used to all the noise anyway. He had to smile. *Even our little one got used to it. She called the jets "vrooms" every time they roared above us. "Daddy's vrooms."*

His smile faded. *My little one. What happened to you? Are you still alive?* Pain washed over his face and clouded his exotic eyes. *It's almost June. The month of my daughter's birthday. She would have turned two, just two years old, but she disappeared right before we could even celebrate her birthday.* He sighed. He couldn't wait to go back to the police and open the cold case again.

With her. With Elisabeth.

He smiled and picked up his phone to text her. *Good night from DC. Flying out to Eglin tomorrow.*

"Can't believe you're leaving for Eglin tomorrow, man. Good luck, man," Nick said, trying to speak clearly and not slur his words. The group of friends was standing outside of the nightclub that had just closed. The time had come to say goodbye to one another.

"I can't believe it, man," Jim said, and suddenly felt sober.

"Can't believe we won't see each other anymore." The boys all looked sad, then looked right at Aaron and piled in for an awkward hug.

Nick patted Aaron's shoulder. "Gonna miss my roommate."

"Yeah, we'll miss you, bro."

"I know, guys, I'll miss you, too. Stay in touch, second lieutenants. We youngsters gotta stick together, even across duty stations!" They all nodded and fist-bumped each other.

It was Brandy's turn. "Good luck, darlin' Aaron. Stay safe. Have fun. Stay in touch."

He nodded, let go of Brandy, and gave Keisha a hug. "Yeah, boy, stay in touch. Good luck with your new job. You got this."

"Yeah, she's right, you got this," Jim said as he put his arm around Keisha. "And Eglin sounds like a very cool and quiet place. Enjoy the Emerald Coast."

Maria and Aaron's Uber arrived and they got in, waving goodbye to their friends. Little did they know the Emerald Coast wouldn't be enjoyable at all.

CHAPTER 65

"**N**o, I'm not at all surprised Emma is still up." Maria smirked and winked an eye. "Come on, Aaron. You shouldn't be surprised either. Of course the lights we see from out here are coming from the TV. Emma is probably watching a show."

Aaron took out the key to his apartment door to let them in, and they found Emma on the couch in the living room, staring at the glowing TV screen. She briefly looked up. "Oh, hi guys. Did you have a good time?"

"Yep, we did," Maria answered while taking off her shoes in the small mudroom at the entrance.

"Emma! Why are you still up? It's almost three a.m.! What are you thinking?"

"Shhh . . ." was the only answer he got from Emma. "This is a good part. You can watch too if you want."

Maria laughed when she saw that Aaron looked upset. "Come on, Aaron, she's fourteen! Let her binge-watch her Netflix shows!"

Aaron sighed. They both sat down to finish watching the show with Emma. But as soon as he sat on the couch, he fell asleep and didn't even get five minutes into the show. Both Emma and Maria rolled their eyes.

"Typical Aaron," Emma commented.

Maria grinned. When the show ended, Emma turned off the TV. "Well, good night, Maria."

"Good night, Emma."

"What will you do with Aaron?"

Maria and Emma were looking at him. He was in a deep sleep, sitting straight up on the couch in the living room.

"I'll try to wake him." Maria gently shook him, but it was useless.

Aaron reacted and answered her clearly. "Sure, I'll be right there." But immediately after uttering that sentence, he closed his eyes, fell into a deep sleep, and started snoring again.

Emma and Maria rolled their eyes and laughed together. "Well, obviously none of us can carry him to his room, so just leave him on the couch," Emma suggested.

Maria nodded. "Yeah. Guess we'll have to." She pulled out a blanket for him and laid it over him.

"Aww, that was sweet of you, Maria." Emma smiled from where she stood in the doorframe to Nick's room. "Good night now, sis. Thanks for letting me stay here."

Maria smiled. "You're welcome, Emma. Good night."

Emma closed the door and Maria headed over to Aaron's room, found the mattress on the floor in between all those packed bins, and fell onto it. She was tired, very tired. *I need to sleep. It'll be such a long day tomorrow—well, today. We need to get up on time to pick up the Penske truck, pack all the furniture and bins inside, deep-clean Aaron's room, drive his mom and sister back to the airport, then drive to Eglin AFB.*

Aaron's new home. Eglin.

Maria shuddered just thinking that word.

She didn't want to think about it anymore and distracted herself by texting her Mamá to let her know they'd gotten back home safely.

Nosotras estamos de vuelta. Te amo, Mamá, she wrote.

She turned on her alarm. *Five hours to sleep. Not bad.* She hadn't expected an answer to her text at three thirty in the morning, but her phone pinged with a text message: *¡Muy bien! Te amo.*

Maria had to smile. *Mamá has always been there for me. Can't imagine anyone else being such a good mom as her. Love and miss you, Mamá.* She fell asleep.

"Miss Mama?" she said in a tiny voice, "Mama?" She looked all over in every room. There were lots of packed bins and boxes and she made sure to look behind every box, just in case her mama was hiding behind one of them. "Mama? Mama?" Her small voice echoed inside the empty rooms.

Where's Mama?

She didn't know and it made her feel uneasy.

Mama is always there for me, but now she's gone. That's not good.

"Mama?" She was a bit panicked now and ran all over the big, empty house looking for her.

A house. Not apartment?

She looked at the packed boxes and bins. They looked very big—well, big compared to her. She looked at her running feet that didn't seem to be getting her around that fast. They were small, so small. Barefoot on the gleaming wooden floors.

"It's okay, sweetie, Mama will be back tonight," a low male voice said from behind her.

She turned around and then she saw him. A big man, standing in the doorframe to this big room with all the packed boxes and empty bins. He was tall, had dark-brown hair, and wore camouflaged military pants with a black undershirt.

"Mama gone?"

"Yes, sweetie, but not for long. She's just saying goodbye to some of our friends before the move," he explained in a soft voice, and bent down to be at eye-level with her.

Why am I so small? Who's that man?

"It's okay! Daddy is here," he said and opened his arms. *"Come here, sweetie, Daddy wants to give you a hug!"*

Daddy? That man is my dad? No, no, he can't be!

She was so confused yet her tiny feet moved automatically, and before she knew it she flew into his arms. Into his strong arms. *"Daddy,"* she heard her tiny voice say, and her mouth smiled widely.

"Hi, sweets." He squeezed her tight in a big hug.

She felt safe, secure, warm, loved. Happy. Just happy to be with Daddy. Her daddy. She looked at him. He was very handsome. He had a straight nose, nicely formed soft lips, and very interesting eyes. They were hazelnut brown with a mosaic of golden-and-emerald-green flecks in the dark-brown center encircled by a blue rim. So exotic. Yes, she heard people say that all the time. Exotic eyes.

They say it to me, too, since I have the same eyes as Daddy.

Wait, what? Same eyes?

She kept looking at him and he smiled. *"While we wait for Mama to say goodbye to her friends, why don't we play together?"*

She nodded excitedly. *That would be fun!* And before she knew it, he had pulled out a toy plane from his pocket.

"Look, this is for you."

"A plane, a plane!"

"Yes, a plane. A jet. A fighter jet, actually. It's called an F-16."

"Like Daddy's? Daddy's vrooms?"

He laughed a warm laugh. *"Yes, smarty pants, a jet like Daddy's. Like Daddy flies for the Air Force!"*

"A vroom! Have it." She stretched out her hand to reach for it when she saw his eyes looking at her, as if he was now scolding her for something. Oh, she knew. *"Have it, please!"*

His mouth turned into a wild smile. "That's right, my little one. We always say 'please.' Just like Mama taught you."

"No, Mama sagt 'bitte.'" She looked at him while taking the toy jet out of his hands.

He laughed again and smirked. "You're so right. Smart girl. Mama says bitte, not please, doesn't she?"

She just nodded and started playing with the jet, flying it around the room, in between all the boxes, and then landed it on one of them. The plastic bin had writing on it. She wasn't able to read yet, but the letters jumped out at her. The big black letters on the red plastic bin formed a word.

EGLIN. The letters spelled "EGLIN."

She stared at the writing, the big black letters on the bin, and felt chills running down her spine. Her toy jet stood right next to that word on the bin. EGLIN.

Oh no. No, no, no!

She turned around to see her Daddy walking over to her, but before he could reach her, the letters swirled around her, got bigger and bigger, and she got caught in them, caught up in the big black writing. EGLIN. They were pulling her, pulling her to Eglin AFB. But most importantly, they pulled her away from him. Away from her daddy.

Where is Mama? Why the heck isn't she here to save me? Mama? Daddy?

The bin next to her suddenly opened up, the lid was open, and all she could see was a big, black, gaping hole, ready to swallow her up. The letters tugged on her little body, and she plunged right in, right into that hole.

No, no! Help! Help me! Please! Please, help me!

She saw the exotic eyes of her dad looking into the bin, into the hole, clearly looking in. She reached up with her tiny hands, but she couldn't reach him. Mucky, murky water pulled her down, surrounded her. She couldn't breathe, she just kept swallowing that water, more and more and more.

"Daddy," she whispered, "Daddy, please . . ."

But it was too late, and everything went black around her.

She heard voices, muffled voices, and felt that she was being shaken. *Who's here to save me? Daddy? Mama?*

She opened her eyes and looked straight into four blue eyes. *Wait, what?* She closed her eyes again then reopened them, and saw that the four blue eyes belonged to Aaron and Emma; each had a set of blue eyes, of course. Aaron and Emma were here.

Aaron and Emma? She was confused and looked from one face to the other.

"Are you okay?" Emma asked.

Maria couldn't answer. She had a bad headache. She looked around and realized she was on the mattress in Aaron's room, in between all those packed bins ready to be loaded onto the truck they still had to get. Ready to go to Aaron's first job, his first military assignment. Ready to go to Eglin AFB.

Eglin AFB.

Chills ran down her spine, her head was throbbing now. *Eglin AFB. Oh my gosh! "EGLIN." The word on the bins.*

Suddenly, she stood up and almost bumped heads with Aaron and Emma, who had been sitting on the end of the mattress, worriedly bent over her prone form. "Sorry," she mumbled, and hopped up.

She walked in the lit-up room and looked at the bins. They were labeled by room and contents, but none of them said "EGLIN" in big blocky letters. It wasn't written on the plastic lids. And the lids weren't red—they were teal. The bins themselves were see-through, not red. *Strange!* She kept searching and ran from one bin to the next.

Aaron got up and followed her as she walked from bin to bin. "Maria, what are you doing?"

By now, Maria was frantic. *The label, the label is gone!* The boxes had been clearly labeled "EGLIN." She knew that. She just knew it. Her fingers touched the writing on each box, the writing that only mentioned the room and content. Her eyes widened as she read each written word on the bins.

"Maria . . . what are you looking for?" Aaron asked her, his eyebrow raised.

She still intensely scanned the bins, trying to make sense of why they had changed color or why they were now labeled by room and content. *There has to be a good explanation. There just has to be.*

"Maria?" Aaron was now next to her, grabbing her arms that limply hung by her side. He turned her around so that she was face-to-face with him. "Maria, you *have* to wake up! Wake up!" she heard him say, and felt herself being gently shaken. "Maria, what are you looking for?"

She now stared at him, an empty, wide-eyed stare. "That word. Those labels. Where did they go?"

"The labels? What labels?"

"The labels on the bins. Handwritten labels. Labels saying where all those bins were going," she explained, still wide-eyed.

Emma looked at Maria, confused. "You mean the labels of what room they're going to?"

Maria still stared at the bins, her face ghostly white. "No, one place. *The* place. The red bins. . . ."

Both Aaron and Emma stared at Maria. "What? Red bins? Aaron, what in the world is Maria talking about?"

Aaron shushed his little sister and looked at Maria again, still holding her arms. "What did they say, the labels?" He looked deep into her wide-open green eyes.

"Eglin. Handwritten on the red bins with black marker, black sharpie."

Aaron studied her face intensely while Emma didn't understand a thing. "Who wrote them?" he said.

"What are you guys talking about? Some sort of secret grown-up code or what?" Emma asked, confused, but was shushed by Aaron again.

"Who wrote those labels on the bins?" Aaron asked again. Maria seemed to stare right through him, her eyes green.

Then she whispered, "*Mama* wrote them. Mama did. For Daddy's new assignment."

Emma stared. Her mouth dropped wide open. Aaron did the same. Then Maria's eyes suddenly crossed, and before he could do anything else but stare, Maria had fainted.

CHAPTER 66

The next time Maria opened her eyes, she found herself looking directly at Emma, who was kneeling next to her head, still staring at her. She felt something wet on her forehead and suddenly realized that Aaron was holding her legs up. She was lying on the floor of his room.

She sat up abruptly and the wet cloth slid down into her lap. Both Emma and Maria stared at it until Maria picked it up. "What's that? Why was there this weird wet cloth on my head?" She looked from Aaron to Emma, back and forth. "And please stop holding my legs like that. It's super uncomfortable."

Aaron let go of her legs so that she could sit up properly. He was still dressed in the clothes he had worn to the nightclub, while both Emma and Maria were in pajamas. Emma just stared at Maria.

"Emma, stop staring! What's going on here?"

"You don't remember?"

She shook her head, then looked at Aaron and she saw it. The worried look. The crinkled forehead and raised eyebrow, just one of them, the way only he could do it. She looked around, saw the wet cloth, the packed see-through plastic bins with the teal lids, and suddenly remembered. "I fainted, didn't I? Had another dream?"

Aaron nodded.

"Dream? Nightmare, I'd say," Emma exclaimed. "I've never heard a scream like that before in my life. Never ever! Oh my gosh, Maria!"

For a minute, the three of them just sat there. Then Emma got up. "I can't kneel anymore. Both my legs are already asleep."

Maria got up too and they all stood there in the room, the lights all turned on, the shutters closed. It was still nighttime.

"So, what in the world was that dream about?" Emma said.

She looked at Maria, who quickly glanced at Aaron. He slightly shook his head. Maria understood and turned back to Emma. "I don't really remember.

"Too bad. 'Cuz it'll be nice to know. You were so weird. Acted so strange. Screamed so loudly, it woke me up. When I rushed out of Nick's room, I bumped right into Aaron in the hallway, then we both came in here. We turned on the lights and tried to wake you up, but you were in a real funky mood. Real scary, actually. Like sleepwalking or something like that. Looking all over the bins for some words your mom apparently labeled for the move. For the move to Eglin AFB. But she really didn't label anything. And then you just fainted all of a sudden."

Maria looked at Emma in surprise. She had just summed up her strange moment before she fainted. Those letters on the bins. She took a deep breath. She now realized the labels had been part of a dream, her drowning dream. *Why? I need to talk to Aaron. Alone. Without Emma. I fainted again. Fainted from dreams. Memories? That's absurd!*

"You're okay?"

"Yeah, yeah, I'm okay. Thanks for the wet cloth, Emma."

"You're welcome. I thought it might help you after you fainted. So, do you remember what exactly you dreamed about?"

"Well, I keep having these weird drowning dreams. Not sure why." She really didn't want to get into it with Emma, as Emma would surely tell her mom. *And then Aaron's whole family would know about my strange dreams, that I might possibly be crazy, all of that. I don't want them to know. I need Emma to stop.*

But Emma wouldn't stop interrogating her. "*Drowning* dream? Why drowning?"

"I don't know. I asked my mom if I ever almost drowned, but she said no. She just thought it was a metaphor or a symbol, for all the recent changes in my life."

"Like the Freudian dream theory?" Emma was excited now. "Oh, I love psychology. It's so interesting to learn about your mind, the tricks it can play on you, and—"

"*Yes*, Emma, like the Freudian dream theory," Aaron said, "Google 'drowning in dreams according to Freud' and you'll know everything we know."

"Okay, I will. Great idea. Just let me get my phone." She made to walk out.

"Emma, not now, silly!" Aaron laughed. "We all need to get back to sleep. We have to be up in a few hours."

Emma sighed. "Fine, big bro, I get it. You're right. As always."

"Good girl." Aaron smiled as Emma walked out of the room.

Maria had just turned off the lights when Aaron came back, dressed in pajamas, his teeth freshly brushed. He found his way to their mattress in the dark and lay down next to her. "So, you're okay?"

Maria said nothing. In the dark he felt her face and found silent tears running down her cheeks. He leaned over and hugged her. Her head on his strong shoulder, she cried helplessly. "Aaron, I just don't know what all of this means. I don't know. I'm so confused. Maybe I am crazy after all?"

He shook his head. "No, you're not. I know you're not."

"How can you be so sure? I know the Freudian interpretation makes sense, but I feel like there's more. Isn't there more?"

Aaron stiffened up. *I can't tell her yet. I need more proof.* Maria noticed his muscles tightening under her head.

"Aaron? What is it?"

"Nothing," he said quickly, maybe a little too quickly. Her tears ran dry, and she now looked at him. Even though it was dark, he could feel her stare. She wiggled out of his hug quickly.

"Aaron, what aren't you telling me?"

"Nothing," he squawked, and turned around to lie down on his side, his back to her.

"*Seriously*, Aaron? You think I'll believe that?"

"Let's just sleep."

Maria bent over him, he felt her warm breath in his face. "I know it's dark, but I swear I can see you blushing. Come on, Aaron, don't lie to me. What is it? I feel like you know something, have a theory or something."

He was silent. *What should I say? Your mom might not be your mom?*

"Aaron, come on. Please, don't lie to me. I'm your fiancée. You shouldn't withhold what you're thinking. Even if it's something bad, we need to stick together, we need to tell each other." Her voice was shaky now. He knew she had started crying again. "Please, Aaron, please, just tell me."

"Maria. . . ." he said slowly to buy himself some time. "I don't know exactly yet. Please, just let me find out more, and then I'll tell you."

"No!" Maria said, her voice sharp. "You will tell me *now*. Whatever it is you know, you will tell me now!"

Aaron sighed and sat up. "Okay, I guess. But you need to promise me you won't get upset."

Maria peered at him through the dark. Her eyes had adjusted to the gloom and she could see his whole face. She nodded. "Sure, I promise. Well, I'll try. So, tell me, what is it? Something about my dad?

Jonathan Smith? Did you find something out about him? Was he in the Air Force?"

No, it's about your mom. And I know you'll be upset. Who wouldn't be, when they've been betrayed by the one person they love the most? He took a deep breath and was ready to start when he suddenly had an idea. An idea on how to give Maria some of the info she sought, but not share the one assumption that would break her.

"Well, I did some more research, and I hate to say it but Jonathan Smith doesn't exist."

Maria gasped. "*What?*"

Aaron nodded. "I searched the military database. And took your dreams into consideration. You're clearly dreaming of a guy in the Air Force. We both know that." She nodded and swallowed hard. "Well, I found a guy who might be your dad. A guy in the Air Force. A guy that has gone on many deployments. And he has your unique exotic eyes. You know, his eyes kinda gave it away. Yeah, I found a guy with the same eyes as you."

Maria stared at him. "You did?" she whispered.

He nodded again. "Yeah, it's safe to assume *that* guy's your dad. Not Jonathan Smith."

Maria swallowed hard. "Who is it?"

"General Brad Collins."

"Brad?" Maria now whispered.

"Yeah, Brad. The name you mentioned before, in your dreams."

"I did?"

"Yeah, that one time." Aaron realized she didn't remember her Freudian slip. "Anyways, I think he's your dad."

Maria was far away now, deep in thought. They were silent for a while until she spoke again. "But Mamá clearly said his name is Jonathan Smith."

Aaron nodded. "Yeah. I know."

"Brad Collins. Sounds familiar. Do I know him?"

"Well, you've seen him before. At the ROTC ball. He was the guest speaker."

Maria gasped. She remembered him. *Charismatic guy. Likable guy. The guy at the water fountain.* "And you really think he's my dad?"

"Yeah."

"But why? Other than the eyes?"

Aaron shrugged. He didn't want to get into that part of the story. First, he needed to put the pieces of information he'd gathered so far together. He started thinking about how best to get out of this situation when Maria interrupted his thoughts.

"Is he married?"

"Not anymore, I think," Aaron said. "Why?"

Maria was silent for a bit, then let out a grunt. "Then he must have cheated on his wife with my mom. He must have given Mamá the wrong name. A fake name. Oh my gosh, what an idiot. What an asshole! No wonder he's divorced now. He was probably a player, a total player."

Aaron was perplexed. *That's what Maria thinks? She still doesn't suspect her mom is the bad guy here? She doesn't even consider her mom would lie to her? Oh my, their bond is strong, very strong. That's not good.*

He heard Maria's voice again, her defiant voice. "Right, Aaron? It makes sense, doesn't it?"

"Yeah," he said quickly, trying not to sound too shaken.

"Oh, Aaron, I thought my dad was a nice guy. And now this. It's crazy!"

Aaron just nodded and then yawned. He was tired.

"Aaron, why didn't you tell me all this earlier?"

He could tell how upset she was. "Because I didn't want to upset you. I wanted you to enjoy this weekend."

She nodded and let out a sigh. "Makes sense, I get it."

Thank goodness. He gave her a kiss on the cheek and was ready to sleep.

But Maria wasn't done yet, not by a long shot. "So, why do I remember this Brad guy in my dreams? In those memories?"

Aaron took a deep breath. *Because you grew up with him. But I can't tell you that.*

"Did Mamá and I see him again when I was little? Did he come back to Florida after I was born?"

Aaron looked at her and decided to share a few more details about what he knew. "He was stationed at Eglin AFB in the early 2000s, when you were just a toddler."

Maria stared at him now, then the words came tumbling out of her. "Maybe we saw him then? Did Mamá somehow find him and see him there? Maybe she wanted to move in with him? Is that why she had labeled those bins, in my dream? And then something happened that she still won't tell me about? Maybe he was abusive? Or maybe he wanted nothing to do with me, was mad, so mad I existed. Maybe he tried to throw me off a boat? And that's why I'm drowning in my dreams? Or did he do something to Mamá? Maybe I experienced something bad there when I was a toddler. Maybe that's why I'm so afraid of Eglin AFB?"

Aaron stared at her, shocked by her torrent of speculation. He didn't know what to say. He sighed. "I don't know Maria. You'll have to ask your mom those questions. But let's move there first. Maybe more memories will come back then." He truly hoped they would. *More memories. But those memories will likely prove that Martina is a criminal, not that Maria's dad is a cheater or a bad guy. No, it's Martina who seems to be the bad guy here.*

Maria sighed. "Yeah, maybe I'll have more memories once we're there. Then I can ask Mamá again." She saw Aaron yawn again and yawned herself. "Okay, sleepyhead. Let's try to get some sleep."

Aaron nodded. "Yeah, sounds good. Good night, my love."

Maria gave him a kiss and turned around. She was exhausted and closed her eyes. Both of them were deep in thought, but then Maria drifted off to sleep and it was only Aaron still awake, thinking.

That went well, all things considered. He looked over at her, saw her breathing quietly, in and out, in and out. *My sweet Maria. Still not sure what happened to you. But yes, General Collins must be your father. But he's not a cheater. He's a man whose daughter was kidnapped. A man who lost his child.*

Aaron wasn't sure what to do. *Maybe I should contact him?*

CHAPTER 67

Brad woke abruptly. He hadn't slept well at all last night. *Of course not. Way too much going on, way too many thoughts circling, swirling around in my head. Not sure what to think, how to feel, what to do. Guess I just have to put on my poker face and go with the flow. I can do it. Yes I can. I can manage to go back and not break down. I'll try, at least. Try hard.*

And I'll have her with me by my side. Elisabeth.

He smiled and grabbed the alarm clock off his nightstand to turn off the alarm he no longer needed. He got out of his big king size bed. *Why did I even buy this big bed? Way too big for one person. We only needed such a big bed when we shared it with each other. And with our little one. She joined us in our big bed almost every night. Some days, she'd just fall asleep there before we did. Either way, she'd always end up in the middle of the bed. Like a queen surrounded by her court. The focal point, the sweet middle.*

He smiled. It was a sweet memory. But it also made him sad, so he quickly headed to the kitchen. He turned on his coffee machine and brewed a big cup of black coffee. When it was ready, he sat down at the kitchen table, cup in hand, and went over his packing list. As though he were about to be deployed and had been issued a military-mandated packing list, he meticulously went over his handwritten list to make sure he hadn't missed anything. He ended up taking both coffee and the list upstairs to inspect each item on the packing list in person.

He completed his inspection and still had time to waste before Drew would be there to pick him up and take him to the airport. He decided to go for his usual morning run. It always made him feel better, made him feel *something*. He felt less like an empty shell while running. He ran every day, every morning. One cup of coffee, a run, a quick breakfast, work. That was his day. He tried to do the same today.

When he returned from his run, he quickly grabbed a breakfast bar—his usual fare—then jumped in the shower. Once clean, still in his towel, he brushed his teeth and shaved. He always preferred to do a wet shave, even though it took longer. Somehow, the wet shave worked better for his beard growth, and he liked to see where exactly he had already shaved as he moved the razor side to side across his face, cutting tracks through the shaving cream.

My little one was fascinated by shaving cream. She loved watching me shave. She loved playing with it and often smeared it all over in the bathtub or sink. Annoying, but so adorable at the same time.

He smiled, then winced as he nicked himself. He sighed again and washed all the shaving cream off his face. Then he dried it with a towel and stared into the mirror. Into his exotic eyes. *She had the same eyes as me.*

He stared into the mirror and watched them change from brown to green. Emerald-green eyes, matching the water of the base he would be flying to in a few short hours.

"You're not looking forward to this, huh?"

Brad turned around and looked at his friend. "Me? *Looking forward to it?* To a trip to Eglin?" He laughed a coarse laugh.

"I know, I know. Just trying to start a conversation about the obvious," Drew said. "I know you hate that place, Cave Man. But I'm glad you finally decided to go. It's a big program. They'll love showing it off to you."

Brad considered his friend's words. "Yeah, I know. It'll be good."

"Yeah, it'll be okay, Cave Man, it'll be okay." Drew focused on the road again while Brad stared out the window on the passenger side.

"We should be at BWI soon, Cave Man."

Brad nodded, then sighed. "Just don't know why we have to go all the way to BWI. It takes forever. Why not fly out of Reagan? It's literally right across the road from where we work."

"Yeah, I know, Reagan would've been more convenient. It's silly."

"No kidding. And then we don't even get a nonstop flight to Valparaiso. We'll have to transfer."

Drew laughed. "You know the government, man. Why give us a nonstop flight straight from Reagan Airport? You know they look for the cheapest flight instead."

"Even for a general?"

Drew glanced over at his friend. "Even for a big shot general like you. Yep. Afraid so."

Brad laughed. "Too bad, man, too bad."

Drew glanced at him again. "Glad you're in a good mood, Cave Man. Didn't expect that."

"No? Well, guess I'm trying to move on, finally."

"Are you?" Drew raised his eyebrows and glanced over again.

"Yeah, sure," Brad said quickly, and stared out of the window. He watched the trees and bushes fly by and felt bad lying to his best friend. *Can't tell you I'm meeting Elisabeth there to reopen the case. You'll think I'm crazy.*

Drew glanced over at Brad again. "You sure you're alright, man?"

"Yeah. No worries, Drew, no worries." He tried to sound as convincing as he could. "Hey, there's the exit. Don't miss it!"

Drew quickly changed lanes without blinking and took the airport exit ramp. Soon after, they arrived and parked the car at the long-term parking lot. The two men got out, grabbed their bags, locked up, then looked for the closest shuttle stop.

"There it is," Drew said, and pointed.

Brad took a deep breath in, clutched his bag a little tighter, and started walking. "Okay. Let's go then."

CHAPTER 68

"Okay, let's go then," Grace said after Maria had parked her car at the departure drop-off area at the Orlando airport. She opened the passenger door and got out. Maria popped open the trunk from the inside and got out as well. Emma was so tired that she moved a lot slower than both Maria and Grace, but eventually joined them at the trunk and helped lift out their small carry-on suitcases.

The three women sighed. "The morning has just flown by, hasn't it?" Grace looked at the girls. Emma and Maria just nodded.

"Honestly, the whole weekend did. It feels like you just arrived," Maria said. "Thanks for helping with the packing this morning, and for letting Mamá and I tag along for Aaron's commissioning and graduation this weekend."

"Nonsense! 'Tag along,'" Grace scolded Maria. "*We* should be thanking *you* for putting up with Aaron and his new, crazy Air Force life."

Emma agreed. "Yeah, thanks for putting up with my big brother!"

Maria laughed. "You're welcome. Maybe thank him for putting up with me?"

"Nah, you're pretty easy to get along with," Emma smiled. "Except for those weird dreams of yours! Better get a handle on that!"

Maria froze for a second, but then calmed down, telling herself that Emma kept bringing it up because she really cared about her. *Probably scared poor Emma to death last night. Can't hold it against her when she means well.* Maria was still occupied thinking about everything Aaron had told her last night when Grace pulled her in for a long hug.

"Maria, we're so excited to have you in our family. I know you'll take good care of my boy. Thanks for being willing to move with him, put up with his military lifestyle, and always be there for him. We really, really appreciate it."

Maria felt Grace's sobs on her shoulder and tears rose in her eyes as well. "You're welcome. Thank you for taking me in so warmly as a part of your family."

"We love you, Maria. Good luck with the move. And thanks for having us this weekend."

Emma came over and gave Maria a big hug as well. "Yeah, thanks for having us this weekend and letting us stay at your place. And me at Aaron's place. It was such a fun weekend. Great meeting your mom too."

Grace nodded. "Yes, please tell your mom we said hi. And tell her to call me!"

Maria nodded and gave Emma one last squeeze.

"Bye, new sis," Emma said, and picked up her suitcase. She started walking away with her mom.

"We love you, Maria," Grace called over her shoulder and waved.

"Yep, we love ya, sis!" Emma yelled and waved also.

Maria closed the trunk and waved back while wiping away her tears. *Wow, what a sweet family.* She got in her car and drove away, thinking of her new family, then her mom. *Why didn't Mamá tell me that Brad Collins is my dad?* The whole day, she had been wondering about that and had come to a conclusion. *Pretty sure Mamá took me to see him at Eglin AFB. That's why I remember him and that base.*

And then something must have happened. Something bad must have happened. Something bad right there at the beautiful Emerald Coast.

CHAPTER 69

"We'll be landing shortly on the beautiful Emerald Coast," Brad heard through the airplane loudspeaker. He had a bad feeling in his stomach.

Valparaiso airport. The local airport shared the same runway with the base and he had often landed here himself. He remembered it. Remembered it all too well. *I flew around here a lot right after the "accident." High above the clouds, to get away from everything on the ground: my thoughts, the constant questioning, the constant reminders of our missing child, the look on her face. . . . Eventually I couldn't stand to look at her anymore. Couldn't stand seeing the pain of a mother whose child was gone.*

It was only when he felt a hand nudging him that he noticed they had landed.

"You okay?" Drew said.

"Yeah." Brad Collins looked out of the window. The bad feeling in his stomach came back suddenly, violently. He swallowed hard so he wouldn't throw up.

Ugh. Embarrassing.

Drew gave him a pat on the shoulder. "It'll be alright, Cave Man, it'll be alright," he told his friend as the plane taxied to the gate.

"Nice house," Drew said. They were walking through the Distinguished Visitor's Quarters on Eglin AFB. "But I guess they only give their VIPs the very best, don't they?"

"Yeah, they do," Brad said, and kept walking, then stopped in front of a large bay window. "It's very nice for sure. They must have upgraded it."

Drew laughed. "Of course they have. It's been like twenty years, Brad."

"I know." He got quiet.

"And back then, you would've been the driver dropping people off here rather than the person being dropped off. Wait, have you ever even been to this part of the base? As far as I can recall, you weren't allowed back then."

"No, I wasn't. But I've been here before anyway." He stared outside the window.

"Don't tell me you actually snuck in one time? Boy, you had nerves of steel," Drew said and whistled through his teeth.

"Only once," Brad said. "I've been on this side of the base only once."

As he stared out of the window, the memories came back, suddenly, violently. He closed his eyes, and when he opened them, he found he was watching himself.

He was running along the road to the Distinguished Visitor's Quarters, running in the misty, warm weather. Slight rain was hitting his face, mixing with his own, salty tears. He heard himself screaming, searching as he was running, screaming his lost daughter's name, looking all over for her. He watched this young man, desperately looking for his daughter that was suddenly not in her bed anymore.

He became one with that young man of the past and sank to his knees, sobbing, screaming her name. "No, Moana, please, please come back! Where are you?"

His tears dripped on the ground and only when someone shook him did he realize he was kneeling on the floor of the Distinguished Visitor's Quarters, no longer looking for his daughter. He had given that up more than twenty years ago.

The hand on his shoulder moved, and he looked up, right into the face of his friend Drew, who was standing next to him with a concerned look on his face. "Brad, are you okay? You okay?"

He took one last look outside at the empty street, then got up and hastily wiped his face. "Yeah, sure, I'm okay. Just memories, man. Just memories. Let me use the bathroom real quick, then we can go eat. I'm hungry."

With that, he walked into the nearby restroom and closed the door behind him. Drew stared after him at the closed bathroom door.

Brad looked in the mirror and saw his now green eyes. He was still shaken from reliving that haunting memory. *I just have to hold on. Gotta keep it together. Even if every corner of Eglin AFB reminds me of the loss of my daughter. Every part of it, every freaking corner of Eglin AFB.*

CHAPTER 70

"Eglin AFB, here we come!" Jack Heikinnen stood outside Aaron's apartment with Maria and Aaron, ready to lock up and get on the road. He was excited to drive the truck with Aaron to his son's very first duty station.

But Aaron and Maria just stood there, staring at the apartment door. Jack cleared his throat. "Lots of changes, huh?"

"Yeah," the couple agreed.

Then Maria smiled. "Well, it is what it is." She looked at the men. "We got everything? Are we ready to go?"

"Yep, I'm ready," Jack said, and then looked at Aaron in his new uniform pants and greenish-tan undershirt. "Where's your jacket, Aaron?"

Aaron seemed absent-minded. He was still preoccupied with Maria's past. He had thought about it all day and still wasn't sure what to do.

"Aaron, *where's your uniform jacket?*" Maria repeated Jack's question.

Aaron looked down to see what he was wearing. "Oh. It's on my computer bag."

"And where's your computer bag, son?"

Aaron now looked at his dad. "Didn't you put it in the truck already?"

"Nope, I didn't. Did you?"

"No, I didn't." Aaron stared at the door. "Wait, don't pull the door shut yet. Must still be inside."

Maria and Jack looked at each other, eyebrows raised.

"Since when did you get so disorganized, Aaron?" Maria teased him, and Jack started laughing.

Aaron ignored them both and walked back inside. He looked around and found his computer bag in the corner. His phone was there as well, still charging. He unplugged it and quickly opened a web browser. *I just have to know more. Just a quick look.*

He started googling General Collins. He had an impressive résumé. He'd been stationed all over the place but was in DC now. Aaron skimmed the résumé. Hill AFB. *Hill AFB? That's in Utah. Maria had a dream about Utah. The dream with the flowers!*

His hands were immediately sweaty. *Dang it. I have to contact him. Have to find a contact number for him. But how?* Then he had an idea. *The Air Force email network. It would have his number.*

Quickly, he grabbed his laptop and pulled up the email network, then searched for General Collins. *There it is, a phone number. A work phone number. Should I call him now? No, it's Sunday. He wouldn't even be at the office today. Or is it a cell phone number?*

"Aaron?" he heard Maria calling him. "Where are you? We've been sitting in the truck forever waiting for you. What's taking so long?"

He saw the door open, and Maria stood in the door frame. "Oh my gosh, Aaron. Why are you on your laptop? There's no time for that! Come on, let's get going. Now!"

"I'm coming," he told her, then quickly saved the general's phone number in his cell phone, shut down his laptop, and packed everything away. He put on his camouflaged uniform jacket and stepped outside, bag in hand.

"Wasn't it a great idea to stop by here at Aaron's favorite restaurant to eat something before hitting the road?" Maria said with a smile.

The guys agreed. The two men got into the Penske truck and waved down from their high seats at Maria. *If Aaron hadn't worn his camo uniform, he could have passed for a real trucker. His dad in that flannel shirt of his definitely does.* She smiled up at the two excited wannabe truckers.

They yelled down through the window. "Ready to follow us?"

She gave them a thumbs-up.

Aaron honked the horn. "Let's go! Eglin, here we come!"

The moving truck rolled out of the parking lot with Aaron's car towed behind it, and Maria followed. *There's those spine shudders again.* She turned up her radio to tune out the little voices in her head telling her she was going to a dangerous place.

CHAPTER 71

Jonathan Sullivan followed them in his truck and made sure to keep enough distance so that they wouldn't notice him. *So glad I brought my personal car, not the work car with that store branding plastered over it. Would've been hard to blend in with that. But my good ol' Dodge Ram blends in well, very well.* He smiled, knowing nobody would notice him.

It was a quiet drive up north. Not too much traffic. He made sure not to lose them. But that was easy. The yellow Penske truck with its car trailer was very easy to see and find again whenever his vision was obscured. Sometimes he even passed them, for fun. He knew where they were headed to, anyway.

Seems like I might not need to be too worried about Problem Child after all. She was so little. Doubt she'll remember anything. At least that's what he was hoping. *I'm a good guy. Never wanted a piece of that crazy situation. Wasn't even my idea. No, it wasn't. It wasn't my fault.* He sighed. *Wish I never met them. Wish I never talked to them.*

Well, they did help me get sober, that's for sure. I had no other choice.

He saw the Penske truck turn into a rest stop, but he kept on going. *I'll take the next one then wait there for them there. They shouldn't be too long.*

He kept driving, then turned off at the next stop and parked. He decided to compose a text message to Ms. Carmal telling her he was still sick and couldn't make it to work tomorrow. He sighed. He loved his work. Loved his store, his business. *Yeah, I made it. After so many tries in life, I finally built a good thing.*

His phone blinked with a reply. *I like her. Carmal's a good employee and a nice lady. Responsive.*

He longed to have someone, someone who would be there for him, a partner in life. But he hadn't found anyone. He liked exotic women. Martina had fit the bill back when she was young.

He thought back to all those women that had passed through his life. There had been a lot. He sighed. *Women. And alcohol. And gambling. Hard to say no to, easy to get addicted to. Never had the strength to say no. I should've. And I definitely should've when I met* them.

That group of four who saddled me with all that trouble. With Problem Child. "The Fearless Four" they called themselves. Should've said no to them.

He sighed. *If I'd said no back then, I wouldn't be following that dumb Penske truck right now. Thought it was a great idea back then, a fine idea. Thought I'd taken care of everything, taken care of it my way. The better way. The less brutal way. But seems like you only get punished for being too nice.* He sighed again and took out a sandwich and a coke.

It was going to be a long drive through the peaceful, quiet, starry Florida night.

CHAPTER 72

The peaceful, starry Florida night surrounded them on the highway. They'd been at it for almost six hours and the drive was starting to feel long and tiring, but they were doing their best to hang in there. Their destination was getting closer and closer.

Soon, Maria saw the truck blink to signal an exit off I-10 toward Niceville. She thought about that name for a bit. *Funny name for a city. Must be nice in Niceville.*

"Nice in Niceville!" a tiny voice seemed to say in her head.

At first Maria giggled, but then the voice wouldn't leave her alone. It kept repeating the same sentence over and over.

What in the world? It isn't even that funny. She had no idea why that sentence kept echoing down every slope of her brain. Though it felt as though she'd heard that joke before. A long time ago.

No, that's crazy. Aaron probably said it when we were researching apartments for him or something. Yes, that must be it. She turned up the music even louder to drown out the silly little voice in her head as she exited I-10 toward Niceville.

She found herself on a smaller road. It was very dark out. It had gotten late, and Maria's bottom was hurting from all that sitting. Almost felt like it was going numb. Impatiently, she shifted in her seat and waited for them to finally arrive.

There! The sign told them they were very close. *Eglin AFB – Main Gate*, it read. The green sign's reflective white letters jumped out at her. Maria stared at them and took her foot off the gas pedal without even noticing it. A shudder ran down her spine as her car crept along the road leading to Eglin AFB's main gate.

Honk!

She was startled out of her trance and noticed a car tailgating behind her. It honked again. She looked ahead and saw that the moving truck had gotten far ahead and was already stopped at the next light, blinking a left again.

Honk!

"Just calm down, idiot."

She sped up to catch up with both the speed limit and the moving truck. Luckily, the other car soon turned right and was no longer behind her.

Then she looked left and saw it. The main gate. The illuminated gate to the base. It had two lanes going in, but one lane was closed off to traffic with cones. There were metal roadblocks to drive around on either side. The exit lane had a row of spikes that looked like they could pierce through any type of tire if anyone tried to go the wrong way.

In between the entrance and exit lanes was a little house, almost just a hut with windows. Just then a car pulled up to the gate and Maria saw the door to the little house open. An armed military guard stepped out. The car's window rolled down and the driver handed the guard something. He looked at it, gave it back, saluted, and the car rolled past.

What is that all about? She wondered for a second, then understood. The ID checkpoint.

"*No ID, no go,*" said that strange tiny voice in her head again.

Go away! Go away, silly voice! Learn to speak correct English and go away!

The light turned green and Aaron made a wide turn. He tried to drive into the parking lot next to a little house located just before the gate and Maria followed slowly, and saw the tiny building said *Visitors' Center* on the front.

But Aaron was having a hard time getting the truck into the tiny parking lot and suddenly, he had two military officers trotting out, gesturing him to back up.

Oh dear!

One of them jogged up to Aaron's window and talked to him. Then Aaron started backing up, and Maria wasn't sure what to do since she was occupying the street behind him. The military personnel that Aaron had talked to now waved her down and signaled her to go around the moving truck and pull into the small parking lot. She saw another sign that read "One Way Only," but assumed she had permission to break that rule since the military guy in uniform was waving her in. The other military guy helped Aaron and his dad back up and had him park in the lane that had been blocked off by cones.

Maria parked her car in one of the few parking spaces then jumped in surprise when she noticed a uniformed man standing right next to her window. She rolled it down.

"Hello, ma'am," he said, and Maria looked at him, a little stunned. *"Ma'am?" Guess I'll have to get used to that.*

The little voice in her head came back suddenly. *"Ma'am, ma'am,"* it repeated.

Maria rubbed her head.

"Are you traveling together?" She had almost forgotten about the man by her window who now pointed to the big moving truck.

"Yes, we're traveling together. My fiancé, his dad, and me."

"Ah, your fiancé?"

"Yes. Correct. I mean, yes, sir!"

He smiled even wider. "New to the Air Force?"

"Yes. Yes, sir, I mean."

"Alright, ma'am, I'm gonna have to ask you to get out now so we can get you a visitor's pass. Don't forget to bring your ID. Please follow me."

"Oh, okay." Maria unbuckled herself. She grabbed her purse off the empty passenger seat and got out of the car. Aaron and his dad also got out of the truck and met Maria in the small parking lot.

"Hey there! You okay?" Aaron took her hand and pulled her in for a quick kiss.

"No kissing in uniform, Second Lieutenant!" one of the checkpoint Airmen scolded him.

Aaron immediately let go of Maria's hand and stiffened up. "Yes, sir, understood!"

The other Airman held the door open and smiled. "Well, Lieutenant, lots to learn, huh?" He winked and led Jack, Maria, and Aaron inside.

"Welcome to Eglin Air Force Base," an older uniformed man behind the desk said. "Now, Lieutenant, let's see your orders, please."

Aaron handed him a piece of paper. The man working the desk studied it, then asked for Aaron's ID before printing another piece of paper.

"You'll need to go to the CAC Card Center first thing in the morning, Lieutenant, to get your official Air Force ID. Make sure to get your beauty rest—they'll be taking a picture." He winked.

They sure are in a joking mood. Or maybe just excited to have a visitor stop by in the middle of the night. Or both? Either way, Maria and then Jack handed over their IDs, punched in their social security numbers, and after looking at the computer screen for a little while, the older man printed a slip of paper for them as well.

"You two will need to stay close to your sponsor, our new second lieutenant here. Avoid walking around on base alone. Always have your visitor's pass with you at all times," he explained to Jack and Maria, who just nodded. "Well then, you're all set. Welcome to Eglin."

Aaron quickly asked for directions to the TLF check-in and received a map of the base. They opened up the lane that had been closed so the truck had enough room to fit. As a formality, one of the same guards that had chaperoned them came over to look at their newly printed visitor's passes before waving them through.

CHAPTER 73

Jonathan Sullivan helplessly watched as they were waved through and drove onto base. *Fuck! They're staying on base? I can't get in there!* He scrambled to think about where to go now and what to do. Was he being too optimistic to think they'd step foot off base again? *No. I'm sure they will.* He decided to stay close to the base and get a cheap motel.

After driving around for a while, he found something. He was tired, longing for a drink, but knew he had to hold back. *I still need to stay sober, as sober as I can. Can't relapse. Wish I had brought my punching bag.* Obviously, he hadn't.

He parked his pickup truck and got the keys to his room at the motel. He walked inside and started punching a pillow.

Punch, don't drink. Punch, don't drink.

After a while, he felt better. *Man, my shrink was right. Punching helps take care of that anger. I don't need to drown it in drinks.* He smiled and fell onto the motel room bed. He was tired, but knew he had to get up early.

I need to make sure I spot them whenever they leave through the gate. I'll look out for a Penske truck or her car. Whatever they might drive off base with. At least I know what kind of car she drives. A blue Oldsmobile.

He stretched out on the bed and tried to relax. *It'll be fine. It's fine for her to be back on base. She won't remember Eglin AFB.*

CHAPTER 74

Eglin AFB. Here they were, on the grounds of Eglin AFB. Maria shuddered. *It's a bit freaky being here after everything that's been going on.*

She followed the Penske truck with its trailer and kept going, ignoring the little hairs on her arm standing up alert, ignoring the sweatiness of her palms, the continuous shudders that kept running down her spine. She concentrated on following Aaron and Jack. It was so dark here. Hard to see anything at night with barely any streetlamps to help them find their way.

Without signaling, Aaron turned a sharp right. Maria saw the car trailer hop the curb and cringed, but the one wheel that had jumped it just plopped back down onto the street again. *Good. Nothing bad happened. Still, this is exhausting. I know Aaron is pretty tired, too. Hopefully, we can go to sleep soon in our beds at the hotel.*

Well, the TLF.

Her hands slipped off the wheel the moment she thought of the TLF. *"Eglin's TLF, Eglin's TLF,"* that tiny little voice in her head repeated over and over.

Maria grew more and more uneasy. Suddenly she was right on top of Aaron's towed car and had to brake hard—she hadn't even noticed that he'd stopped the truck.

She was breathing heavily after the near miss. *Where are we?*

She stopped the car and then saw Aaron jump out of the truck's driver's seat with a bunch of papers in his hand. He waved her over, so Maria pulled up next to the truck and rolled down the passenger window.

"This is the check-in for the TLF," Aaron explained.

She looked around and now realized they were in another parking lot, though she didn't see any water.

"I thought it was right by the water?" Her tongue felt heavy for some reason as she said those words.

"Not the check-in. Gotta get our keys here first, then keep driving. Right to *here*."

He bent down to poke his lower body in and showed her the map of the base. The building where they would be staying was at the opposite end of where they were at now. *How annoying! More driving and looking for directions.*

"Do you want to come in?"

"Do I have to?"

Aaron shrugged his shoulders.

"Well, sure, I'll go with you. Can't sit anymore anyway." She got out of her car, but made sure to bring her purse with the visitor's pass and her ID.

Jack got out as well and the three of them walked inside. It was a modern-looking building with glass sliding doors leading inside. Not at all like the antiquated pictures they had seen online. But maybe only the check-in was modernized? They stood in front of a desk and rang the little bell on the counter.

"Good evening," they heard from a room behind the counter. "I will be right there." Soon after, a friendly lady came out and greeted the three of them. She looked at Aaron's papers and the reservations. She then printed something and had Aaron sign it, ran his credit card, and soon they were all set.

"Enjoy TLF," she said with a slight accent. "You're third row down, apartment right next to water. Look, right here."

The woman pulled out a map of that part of the base and circled the building they needed to go to, then the apartment they would be in.

"Good luck with house hunting, and please let us know if you need move out earlier or if you like extended stay. We kept apartment open for you after just in case. You can extend reservation. Not too many movers this early in summer," the friendly clerk explained, and smiled widely. "Welcome to Eglin Air Force Base!" Maria stared at her. "I remember when my husband and I moved here. We were young like you and Eglin was my first station with him. We came from Korea." She laughed. "Long time ago. And now we're retired here. It's good place! You will like it at Eglin."

She winked at Maria, and Maria smiled back. "Like Eglin, will like Eglin," Maria said loudly, the little voice in her head taking over.

The lady's smile vanished, and both Aaron and Jack stared at her. Maria didn't notice what she'd done; all she heard was the small little voice in her head egging her on.

"Like Eglin. Yes! Nice Eglin."

Before she knew it, she was being tugged away by her hand. She felt so small, so little. She turned around and found the desk suddenly looked very tall, the small, slender woman behind it even taller. Maria waved goodbye. "Bye-bye! Will like Eglin!"

Maria felt the hot, humid air on her face the moment they left the air-conditioned check-in building and suddenly wasn't pulled along anymore. She looked at her hand, her grown hand with the shiny engagement ring on it. She was confused and felt a headache coming on. She rubbed her head.

Aaron stopped her to look her into the eyes. "What was *that*? How dare you insult that nice lady?"

Maria stopped rubbing her head. "Me? What? I didn't insult her! Why would you even say that?"

"Because he's right," Jack said, his voice stern, his look cold, "You insulted her and made all of us look bad. How can *you* out of all people make fun of someone's accent? You're the daughter of an immigrant. I am *very* disappointed." Jack pressed his lips together and opened the moving truck's passenger door, climbed up the steps, got in, and slammed the door shut.

Bam!

The loud noise made Maria jump, her thoughts clear for a moment. "What did I do? I made fun of her? Oh no, no. Really?"

Aaron nodded and gave her a funny look. "You don't remember that, do you?"

"No, I don't. Really, I don't. I'm so sorry, Aaron. I should walk back in and apologize." Maria turned around and started walking toward the check-in building.

He grabbed her arm and held her back, then shook his head. "No, don't apologize. That'll be even more embarrassing."

Tears started dwelling in her eyes. "I'm so sorry." She rubbed her temples.

While studying her face, Aaron raised an eyebrow. "Well . . . it's okay," he said, "Let's just go. Sure you can drive?"

"Yeah, I can. It's just a headache. I'll be fine."

"Hmm. Okay then. Follow me."

Maria got back into her car while Aaron climbed up the steps of the truck into the driver's seat. Maria heard him start the truck. Her head was throbbing, but she concentrated on following Aaron. As they rolled down the roads on base that dark night, yet another shudder ran down her spine.

They drove further down the winding road. On the left-hand side of it was the bay while the right-hand side of the road showed big open fields surrounded by trees. There were not just palm trees but pine trees. Big dark pine trees on those dark, open fields, throwing strange shadows on the road that Maria was driving on, slowly following the big yellow truck in front of her.

Her palms were so sweaty, her head throbbing with a headache, the little hairs on her arms standing up. She cracked the window to let a breeze in, but despite being right there by the water on the bay in the middle of the night, the air was hot and humid. Not much of a breeze at all.

She concentrated on the road. *Not many streetlamps in this area.* They passed a large lot full of campers and boats, all fenced in. *Strange.*

"For people who have RVs or campers or boats," Maria heard a voice explain.

Who's there? She looked around in bewilderment. *Nobody. There's no one.* She turned on the radio again to distract herself. *This place is creepy!*

They crept along the winding road at only fifteen miles per hour. Then she saw them. The TLFs at Eglin AFB.

CHAPTER 75

The TLFs were a few rows of old-looking, one-story buildings with a half-sandy, half-grassy area in between each row. The rows faced the water, the last apartment of each row was closest to the water. Each row contained four doors, every one of them facing the half-sandy, half-grassy area meaning that two buildings shared the grassy and sandy area as well as a common sidewalk that led to the parking spaces. There were parking spaces right next to the road. One building in particular was lit in bright light. Through the windows, Maria could see rows and rows of white washing machines and driers.

Laundromat, the sign above the glass door said.

Her left hand slipped off the steering wheel. She stared at the building and saw a little waiting room right behind the glass doors with a round table and TV hanging from the ceiling.

As she slowly drove past, she saw a friendly-looking Hispanic woman who was enjoying a snack at the round table while watching TV. Then she looked up at Maria. "Hola, mi niña," she heard her say.

What? How am I able to hear that woman through the closed glass doors? And how is she able to see me while I'm driving by? Maria turned her head to look closer and suddenly, the woman was gone. The TV wasn't even running.

Maria's head wasn't merely throbbing anymore, it was hammering, a relentless pain right behind her temples. She had to brake hard again as she hadn't been paying attention to her driving and didn't notice that Aaron had turned to the right, into a sandy parking area. He turned the truck around and parked it sideways along the tree line surrounding the empty parking lot. Only a few other cars were parked in the parking spaces by the streets, and this lot was completely empty.

Maria turned in and came to a stop next to Aaron. He gestured for her to park on the opposite side of the truck, so she pulled in backward into a parking spot right by the entrance to the parking area. This part was still tarmacked—the asphalt started breaking apart the further you went into the parking lot.

She got out of her car and waited by the driver's door, holding on to the open door while looking across the street at the TLFs. She saw the entrance to the rows of little one-story buildings. Each row had a number. One, two, three. Number three.

The lady had said three.

Maria stared at it. Three was located on the left-hand side and shared the grassy, sandy area in between with building number four. Each building had four front doors, meaning each contained four apartments inside. The doors to the apartments were white, each with a light and a little overhang supported by two white pillars to provide shelter. The entrance of each apartment was connected to an asphalt walkway. A long window could be found by every front door. Most of the windows were dark, but a few were lit up with curtains pulled shut for privacy.

Maria was leaning on the open car door now, more for support than anything. She stared at the buildings. A cold shudder ran down her spine. She stared at the half-grassy, half-sandy area in between the buildings and followed it to the end. The buildings stopped, but the sandy area went on. She squinted to see where it led to.

And then she saw it. The shadowy silhouettes of boats. The silhouette of a small, little marina. *No. A marina? Then there must be water. The half-grassy, half-sandy area leads right to the water! Yes, it does. No fence, no nothing. You can walk right into the water from here.*

Oh no. Walk right into the water? From the apartments? No, no, no! Not the water. The dark, mucky, murky water. Her hands tried to grip on to the open car door, her knuckles white from holding on so tightly, but at last they slipped, couldn't hold on anymore as she stared at that water in the distance, the dark water of Choctawhatchee Bay at Eglin AFB, and everything went black around her.

"Maria! Maria! Are you okay?"

Slowly, she opened her eyes and realized she was sprawled flat on the hard ground. She felt the ground with her hand and touched what felt like asphalt, like a street, but with lots of fine sand on top.

What in the world?

She looked around and saw she was lying next to her car.

Wait. Is this a dream? Have I been in an accident?

Her thoughts started racing, retracing her steps before this strange moment, when she saw the open door of her car, and through its window a yellow truck. *Oh yeah, the moving truck!*

"Did you hurt yourself?" Jack asked.

She looked up and saw Jack kneeling next to her, then realized Aaron was sitting there as well. Aaron in his camo uniform, peering down at her in concern while holding her legs up. She sat up slowly.

"I'm okay, I think." She felt the back of her head. *Autsch! A bump is already forming. Oh no. I must have really hit my head hard.*

"Are you *sure* you're okay, Maria?" Aaron said, his voice stern.

She nodded. "Yeah. I guess I hit my head a little, but I'm okay. Did I faint?" They all looked at each other.

"Not sure. We were getting out of the truck when suddenly, we saw you drop to the ground. We came running as fast as we could," Jack explained.

Maria shrugged and got up. She dusted off her pants and found she felt fine.

"I'm okay," she said, "No worries." She smiled at the two men.

Aaron raised his eyebrow, but Jack got up and shrugged his shoulders. "Well, if you are sure, then I guess we need to bring in at least the essentials." Jack turned around and started walking away.

Puzzled, Maria looked at Aaron. She saw the concerned look on his face, his blue eyes resting on her. *Wait? Get the essentials? Aaron in a camo uniform? Sand on the asphalt?*

She turned her head and saw *them* across from the parking lot they were in. Those little one-story buildings. She stared directly at row number three.

She wasn't sure what was happening, but suddenly she couldn't hear Aaron and Jack anymore. Their voices faded, faded as she went further and further away into her deep, deep memories, trying to make sense of it all.

I know this place! I know it. I've been here. Reaching for her car door and holding on tightly was all she could do—the memories came flashing back so violently that they almost swept her off her feet again. She couldn't feel the car door in her hands anymore, though. Instead, she felt an arm. She looked down and saw it—a strong arm in a camouflaged uniform.

Oh my gosh, no! Her mind started swirling, mixing up past and present.

No, don't carry me again! Go away! Go away stranger in the uniform! She screamed a high-pitched scream and heard two voices, two low voices trying to shush her. The man in uniform was trying to grab her again and she knew she had to get away, get away from this guy who was here to hurt her. The guy who had taken her away from her family. The guy she didn't know, the guy who wasn't her dad.

Daddy? Mama? Where are you? She fought with all her might against the man in the uniform, and he suddenly let go of her and she ran away, ran away trying to get back to her parents. She heard them yell something after her, but she wasn't listening and had completely crossed over, crossed over into her former self, the little one. All she knew was that she was a child and should be with her parents, not with these guys.

Not with these strange guys! How did they get to me anyway? And why am I so weak? And where is Enti? I always have Enti! Tears were streaming down her face as she ran, ran away from the bad guys. The guys who had hurt her, held her underwater.

I don't know how to swim yet! Don't they know that?

She felt weak, her head throbbing, her little legs trying to take her away from the danger. She heard them run after her and knew she wouldn't make it far. They were much bigger, much faster, could easily lift her up and throw her into that small little area with the blanket again. But she needed to get away. Get away quickly. *Get to Enti, Mama, Daddy. But what's that? No way! Could it be? Sure looks like it.*

She recognized this particular half-grassy, half-sandy area in between the one-story buildings. It looked exactly like the place she was staying at with her parents. *Yes, that place. Eglin something. Eglin TLF. The place before the bad guys took me.*

Wow! She was proud of herself. *I ran that far? But isn't there water? Didn't we go through the water?* She couldn't remember, didn't want to remember. She was here now. *Or is all of this a bad dream?*

"Mama! Daddy!" she cried out.

She ran over the grassy, sandy area to the last door in the building. There were no lights on, but she ran there anyway, toward the white door underneath the little roof. *That's it! Our apartment!* She was sure about it now and felt so relieved. She was crying out of sheer joy, overjoyed she would soon see her parents again. After all that time with the bad guys. She didn't know how much time had gone by, but it had felt like forever.

She had created a dreamworld, a dreamworld to escape to during the long hours in darkness in that tiny wooden cage. She barely felt hunger anymore. Her uncombed hair and stinky, dirty clothes became a beautiful, fancy dress in her imagination.

But the bad guys always ripped her out of that world, out of her place of escape. But this time, *she* had escaped.

So smart! Daddy had told her she was so smart. And today, this dark night, she really felt smart. *So smart!* She had escaped them. Still heard them running after her, but she had reached her safe haven! That apartment door! The apartment where her parents were waiting for her.

She knew she would have to make herself real tall to get to that doorhandle, but just as she was about to stand on her tippy-toes, she realized she was able to reach the doorhandle easily.

Did I grow?

She looked at her hands and stopped to stare at them. They looked so big!

What? Why?

There was a shiny, sparkly ring on her left hand, the hand that had easily reached the doorknob. It looked like a grown-up's hand, like her mama's.

But I'm small, aren't I? How long have I been in the darkness with the bad guys? For so long that I grew up and got big? No, no, no. . . .

She choked on her tears, her hand reached for the doorknob again, but then the darkness took over again and everything went all black around her.

"Maria! Oh my gosh, Maria!"

She heard a faint voice and felt herself being shaken. She also heard low, muffled voices and made out phrases such as "not normal," "out of her mind," and "need to get a doctor."

She opened her eyes and looked directly into Aaron's blue eyes. His pretty, calming, ocean-blue eyes. But she realized they didn't look calm at all. They looked rather like a storm that was brewing over the ocean. She realized her head was being held by Aaron—she was lying in his lap, her body stretched out over hard concrete. There was hot, humid air all around them. Then she heard a faint sound. *What is that? It sounds like water. Water? Yes, like waves crashing ashore. But little waves, quiet waves. Where am I?*

"Aaron?"

"Dad, she's awake. Maria, oh my gosh, are you okay?"

She saw Aaron's dad bend down to look at her. He looked not only concerned, but disturbed. Disturbed and confused.

"Aaron?"

"Yes, Maria, I'm here. I'm here. You're okay. I think. You collapsed again."

"I did?" She now looked at Jack.

"After you . . . ran from us screaming," Jack added.

"I did?"

Why can't I remember anything? She sat up and saw that she was sitting on a square slab of concrete in front of a white door. *Where am I?*

She looked back at Aaron, who was still kneeling, and saw red on his hands. *Red? Blood?* She couldn't get any words to form, so she just pointed at his hands. He looked at them.

"You collapsed sideways and somehow must have hit your lip," he explained.

Maria felt her lips with her tongue and sure enough, she felt a little gap and tasted a warm, metallic liquid there. Blood. Her blood. Her blood on his hands.

He came closer and took her face in his hands and peered at the injury. "I don't think you need stitches, but you can't lick it. It will open up the wound again."

Jack just looked at her with that puzzled look on his face.

"Does it hurt?" Aaron wanted to know, and Maria shook her head. *No, my lip doesn't particularly hurt. My head does. No, somehow every inch of my body is hurting.* She had the strangest feeling that she couldn't explain.

"Dad, how about you get our essentials and then we go in? At least Maria found our apartment. I'll stay here with her. Okay?"

Jack just nodded and turned around, walking slowly, dragging his feet as if he were carrying some heavy burden.

Maria looked around. She saw the half-grassy, half-sandy strip nearby, heard the water lightly splashing ashore, then noticed the silhouettes of boats slightly rocking back and forth in the waves. *The marina!* A feeling washed over her that she just couldn't explain. She had no words for it. *I feel so strange, I feel like I'm not myself anymore.*

Who am I?

CHAPTER 76

Aaron was looking at Maria when he saw it. The bewilderment that blanketed her expression. He couldn't help but stare; his heart sank as he studied her beautiful face that now washed over in blank fear, bathed in bewilderment and fear. That bloodied lip, those intense green eyes staring back at him as if she didn't even know him anymore. As if she wasn't even herself anymore.

He knew that she had just crossed over again into her deep, hidden-away memories. Yet he suddenly had an idea. An idea that might help her unlock that secret place, those hidden-away, dark memories.

"Come on, sweetie, let's go in," Aaron said to Maria, and opened the door for her.

Just like in a trance, she got up and walked in.

They peered about the shadowy hallway of the TLF. "Do you remember?"

She nodded faintly. Aaron turned on a light and she truly saw it, her eyes wide, her mind confused.

Their apartment. *Of course I remember. We arrived just a few days ago. What a silly question!* She saw the tan-and-greenish-looking couch on the left, a little half-table facing a kitchenette composed of old-looking white cabinets, then two bedrooms to the right of her—one with a king size bed, the other with bunk beds—and a hallway connecting them to a small bathroom with tan tiles. She took off her shoes by the door and felt the greenish-brown carpet under her bare feet. It wasn't soft, seemed rather sticky, but she didn't mind.

"Come on," she said, and grabbed his hand, dragging him along, giggling, her little feet shuffling across the sticky carpet.

She walked into the kitchen and looked at the tall cabinets, too tall for her to reach. Then she pointed. "Look! Door!" She pointed at another door that led from the kitchen to the outside. She was too small to look through its window, and the window was covered in white, fluffy curtains anyway.

"Come on! Go my room!"

She grabbed the hand again, giggling. She ran across the living room by the front door and got distracted by the TV that hung on the wall across from the couch, close to the front door. But it was turned off, the front door still open. She pushed the door shut, then kneeled down on the carpet to open a drawer on a piece of furniture that looked more like a dresser than an actual TV stand.

"Find big blocks," she said, opening the lowest drawer.

But it was empty. *Why empty?* She knew she had cleaned up like she had been told and put her big building blocks in this drawer. *Maybe next one up? No, that's the one with the puzzles and the doll clothes.* But it wouldn't hurt to check. So, she got up and found the second drawer from the top. When she pulled that one out, she was again disappointed. *It's empty too! How can this be? It's not right!* She was confused now.

"Where toys?"

Maybe Mama moved them all to my room? She walked through the first door on the right, into the bedroom with the bunk beds. She smiled. She liked this room. She *really* wanted to sleep up top, but Mama always said no, said it was too high for her. So, she had to sleep on the lower bunk. But Mama let her play up on the top bunk during the day whenever there was someone who could watch her and make sure she wouldn't fall out. Her little baby doll Betty slept up there, though. *She* was allowed to sleep up there.

Yes, Betty's mama allows her to sleep up there. She giggled. *Of course she does. I'm Betty's mama!* She grinned widely and climbed up the ladder to see if Betty was still there.

"Betty?"

When she reached the top, she didn't see Betty. Or any other toys. *What in the world? Where are all my toys?* She knew Mama liked it neat and orderly, but she always let her have toys. Mama would never hide her toys. She was so confused.

"No toys?"

She took one last look before climbing down again. She got on all fours and checked under the lower bunk. *Maybe Mama pushed all the toys under here? Sometimes, after she trips on toys, she gets mad and just pushes them away until it's cleanup time. Maybe they got pushed under the bed and were forgotten about?*

But there were no toys. It looked perfectly clean under there as well. *Where did all of my toys go? So strange! They have to be here somewhere.*

She now stood up again and looked at her lower bunk bed. At the very least Kissen and Enti had to be around there. Her little pink pillow and the sweet duck she loved so much. But the bed looked perfectly made, as if nobody had ever slept in it.

She was getting angry now. *Where are all of my toys? Why would they take all my toys? I've been a good girl!* And even when she was naughty, they never took away everything. Some toys might go into "toy time-out," but mostly *she* went to regular time-out until she'd calmed down and thought about her behavior.

Why would they take all the toys? Even when they had moved here, they hadn't packed up and taken all the toys. *Nope.* They had packed up lots of them, but left her favorites out to play with. To play with right here in this apartment, on the greenish-brown carpet. *And Enti! Enti is always with me! I can't go anywhere without her! Did I leave her in the car in my car seat?* She wasn't sure but searched the lower bunk one more time to be safe.

"Enti, come out!"

She crawled into the bunk bed and checked the side by the wall in case they had fallen through the crack—and then she heard it. The door. The front door. Someone was at the front door!

Panic swept over her. *But Daddy's right here.* She was sure of that—she had dragged him into her room. She looked up, but there was nobody there. *Where did he go? Wasn't he just here? And why is it so dark now?* She only saw a light outside of her room now. *Why so dark? Didn't Daddy turn on the light when we came in?*

Her door was almost closed also, just a little crack still open, and all of the sudden she was under the covers, in her pj's. *What happened? Wasn't I just looking for my toys with Daddy?*

She was so confused. *It's weird that all my toys are gone, but why am I in my pj's in bed now? Or did I lose track of time? It's late now? Been hours since the last time I was with Daddy?*

She now heard voices at the door. Unfamiliar voices. Two male voices, low, dark voices.

She trembled. *Who's that?*

She heard footsteps come closer and closer to her door, heard something dragging along behind them. *What's that? A suitcase? Oh no. . . .*

Had they come back again for her? Did they come back again to take her? *No, no, don't take me away again. I don't like having no toys, but I want to stay here. Please! Please let me stay here, don't take me away again! Please no!*

The door opened and the light streamed in. She saw the silhouette of a man in uniform, a strong man in uniform.

"Daddy?"

Another man appeared behind him. A man so unfamiliar, she had never seen him before. Her eyes widened in panic. She knew what they were here for. She knew that they would carry her out of her bed to the water, the cold, dark, mucky, murky water that was right outside of this apartment.

"No, please, no, don't take me! No, please, please! Don't take me! Don't hurt me! Mama! Mama! Daddy! Help me!"

She was crying now, backed up against the wall in the bunk bed. *They can't get me, they can't take me away again. Please, don't do it. I want to stay here. I want my Mama and Daddy! And Enti! Where the heck is Enti?* She searched the bed in panic for Enti. *At least Enti will protect me. Enti will help me.*

But it was too late. The guy in uniform grabbed her by the arms and tried to drag her out of the bunk bed. She kicked and screamed and the guy let go of her in surprise.

It worked? It worked! Oh my gosh, it worked! He let go of me! That's surprising! Surprising, shocking . . . liberating. I'm free, he didn't take me, not this time.

Not this time? What? What does that mean, "not this time?" Has this happened to me before? But I'm so little. It couldn't have happened twice. We just got here a few days ago, didn't we?

But she knew. This was the day she had been dreading, the day she was taken, taken away from her parents. *How can I dread a day I know nothing about? What's happening?*

She stared at the guy in the uniform still standing there in front of her bed. She realized she was screaming and suddenly stopped.

What's going on?

She heard him speak to her in a low voice, but it was as if he was speaking through a wall, far away. So far away.

"Maria?"

Maria? Who's Maria? Is there another little girl?

The man in uniform was still speaking to her. He didn't take her. He was only speaking, in a soft voice, as if he was trying to calm her.

What's happening?

She cowered lower, pushed her side into the crack of the bunk bed, not sure what to do. She pulled in her knees closer to her chest to make herself as little as could be.

Then she saw it. The light. Little flecks of light reflecting onto the walls around her.

Reflecting from what?

Then she saw the source of the light. The ring on her left finger. The sparkling diamond ring on her finger.

She stared at her hands. They looked so big. So tall. Like the hands of a grown woman.

"Maria?"

Maria? The strong man in uniform sat down on the lower bunk bed, on the same bed she was hiding in. "Maria, you've been here before, haven't you?"

What is he saying? I'm not Maria! My name is not Maria. I'm a little girl, definitely not named Maria. The ring kept throwing speckles of light all around the room. *So pretty. Why do I have this ring? And why are my hands so big?*

"What are you afraid of?"

Afraid of? You! But this guy seemed different. He seemed different and not so scary after all. But she knew that wasn't right. She knew the unfamiliar man in uniform was scary. Not a nice guy. A bad guy! The guy who had taken her!

"What are you afraid of?" She heard the soft voice again, a voice so loving, so full of empathy. So sweet. A voice trying to protect her, it seemed like. "You can tell me. What are you afraid of?"

That sweet voice, low, soft, full of love. All of the sudden, she wasn't sure anymore who exactly this guy was. She somehow trusted him. *It isn't Daddy, but it also isn't one of the bad guys.*

"What are you afraid of?"

"Bad guys. Bad guys taking me!"

And before she could see his reaction, she heard the small waves crashing onto the shore, then those waves suddenly reared up, formed a wave so big that it swept over her and she was surrounded by dark, mucky, murky water, so much water, so deep, and she swallowed a bunch of it and coughed but more came, more and more came, and she couldn't breathe, struggled to breathe, and it all went completely black around her.

The first thing she heard was a low whispering that faded in and out.

"Can't leave her here."

"This is crazy!"

"Might need to call the police."

"Can she even be left alone?"

She realized she had a wet cloth on her face and was lying in a big, unfamiliar bed on top of a quilt. It was a king size bed facing a white closet. Next to the bed was a brown dresser with a TV on top of it. The carpet was greenish brown and the quilt was in a matching tan color with green designs on it. The whispering came from the living room outside of her door that was open just a crack.

She took the wet cloth off her forehead and looked around. She had a splitting headache when she sat up. She lay back down again. The voices were getting clearer now.

"How long have you suspected?"

"A while now. But after tonight, I'm positive. Pretty sure, at least. But I still have no proof!"

"That's the police's job. We can report a suspicion!"

Silence for a bit. "I need to speak to her myself. I can't just go to the police!"

"Aaron, come on. You can. And you should. You have to!"

"No, not yet. I need to talk to her first. To both of them. Maria and Martina."

Maria stared at the door. *Aaron needs to talk to me? About what? And Mamá? And the police?* She was confused, her headache unbearable.

"Aaron, this might be a kidnapping case! You gotta report this."

"Dad, I can't. Not yet. They won't believe Maria. We've got no proof. Please, trust me. I have a plan. Let me just wait and see what happens tomorrow during my security interview. If they found something while checking my background—and therefore Maria's— they'll tell me. They said something was fraudulent, and I'm sure it's her birth certificate. Then we'll have our proof."

"Aaron, at least call that guy, that general! At least report that you might have found his daughter. Alive!"

"I guess. That's fair. I'll report my suspicions to him. But he'll have to understand that I don't have *proof* yet. Okay. Yeah. I'll call him tomorrow morning, explain what I know."

"Sounds good, son. Sounds good. But for now, we need to get Maria out of here. I don't think she can handle staying here."

Silence.

Maria sat up again in her bed. *What in the world? Can't handle staying here? Where am I anyway?* She looked around and searched for clues. Then she heard the soft waves crashing onto the shore. *Waves? Right here?* She saw the carpet, the TV, the drawers. *Socks. Socks are in there. And underwear.*

Wait. What?

She stared at the drawers. She got up and her bare feet touched the greenish-brown carpet. It was kind of sticky. Not soft at all, just sticky. Sticky from the humidity. The room was cold, though. The A/C had been running.

She stared at the drawers. *Don't take out the socks. Mama will be mad. Not to play with!*

What?

I'm going crazy!

417

For a moment, she thought about it, and suddenly it all came rushing back to her.

I'm in the TLF.

She peeked through the crack in the door toward the light and saw Aaron and his dad sitting on an old-looking green couch. *Eglin's TLF. We are at Eglin's temporary lodging facilities. I know now. Yes, here we are. At Eglin's TLF.*

Her unbearable headache got worse, if that was even possible, and she started getting dizzy. Her vision got blurry. She saw Aaron in his camo uniform with the boots. She closed her eyes for a second to make the spinning stop, but when she opened them again, the spinning was still there, and her mind fixated on a memory from long ago.

She looked again at the people on the couch. The man in uniform was now wearing a flight suit. In his arms was a woman, a beautiful brown-haired woman with long, wavy hair. She had freckles all around her elegantly formed nose and on her high cheek bones. They were laughing together, having a good time cuddling and talking.

It was Mama and Daddy.

They often stayed up late to talk and sometimes she would peek out of her room just to see them and make sure they were actually there. Then she could crawl back into her bed, knowing she was safe.

But Eglin AFB isn't safe. The TLF at Eglin's AFB is not safe at all! It's dangerous. She somehow knew. *Kidnapping. It's a case of kidnapping.* That thought crossed her mind and before she knew it, her head exploded with pain and everything went black around her—again.

CHAPTER 77

Aaron was sitting next to Maria's bed. It was way past midnight and he really needed to get some sleep. *Not sure how I'll manage to survive tomorrow. My first day at work, on no sleep. I'll meet my sponsor at seven thirty a.m.—in less than four hours.*

Want to leave a good impression on the first lieutenant I'll be working with. But can I? I'm exhausted and it'll be a busy day. He'll show me around base, get my ID card set up, PC access too, then drop me off at the security clearance interview.

The interview. Honestly, it was the only thing Aaron could think of right now. *It'll give us clues to the unknown. Clues for what seems to be a huge case. It'll also most likely end my interview and lead to denying me access to secure information for my new job.* He sighed. *Don't really care, though. All I care about right now is Maria. My fiancée. The love of my life. What happened to you?* He wondered that over and over again as he gazed at Maria.

Suddenly, she opened her eyes and looked at Aaron.

"Hey there, my love." He smiled at her, then moved a strand of hair away from her eyes. "How are you feeling?"

She looked at him with a weak smile on her lips. "Okay," she said. "I've a bad headache and I had the weirdest dreams, but—"

Aaron snorted, interrupting her. He just couldn't help it.

"What?"

He had no idea how to explain it all to her. He felt his phone in his pocket. *She doesn't know I recorded her this time, when we were in the TLF. Not sure yet what to do with the footage, but I've got her whole strange, insane episode recorded. But it really isn't insanity. Nope, it's part of the truth that needs to be found. But right now, I need her to stay calm and get some sleep. Both of us need sleep.*

"What, Aaron? Why would you act like that? That was almost cruel. What's going on with you?"

He now had to laugh. *She's funny! What's going on with me? What in the world is going on with her—that's the much bigger question!* He suppressed his nervous laughter and thought for a moment, then looked at her. "Maria, do you know where we are?"

She was still confused and looked around. She saw a nice teal wall with a big picture of a white sandy beach and emerald water, a big king size bed with a tan quilt and teal sheets, a modern-looking nightstand with soft white light, and a hallway leading to a front door and the bathroom. "Looks like a hotel room."

"Right. We're in a hotel room. The Air Force Inn *at Eglin AFB*."

The little hairs on her arm stood up, but she stayed calm. "'Air Force Inn?' I thought you didn't want to stay here?"

"No, I didn't. I booked the TLF for you, me, and my dad."

Maria nodded. *That's right. He booked the TLF.* Her breathing started getting heavy, her forehead glistened with sweat.

"Maria, we *moved* you. You couldn't stay at the TLF. So, we moved you here. To rest and sleep. My dad's in a separate room here at the Inn. The nice check-in lady was okay with all three of us staying here instead."

Maria looked at him, still not understanding.

"Maria, you didn't have a *weird dream*. You had a flashback."

"A flashback?" She sat up and wiped the sweat off her forehead.

"Yeah, something like that. You fainted three times. I can't let you keep fainting. It's dangerous. You might end up in the hospital at this rate. You already hit your head, and cut your lip. Not safe. So we decided to book a room for us here at the hotel on base. Away from the TLF—and the water."

The water? Now her hands started to get sweaty also.

"Maria, focus on me, please! You're safe here. You are. I'm here with you. Whatever happened over there, it's done now, and you're safe now."

She stared at him.

"Maria, we have to sleep. I need to go to work tomorrow. For the first time. Less than four hours from now."

She nodded, her tongue dry, her hands slippery.

He gently stroked her cheek. "Let's get ready together, okay?"

She nodded and got up. Her legs were wiggly, her head still hurting from the pounding headache. She managed to find her suitcase and her pajamas. She walked into the beautiful modern bathroom. Stared at herself in the big mirror.

She looked horrible.

Her face was so pale, her freckles almost seemed to jump off her face. Her eyes were freakishly green, the blue rim so prominent that it contrasted the whites of her eyes immensely. Her hair was a mess—and was that *sand and pine needles* she saw stuck inside it? Her lip was bloody. Swollen with a small, bloody streak on it. As she touched the cut, Aaron stopped brushing.

"You hurt it when you fell on the concrete," he just said, then spat out his toothpaste.

"What?"

"You don't remember any of it?" He turned to look at her directly, his eyes showing deep concern.

Maria shook her head. "I only remember that we arrived and parked the truck in the sandy parking lot across from those buildings."

Aaron nodded.

Maria kept thinking. "Aaron, when did I faint the first time tonight?"

He had just washed his face and was drying it on one of the towels. "In the parking lot, as soon as you got out of the car."

"Interesting. I only remember arriving." She washed her face as well and put cream on it afterward, especially on her bruised lip.

Aaron nodded. "I think you crossed over after that." He took her by the hand, sat her down on the bed, and turned off the light. He hopped in after her.

"*Crossed over?*"

"Yeah. That's what I'm calling it, because when it happens it's like you're not yourself anymore, but little again. You take on a different personality."

Maria laughed out loud at first, then stopped immediately. "You're being serious? What? That sounds insane. Like bipolar or something."

Aaron shook his head. "No, more like PTSD. Remember, I told you that before." She nodded. He touched her face, stroked it gently. "I truly believe you've been here before, Maria. You've been right here, inside Eglin's TLF. And something bad happened."

He didn't want to get into details. *Not yet, anyway. Need to see what the agents have to say.*

"Aaron?"

He heard Maria's voice and came back to the present, pushing his disturbing thoughts away. "I don't know enough yet. We'll find out, but we need more time. And you need to be strong. You can't keep fainting. My dad and I are very concerned about you. So, let's get some sleep. Please. No more questions. Let's sleep, both you and me." Aaron was exhausted. As soon as he got under the covers, he fell asleep.

Maria looked at him. She wasn't sure what to do or think. She fumbled around in the dark for her purse and found her phone. It had a bunch of messages from her mamá.

"Oh dear. Forgot to text her we arrived," she exclaimed, but Aaron's only response was a snore.

Maria quickly texted her. Only a few seconds after, she already had a response.

Mija, gracias a dios. Estaba preocupada y no podia dormir.

Maria smiled. *Poor Mamá has been worried and couldn't sleep.* She texted her back.

Yo también te amo mucho, her phone flashed back.

Aw, Mamá. Love you as well, with all my heart.

She put her phone on the nightstand and switched off the light. She felt much better already.

"*You've been here before.*"

Aaron's sentence came back to her, and she fixated on it. *Did Mamá take me to Eglin AFB? To see my father?* As she was pondering this, her headache came back and was pounding, pounding down every slope of her brain. And even when she fell into a deep sleep out of sheer exhaustion, her brain kept telling her that something wasn't right with her and her mom. Because deep down inside, she knew she had been here before—but not with this mama.

CHAPTER 78

Elisabeth had had a restless night. Memories tangled with what-if dreams, and everything mixed together. She woke up before the sun and made herself a cup of black coffee using the hotel room's small coffee machine. Then, Styrofoam cup of coffee in hand, she softly opened the sliding door and sat on the balcony overlooking the emerald-green ocean and watched the sun rise.

The sun rose as it had every single day of her life. A new day had always come, bringing with it daylight, a light against the darkness. Her life had been so dark, so sad and lonely these past twenty years.

Today, however, it's different.

The sunlight reflected against the transparent emerald-green, bringing with it brightness and warmth. It brightened her day, her mood, her heart. It made her see things clearly. *We'll go to the police today. Yes. We'll ask them to pick up the cold case from over twenty years ago. And we will find answers. Both me and Brad.* Elisabeth couldn't help but smile.

She sipped her black coffee and felt the warmth stream down her throat. And for some reason, today, the warmth seemed to touch her heart as well. She smiled a big smile. The warmth and brightness gave her hope, so much hope, a strong feeling, a sense of knowledge. *My lost daughter is near. So near I can almost touch her.*

She held the image of her little toddler in mind and tried to imagine what she would look like now. *If she's really still alive.*

But somehow she knew that she was, had known all along. *And I know I'd recognize her right away. A mom always recognizes her child, no matter what has happened. Never lost the feeling of being a mom, the lightning-fast reactions, the deep, deep love that only a mom can feel for her child.*

She had the biggest smile on her lips. Because that morning, that special love, that motherly love, was rekindled right there on that balcony. It streamed down her body with such an intense warmth that she knew she would find answers on this crazy trip.

◦◇◦◆◦◇◦

Brad sipped his warm coffee while watching the sun rise over the bay, sitting on the back deck of the VIP house. It had been a rough night. Confusing thoughts, strange dreams, intense memories. The golden sun came up over the emerald-green water in the bay and flooded the deck with light, and warmed his heart. He had a big smile on his face as he dialed her number.

"Good morning. I was just thinking of you," he said.

"Oh, were you?" he heard her say.

"Yeah. I'm watching the sunrise and it made me . . ."

She laughed a warm laugh that made him smile. ". . . think of me?"

"Yeah!"

"Well, looks like we still have a lot in common. Don't tell me you're sipping a cup of black coffee at the moment?"

Brad laughed lightheartedly. "I sure am. And so are you, I assume?"

"Yeah, of course. This hotel coffee is not very good, but it'll do."

He nodded. "Well, I'll get you a great cup of coffee later. And wine. How about that?"

"Sounds like a plan. But what exactly *is* the plan? You're still meeting me at the police station at lunchtime, correct?" He heard doubt in her voice.

"Of course, I will. Why wouldn't I?"

Silence for a bit. "I . . . I was afraid . . ."

". . . that I would end up changing my mind and not believe you after all?"

"Yeah, maybe."

"Elisabeth, you have to trust me. Trust me again like you used to. And I'm telling you, we're gonna go in there together and pick up that cold case. We will not give up. Won't let them give up. And this time, we *will* find answers. Heck yeah, we will. Find answers and find her!" He continued to make plans with her while sipping his coffee.

CHAPTER 79

"Coffee? Yeah, I found a small coffee machine. I'll make some right away, no worries," Aaron heard Maria tell him while he was still in the bathroom fixing his blue uniform. He looked in the mirror and saw dark circles under both his eyes. *Man, I look tired. Gonna make for such a fun first ID card picture.*

He frowned and stepped out of the bathroom. Maria was waiting for him. She smiled. "Good morning, my love. You look stunning. Well, perhaps a bit tired, but handsome all the same. Here's some coffee for my good-looking second lieutenant."

"Thanks," he said, and took the cup. He looked at the dark black liquid and groaned. "No creamer?"

"Nope, no creamer. Couldn't find any. So, this is Maria-style coffee. Best way to wake you up after a short night and a long day ahead."

He tried a sip and shuddered. "I don't know about this. Not sure I can handle Maria-style coffee. You know that."

She laughed. "Yeah, I do, but I'm afraid it's either this or no coffee at all."

He frowned. "Fine then, I'll have this."

They sat on the bed together and sipped their coffee out of Styrofoam cups. They were quiet. The terrible night was still looming over them. Maria looked at him, her eyes sad. Then a ray of sunlight shone through the curtains across from them. Aaron got up and walked over to open them. The sunlight flooded the room and filled it with such warmth that it encouraged him, gave him strength.

"Maria, how are you feeling today?"

She shrugged her shoulders. "Good, I guess." She looked up at him, her exotic eyes clouded over by pain and sadness.

He sat back down. "Hey, my love, don't worry."

She grunted, took another sip of her coffee, and looked at him. "'Don't worry.' Hah. I know I've been nothing but trouble, nothing but crazy, absolutely insane trouble. *Of course* I'm worried."

He nodded, but before he could say anything, she continued. "Look, I'm so, so sorry that I made you so tired. You must be exhausted. And it's your first day today. I'm sorry." A tear ran down her face and was lit up by the sunrays shining into the hotel room.

Aaron looked at her. "Well, I won't be exhausted for long with this Maria-style coffee!"

She looked up and smiled a weak smile. "Are you sure?"

"Yes, I'm sure. It's just a bunch of in-processing today anyways."

"'In-processing?'"

"Yeah, it just means I need to let everyone know I'm here. I'll get my military ID, get my pay set, get access to certain programs and buildings, get my computer set up, and so on. A bunch of bureaucracy today. And then my security clearance interview early this afternoon."

Maria nodded, the sad look still on her face. "Full day. I'm sorry you didn't get a good night's sleep because of me."

He pounded his coffee and gave her a kiss. "Please don't worry about it. I'm all set now after this cup." He grinned and pointed at the empty Styrofoam. "And I promise we'll deal with you later. Understood, ma'am?"

She smiled weakly and nodded.

"Until then, I figure you and my dad can explore the area outside the base? Maybe drive by some of the apartments we'll start looking at tomorrow?"

Maria looked at him and smiled. "That's a great idea. I really don't feel comfortable here on base."

"See, perfect. Well, you better get ready and showered quickly or you'll miss breakfast."

"Breakfast?"

"Yep, I'll go get my dad now from the next room. We need to go back to the . . . you know . . . the other place we were going to stay at and get my car. Need to move it off the truck's trailer and then bring both cars back here. I'll leave your car with you and my dad and will take mine to work. But before I head off to work, I'd love to have a quick breakfast with you both. So you have about half an hour to get ready for breakfast."

She nodded and looked at her phone to check the time. "But Aaron, it's super early!"

He laughed. "It is. But I need to get all of that done and eat breakfast before leaving here at seven fifteen a.m. to meet the first lieutenant. Welcome to work life!"

Aaron was sitting in his car in the parking lot in front of the flight line. He had collected both his thoughts and papers and was ready to meet his sponsor. He looked around. So far, he was the only one in the parking lot. *I'm early.* He stared at his phone in the phone holder for a while. Suddenly, he grabbed it. *Yes, now is the time. I have to try.*

He took a deep breath and dialed the phone number he had saved earlier. General Brad Collins's number. The phone started ringing.

"Hello, this is Major Starke, General Collins's exec," Aaron heard, and sighed. *Only the phone number to his exec. But I really need to talk to the boss. Have to try.*

"Hello, this is Lieutenant Heikinnen. Could I please talk to General Collins?"

"What matter do you need to discuss with him, Lieutenant Heikinnen?"

"It's a personal matter that will really be of interest to the general."

"I see. Well, all calls go through me first, and then I decide if they are of interest to the general."

Aaron sighed. *Of course. Can't tell his exec, though. Need to talk to the General himself. But how?*

"Well," he said to buy himself some time, "it's about the general's family."

"The general doesn't have a family, Lieutenant. And if he did, it would be none of your business."

How rude! Aaron had to calm himself down. "Could I please set up a meeting with the general?"

"An in-person meeting?"

Aaron thought about it. "Preferably."

"Well, we still need a reason for the general to see you."

"It's of urgent personal interest regarding the general," Aaron explained again, getting a little annoyed. The exec was really protecting his general. *Guess that's his job, though.*

"Well, Lieutenant, I'm afraid I can't help you if you won't explain your motivations better. The general is not here at the moment anyway. He's on a TDY in Florida."

"In Florida?" Aaron asked, his interest sparked. "Where in Florida? At Eglin?"

Major Starke paused then said, "Huh, yes, Lieutenant, that's correct. At Eglin. He won't be back until next week. If you're still interested in meeting with him, I need you to state your reasons, and only then can we think about setting something up within the next few weeks."

Aaron's thoughts were racing. *If he's here, maybe I can just meet him here? If only I knew where. How can I find out?*

"Lieutenant?"

"Ah, yes, sir. I understand. I apologize for not being better prepared for this conversation. I'll call back later to give you more details."

"Okay. Goodbye, Lieutenant."

"Goodbye, and have a nice day," Aaron said and hung up.

He's here. Right here on base. Awesome. Have to find out where.

Aaron saw another car arrive, and a young-looking lieutenant stepped out in his camo uniform. *That must be my sponsor. First Lieutenant Marc Snyder.* Aaron had an idea. *I'll ask him. Maybe he'll know?*

Then Aaron looked at the first lieutenant again. *Wait, he's in camo uniform? Gosh, I put on my blues. Stupid me!* He sighed. *Oh well, gotta roll with it.* He took a deep breath and got out of his car. He waved at the other lieutenant.

"Hi. You must be Aaron Heikinnen." The first lieutenant smiled. "I can tell by your uniform. Rookie mistake!"

Aaron laughed, even though he didn't think it was funny at all. He shook Lieutenant Snyder's hand and they got started with their day.

◦◇◈◇◦

After seeing his new workplace, Lieutenant Snyder then drove him around base, not only to show him where everything was located but also to make sure they stopped by the necessary offices for all of Aaron's enrollments, ID cards, and access cards. While riding in the car, Aaron thought it would be the perfect opportunity to bring up General Collins.

"Yeah," his sponsor said, "I know the guy. Impressive résumé. He was stationed here at Eglin at one time. As a captain, I think."

Aaron nodded and kept listening.

"I heard he's in town this week."

Aaron perked up, but tried to hide his excitement. "Oh yeah? That's cool. What does he do here?"

"Well, he's overseeing the F-35 project. He's meeting some of our bosses. TDYs are pretty fun, you'll see."

Aaron nodded. "What do you do during TDYs?"

"It's a bunch of meetings. My favorite are the work dinners, though."

"Are dinners just for young guys like us or does everyone go to those?"

"It depends. But it's usually everyone. Like tonight. I heard they'll be taking General Collins to a fun, famous restaurant around here."

"Oh yeah?" Aaron said casually to hide his immense interest. "You have a famous restaurant around here?"

"Yup. It's called Compass Rose. You should check it out sometime."

"Yes, I will." Aaron smiled. *I definitely will. Tonight. I'll meet the general there.* He grinned contently, and before he knew it, it was lunch time. Lieutenant Snyder took him out to the BX Food Court for lunch.

CHAPTER 80

"Lunch at the BX, General?"

Brad looked at the wing commander. "I'm sorry, sir, but I can't. I have another important meeting to get to." Drew Markas looked at him, puzzled. "But Mr. Markas can grab some lunch with you."

Drew looked at his friend again, then declared: "Actually, I'll have to decline as well. I must stick with the general here. You know, keep him out of trouble."

The men laughed, then parted ways. When they walked out, Drew gave his friend an elbow bump.

"So, General, what important meeting are you off to?"

"A personal matter," Brad replied and kept walking toward the car without even looking at Drew.

"So, will I be attending this *personal matter*, boss?" Drew looked at his friend.

"You don't have to. I can take you back to the visitor's quarters." Brad got into the car and started the engine. Surprised, Drew jumped in and buckled up quickly. Then, they started driving.

"You're just dropping me off at the visitor's quarters?"

"Yeah."

"By myself, with an empty fridge? What am I supposed to do for lunch?"

"Told you. You should've stayed at the BX," Brad said without even looking at his friend.

Drew raised his eyebrows. "Seriously, Cave Man?"

"What?"

"What in the world are you not telling me?"

"Nothing," he said, and felt color flush his face.

"You're a bad liar, man. Tell you what, I'm going with you, whether you like it or not."

"I won't like it," was Brad's short answer.

Drew looked at him, stared at him. "What in the world, man? So, tell me, what the heck is this all about?"

Without looking at his friend, Brad explained briefly. "I'm headed to the Niceville Police Station. I need them to open up the case again."

Drew stared at him and sighed. "Brad, I don't think it's—"

"I *know* you don't," Brad cut him off, "that's why *I'm not asking you*. I'm *telling* you that's what I will do, and I can either drop you off at the Distinguished Visitor's Quarters or you can shut up and come along."

There was silence in the car. Drew looked at his friend and knew well enough that there was no reasoning with him. He sighed.

"What?"

"I didn't say anything."

"Exactly, you didn't. So, you coming or not?" Brad glanced at Drew.

"I'm coming, Cave Man, I'm coming. I'll always be there for you."

"That's what I thought," he said, his voice softer now, almost shaking, as he sped off the base to Niceville's Police Station.

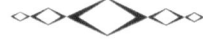

They soon arrived and for a while, Brad just sat there in the car behind the wheel, staring at the police station.

"If we don't go in soon, I'm pretty sure they're gonna come out and arrest us for suspicious activity," Drew joked.

Brad looked over abruptly, straight into the smiling face of his friend. His best friend.

Drew sobered up. "Come on, Cave Man, let's do this."

"I can't yet."

"Excuse me?"

"She's not here yet." Brad looked at his personal cell phone.

"Who's not here yet?"

"Elisabeth."

Drew raised his eyebrows. "What? Are you delusional? Brad, we're here and now, not twenty years ago. Elisabeth isn't here. Your ex-wife hasn't even been stateside in years. She's not coming. Man, are you daydreaming or what? You having a nervous breakdown?"

But then they saw her. She had just parked her car and stepped out immediately.

Elisabeth.

Brad and Drew recognized her immediately. Her auburn hair in a short pixie cut, the perfectly straight nose with the freckles, her elegant neck, her slender figure. Drew's jaw dropped while Brad let out a deep breath, then stepped out of the car.

"Hi, there."

"Hi, Brad," she said as she walked over to him. "I see you haven't changed much. Not much more than that camo uniform I see you're still wearing."

He laughed, his exotic eyes sparkling, his wide shoulders still as strong as they had always been, his brown hair now mixed with a few grey streaks. "And neither have you," he said. "Except for your hair length."

She laughed. "Yeah, I chopped it off. Much easier to take care of."

Here they were, standing in front of each other, not sure what to do. They just looked at each other and smiled. He stood stiff in front of her, as if standing at attention. Suddenly, she gave him a big hug and his heart jumped, then melted, as he held her slender frame, right there in the parking lot, twenty years later.

"Hi," she whispered, and he felt her breath on his neck.

"Hi," he mumbled, and held her even tighter.

For a while, they just stood there in their embrace. Holding each other, hugging each other, stroking each other's backs, they forgot everything around them.

They were sitting in the big leather chairs inside Niceville Police Station's waiting area, not saying anything. Brad and Elisabeth held each other's hand, Drew next to Brad, Sarah next to Drew.

"Sarah, did you have any idea?" Drew whispered to her.

She looked at him, her eyes wide, then shook her head.

"So, why did you guys even come here? I mean here to Florida, all the way from Germany?"

Sarah looked at him. "It was my idea. I thought Elisabeth needed forgetting."

Drew laughed. "'Closure,' you mean? Well, this is definitely not closure."

"No," Sarah said, and stared straight ahead, then quietly started telling him everything, her words slow, carefully chosen. "A forgetting. I picked this week, this year. Twenty years later. After the—oh, how do you say?—*disappearance*. Yes, after the disappearance. On May twenty-eighth. And then this week, on June second. Their little one's birthday." Drew nodded. "Though yes, I thought she would find *closure* here, too. Bury something. A toy, pictures, anything."

Drew looked at Sarah. "I understand, Sarah. That was a good idea."

"Yes, it was," she said, and sighed. "But why are you here? You and Brad?"

"Oh. Work trip. For the military. We're on base this week."

Sarah looked at him. "This week? That is very much a—oh, how do say?—very much an *irony*?"

Drew looked at her, confused. "Oh, you mean 'coincidence?'"

Sarah nodded.

Drew thought about it. "Yeah, a coincidence. Interesting." His face flushed, and he turned around to look at Brad, then tapped him on the shoulder. "So, Brad, how long have you been lying to me?"

Brad turned around to look at his friend. "Lying? What do you mean?"

"Don't tell me your sudden change of heart about a TDY to Eglin has nothing to do with Elisabeth being here this week. Man, you lied to me. Not cool, so not cool, man."

Brad looked at him. "I'm sorry, Drew, I'm sorry. I started talking to Elisabeth and thought it would be—"

"Mr. and Mrs. Collins?" they heard the front desk lady say. Both Brad and Elisabeth stood up, still holding each other's hand. "Chief Parlot is ready to see you now."

They looked at each other, then at their two friends. They all nodded. Together, hand in hand, Elisabeth and Brad walked back to see the chief. They were determined to open up the case of the missing toddler again that day at the Niceville Police Office.

CHAPTER 81

Niceville Police Office. He shuddered as he drove by, tailing the blue Oldsmobile down the road. *They led the case back then, I think.* He thought about it. *Guess the Niceville Police Office is the reason why we got away with it. They quickly concluded it was an "accidental drowning."*

He saw the blue Oldsmobile signal and then turn into another block of apartment buildings. He sighed. *They're looking at even more apartments? How boring.*

At this point he was no longer sure he needed to follow them everywhere like this, but didn't know what else to do. *Can't call Bill again. He told me to leave him alone. He'd freak if he knew Problem Child is back here in the old hood.*

That meant he had no other choice than to follow them, just in case something happened that provided a clue about whether or not she remembered anything.

Or anyone.

He shuddered again, then parked his green truck behind some bushes to wait until the blue Oldsmobile moved again.

CHAPTER 82

They were on the move again. Jack was driving Maria's blue Oldsmobile and she was in the passenger seat, taking in everything around her. They were quiet today. *Just don't know what to say. I'm so embarrassed after last night. I can only imagine what Jack's thinking. He was so quiet, so reserved at breakfast, and now he's giving me that strange look. A mix of concern and shock. Maybe even a hint of disappointment and mistrust?* She sighed and stared out the window.

They passed a strip mall and then a sign that read "Niceville Children's Park."

"Turn here," Maria said suddenly.

Jack gave her a quick glance but hit the blinker and turned.

"There, into that parking lot," Maria directed, and Jack did what she said. And there they were. Right there in a parking lot facing a black metal gate that led to a bunch of playground equipment affixed to a soft, cushioned rubber floor. There were slides, climbing structures, a sand area for digging, and a seesaw. Maria stared at it while Jack stared at her.

"This isn't the right place," he just said, his eyes resting on her.

But Maria didn't notice his gaze, just kept staring at the big metal gate. The sun shone on it, and it got so bright she had to close her eyes for a second. When she opened them again, a picture from long gone times played out before her eyes.

A tall, slender woman with wavy reddish-brown hair, a perfectly formed nose, and high cheekbones with freckles all over them was holding the hand of a little toddler. The little one was dressed in a brown neckholder dress adorned with purple, pink, and blue flowers. The outside border of the dress was a wavy pink trim.

The little one had her wavy brown hair up in a high ponytail that bobbed up and down, up and down as she hopped from one foot to the next in excitement. The mom laughed as she tried to open the childproof gate to the play area while not letting go of her daughter's hand.

She squatted down to look at her daughter and explain something. "Warte, bitte!" Maria heard, and wasn't sure what language they were speaking, but somehow she knew the mom had told her daughter to wait. The mom let go of her hand so she could use both her own hands to open the tricky metal gate, then gestured her little one to come through.

Without hesitation, the little girl let go of the metal gate she had been holding on to and ran past her mom as fast as she could onto the playground area. Her mom closed the gate and yelled after her, "Langsam, warte auf Mama!"

The little one stopped abruptly and turned around to look at her mom. Her hazel eyes—a mosaic of golden-and-emerald-green flecks in the dark brown center encircled by a blue rim—shone in delight, reflecting the bright Florida sun.

It became so bright that Maria had to close her eyes again. When she opened them, the little girl and her mom were gone. She stared at the metal gate glimmering in the sun.

"Maria?" she heard a male voice ask, and turned her head toward the sound. It was Jack, sitting behind the driving wheel in her car. "Maria, what are we doing here? This isn't an apartment complex. We took a wrong turn. Your directions were incorrect."

Maria looked at him in a daze, then back to the playground area. "Niceville Children's Park" the sign said. She didn't see any other cars parked in the parking lot. She was confused.

Did the mom and her daughter come on foot? She looked around again, a puzzled look on her face.

"Maria, are you okay?"

She nodded. "Where did they go?"

"Who?"

"The mom and her little daughter. The one in the brown dress." Jack looked at her, stunned, as she continued, "The mom who just opened the gate and went onto the playground with her little daughter."

Jack was gobsmacked for a moment, then said, "Maria, there's nobody there. Look, the park isn't even open today."

"What?"

She looked through the windshield at the gate, just as she had done before. There. A big white sign with black lettering on it. "CLOSED" it said in capital letters. The days and hours of operation were listed underneath.

She checked the day and time on her phone. *Monday around noon.* She looked back at the sign.

OPEN:
TUESDAY-FRIDAY, 10 A.M.-7 P.M.
SATURDAY, 9 A.M.-6 P.M.
SUNDAY, NOON-6 P.M.
CLOSED MONDAYS

She stared at it. *Closed Mondays?* She looked at Jack. "But the mom and her daughter. . . ."

"There was nobody, Maria. I swear. Nobody. No other cars here. The locals know it's closed on Mondays."

She looked back at the gate, then around the parking lot. *He's right, it's only us here. But who was that lady with her daughter? They were so clear. So real.*

Jack looked at Maria, who was still staring at the gate, and asked, "What did they look like?"

"What?" She started rubbing her head.

"What did the woman and her daughter look like?" Jack turned off the car and sat back, relaxing.

"I thought you said you didn't see anyone and—"

"I'm asking what *you* saw. Please, Maria, sit back with me. Close your eyes and tell me what you just saw. Don't question it, just tell me."

Maria looked at him, confused. His voice had taken on a different tone. Almost sounded like a professional. Just like a lawyer. Calm, very calm. His eyes rested on her.

Close my eyes? Why?

"Just go ahead, Maria. Tell me what you saw."

She heard his calm voice and sat back, ignoring the oncoming headache, and thought back. She told him about the tall slender woman with the wavy reddish-brown hair and the little girl in the brown flowery dress with the pink trim around it. She told him about the little one's bright eyes, the unique eyes.

Maria was smiling when she suddenly heard a snap. She abruptly opened her eyes again.

"Well, Maria, thank you for telling me that," Jack just said, and put a little notepad back in his pocket.

What in the world? Was he interrogating me? Like one of his clients? He sure sounds just like a lawyer right now. Calm, deliberate. Her headache came back.

"Well, Maria, I suggest you close your eyes to rest your head before we see the next few apartments. Get a bit of rest. We still need you present for this task. How does that sound?"

She was stunned, but just nodded. *He has such a calming voice, just like Aaron. Aaron! I miss him. Wonder how he's doing.*

Quickly, she texted Aaron. She was surprised to get a response from him right away and smiled. "Oh, Aaron texted back. He's doing lunch at the BX with his sponsor and about to see more of his new office before going to the security clearance interview."

"Good. Tell him good luck, and that everything is under control here," Jack said, and saw Maria text.

"All sent," she said and smiled at him. Her headache was waning now.

Jack started the car and pulled out of the parking lot. He looked at her and noted her wavy reddish-brown hair with the perfectly formed nose and high cheek bones, all the freckles, and the exotic hazel eyes with the blue rim around them.

"The little girl has grown up," he mumbled, and turned onto the street. He almost ran into a green pickup truck that was illegally parked right there under the tree by the entrance to the Niceville Children's Park.

"Gosh, what the heck? Where did that truck come from?"

Maria shrugged her shoulders and looked at the truck parked there. She couldn't see anyone inside. But something nagged at her. *Have I seen that truck before? I feel like I have.* She thought about it, but couldn't be sure.

CHAPTER 83

"I'm not sure we can do anything else now," Elisabeth said, tears dwelling in her eyes. "I just don't understand how they could refuse to open up the case again!"

"Because it's not a cold case—it's a *closed* case. You heard the man," Brad said, his voice low, his eyebrows crunched in. "We all know that the investigation was closed after they determined it was an 'accidental drowning'"—Brad mocked the police chief's words—"but *we* know there's too many loose ends dangling about. It's ridiculous! I even gave him a new suspect! And such good reasons as to why they were wrong about calling it an accidental drowning."

Elisabeth nodded. Sarah and Drew watched on as they all stood in the parking lot of the Niceville Police Station.

"I just don't understand. The Chief even remembers the case. He was young, a brand-new police officer back then, and worked the case. He should understand," Brad mumbled, his voice low. Dangerously low. "Sure, he promised 'to think about it.' Yeah, right. As if he's going to do that. I bet he's already forgotten all about it."

They looked at one another, Elisabeth crying silent tears.

"I'm sorry, guys," Drew said, and squeezed Brad's shoulder.

"I, too. I am sorry, too," Sarah said, then turned to Elisabeth and gave her a hug. "Tut mir leid, Elisabeth."

Elisabeth nodded, but suddenly started sobbing loudly. Sarah hugged her tighter. For a while, they just stood there like that, then Brad started rubbing Elisabeth's back, gently.

Elisabeth got out of Sarah's hug and turned around to look at her ex-husband. "Brad, I just *know* she's out there somewhere. I *know*. I can't explain it, but it's a mother's intuition. Just like it was back then. I knew she was kidnapped, but nobody believed me. And I know now she's alive even now."

Drew and Sarah exchanged a glance in secret.

Brad hugged her, hugged her tight. "I believe you. I do. And I swear to you, we'll find her. This time, we'll find the answers, and they'll lead us to her. I told you that before. You gotta believe me. You gotta trust me."

Elisabeth suddenly smiled and looked up at him. "I do trust you. And I'm so glad that you're here with me."

Brad looked at her, his heart skipping a beat then beating faster. "You are?"

"Yeah, I am," she said, then gave him a kiss. At first, he was shocked, but then closed his eyes and kissed her back.

"Well, at least they found each other again," Drew whispered to Sarah as they both watched them.

Sarah smiled. "Ja. That's not bad."

Drew laughed. "Yep, not bad at all." He checked his watch and looked over at Brad. He waited a good moment, as long as he could, before tapping his friend on the shoulder. "Sorry to interrupt, Cave Man, but we gotta go. More meetings."

Brad looked at him. "Drew, can't you just—"

"No, Brad," Elisabeth interrupted, "Drew can't just go by himself. You're here for those meetings, too. And like I said, I don't think there's anything else we can do right now."

"I know, but—"

"No, hun, just go. Seriously. I'm not mad. I think it'll be good for you, actually."

He looked at her while still holding her, his hands around her waist. "'Good?'"

"Yeah. You take your mind off this disappointment for a bit, and we'll meet again tonight to figure out next steps."

"Okay. But what will you do while I work?"

She smiled. "I don't know. Guess Sarah and I can go to the beach. I have my best ideas when I'm in nature. I might think of another solution to our problem. Like you said, this time we won't give up, right?"

He smiled broadly. "No, this time we won't give up! That's right."

"Okay then. You guys go and we'll see you tonight. We'll come up with a new plan. Tonight, at the restaurant."

"Yeah, tonight. At the Compass Rose. After my work dinner." He smiled and waved goodbye to her and Sarah, his hands still sweaty.

CHAPTER 84

His hands were sweaty. Aaron had just met Special Agent William Barrett and his colleague Special Agent Kayla Smith, both Top Secret Security Clearance interviewers.

"Please follow us, Lieutenant Heikinnen."

The special agents took him to a secure room on one of the floors in their office that Lieutenant Snyder hadn't shown Aaron before. *Of course not. It's a top-secret floor. Intense.* He inhaled deeply. The agents weren't people of many words and just gestured Aaron to sit down at the table opposite them. The room was darkened with shades to block out the sun and had a single light on. Aaron felt uneasy already. *Interview?* He almost chuckled. *What a wrong word for this. This is an interrogation!*

"Lieutenant Heikinnen, welcome to Eglin Air Force Base, and to your Top Secret Security Clearance Interview," Special Agent Smith started.

"Thank you, ma'am," Aaron said, and smiled.

"We didn't ask you to speak," Special Agent Smith scolded him.

"Oh, I'm sorry, ma'am." Aaron looked at her. *Jeez. I was just trying to be nice.*

He quickly learned to stiffen up in his seat and follow orders and only answer questions when asked directly. They went over all of his personal information. He confirmed everything and swore that he had only stated the truth to the best of his ability in the paperwork he had handed in.

They grilled him on his travels, his social media accounts, and most of all, his foreign contacts. Mostly Maria's family. Luckily, he remembered their occupations, where they lived and worked, how long they've been living in the states already. He felt like it was going great until Special Agent Smith started asking him about Maria. Aaron had a hard time not being biased—not telling them how great and special she was to him—and just sticking to the facts about her.

"So, Lieutenant Heikinnen, would you say you know your fiancée well?" Special Agent Smith looked at him.

He nodded. "Yes, ma'am."

"And you said you filled out your paperwork truthfully to your best knowledge?"

"Yes, ma'am."

"You are about to marry Maria Gabriella Sullivan?"

"Yes, ma'am."

"And you're sure she's trustworthy?"

"Yes, ma'am." *What in the world? What do they know?* He stayed as calm as he could.

"Are you sure she's not just using you, Lieutenant Heikinnen?"

Aaron didn't know what to say to that. *What kind of question is that?* "No, ma'am, she isn't 'just using me.' Using me for what?"

Special Agent Smith got up and started pacing back and forth while fixating her eyes on Aaron. Agent Barrett remained sitting across from Aaron, intensely studying his face.

"Well, I don't know. Maybe for a cover-up?"

"A cover-up?"

"Yes, a cover-up," Agent Smith said.

"Or maybe citizenship?" Special Agent Barrett now threw in.

"Citizenship?" Aaron was confused.

"Yes, citizenship," both agents said in unison, and Agent Smith stopped pacing. They both just looked at Aaron.

"Ma'am, sir, Maria is a US citizen already. She was born in the United States. Born to a United States citizen—her dad—and her naturalized mother," Aaron stated, a smile on his face.

"Are you *sure* about that, Lieutenant Heikinnen?"

Aaron's mind started racing. *Well, that's the official story, of course. I already know the name of the father on the birth certificate is wrong. And that's according to Martina, Maria's mom. The woman I suspect may have lied about herself as well.*

"Lieutenant Heikinnen, please answer our question!" yelled Agent Smith.

"Yes, sir," Aaron said immediately.

"Yes, sir, what? Meaning 'yes, you are sure about your statement earlier?'"

Aaron looked at her, then at her colleague. *Well, yes, as in I'm supposed to think it's true, but I've a feeling it isn't. But no real proof either way.* He had been hoping they would just tell him what they had found out, but they had confronted him over it instead. *Will they accuse me of lying if I don't tell them my assumptions? Or is it worse to talk about those assumptions?*

"Lieutenant Heikinnen?" They both looked at him, eyebrows raised.

Aaron started sweating. *Oh no, I'm sweating. That probably seems suspicious.* But thinking that only made him sweat more. He took a deep breath.

"Lieutenant Heikinnen, what are you hiding?"

Aaron had to say something. He quickly sorted his thoughts and decided to explain, as briefly and convincingly as he could. "Special Agent Barrett, you called me a few weeks ago telling me something wasn't right with my paperwork."

The agent nodded slightly.

"I kept thinking about what it could be. I know I did everything right. So, I came to the conclusion it must have been one of the pieces of paperwork I didn't triple check." He looked at the agents, who were both silently listening. "I assume this must be about Maria's birth certificate. Is it a fake?"

The agents didn't answer his question. "How well do you know her, Lieutenant Heikinnen?" they asked instead.

"Very well, ma'am. I know her better than myself. And I know that *she* doesn't know anything is wrong with her birth certificate. Except for the name of her father on it."

"Name of her father?"

"Yes, sir. In recent developments, Maria found out that the name of the guy on her birth certificate, her mom's ex-husband, is not her biological father."

"I see. She found that out and told you this?"

"Yes, ma'am."

"And you didn't think to tell us?" Agent Barrett stared at Aaron.

"No, sir. Maria's mother, Martina Sullivan, told us the biological father has the same first name and that it's not illegal to put an assumptive father on the birth certificate."

The agents looked at each other and then at Aaron.

"Doesn't sound like an assumption to me if she knew who she had sexual contact with nine months before," Special Agent Smith said.

Aaron blushed. "Ma'am, according to Martina Sullivan, she didn't want to get the guy who impregnated her in trouble. He was still married. And she never heard from him again."

"Save the sad stories for a different time," Agent Smith commented. "How do you explain the fact that the Jackson Memorial Hospital in Miami never registered the birth of a 'Maria Gabriella Sullivan?'"

Aaron stared at her. *There it is. My proof! Proof that Martina isn't Maria's real mom.* His thoughts started racing, but he forced himself to stay calm and cool. "I don't know, ma'am."

"And how do you explain the fact that none of the other two hospitals in Miami ever registered the birth of a Maria Gabriella Sullivan?"

"I don't know, sir!"

"Lieutenant Heikinnen, how do you explain the fact that *nowhere in Florida* on *this* day of September"—the agent now threw Maria's birth certificate onto the table and pointed at the date on it—"was there *any* baby girl named Maria Gabriella Sullivan born to a Martina Perez Sullivan?"

Aaron stared at her. His heart sank for Maria. *Nowhere in Florida? Not on this day? Oh my gosh, Maria. You're not who you think you are! Maria isn't even your real name!*

"Lieutenant Heikinnen. Explain!"

Aaron shuddered. "I can't explain it." He couldn't tell him his suspicion. His suspicion that Maria was actually the little toddler Moana Marie Collins who had allegedly drowned here at Eglin AFB twenty years earlier. *That's just not explainable. It doesn't make sense. Unless the kidnapping theory is correct. But how—and why—would Martina come to Eglin AFB to kidnap a child?*

"You cannot explain it?" He heard Agent Smith ask, and saw her looking down at him, still standing, hovering, towering over him.

Aaron shook his head.

Agent Barrett stared at him from across the table. "Lieutenant Heikinnen, have you ever been involved in criminal activity?"

"What? No!"

Special Agent Smith came over and bent over the table to look Aaron in the eye.

"How do you explain this fake birth certificate then, Lieutenant Heikinnen? This birth certificate of your fiancée, the one you know inside out?"

Aaron stared back. "I don't know ma'am."

She slammed her fist on the table and Aaron almost jumped out of his seat. *Wow she's intimidating.*

"If her *birth certificate* is a *fake*, who is she *really*? Are you sleeping with the enemy, Lieutenant Heikinnen?"

He couldn't help but let out a quick laugh.

"What's so funny, Lieutenant Heikinnen?"

"I'm sorry, ma'am and sir. Your question just sounded like something out of a James Bond movie."

Both agents stared at him.

"Look, Special Agent Smith and Special Agent Barrett, I can assure you Maria is innocent. Whatever happened to her, she's not a part of it. She's not the culprit, she's the victim!"

"Victim?" both agents asked at the same time, their eyes fixated on him.

He thought for a quick second and decided it was probably best to explain his suspicions. "When I got your call, Agent Barrett, you led me to thinking it might be her birth certificate. Listen, I have no proof, and therefore haven't told anyone yet, but I believe Martina Sullivan is not Maria's real mom. And I think her real dad used to be in the military. Maria's been having dreams—well, memories, more like, I think—of a guy in uniform she thinks is her dad. I believe Maria might have childhood PTSD. She's been showing all the signs of it recently, especially when we came here to Eglin Air Force Base."

Both agents were sitting across from Aaron now, listening, taking notes. "Go on, Lieutenant Heikinnen."

Aaron took a deep breath. "I think she lived here at Eglin at one point. Twenty years ago. She might be the toddler that supposedly drowned here by accident. If that's actually her, then the police got it wrong. She didn't drown. She was somehow taken from her real parents. Maybe kidnapped? I really don't know. It's all just speculation at that point. But knowing all that, I think you'll find Maria is the victim in all this."

The agents looked at each other. "Lieutenant Heikinnen, if what you're saying is true, why didn't you contact the police?"

"Because I have no proof! Just a story. I was hoping you would provide proof today, that you'd tell me more about the fake birth certificate. Then I'd have ammunition to confront her mother."

The agents looked at each other. "Lieutenant Heikinnen, if Martina Sullivan has a child that's obviously not hers, but was raised to believe it is, she has a huge problem! It's a case for the police, not for a second lieutenant to figure out!"

Aaron nodded. "What else did you find out about the birth certificate? Is it a complete fake?"

The agents looked at each other. "Lieutenant Heikinnen, *we* are the ones asking questions here," Agent Smith said.

"Oh, okay. I'm sorry, ma'am. I'm just trying to understand.. . . ."

Agent Barrett smiled briefly, for the first time that day, then nodded. "We understand, Lieutenant Heikinnen. It's definitely an interesting case. Yes, Maria's birth certificate is convincing, professionally faked, but definitely not an original. Martina Sullivan never had a child. We checked her doctor's appointments dating back thirty years."

Aaron's mouth dropped open. *There it is. Martina is not Maria's real mom. Oh my gosh! Martina is not Maria's real mom! Unbelievable.* Even though he had suspected it, the reality of it hit him hard. Real hard. "What else did you find out?"

"Lieutenant Heikinnen," Agent Smith explained, "our job is to look up your background and contacts. We did. We found an issue. We determined the birth certificate was a fake by contacting both the previously mentioned hospitals and the Division of Vital Records, and found neither had a birth registered under that name on that date. The rest is up to the police."

Aaron looked at her. "But can't you—"

"Lieutenant Heikinnen, we cannot. It's a case for the police now. We've already contacted them last week, but we've all decided to wait for today's interview. Just in case you had a different birth certificate or an explanation for this one." Agent Barret pointed at the certificate still laying on the table. "The police are on standby in Miami as we speak."

"On standby in Miami?"

"Yes, Lieutenant. Martina Sullivan broke the law and will therefore be brought in for questioning."

Aaron suddenly got up. He didn't know if he was allowed to, but he couldn't help himself. "But, but . . . you can't just arrest her! You can't just arrest Martina! We don't even know if—"

"Lieutenant Heikinnen, sit down," Agent Smith ordered him.

"Yes, ma'am, I'm sorry."

"We understand it's hard for you, Lieutenant Heikinnen, but this is something the police need to determine. They will also have to question your fiancée."

Aaron looked at them. "Maria?"

"Yes, Lieutenant Heikinnen. She might be a part of it. It's not yet proven she's just a victim. She'll be treated as a witness for now. The police will take care of it."

Aaron jumped up again. "'The police will take care of it?' Ma'am, Maria can't possibly be a suspect here, and we—"

"Nobody really knows who she is! The police will have to determine that. They'll bring her in for questioning soon. We'll inform the Niceville Police Department as soon as we're done here."

"As soon as we're. . . ." Aaron felt as if someone had just dumped a bucket of cold water on him. *This is a mess. My future mother-in-law is about to be arrested, my fiancée will be picked up by the police for questioning, and I'm stuck here getting grilled by these two agents.*

"And Lieutenant Heikinnen, we believe you are innocent in all of this, but we are sure you will understand that we cannot give you any sort of security clearance at this point in time."

Aaron jumped up again. "But sir, I don't—"

"Lieutenant. Sit. Down!"

Fine! What's wrong with standing up anyway? Don't they understand my world is about to fall apart? He plopped down onto the uncomfortable metal chair and looked at them.

"Lieutenant Heikinnen, we cannot give you your security clearance *for now*, until everything gets figured out regarding your fiancée and her family. Thank you for coming in today. You are free to go."

He looked at them. "Okay, fine. I'm free to go. What about Maria and Martina? You said you're—"

"We will inform the appropriate authorities now. They will make contact."

Aaron stood up again. "Please, Agent Smith and Agent Barrett, please let me talk to them before you do that. To both of them. Please!"

"I'm sorry, Lieutenant, that's not our protocol. You are not allowed to talk to Martina Sullivan. Luckily, we have the Miami Police Department on speed dial. By the time you get to your phone, they will have picked her up already. Thanks again for coming in today. Good luck with everything, and we hope to see you again when it's all sorted out," Agent Barrett said, and pointed to the door.

Agent Smith was already opening it. "Have a good day, Lieutenant."

Aaron couldn't believe it. *They're throwing me out and siccing the police on Martina and Maria. Right now! Oh my gosh! That's crazy!*

He felt like he was in a bad dream, but knew it wasn't a dream at all. It was stone-cold reality, and it hit him harder than he would've ever thought. Never had he thought the police would go after Maria. *Holy cow, Maria! I need to get to her. As quick as possible.*

He walked around the table and mumbled a goodbye to both special agents, barely noticing the door shut behind him. He was staring straight ahead at the white wall and only noticed Lieutenant Snyder when he gave him a friendly bump on the shoulder.

"Hey there, you survived! How'd it go, man?"

Slowly, Aaron turned his head and looked into Lieutenant Snyder's face. He had no idea what to say to him, to his new coworker and colleague. *I don't care if I get in trouble for leaving, I have to get to Maria.*

"I gotta go," he said simply. "Gotta go right away and find her before they do." And then he ran down the six flights of stairs without looking back, leaving the baffled first lieutenant behind.

CHAPTER 85

Maria and Jack were just leaving an apartment complex they had toured in Niceville when her phone rang.

"Oh, it's Aaron," Maria told Jack, and picked up the phone while buckling her seatbelt as he started the car.

"Maria—"

"Hi, Aaron! We were thinking of you during your interview. Congrats for making it out alive," she joked. "Wait, I'll put you on loudspeaker so your dad can hear you too."

And before Aaron could say anything he was already on loudspeaker. "Where are you?"

"We were just looking at some Niceville apartments. They sure seemed . . . *nice*."

Both Maria and Jack laughed. That joke was cheesy but never got old. As their laughter died down, they heard Aaron's quick breathing over the loudspeaker.

"Get. Out. Of. There!"

"What?" Maria and Jack looked at each other, confused.

"You. Have. To. Leave," they heard Aaron saying between quick breaths.

Maria and Jack looked at each other again. "What in the world is going on with you? Are you running a marathon while talking to us?" Maria's joke made Jack grin.

"Maria, the police are coming."

Jack's grin faded. Maria stared at her phone screen. *The voice call should've been the first clue that something isn't right. What in the world is going on?*

"Warn your mom also," she heard Aaron say, then heard a door slam in the background.

"Aaron, you're scaring me. You're not making sense at all. What's going on? Where are you?"

Aaron struggled to get his breathing under control. "In my car . . . trying to find you. . . . Where the heck are you?" He turned on his engine. Tires squeaking, he left the parking lot at his new office, checked to make sure he had his brand-new ID card on him, then started driving off base as quickly as he could without risking getting pulled over.

Jack took over now and spoke into Maria's phone. "Aaron, we're in Niceville."

"Okay, stay where you are. I'm coming!"

Through the phone, Maria and Jack heard the blinker and the intense squeaking of Aaron's tires.

"What's wrong with you, Aaron? You have to calm down," Maria pleaded. "Please Aaron. Don't get into an accident. I need you to stay safe. I love you and need you around! Please, take a deep breath and drive safely."

Jack looked over at Maria in amazement. He was impressed. She really knew the right words to calm him. He smiled, then talked to his son. "Aaron, Maria is right. You need to stay calm. You know you tend to get a little hot-headed and anxious when things slip out of your control. And I assume something has?"

"Yes, Dad. It really, really has," they heard Aaron say.

Maria stared back and forth between her phone's screen and Jack. *What is going on?*

"Maria, listen," Aaron said, "you need to warn your mom."

"Warn my mom? About what?"

"The police. They're headed to her house. Or store. Wherever she is. To question her."

"What?" Maria stared at the phone. She had barely ever been this irritated in her life.

While stopping at a red light, Jack glanced at her. "Aaron, we'll turn off somewhere and park. I assume you need us to be in a safe area before you break the news?"

"Yes, Dad. Thanks."

"The news? What news?" Maria stared at them both. When the light turned green, Jack pulled into the next parking lot they came across, in front of a Walmart, then explained to Aaron exactly where they were at that moment.

"Great, thanks Dad. Don't move. I'll be right there," they heard Aaron say, still out of breath. "Maria, you really have to call your mom. Tell her the police are coming to bring her in for questioning. It's about you."

"What? Question my mamá? About me? Why?"

"Because of the agents I talked to just now. They know the secret."

"What secret are you talking about?" Her face was flushed.

"Maria, your mom is not your mom. Not your biological mom."

Aaron's words felt like a punch to the face. Maria stared at the phone's screen and gasped. She turned pale, tears dwelling in her eyes. Then her face turned red, red with anger.

"What in the world are you *talking about*, Aaron? Are you *insane?*" Her voice was breaking from yelling so loudly while she struggled to breathe, to hold back tears.

"Maria, I know it's hard to believe, but your birth certificate is a fake. Martina isn't your biological mom."

Silence. All he heard was silence. He slowed down his car to go through the gate then sped up as soon as he was off base. "Maria? Are you still there?"

Then he heard it. Violent sobs. She was crying now. He heard his dad trying to calm her down.

"You're . . . y-you're . . . you . . . a-are . . . You are *wrong*, Aaron," was the last thing he heard before his phone started beeping.

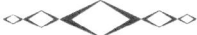

She had hung up on him. *I don't want to talk to him right now. He's wrong, he's insane, he's a liar.* She sobbed loudly. Jack's cell phone started ringing and she heard him pick up and put it on loudspeaker.

"Aaron, your assumption was right?"

"Yeah, I guess so. Martina Sullivan did not give birth to a baby girl in September 2001—or ever."

Jack let out a big sigh; Maria was shaken by violent sobs.

"Is she okay, Dad?"

"Well, she's still here. Let's leave it at that."

"Don't let her go anywhere, Dad. Please, stay where you are. I'll be right there."

"Okay. Drive safely," Jack said, and hung up.

Maria's phone blinked with an incoming text message. Maria stared at it as it blinked again, indicating to her she had just received a text message from Mamá.

Mamá!

"Maria? Please look at it. It might be important." Jack said, and looked at her. His voice was soft.

Maria lifted her heavy head—it seemed to weigh one hundred pounds—to look at Aaron's dad. He was calm. He calmly sat behind the steering wheel of her parked car, giving her an encouraging smile.

"Maria, your mamá needs you now. I know you're confused and you might not want to talk to her, but now is the time to do exactly that. I know you love her. And I know she loves you. No matter what, that love will always be there. Always. No matter what happens after this."

Maria stared at him, her eyes filled with tears, her mascara smeared all over her face.

"Please give this woman a warning, like Aaron said. We're all trying to help. Please, text or call her. Something. Your choice. Remember the love between you and her." Jack put a hand on her shoulder and squeezed. "You can do this, Maria. Check the text."

Her hands felt heavy, felt like weights had been tied to them. She couldn't even describe the feelings she had. It seemed to be a mix of despair, love, hate, confusion, and pain. So much pain. Her heart was hurting.

"Not your biological mom." Aaron's words echoed in her brain, in every part of her brain.

Not my biological mom? How can that be? That can't be right! But maybe it is? I don't look like her at all. I have different talents than her. I'm so much taller than her.

But I love her.

The phone vibrated. "Mamá" the screen read as it vibrated silently in her lap. She was calling now. *I can't talk to her right now. I don't want to. Or do I?* Before she had made up her mind, the vibrating stopped. The call had gone to voicemail.

"Maria, you owe her a warning. She raised you, loved you."

Jack's words make so much sense. Yes, I have to do something.

Maria looked at the text message. *La policía está en mi tienda. ¿Por qué?* it said.

460

She slowly answered. *Ellas te preguntarán sobre mi.* She clicked "send" and within seconds her phone blinked again.

Maria sobbed loudly.

"Maria, what did she say?" Jack asked, still squeezing her shoulder. She took a deep breath and translated the Spanish message on her phone for Jack. "She said the police are already there. She doesn't know why."

"Okay. And what did you tell her?"

Quiet as a mouse, Maria read out her response. "I told her they will ask her about me."

"Good, Maria, good. That'll help. Then she won't be taken so much by surprise."

"By surprise?" She snorted. "She *knows*. No surprise there. You'd know if you gave birth or not. You'd know if you lied your whole life long or not. She shouldn't be *surprised*. I am! I freaking am! She lied to me! She just lied.. . . ." She buried her face in her hands and sobbed quietly now. Jack saw a bunch of tears streaming through her fingers.

"Maria, I know you feel betrayed. But she may have had her reasons. Give her a fair chance. Please. Just text her that the police know about the fake birth certificate. And tell her to request a lawyer," Jack Heikinnen urged his soon-to-be daughter-in-law.

She looked up at him. Her face showed so much pain that Jack felt like he had been stabbed in the back. It hurt him to see her like that. "I like you, Maria. No matter who you really are. I already feel like a dad to you," he said, hoping his words would encourage her.

Slowly, Maria nodded and picked up her phone to text Martina Sullivan. *La policía sabe que la partida de nacimiento es falsa. ¡Conseguir una abogada!*

Within seconds of having sent the text, a simple text message appeared. *Te amo mucho,* it simply said.

"I love you too, I think," Maria mumbled, and started crying again.

Jack couldn't handle seeing her in this much pain anymore and leaned over to give her a hug. It felt as though he were hugging a lifeless puppet that was being jerked about at times by invisible strings as the sobs racked her body. As they waited for Aaron to arrive, they sat there like that in the car. Like a dad hugging, encouraging, protecting his daughter.

A car came rushing into the parking lot and pulled up next to them, brakes squealing.

"Hey, it's Aaron," Jack exclaimed, and Maria looked up to see him get out of his car. He waved to his dad in the driver's seat and ran around the car to get to Maria. He opened the door at the passenger side and found his fiancée crumpled in her seat—the beautiful young woman had turned into a picture of misery. Aaron's heart sank for her. He felt her pain, her confusion, her anger, her despair.

"Oh, Maria," he whispered, and then quickly pulled her up into a long, strong hug. She leaned on his strong shoulder and fell apart—everything fell apart, her life, the whole life that she had thought was hers. It all fell apart, right there in that Walmart parking lot.

CHAPTER 86

In the Walmart parking lot, Jonathan Sullivan was sitting in his truck, feeling confused. No, more than confused. *What the fuck is going on? Why is Problem Child crying like that? Almost inconsolable?*

At this point all he could see was that Aaron guy trying to calm her down while standing outside her car. His face had been flushed when he'd driven into the Walmart parking lot, tires squealing, to meet the old man and Problem Child.

Don't understand. The old man and the girl were happily looking at apartments earlier, now this? Don't get it. What the fuck's wrong with people? He took out a cigarette, rolled down the window of his green pickup truck, and lit it, blowing out smoke while watching the group. *What's their problem?*

His tummy started grumbling. *I need some food. This is exhausting.* He saw that Problem Child was still crying but seemed to have calmed down a bit. *She still looks terrible, far as I can tell. But she sure grew into a pretty little thing.* He smiled and kept watching, smoking his cigarette. He saw her hold up a cell phone to her ear and start speaking.

CHAPTER 87

"Hello?" she said in a fake chipper voice. Aaron and Maria had sat back down in the car, Aaron in the backseat.

"We are looking for Maria Gabriella Sullivan," she heard a male voice say. "To whom am I speaking?"

Maria wrinkled her forehead. *Who would call me by my middle name?* "This is she. Hi, I'm Maria," she said, a bit suspicious, and then took the phone off her ear to put it on loudspeaker so Jack and Aaron could listen in.

"Hello, Maria. This is Chief Parlot from the Niceville Police Department. How are you?"

Maria couldn't say anything for a moment. Jack gestured for her to keep speaking. "I-I . . . I've been better. Thank you. Err, how can I help you?"

"Well, Maria, we heard you are in the area and would like you to come in for questioning," the police chief said.

"Questioning? Me? Why?"

"Well, we've gotten some information from both our partners here at Eglin Air Force Base as well as Miami that concerns both you and your mother, Martina Marie Sullivan."

Maria stared at the phone.

"We would like you to answer a few questions to help with our investigation."

"Investigation into what?"

"Miss, we'll just have to wait and talk about that in person. Please come to the Niceville Police Department now. Unless you'd rather have us pick you up?"

Jack and Aaron looked at Maria and shook their heads, signaling her to tell the chief she would come by.

"Fine, Chief Parlot, I'll come in."

"Wonderful. Looks like you're right around the corner from the police station. So, I'll see you in about five to ten minutes then? Thank you." He hung up.

Maria stared at her phone.

Jack raised his eyebrows. "Sounds like they're already having your phone tracked, Maria."

"What? Why?" Maria was confused and shocked. Her tears were all dried up now and color started flushing back into her face. A reddish color. An angry color.

"Well, a fake birth certificate is a big deal. And it affects the child whose birth was faked as much as it does the person who pretended to be the birth mom and defrauded the government."

The color flushed away from her face again and her lip started shaking. *I just can't believe it. My mamá is not my mom?* She felt like she had been hit by a truck. *Mamá is not my mom?* She stared out the window on her way to Niceville's Police Station.

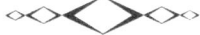

"Well, Miss Sullivan, I suggest you go get some dinner and rest up for the night. At the moment we cannot do anything else here on our end," Chief Parlot said, looking at Maria.

Maria nodded and looked at him, her face smeared with mascara, her hair wild.

Chief Parlot got up. "Please, let me walk you out."

She nodded again and got up, robotically, barely noticing anything around her.

The chief sighed. "Thank you again for coming in for questioning."

Slowly, she lifted her head and looked at him, her eyes empty, freakishly green. She formed her words slowly. "How did that help?"

"Well, you just confirmed what we already suspected. You seem to be the victim in all of this. You were convinced that Martina Marie Sullivan, also known as Martina Marie Perez, was your biological mother and had no reason to suspect otherwise."

Her empty eyes stared back at his. "How do you know that?"

The chief let out a chuckle. "Well, Miss, I don't need to be a police officer to see it. You obviously feel betrayed by this woman you've known your whole life as your mom. You look very confused. Miserable, actually. If all this isn't true and you're just playing this part of a confused woman, I think you deserve an Oscar for your performance."

She just nodded. The chief gently touched her shoulder, and she almost jumped at the slight touch. "I'm sorry, Miss Sullivan. Please, just follow me."

She looked at him and started stammering. "P-please, look at Jonathan Smith. My dad. Special Forces. Air Force. Shiny shoes. Brad. Water. And—"

"Please, miss, let me stop you here. I'll try to make sense of the incohesive story you told me about your biological dad. But for now, go home. Just go home. I understand how hard this must be for you, miss. Let me take you to your fiancé and his dad, okay?"

"Okay," she mumbled, and followed him, mechanically, robotically, her eyes wide, staring ahead.

CHAPTER 88

His eyes were wide as he stared ahead. His hands were sweating, his heart beating fast. *What the fuck are they doing at the police office?* He walked across the street again and around the block, always keeping his eyes on the police station. He had parked his truck a little further down the street. Didn't want to be seen in the area or caught on surveillance cams. It might start to look suspicious, like he was casing the joint, him in his truck parked there for hours.

He smiled. *Well, I'm clever, after all. It's smart to walk by, be a passerby.* Then he frowned. *Why are they in the fucking police station?* He started sweating again. *Did Problem Child actually remember something?* He shook his head. *No, can't be.*

His tummy growled again. *All this walking. I'm hungry, so hungry. But I gotta wait and see what the fuck's going on here.* He kept an eye on the two cars parked in front of the police station.

CHAPTER 89

Chief Parlot walked the young lady through the hallway and out into the foyer by the front desk with the big leather chairs. He saw the young Air Force officer, her fiancé, and her soon-to-be father-in-law waiting there, sitting in the chairs. They got up the moment they saw Maria.

"We're all done," he announced to the group, and stepped behind the young lady.

She just stood there and didn't move. The young Air Force officer walked over and put his arm around her. She put her head on his shoulder and he held her tight, comforting her. He was calm. Very calm.

Chief Parlot analyzed the encounter. *The young man is very poised, almost too poised for a man who just found out his fiancée isn't who he thought she was. Does he know more than he's letting on?* He made a mental note. *Need to look at the transcript of that young lieutenant's security interview when it comes in later.*

"Thank you, sir," the older man said and shook the chief's hand.

"Yes, thank you, sir. We hope to find out who Maria is soon," the young lieutenant said, and shook Chief Parlot's hand as well.

The chief looked at him. *Seems a little too confident they'll figure out who this young lady is soon. Why?* Instead of asking him that, he just said, "Yes, we hope so, too. But for now, there's nothing more we can do. We'll have to wait for our partners in Miami to provide us more information."

The young woman looked at him, tears rolling down her high cheek bones with the freckles on them. She started sobbing.

The chief felt sorry for her. "We *will* find out," he assured her as he looked at her. *She's beautiful, even with a mascara-smeared face.* He stared at her now. *Have I met her before?*

He offered her a box of tissues from the front desk. She took it and started dabbing her swollen eyes, then cleared her stuffy nose, then took another one to wipe away her tears. The chief watched her dab her eyes—those beautiful, exotic eyes. He quickly glanced at the folder he was carrying and looked down on his papers.

All their copies of the several IDs on record for this young lady stated that she was "Maria Gabriella Sullivan." They all had the same description: brown hair and hazelnut-brown eyes. He looked at her again and realized that her eyes were more green at this moment, and had an interesting, unique blue rim around them. *Those eyes! Have I seen them before? And that elegantly formed nose with the freckles on it?*

He thought back to earlier that day. *No. No other young lady has been in today. No other young lady has been in for over a week. It's usually very quiet here. Still, she reminds me of someone.* He checked the time. *Six p.m. Dinnertime.* He closed his folder named "Identity Case: Maria Gabriella Sullivan."

"Thank you again for coming in. We'll be in touch and know where to find you if we need you again. I suggest you take this young lady back to your hotel now. Or out to dinner."

"Yes, thank you, Chief. Thanks for your help," the older man said.

"Thank you, Chief. Yes, we'll definitely go out to dinner," the young man in the Air Force uniform said firmly.

Chief Parlot watched them walk away. *Something is off. What does the young man know? He seems so confident—the exact opposite of Maria. She needs to be stabilized by her fiancé as she's dragging her feet, almost stumbling over them. She looks so frail, so timid. So broken. And that broken walk somehow reminds me of someone. But who?* He just shrugged his shoulders and walked back to his office. He needed to get ready to pack up and go home to his own family for dinner.

CHAPTER 90

Dinner. They were hungry and stood at the entrance to the restaurant. They waited for the hostess to come back to seat them. With a big smile on her face, the hostess returned from having helped another family and looked at Elisabeth and Sarah.

"Good evening, ladies. Do you have a reservation?"

Elisabeth nodded and gave her the name of the reservation.

"Oh yes, you got one of the last tables out on the balcony. Excellent." The young hostess grabbed some menus and told them to follow her.

Elisabeth was glad she had called in advance—the restaurant was pretty busy. The balcony was especially packed, except for one large table over in the other corner of the beautiful outdoor seating area. It too had a large "Reserved" sign on it. Elisabeth and Sarah sat down at their own small table in the opposite corner of the balcony, overlooking the bay.

"Wow," Sarah just said as they sat down.

"Isn't it beautiful?" The hostess smiled at them and gave them a menu. "Your server will be with you in just a minute."

"Thank you," they both said, and started studying the menu.

Elisabeth already knew what she wanted. "I love their blackened Mahi Mahi. You have to try it."

"Okay, maybe," Sarah said, still busy looking at the menu. Elisabeth took the moment to peer inside her purse. *There she is. That old, faded little toy with the duck head. Enti.* She'd felt like she had to bring it. *Enti will help me and Brad come up with a new plan.* She smiled and looked at the sun dipping down toward the horizon across the bay, then looked over at the big table in the corner with the "Reserved" sign on it.

"Waiting for Brad to arrive, huh?"

Elisabeth looked at Sarah and blushed.

"Oh, Elisabeth. I'm glad you connected with him again."

"Ja? Really?"

"Ja, of course. I'm mad at you for lying to me, and honestly, I still think it's very unlikely that your little one is still out there." Elisabeth stared at her friend, her smile instantly gone. "It's very naïve of you to think she's still alive, and—"

"Listen, Sarah," Elisabeth said, her voice cold, harsh, "I did not ask for your opinion on this and need you to stay out of it. It's none of your—"

"Hi, I'm your server for the night," a young man interrupted just in time before the two friends could get into a deeper argument. "How may I help you? Can we start you out with some drinks?"

The two friends dropped their heated discussion and turned toward the server to order their drinks.

The two friends were sipping their drinks quietly, each one of them avoiding to look at each other. Instead, they took in the beautiful view. They turned their heads when they heard a large group make their way toward the balcony, talking and laughing loudly.

"There's your Prince Charming," Sarah finally said when she noticed that the large group dressed in military uniforms was Brad's work dinner. "Cheers to that?"

Elisabeth looked at her friend, nodded, then smiled. They both cheered with glasses of wine raised. They waved at Brad and Drew as they walked through the sliding door onto the deck. The men took their seats at the large reserved table on the other side of the balcony. Elisabeth blushed again and kept looking over.

"So, you think you'll get married again?" Sarah asked, and took a sip of her wine.

"What?"

"You and Brad. Will you get married again?"

Elisabeth stared at Sarah. "Don't be silly. I've only just met him."

"Yeah, met him *again*. You were meant to be together."

Elisabeth smirked, looked over to the large table again, waved a little, and her cheeks turned red.

"Or do you think it would bring back too many memories, too many open wounds?"

"What?" Elisabeth said, distracted.

Sarah sighed. "Well, you're obviously not really a part of the conversation here. Guess you're just using me to pass the time until his work dinner is finally done, huh?"

"Ja. We're at dinner," Elisabeth said, still not paying attention.

Sarah rolled her eyes. "So, I guess you're not mad at me anymore about my earlier comment?"

"What comment?"

Sarah laughed. "Well, cheers my friend."

Elisabeth lifted her glass and the two of them cheered with their red wine right there on the balcony of the Compass Rose.

CHAPTER 91

"A seat on the balcony, you said?" the hostess asked Aaron, Jack, and Maria, who had all just arrived at the Compass Rose restaurant.

Aaron nodded with a smile. "Yes, please."

The hostess looked at the group of three and couldn't help but think how terrible the young lady looked.

"So, any seats on the deck left for the three of us?"

The hostess had to tear her eyes away from the girl and make sure to concentrate on her job. She took on a regrettable tone. "I'm sorry, but the balcony is all filled. Most of the seats get reserved early on, especially on Mondays. We're one of the few restaurants in the area that's open Monday nights."

"Oh, too bad," the two guys said in unison.

The hostess glanced at Maria who didn't say a word and started chewing on her lip. She tried to ignore Maria and focused on Aaron again, then said: "We do have a nice little table for you on the inside, right in the corner by the window overlooking the bay. Would that be okay?"

"Sounds great," Jack said and Aaron smiled. They followed her to the table—though the young woman was practically dragged along by the young Air Force officer.

"Your waitress will be with you in just a minute," the hostess said before she left.

On her way back, she waved her colleague over. "Amanda, do you see that group of three over there?"

"Sure. Handsome young man in his blues?" The waitress giggled. "He must be new here. I've never seen him before. Would have noticed him for sure."

The hostess rolled her eyes. "Yes, you can serve him in a minute, Amanda." Amanda giggled as she continued, "But look at the young woman. There's something strange going on."

Amanda looked at her. "What do you mean?"

"Well, look at how *terrible* that girl looks. Mascara all over her face, her hair going crazy. Look at her eyes. She's totally checked out. And so *pale*. Like she's seen a ghost."

"A ghost?"

"I'm just wondering if that young woman is okay. I don't think she's afraid of any of the men that are with her, but you never know. Please keep an eye on that group."

"Okay, will do," Amanda told her, and went off to serve them.

"Hi, my name is Amanda and I'll be your server tonight."

Aaron and Jack looked at the server and greeted her, then took the menus she handed to them. Maria didn't say a word when she took her menu and laid it down on the table in front of her without even looking at it.

"Are you guys new to town? I've never seen you here before, Lieutenant."

Aaron looked at her. He wasn't used to being called that yet. "Ahem, yes, brand-new actually. Just arrived last night. Had my first day today."

"Oh, wonderful," Amanda said. "We have a lot of military people come through here. They *adore* our food. And we give you a great military discount as well. Maybe that's why so many of them love to eat here, even for work dinners." She laughed.

Aaron looked at her, his eyes resting on her. "Work dinners?"

"Yeah, you know. Like that big military group out there, for example." She pointed to the balcony and Aaron saw it. A big group of higher-ups. He swallowed hard, then heard her ask, "Can I start by bringing you something to drink?" He stopped looking over at the uniformed men and women and concentrated on the waitress again.

"Sure, I'd like an iced tea, please," Jack said, and smiled.

"Make it two, please," Aaron said, and looked up at the young waitress, who suddenly blushed.

"Okay then, two iced teas for the gentlemen. Coming right up. And what would the young lady like to drink?"

They all looked at Maria, but she didn't respond, just stared at the tablecloth. She didn't even seem to notice someone was talking to her.

"Maria," Aaron whispered, "the young lady just asked you what you'd like to drink."

She didn't react.

"Maria, *please*. You need to drink something."

No reply.

"Maria," he said, and gently touched her arm.

She almost jumped at his touch. The waitress looked on in shock. Maria now looked at Aaron, looked into his blue eyes.

His eyes full of worry, full of sorrow, full of pain. Pain for me. She sighed. *I know it's hard for him too. But how could he have withheld his suspicions from me? Why didn't he tell me he already suspected Mamá wasn't my biological mom? I'm so mad at him! Even if it's true I probably wouldn't have believed him.*

She let out a deep sigh and, finally, the sound of his words actually made it to her ears. "Maria, what would you like to drink?"

Suddenly, she realized there was a waitress next to her with a notepad, ready to take her order. She hadn't even noticed her before. "Just water," she whispered without making eye contact. "Just water, please."

The waitress nodded and looked at her. Maria could feel her gaze and realized she probably looked terrible. She looked up at her. "Maybe I'll also take something stronger. A whiskey on ice," Maria said, suddenly having found her voice again. "It's been a terrible day. Yes, a drink like that would do me good."

The waitress looked a bit shocked. "Okay, then. Could I please see your ID?"

Maria pulled it out and gave it to the waitress, who studied it then gave it back to her with an approving nod.

"Thank you, Ms. Sullivan," she said with a smile.

Maria let out a big snort that surprised not only everyone at the table but also herself. "Yeah, if that's even my real name," she said.

The waitress was irritated. "Okay then, well, thank you for the orders. Your drinks will be right out. I'll give you a chance to look at the menu for now," she said and walked away, more than confused.

"Excuse me," Maria called after her, and saw her turn around, surprised. "Where is your restroom located? I desperately need to fix my face."

The waitress looked at her and laughed. "Yes, good idea. Sure, the restroom is located right over there. Just past the entryway and down the hallway to the left."

"Okay, thank you." Maria got up and walked to the restroom, suddenly determined to find out who in the world she really was.

CHAPTER 92

Does she know who she is? Did she figure it out? What the fuck is going on with Problem Child? Jonathan saw her rush past the window into the restroom and decided to finally step inside. *I'm hungry. Bet I can blend in just fine at the restaurant. Same as everywhere else the past few days.*

"Good evening, do you have a reservation?" He looked at the young hostess and shook his head. "Party of one?" He nodded. "Okay, one moment please while I look for a table."

"Okay," he said, and spent his time waiting looking around. He saw the Aaron guy and the older man at a table in the corner. Outside, there was a large group of military personnel. It was very busy in here.

"Actually, you're in luck: we have a very small bistro table open on the balcony. Does that work for you?"

He scowled at her and mumbled, "No, I want to be inside."

"Excuse me?"

"Listen, lady, I said I want to be inside."

The hostess looked at him. "I'm sorry, there's no more seats left inside. And most people who come here prefer to be seated out on the balcony to—"

"I don't. I don't wanna sit outside. I want to be inside."

"Sir, I'm afraid there are no more seats available right now. We can take your name and number and call you when one opens up?"

"No."

Perplexed, the hostess looked at him, seeming unsure of what to say.

"No. Don't call me. Eh. Fine then. I'll take the bistro table outside."

"Okay, perfect," she smiled at him. "Follow me, please."

The hostess showed the rude old guy to his table and exhaled deeply as she walked through the sliding door to go back inside. She almost bumped into the young military guy in his blues uniform.

"Excuse me, sir. Are you looking for your table? It's back over there." The hostess pointed to Aaron's dad and looked mad.

"I know, I was just—"

"We ask our guests to please stick to their tables. If you'd like to take in the view, there's an excellent elevated spot a short walk away from the building, but we'd prefer it if you wouldn't disturb the other guests sitting out on the balcony. Easy to get in their personal space, you know?"

He looked at her. He'd just wanted to step outside and see if General Collins was out there. But the young hostess was pointing to his table again and he didn't want to make a scene. He turned around and walked back to his table. He made sure to keep an eye on the big military group outside. Didn't want to miss them. With a sigh, he slurped his iced tea and waited for Maria to return from the ladies' room.

CHAPTER 93

"I have to run and use the ladies' room," Sarah said, looking pointedly at Elisabeth, who was busy watching the group of military personnel at the table on the other side of the deck. "Seems like you don't need me anyway."

Elisabeth looked up, irritated, as Sarah got up.

"Enjoy watching your handsome military guy," she teased her friend and left with a grin on her face.

Elisabeth watched her go, but then did as suggested. She couldn't help but watch her ex-husband. *He's still so charming. Love those little grey streaks in his brown hair. He's still so fit, so strong, yet gentle.* She stared at the perfect V-shape of his upper body and then felt so silly about all of it.

She caught him looking back at her. Shyly, she waved to him, and he returned a quick wave.

"Hi there, Brad," she whispered to herself.

"Oh, hi there!" Sarah said as she almost bumped into a young lady in the bathroom. The lady had been standing around the blind corner just past the entrance, leaning against the wall that led to the sinks and toilets. "I am sorry, didn't see you there." She snuck past to use the restroom.

After Sarah was done and exited her stall, she found the young girl still standing there. She walked by her to the sink to wash her hands.

The young lady was crying silent tears. Her face was streaked with lines of mascara that ran down to her chin. Sarah inspected her in the mirror. Her long, wavy reddish-brown hair looked uncombed and wild. She was very slender but had a great figure. Long legs, elegant fingers.

Sarah now had to use the hand dryer on the wall next to where the young lady was leaning. She didn't want to scare her and was searching for the right English words to convey that, but couldn't think of what to say.

"Entschuldigung," she just mumbled in German. "Ich muss mir die Hände trocknen."

Suddenly, the young woman looked up straight at Sarah. Sarah saw her face. High cheek bones, an elegant, perfectly formed nose with little freckles all over it, and the most interesting exotic eyes. She stared.

"I'm sorry. I'm blocking the hand dryer, aren't I? Please go ahead and dry your hands." The girl moved over to the sink. She took out a tissue and dabbed at her eyes, then wet it and tried to wipe off the smeared mascara.

Sarah found she felt irritated. After the loudness of the hand dryer had faded away, she turned around and asked the girl, "Sprechen Sie Deutsch?"

The young lady was still dabbing her eyes. "No, I don't speak German. Only Spanish." She took out a comb and started brushing her hair.

Sarah was even more irritated. "Sie sprechen nicht Deutsch. Aber Spanisch? Toll."

The young lady nodded. "Yeah, Spanish. It's pretty cool." She carried on the conversation without issue.

"Wo haben Sie denn Spanisch gelernt?"

"My mom taught me. She's from . . ." The young lady faltered and her voice broke. She stopped brushing her hair and looked down.

"Ist alles in Ordnung?" Sarah went on, intrigued.

Again, the young lady answered perfectly in English, "Yeah, I'm okay. Tough day." It looked like she was trying to keep her poise, trying not to break down in tears.

"Dann hoffe ich, dass der Abend besser wird!"

"I hope so, too," the young woman said, her lip quivering, "I hope this evening will only get better."

Another perfect match. Sarah stared at her, her mouth open. "Haben wir uns schon mal getroffen irgendwo?"

The young lady's lower lip was still quivering. "No, I don't think we've ever met before."

Sarah looked at her again. "Okay. Dann tschüss."

"Bye," the young lady said, as if that colloquial German goodbye was something she heard every day.

Irritated, Sarah left the ladies' room and wondered about that strange conversation she'd just had.

Maria now stared at herself in the bathroom mirror. *I look a bit better now.* She rubbed her temples. There was that headache coming on again. *The lady was irritating. Not sure why, but there was something weird about her. Something about the way she talked, maybe? Yeah, that's it! Why in the world did she ask me if I knew German? What a strange question.*

Her head was pounding now. She looked in the mirror again and saw her now green eyes. They had changed color again. She was agitated, she felt it, but looking at herself in the mirror, she knew it. Her eyes always told the truth. The pain in her head spiked so sharply, she had to close her eyes for a second. When she opened them again, she saw it, a picture from a long-gone time.

Herself as a toddler. Being held by a guy in uniform, a strong guy, laughing. His eyes sparkled in happiness, his exotic hazel eyes with a mosaic of golden-and-emerald-green flecks in the dark-brown center, a blue rim around them. Just like her eyes.

"Say goodbye to Mama," he said, and waved along with her. "No worries, she'll be back. She's just going out with her friends. Daddy will stay here with you."

Daddy?

He waved again and encouraged her to do the same. "That's right, say goodbye to Mama!"

"Tschüss, Mama, tschüss," she heard her toddler self say.

Tschüss. Goodbye. Tschüss means goodbye? What language is that? Have I heard it before?

Her head started spinning, the image of her toddler self waving goodbye, yelling "Tschüss," started fading, fading away, and suddenly she replayed the conversation she's just had with that lady in her head. She heard her ask, "Do you speak German? Deutsch? German?"

"Tschüss," she heard herself say.

"German," she heard the unfamiliar lady who had just left the restroom say.

Tschüss is German!

The pain in her forehead was unbearable and she had to close her eyes. When she opened them again, she was sitting on the cold restroom floor underneath the sink, her head hurting intensely. *What happened?*

Before she had a chance to think about it, she heard a knock on the door. "Maria?" she heard. "Maria, are you okay?"

Aaron? Yes, definitely his voice. I know that voice well. He sounds worried. Worried? Probably about me.

"Maria, are you okay?" she heard him ask again. "You've been in there for a while now. If you don't come out soon, I'm coming in!"

He sounds determined. Yes, Aaron would *bust into a ladies' room just to get to me. Check on me, make sure I'm okay. Yes, he'll always make sure I'm okay. He'll always be there for me.*

"I'm okay," Maria yelled, "I'll be right out!"

"Okay! I won't move, though, until you're safely out!"

She had to smile. *No matter what happens, no matter how bad a day I'm having—and today certainly counts as the worst one ever—he's always been there for me the past three years. And he'll be there for decades to come. My Aaron, my fiancé.*

No matter who I really am and what may come tonight, tomorrow, the next few days, years from now—he'll be there. For me. With me. Always. With that in mind, she felt stronger again. Strong enough to go out and face the world with Aaron by her side.

CHAPTER 94

"**N**o dinner? Please, you have to eat something."

Jack nodded. "Yes, Maria, please. Aaron is right. You need to eat something."

She looked at them. *I really don't feel like eating anything, but I know they won't take no for an answer.* The waitress was idling close by, right next to Maria, still waiting to take their order.

"Might I recommend something?" The waitress smiled at Maria, who looked better after having visited the ladies' room.

Maria nodded.

"If you don't have much of an appetite, I recommend the blackened Mahi Mahi. It's a local fish that's light on the stomach, and the way we prepare it is just delicious. And it tastes great the next day if you just reheat it in a pan. Would be good leftover if you really aren't that hungry."

Maria looked at the young waitress. "Amanda," her name tag said. "Sounds good," Maria agreed. "One blackened Mahi Mahi then." She smiled weakly as Amanda took her order.

"And don't forget your whiskey," Amanda said with the wink of an eye before she left the table.

True! Haven't even touched it. The ice is slowly melting away. Well, time for that now. She took the whiskey in her hand, Jack and Aaron both watching her.

"Cheers," Jack said.

"Cheers to what?" Maria swished the whiskey around in her glass.

Jack lifted his iced tea. "Cheers to finding the truth, and to new beginnings."

"Yeah, that sounds like a plan." Aaron lifted his glass as well.

Maria shrugged her shoulders and they all clinked glasses. Then, she took a sip so big, she immediately felt it burning her throat as it went down her esophagus, leaving behind a strong burning sensation that brought tears to her eyes. *Wow! That is one strong drink!* She trembled in disgust. Both Jack and Aaron couldn't help but grin.

"A little too ambitious, huh?" Aaron laughed. Maria looked at him then tried another big gulp. Same thing. Her eyes were stinging.

Jack couldn't help but laugh as well. "Too strong? Hope it helps burn away the bad day, Maria!"

She looked up. *Bad day? Yeah, for sure. Maria. Maria? She took another sip. Is that who I am? Maria?*

Aaron picked up on her quietness, her brooding. "Hey, you okay?"

She shrugged her shoulders. "I just don't know who I am anymore. No longer wondering who my dad is but who my mom is. Who I am."

Maria looked at both Aaron and Jack. She felt so sad. Aaron got very quiet. He glanced over at the balcony. The military group was still sitting there. He knew what he had to do to help her. "Well, Maria—"

"Am I even 'Maria?'" she interrupted him, defiance in her voice. "Should you guys even be calling me Maria?"

Aaron looked at her. "Well, I guess that's up to you."

"Up to me? What? I should just *name* myself? Like what? *Peggy?*" Her eyes were narrow.

Aaron looked at his dad. He just quietly sipped his iced tea. Aaron then turned back to Maria. "Well, you know, maybe for now, you're just . . . *you*. Yes, you are who you are, Maria."

Jack nodded and took another sip of his iced tea. He was deep in thought. Suddenly, he blurted out, "Maria, your mom might've had her reasons. We just have to wait and see. All we know is that she loves you, loves you as her own child."

Maria looked at him, her eyes sparking with anger.

"My dad's right, Maria. She does love you. There's no doubt about it. You will have to see what the police have to say. She did say she's never been to Eglin AFB, so she may be innocent."

"What? What are you *talking* about, Aaron. 'Innocent?' Even if she's never been to Eglin, what does that have to do with the fake birth certificate?"

Aaron took a deep breath and looked at her. "Well, Maria, I have a theory.. . . ."

She stared at him. "What? What do you mean? I know you think that the Collins guy is my dad." Maria took another sip of her whiskey and shook herself.

"Yeah, but I also think that his ex-wife is your real mom."

Maria stared at him. "What?" Her green eyes looked as though they were about to laser his face off.

"Well," Aaron continued, "remember how we think you have PTSD? Because of something that happened to you here at Eglin?"

She nodded slightly.

"Well, I think you almost drowned here. The little daughter of Brad and Elisabeth Collins reportedly drowned here at Eglin AFB."

Maria stared at him, then shook her head and dumped the rest of the whiskey down her throat. She couldn't say anything.

Jack took over. "I think Aaron is right. And your dreams might be more important now than ever. They might help us prove you're that little girl."

Maria gave them a blank stare. She lifted her glass again, but the whiskey was gone. Silence for a bit. Then she looked back and forth between the two of them. "But I'm *alive*," she whispered.

"Exactly!" Aaron said, and slammed his fists down on the table, making Maria jump. He saw it. "I'm sorry, my love. But what I'm thinking is that maybe you *almost* drowned, and then maybe your mom—I mean, Mamá—err, I mean, Martina maybe . . ."

". . . saved me?" A glimmer of hope shone in Maria's eyes.

"Err, yeah. Sure."

Jack spoke up again. "Drowning. Yes. Interesting."

Maria looked at him. "What do you mean?"

"Well, PTSD occurs when you've lived through a traumatic experience. We need to find out what exactly that experience was in your case. Was it a near-drowning? Or something that happened at the TLF? We need to look at the evidence. We need to look at the articles Aaron found online about the 'missing toddler at Eglin AFB.' And we need to examine your dreams. They might tell us more of the story when we put them all together. Aaron said you have them written down?" Jack spoke as if he were preparing a jury statement.

Maria looked at Jack. *Makes sense. He might be on to something.* "I have the book with me in my purse."

"Fantastic," Jack smiled. "That's a start. Should we take a look now, or later?"

Maria wasn't sure what to do or think. But she had nothing else that needed doing and felt the need to do something at least. Determined, she pulled the notebook out of her purse. The notebook labeled *My Past.*

They all agreed the time was right. Looking at the book might help in solving the mystery. And there was still a lot that even Aaron didn't understand. He pulled out his phone and glanced over at the balcony. The military group was still there. He turned his focus back to Maria and his dad. They huddled over the notebook, right there in the corner of the restaurant.

CHAPTER 95

In the corner of the balcony, Brad's work dinner was coming to an end. He and Drew said goodbye to the others and then both went and joined Sarah and Elisabeth at their table.

"Hi there, ladies," Brad said, and smiled. "Would you ladies care for another wine?"

"Sure," they said in unison.

Brad waved the waiter over. "A bottle of your finest red wine for all of us, please."

He nodded and left to go inside. A few minutes later, he returned with the bottle of wine. The four of them shared it, savored it, and started chatting.

Sarah kept looking at Brad. He was completely focused on Elisabeth and his eyes were sparkling. His exotic hazel eyes. Such a unique feature. Those dreamy eyes. They sure were striking. She kept staring at them. Were they so unique though? She had a feeling she had seen them before, in someone else.

Her thoughts began to take her elsewhere, and she had a hard time following the conversation in English, a language she had learned a long time ago in high school but had rarely spoken since. She was getting tired. She tried to hide her yawns, but they didn't go unnoticed.

Drew looked at her. "Long day?"

She shook her head. "No. Jet lag."

"Oh yeah, I forgot about that," Drew said, and turned to Elisabeth. "You must still be jet-lagged, too, huh Elisabeth?"

"Not too much."

"She doesn't sleep much in the first place," Sarah explained.

Elisabeth laughed and nodded. "True, I don't. At least I haven't in a long time. Kind of gave up on sleep."

"Me, too," Brad agreed. "Too many bad dreams, too many memories."

The four of them were silent for a little bit. Elisabeth nodded. "Yeah, you're right. Ever since . . . ever since, you know, ever since—"

"I know. I haven't slept much since then either."

"I tried to forget, but I couldn't. I just couldn't," Elisabeth said.

From across the table, Brad took her hand. "And I know now that I should've been there for you. I should've stopped working and listened to you. Because you were right. No matter how much I worked, I couldn't forget. Never. Neither her, nor you."

Elisabeth let him hold her hand and listened intensely, forgetting the world around her. "Oh Brad. I know. But we're here *now*. And this is the moment I've been waiting for. The moment I've dreamed of. Meeting, seeing you again. We both know our love is still there, don't we?"

"Yeah, we do," Brad said, and leaned in to kiss her.

Sarah blushed and looked at Drew. He nodded and rose to his feet. "Okay, guys, you enjoy the sunset out here; Sarah and I will be inside by the bar."

Brad and Elisabeth Collins forgot everything around them. They neither noticed that both Sarah and Drew got up and left, nor that they were being watched intensely.

Out of the corner of his eye, Aaron noticed the senior military personnel were making their way through the restaurant to the exit—their dinner had come to an end. He got up quickly. "Dad, Maria, I'm headed to the restroom. Be right back."

They barely noticed him, so engrossed they were looking at the notebook as well as the articles about the "missing toddler" on Google. Maria was staring at the pictures. *Good. They're busy. I need to talk to General Collins. Alone. Without them. Maria doesn't even know yet he's here. Hope he's actually here.*

Aaron pretended he was walking to the restroom but then slipped out of the restaurant's front door just in time. He politely made sure the sliding door stayed open for each and every one of the military people as they walked out. Since he was in uniform, they all saluted one other. Each salute lasted long enough for Aaron to read the name tag on their uniforms.

"No General Collins," he mumbled. *What gives?*

He walked back inside, then strolled over toward their table. Jack and Maria were still looking at the notebook and his phone. *Okay, good. They're still occupied.* He looked over at the balcony. *But where is Collins? He must be here.*

He noticed a single guy in uniform still sitting outside, but at a different table now, talking to a lady in a pixie cut. *Did General Collins just pick up a lady at this restaurant?* He saw them holding hands, deep into conversation. *Guess I'll just keep an eye on him. Gotta wait for the perfect opportunity to talk to General Brad Collins.*

CHAPTER 96

He almost choked on his coke as he read the name tag on the older guy's military uniform. *Collins? What the fuck?* As he was coughing, both the guy in the uniform and the lady in the pixie cut Jonathan had been sitting close to this whole time looked at him.

"Are you alright, sir?" he heard the military guy ask.

He looked up and had to take another deep breath in. A pair of hazel eyes with a mosaic of golden-and-emerald-green flecks in the dark-brown center and a blue rim around them were staring at him. *Fuck! That's* her *eyes! Problem Child's eyes.* He was still coughing.

"Do you need help?" the lady in the pixie cut asked him. He looked at her and coughed again and again. *Oh shit! Those freckles. The same fucking freckles. Are these people the Collins? I've never met them, but they must be.*

The couple got up to aid him but he held up his hand. He closed his eyes for a second, rubbed his belly, did a quick breathing exercise, and was ready to perform as if going on stage. "I'm alright, I'm alright. No worries. Coke just went down the wrong tube." He managed to laugh a convincing laugh. "Silly, isn't it? An old man like me apparently can't even drink a coke anymore."

The couple laughed. "Well, we're glad you're okay," they said, amused.

"Oh yeah. I am, I am. Please, don't let me disturb your date-night dinner. Just ignore me."

"You didn't disturb us at all. No worries, sir."

He looked at them. "Good, good. Well, I'll be on my way soon. Nearly done. Then you two can get on with enjoying your evening without having to worry about an old man croaking on your watch. Just need to use the men's room first. No worries, I won't run off without paying." He winked.

They smiled and nodded at him. "We wouldn't dare judge you either way. And please, no rush to leave."

He smiled back. "Alright then, thank you. Please, enjoy your night."

"Thanks." They smiled and went back to their conversation.

He glanced at them again. *The Collins. The fucking Collins. That's definitely Problem Child's last name. Shit! Why are they here now? How the fuck did this happen?*

He swallowed hard, took his last sip of coke, then looked over at the other table inside. Problem Child and the two guys were still huddling over something on their table. *They sure don't look like they're leaving any time soon. Good, 'cuz I have to pee real bad.* He stood up and left the balcony. *Gotta think of what to do while I hit the head. 'Cuz one thing is for sure: they can't fucking meet each other!*

CHAPTER 97

Sarah and Drew looked at the couple sitting on the balcony by the water. Holding hands, chairs close together.

"I still can't believe this is happening," Drew said. "It's as if it was meant to be. Both here at the same time. And look at them. Still a handsome couple. They just need to be together."

Sarah nodded and said, "Elisabeth is very happy now."

Drew sipped his coke and nodded. "Yeah, I haven't seen Cave Man—I mean Brad—this happy in a long time. He can have quite the temper, you know." Sarah looked at him. "He was hurting. Hurting real bad after losing both his girls."

Sarah nodded. "Yes, it was hard. *Is* hard. Elisabeth, too. She was sad."

Drew nodded. "Yeah. I'm not sure if it'll help them to open the case again. To keep researching. To keep looking for her, clinging on to some idiotic hope that she's still alive."

"Not good," Sarah said, and sighed. "Crazy."

Drew laughed. "Yeah, crazy. Well, cheers to two crazy people, then."

They toasted to that and sipped their drink, looking around. The restaurant had gotten pretty empty. The balcony had only one other table occupied now. On the inside, there was only a group of three huddling in the far corner, seemingly very busy reading and writing something.

Suddenly, the young woman from that group got up, cell phone to her ear. She started pacing back and forth along the wall in between her table and the other empty tables on that side of the restaurant. She was talking fast, heatedly at times, but neither Sarah nor Drew could hear her clearly. She suddenly signaled to the two guys at her table and rushed outside, past Sarah and Drew sitting at the bar.

"No, sí, no," they heard her say as she rushed past them.

Sarah's eyes followed her as she left the restaurant through the front door to talk outside of the entrance, wildly gesturing, even though it was a voice call. Sarah recognized her.

"That woman there"—she pointed briefly to the girl outside—"knows German."

Drew took a sip of his coke. "No, I don't think that was German. Sounded more like Spanish to me." He took another sip, now peering at the girl through the restaurant's tinted front doors.

"Yes, it's Spanish *now*. But she speaks German, too." Drew looked at Sarah, puzzled. "I met her in the bathroom earlier."

"Oh, that's nice. Talented young lady to speak two foreign languages."

Sarah nodded and kept watching her, pacing back and forth outside. "But it was strange. She said she speaks no German. But she answered my questions correct."

"What do you mean, 'correct?'"

"I asked them in German. Her English answers were correct answers."

Drew looked at Sarah, then outside at the young lady, gesturing, pacing, chatting away. "Hmmm . . . not sure I understand. I'm sorry."

Sarah looked at him, sipping her wine, frustrated by her own language barrier. "She is strange. Something is strange with her."

Drew nodded but didn't understand. Sarah's English wasn't the best. He looked over his shoulder to the balcony. Elisabeth and Brad were still talking, so engaged and happy that they didn't even seem to notice that everyone around them had left. Drew finished his coke, and Sarah's glass of wine was almost empty as well.

"I tell you what, Sarah," Drew said, "how about I drive you home? Brad can hitch a ride with Elisabeth. I've a feeling it'll be a long night. We should let them catch up and just enjoy each other. What do you say?"

Sarah looked at him, then at the couple outside. She nodded. "Okay. Yes. Good."

"Great. Then let's pay and I'll let Brad and Elisabeth know."

Sarah nodded and finished the last sip of her wine, then was ready to get up. She pushed back her bar stool at the exact same moment Maria came rushing in, cell phone in hand, sprinting past the bar to get back to her table.

Maria tripped on the leg of the bar stool chair, and before Sarah or anyone else could do anything, she fell. Her phone flew out of her hand and crashed onto the ground a few feet away from her. Maria hit the ground flat on her face with a loud bang.

Little did anyone know this wouldn't even be the loudest bang of the night.

"Oh my gosh!" Drew jumped up.

"Du meine Güte!" Sarah bent down to help Maria.

Aaron and Jack came running over from their table. Sarah squatted down next to Maria and started talking. "Ist alles okay? Haben Sie sich verletzt?"

Maria was slowly sitting up, rubbing her elbows. "I think I'm fine."

"Sie haben sich nicht verletzt?"

Maria shook her head. "No, I'm not injured. Might get a few bruises on my face, but I really didn't hurt myself that bad."

Aaron had just arrived at the bar. "You okay, Maria?"

Maria just nodded. Drew, Jack, and Aaron were standing by Maria's head while Sarah continued to squat next to Maria's feet.

"Es tut mir so leid," Sarah continued to babble in German. "Es ist alles meine Schuld!"

Maria looked at her. "No, it's okay. It's not your fault at all. It was just bad timing," Maria assured her. She smiled. "Unless you pushed the chair into me on purpose?"

Sarah quickly shook her head. "Nein, nein, natürlich nicht!"

"I figured. No worries, it's okay. Kinda funny, actually." Maria chuckled.

"Witzig? Ich finde das gar nicht witzig! Ich weiß gar nicht, wie ich das wieder gut machen kann. . . ."

The German woman looked so sad. *Poor lady*, Maria thought. *It wasn't her fault. I should try to cheer her up.* "Maybe you can buy me a drink? That would probably make up for it!"

Maria grinned and got up. She finally noticed the three guys staring at her. She brushed the dirt from the floor off her. "I'm okay. Really!" But Jack, Aaron, and the older man that had been sitting with the German lady just stared at her. "What? I'm okay," she insisted.

Sarah stood up as well. "Eigentlich wollten wir gerade gehen, aber ich kaufe Ihnen gerne noch etwas zu trinken. Was denn? Einen Wein?"

Maria thought for a moment. "If you were about to go, please don't worry about buying me a drink. You really don't have to."

But Sarah insisted. Neither of the two ladies realized that Aaron, Jack, and Drew were staring at them, mouths hanging wide open.

"Okay then," Maria winked. "It's been quite the day, so I guess wine won't do. I'll go with another whiskey on the rocks."

"Okay," Sarah said. "Und Sie sind sich sicher, dass es Ihnen gut geht!"

Maria nodded. "Yes, I'm sure. I'm completely fine."

Sarah turned to flag down the barkeeper while Maria continued to straighten out her clothing. "Oh no, my phone." She looked around, searching for it.

Aaron held it up. "Right here. Found it on the way over from our table."

Maria sighed. "Oh good." And then she noticed the men wouldn't stop staring at her. "I'm *fine*," she repeated.

Jack finally closed his mouth. "What was *that*?"

"That? That was just bad timing. I fell over the bar stool."

Without even knowing each other, Drew, Jack, and Aaron looked at one another, flabbergasted.

"Not that," Aaron said. "No, I think we were all just wondering about that conversation."

"The conversation?" Maria looked at them all.

Sarah, who had just ordered two whiskeys on the rocks, one for her and one for Maria, turned around to follow what was being said.

"This lovely lady here was just wondering if I was okay and feels bad about me tripping over her chair, so she's buying a drink for me," Maria explained.

"Yeah, I get that. *We* get that," Aaron said, and gestured at all three of them, "But how did you *know* what she was saying?"

"What?" Maria looked at Aaron.

"Yes. Wondering the same. I didn't understand a word," Jack said.

"I didn't understand either, but to be fair I don't speak German," Drew said, then turned to Maria. "You, young lady, must be pretty good at it, though. Sarah mentioned that earlier. She must be right. You do speak German, don't you?"

Color left Maria's face and she slowly shook her head. *No, I don't speak German.*

Jack and Aaron were now staring at Drew. "What? German?"

"Oh no," Sarah said, "Did I do it again?"

Drew just nodded.

"Do what?" Maria was puzzled.

Sarah looked down and shook her head. "I'm sorry. I . . . I . . . I have a hard time to speak English," she explained, her accent clearly audible. "More hard in stress." Everyone looked at her.

"Two whiskeys on the rocks," the bartender announced, and put the drinks in front of Sarah.

She turned around and thanked him, paid in cash, then continued the conversation while he was getting change for her. "I forget English sometimes. Long ago I learned."

Maria stared at her. *That lady was speaking a foreign language? With me?*

"And you speak what language again?" Aaron just wanted to make sure he had the story completely straight.

"German. I speak German. I'm from Germany."

Drew nodded. Jack stared. Aaron swallowed hard.

"I speak German when I don't remember English words. Did I again?"

The three men nodded, then all eyes rested on Maria.

German? She speaks German? Maria pointed to Sarah. "This lady was speaking German to me?"

"Yes. And you seem to have understood her perfectly," Drew said.

She stared at him. "I did?"

"Ja! You must speak German," Sarah said.

Maria shook her head, first slightly, then more violently.

"Sie sprechen nicht Deutsch?" Sarah prodded.

German? Deutsch? Maria's head started swirling, her thoughts all jumbled up. *Deutsch? Sprechen?* She looked at everyone and felt her headache come on, suddenly, violently.

"No, no, I don't speak German," she whispered, but then scolded herself. Deep, deep down in her brain, she knew that wasn't correct.

She closed her eyes and held on to the back of the bar stool. *German? Deutsch? Sprichst du Deutsch? Ja, ich spreche Deutsch!* Her thoughts were hurting her, causing so much pain that she couldn't take it anymore.

499

"Hallo, Mama! Gute Nacht! Hab dich lieb."

All these German sentences came flushing in, flushing in all at once. It made her feel dizzy, so dizzy that she could barely hold on to the chair. Her brain blanked out to shut out the pain, the deep pain. She felt so small again.

"Mama, ich hab dich lieb!" was the last thing she thought before her brain shut down completely and her legs gave out.

CHAPTER 98

Aaron had enough experience by now to see it coming. This time, he was fast enough to catch her before she hit the ground. He even managed to kick the bar stool Maria had tugged down with her so that it didn't fall and just wiggled back in place. The German lady just stared, her mouth open, and the guy in the nice-looking suit also watched helplessly, while Jack rushed over.

"She's fainted again," Jack stated the obvious, then yelled out, "Water. We need water! And a wet cloth. Quick!"

Drew started moving fast. He was torn out of his trance and jumped over the counter of the bar to grab a cloth off the sink. The bartender was staring at him but didn't say anything. Sarah now had both hands over her mouth. Two waitresses came rushing over, one with a glass of ice water. Everyone was talking over each other, not sure what to do. They were all staring at Maria. Aaron laid her down, took off his blue uniform jacket to let her head rest on it, while propped up her legs on his shoulders.

Drew kneeled next to her and held her arm, reading her pulse. "She's stable. Pulse is fine."

One of the waitresses asked, "Do we need to call 911?"

"No, not yet. I'll continue to monitor her pulse. Lieutenant, you will continue to hold her legs up. You, young waitress lady, I need you to keep the cloth on her forehead wet and cool. Everyone else, stand back!" Drew gave his orders. He was in his element, taking the lead, his Air Force training taking over in this moment of distress. "Lieutenant, tell me more about this young lady. Does she faint often?" He looked at Aaron.

"Well, I wouldn't say *often*. I think she—"

"This is a yes or no question, Lieutenant."

"Then yes, sir, she faints often, lately."

"Any reason for it? Medical reason?"

"Sort of, sir," Aaron said. "A psychological one, sir!"

Drew looked up at the young lieutenant. "Explain, Lieutenant."

"Yes, sir," Aaron said, "I'll try. It's complicated. My fiancée Maria here just learned this afternoon that her birth certificate was faked. She's not who she always believed she was. Lately she's been having dreams—well, memories probably—from her early childhood. Snippets of the past. And that German she was speaking just now, it was in her dreams, too, even though she doesn't speak it. But whenever anyone confronts her about her dreams, she just faints. Can't even help it."

Sarah still had her hands in front of her mouth, but now turned around and downed the whiskey on ice in one gulp.

Drew looked at Aaron. "Have you been to the police?"

"Yes, sir," Aaron answered. "Before dinner here. We literally just came from the police station. They called her in after the special agents discovered that her birth certificate is a fake."

"Special agents?"

"Yes, sir! The agents that administered my security clearance interview, sir."

Drew looked at him. Blues uniform. No ribbons on it. He put two and two together. "Rough first day, huh, Lieutenant? I'm sorry you're having to go through all this."

"Thank you, sir." He nodded and looked at Maria stretched out on the floor. *German. She knows German. She must be the Collinses' daughter! General Collin's wife is from Germany. Her mom. Maria's real mom.*

I need to talk to him.

He looked outside. General Collins was still sitting there with that lady. He looked back at the man who had been questioning him. *He has the same short military haircut as the rest of us but wears a suit. Probably a civilian? I thought I saw a civilian at the military dinner table. Was it this guy? Does he know General Collins?*

He decided to introduce himself. "Sir, I'm Aaron Heikinnen. Newly commissioned into the Air Force. Just got in last night."

"Nice to meet you, Lieutenant Heikinnen. I'm Drew Markas, retired lieutenant colonel in the Air Force. I'm here on a TDY with my boss. He's still sitting outside."

Aaron stared at him. *His boss is still outside? I knew it! This guy works for Collins.*

Before he could say anything else, the waitress holding the washcloth across Maria's forehead yelled, "She's waking up!"

Maria's eyes fluttered as everyone around her watched on. Drew let go of her arm and put it on her belly. He looked at her face. The high cheek bones, the freckles around her perfectly formed nose, the long, wavy reddish-brown hair. Her eyes opened, and Drew's mouth fell wide open for the second time that night.

"Holy cow," he said, and got up abruptly.

Aaron looked at him, confused. *The lieutenant colonel has been very professional and calm all night, but now he looks as if he's seen a ghost.* But before Aaron could worry about him, he had to worry about his fiancée, who was still lying on the ground.

"Aaron?" Maria's eyes met his. He let go of her legs and scooted up by her head where the waitress had been sitting. She had since gotten up and taken the wet cloth off Maria's forehead, wringing it tight in her hands as she watched the scene.

"Hey there." Aaron smiled and took Maria's hand. "How are you feeling?"

She gazed at him, then looked around. On her left-hand side she saw Jack standing behind Aaron, and two waitresses, one clutching a cloth. To her right she saw a shocked-looking guy in a nice-looking suit and a middle-aged lady. "Aaron? Where am I?"

"You're at the restaurant, still," Aaron said, his blue eyes smiling, calming.

She sat up and her long wavy hair fell around her face. She got up, her head clear, and acted as if nothing had happened.

Aaron was still holding her hand when she scolded him, as she needed it to dust herself off. He let go and grabbed his blue uniform jacket that was all scrunched up on the floor, having served as a pillow for Maria's head. Seeing Aaron and Maria busy themselves dusting off, the waitresses left the group, feeling assured the young lady was fine.

Only Drew and Sarah were still standing by the bar, both intensely watching Maria.

"You fainted again," Aaron whispered in her ear.

"I figured as much. Who are these people at the bar?"

Aaron put his jacket back on and started introducing them. "This is Lieutenant Colonel Markas, who reacted quickly and calmly as you fainted. He helped organize the crew to aid you. Lieutenant Colonel Markas, this is my fiancée Maria."

Maria looked at the lieutenant colonel, who looked anything but calm. "Nice to meet you, sir," she said with a smile and held out her hand to Drew. "Thank you for helping with my fainting episode."

He continued staring her straight into the eyes as he shook her hand absent-mindedly.

"And this is Sarah," Aaron explained, "the woman from Germany whose bar stool you tripped on earlier."

Maria looked at Sarah and stretched out her hand. "Hi, Ms. Sarah, it's nice to meet you as well," Maria said, smiling, looking her into the eyes.

Suddenly, Sarah looked bewildered. Her hand slipped out of Maria's.

Maria looked back and forth between Drew and Sarah, who both stared at her. Before anyone could say anything, Drew reached behind him and downed the other whiskey on ice in one big gulp.

Maria started laughing. "Sir, I think you just had my drink." She winked at him with a big grin. "I don't remember much before I fainted, but as far as I can recall, Ms. Sarah here bought that drink for me after I tripped over her chair."

Sarah's eyes were wide, her mouth open. She now pointed at Maria. "Ihr Gesicht," she mumbled in German, then translated for Drew. "Her face! Her hair!"

Maria's smile faded now. "Excuse me? Stare at me if you must, but the pointing is downright irritating, and offensive!"

"And those eyes," Drew just said, ignoring Maria's protests. She was about to say something else when the lieutenant colonel suddenly yelled, "Cave Man!"

Maria, Jack, and Aaron didn't know what to say. The lieutenant colonel seemed to have completely lost it. *Cave Man? What in the world?* Maria thought.

Then he yelled again, this time louder, looking straight out at the balcony: "Cave Man! Hey! Get over here!"

CHAPTER 99

"**C**ave Man!" he heard someone yell as he stepped out of the men's room.

What the fuck? Did someone have too much to drink?

Quickly, Jonathan walked down the hallway to see what the commotion was all about.

He stopped and saw a middle-aged man in a suit standing by the bar, still yelling "Cave Man." He chuckled. *What a crazy old man!* He saw a middle-aged lady by the bar as well. She was ghostly white, her eyes wide, her mouth open. Both her and the crazy man stared at Problem Child.

That Aaron guy and his dad seem confused. What's going on here? He made sure to stay hidden by the corner of the bar to watch the scene unfold and overhear what was being said.

And then he heard it. The two middle-aged people kept mumbling the same words over and over again. "Just like him. Those eyes. Those freckles. That hair. Just like her. Just like them. Holy cow! Just like *them.*"

Jonathan started sweating, his heart beating faster. When the sliding door to the balcony opened, his heart skipped a beat. He turned ghostly white as Elisabeth and Brad Collins walked through the sliding door, approaching the group by the bar.

Holy shit! Fuck! What the fuck should I do? They can't meet, they just can't meet!

His feet were sweating now, too, and his legs seemed ready to give out underneath him. He held onto the bar to not tip over.

"What would you like to drink?"

What? What the fuck?

He turned his head and found the bartender standing before him, smiling.

"How may I help you? What would you like to drink?" he heard him ask again.

Nothing! Just leave me alone! I need to stop what's about to happen! He closed his eyes quickly, exhaled deeply, rubbed his belly, and was ready.

He looked at the bartender. "Whiskey on ice, please," he said, even though he knew he shouldn't drink. *I just need something. Just one drink. Now.*

He paused.

"You know what? Make it two," he heard himself say.

I lost. I lost it. I've lost it all. What the fuck should I do now? The first of the whiskeys arrived, and he stared down at it. *All I can do now is watch, watch what happens.* In one sip, he downed his first whiskey and watched the scene unfold.

CHAPTER 100

"What's going on here?" they heard an amused low voice say, and Aaron turned around. He recognized the speaker right away. *General Collins, the one I googled. Brad Collins! The guy who spoke at the ROTC Ball, the ball I proposed at. The one I* really *need to talk to so I can tell him my fiancée is most likely his missing daughter.*

Before he could say anything, the general saluted him. Ingrained and trained into him, Aaron stood at attention and saluted back. As he saluted General Collins, he saw it, at that moment, that second. His salute suddenly dropped, and he had to take a step back so he wouldn't fall over in shock as he stared into Collins's eyes. Those eyes. He had no doubt this man was Maria's father.

The dreams of her dad in uniform finally make sense.

He heard a female voice ask, "What's going on here?" and turned to see who was talking. He staggered back another step. Except for the short pixie cut and the wrinkles on her forehead, he felt as if he were looking at a doppelgänger who shared Maria's face. The resemblance was uncanny.

Her German mom is here with the general?

He felt his dad hold on to him as though he too needed help stabilizing himself. Both Heikinnens stared at Brad and Elisabeth, shocked.

Elisabeth saw a young woman facing the other way. She had long, wavy reddish-brown hair that fell over her shoulders. A slim figure, a nicely rounded butt, long legs. *Like I used to have.* She sighed.

When the young woman turned around, it hit Elisabeth like a truck. She let out a cry and sank to her knees.

She knew. At that moment, she knew. She knew when she saw that younger version of herself, a reflection in the form of a young woman.

And then she saw the woman's eyes. Brad's eyes, Brad's unique eyes. *I've only known two people in the world with these eyes: my ex-husband and my daughter. Oh my gosh! Is this real?*

Brad watched Elisabeth go down on her knees. *What's wrong with her?* He looked at Elisabeth and saw her crying silent tears, her gaze fixed on the young woman standing in front of him. He looked at the young woman.

She turned her head quickly from left to right to look everyone in the face, her long, wavy reddish-brown hair wildly flying around her. Her slender figure looked almost broken, her freckled cheeks flushed in anger and embarrassment as everyone stared at her. *She doesn't seem to understand what's going on here. And neither do I!*

Until he heard Elisabeth whisper, "Moana," tears now streaming down her face.

He stared at Elisabeth, then looked up again at the young woman in front of him.

He saw it.

"Holy cow!"

He took a step back. *She looks just like Elisabeth did over twenty years ago.* And then he touched his own lips—"those kissable lips" Elisabeth used to call them, with the pronounced groove between the base of the nose and border of the upper lip forming the wonderful curve of the lips. Full lips, kissable lips. *That young woman has my lips! Lips just like mine.*

As she focused her gaze on him now, tears of joy started streaming down his face. *It's like looking into a mirror. She has my eyes. There's no doubt about it. It* has *to be her! It's her! My lost daughter! Oh my gosh!*

He sank to his knees, right next to his ex-wife, sobbing. "Moana! Oh my gosh, you're alive! Moana!"

CHAPTER 101

Moana? Did I just hear them call me Moana? Maria stared at the couple kneeling before her, sobbing, crying. *What in the world is going on? I'm so confused. I've never been this confused before in my life.* She had to chuckle. *Well, not true. I was just a few hours ago, when I learned that Mamá is not actually my mom. This day is getting weirder by the minute.*

She heard the couple cry out again. *Moana. That name. Why does it seem so familiar?* She shook her head. *No, my name is Maria.*

Then she heard something else. A faint voice made it to her ear. "Moana, mein Engel. Mein kleiner Engel." *Moana, my little angel,* her brain translated automatically.

What?

Within seconds, a feeling washed over her that was so powerful, she didn't know what was happening. Her little arm hairs stood up. Her heart started beating, fast, faster, so fast. Her legs went numb. She was staring at the sobbing couple kneeling on the ground, on the same ground that she had fainted on earlier. On the same ground that she had landed on after tripping over the legs of the bar stool.

Wow, what an intense ground!

She felt everyone staring at her, but she could only focus on the couple in front of her.

Moana?

Her knees gave out and she became one with the ground as well, only inches away from the man and woman's faces. She stared at them, stared into the man's eyes. He had exotic hazel eyes that had turned more green at this moment. Hazel eyes with a mosaic of golden-and-emerald-green flecks in the dark-brown center encircled by a blue rim.

His eyes? No, those are my *eyes! Mine! Only mine!* Confused, she looked at the name tag on his uniform. "Collins," it said.

"Moana," he whispered, and suddenly, a bright light shone from his uniform, so bright that she had to close her eyes. Her mind was transported.

The light reflecting off the name tag was so interesting. She just had to touch it. As she reached for it with her little hands, the light shifted. She now saw the shiny metal name tag had blue letters on it. Her little hand touched the cold metal, traced the letters. It felt so nice. So fun.

Her little hand now pulled at it. "Oh no, no, don't pull on that tag, Moana. Daddy needs that to stay on his uniform. Will you do that for Daddy?"

For Daddy?

She heard giggling, a little toddler's giggling.

Confused, she closed her eyes and opened them again and found she was touching the general's uniform, stroking his name tag. Embarrassed, she moved her hand away and looked up at him, straight into his eyes. Tears were streaming down his face, but his eyes were sparkling, looking at her with love, so much love.

She had the strange feeling again. "Daddy?"

She saw him nod.

In a trance, she forced herself to look at the woman. The middle-aged woman with the pixie cut. *She has reddish-brown hair, just like mine. She has high cheek bones and a perfectly straight, beautifully formed nose with freckles all over it.*

Freckles?

Instinctively, she touched her own face. Her own high cheek bones. Her own nose. Her own freckles. *Freckles? Those are my freckles!* She stared at the freckles and suddenly they shone so bright. She blinked against the glare, eyes watering, until it faded.

Her little hand was touching every single freckle on the woman's face, which had long hair now that fell nicely around it.

She tried to scratch at the freckles. "Oh nein, das macht aua," she heard the woman say, laughing.

She took her little hand and moved it away from the woman's face. She now felt sad. She didn't mean to hurt her.

"Ist okay," she heard the woman say, then reach out to take her hand. "Das sind Mama's Sommersprossen. Die gehen nicht ab!"

Mama's freckles? Can't take them off?

"Du hast die auch."

Really, I have them too? Instinctively, she felt her own face, but couldn't feel anything. She heard laughter.

"Du kannst die nicht fühlen. Wir brauchen einen Spiegel!"

Oh, that makes sense. You can't really feel them, you can only see them. We need a mirror. And she was carried to a mirror, a mirror that showed a tall, slender woman with long, wavy reddish-brown hair, high cheek bones, a perfectly straight nose, and small little dots, little freckles all over her face. And it showed another, smaller face—the round face of a toddler with the same nose and the same freckles.

"Guck! Wie die Mama!"

Yes, just like Mama. Fun, little freckles all over.

Suddenly, the freckles started glowing, turned so bright that she had to close her eyes.

And when she opened them, her hand was on that woman's face, resting on her freckles. She was confused. She stared at her, into the woman's blue eyes. The woman raised a trembling hand and laid it against her own. The woman then slowly shifted Maria's hands away from her face until she was clutching them in her own, against her bosom.

"Moana, bist du es wirklich?"

Is it really me? Me? Moana?

As confused as she was, she heard herself form the most surprising sentence. "Ja, Mama, ich bin es!"

"It's her, it really *is* her!" the general cried out, and before she knew it, she was being squeezed tightly, hugged so tightly that she felt like she couldn't breathe anymore. *No, not again! Not again! Help, help, help! I need help! I can't breathe! It's all over me, the water, it's all over! I'm swallowing it, mouthfuls of water, more and more. It's taking me away, away from my parents. The water. Help me! Mama! Daddy!* And with a scream, it all went black around her.

CHAPTER 102

He almost screamed when he saw the Collins hug Problem Child. *Fuck! This is bad, real bad. Holy shit! This is the worst thing that could have ever happened. How the fuck did this happen? Oh, shit! They'll get me, they'll catch me. They'll fucking arrest me! No, no, no.*

His thoughts were racing. He jumped up from the bar stool. With shaky hands, he took out cash and a pen. Quickly, he scribbled a note on the napkin: *Thanks for the drinks. Thanks for the food. Table outside. Keep the change.* Then he left the napkin and the chash by the two empty whiskey glasses.

Nobody noticed him. Quietly, he slipped out of the restaurant into the darkness.

CHAPTER 103

Darkness surrounded him except for the little light on his desk. Chief Parlot was sitting inside the Niceville Police Station, staring at the folder named "Identity Case: Maria Gabriella Sullivan." He somehow couldn't stop thinking about it and had returned to work after dinner, much to the distress of his wife. *There's something about that young woman. She reminds me of someone. Just can't pinpoint it.*

He was looking at the copies of her ID when his phone rang. "Niceville Police Department, Chief Parlot speaking."

"Hi, Chief Parlot. This is Aaron Heikinnen, Maria's fiancé."

He looked at his watch. *It's late. What does he want?*

"We figured out who Maria is," he heard the young man say. "She's Moana Marie Collins."

He gasped. *What? Moana Marie Collins? The little toddler? But Moana Marie Collins drowned a long time ago!*

He listened as the young man on the phone continued. "Chief, I did some research, had an inkling that Maria was possibly that little toddler who went missing on base twenty years ago."

Aaron Heikinnen had an "inkling." Seriously? "Why didn't you *say* something?" he barked.

"I'm sorry, Chief, I just needed proof. I knew General Collins had a work dinner at the Compass Rose, so I steered us to have dinner there as well."

They ended up at the Compass Rose? The general? His kid? All at the restaurant?

He listened again. "I didn't know his wife—well, ex-wife—was in town also. But we all just stumbled across each other. They're convinced Maria is their daughter. Maria recognized them too, I think."

"You *think?*" The chief couldn't believe it.

"Yeah. It's just that she fainted. Oh wait. She's waking up! I gotta go!"

The phone clicked. Aaron Heikinnen had hung up on him.

The chief stared at the beeping phone. *Maria is Moana Marie Collins? She's alive? And didn't drown?*

He thought back to twenty years ago, when he was a young police officer. He remembered it all too well.

I had just started my career when that case came through here. The base police called us in because they thought the little girl could've left the base. Alone or with someone.

I remember how bad I felt. For the parents. I wanted to help.

He sighed. *That case should've been my first major case, but then the Feds took over. The FBI. Of course, they snatched it away. Only my boss, the former chief, was allowed to help.*

And then, within a few days, they "solved" it. Declared it case-closed, an "accidental drowning." Said there was overwhelming evidence that the little one had walked out and drowned. Convinced everyone but the mom.

And then it dawned on him that Elisabeth Collins had been right. Back then *and* this morning, when she and her ex-husband had marched into his office, begging him to open the case back up. *Shoot! Both us and the FBI were wrong all this time?* He gasped. *This morning the parents gave me three reasons why they were convinced their daughter had been kidnapped. They've been right this whole time?*

Suddenly, Chief Parlot got up. *Maria Gabriella Sullivan is Moana Marie Collins? I need to know for sure.* He grabbed the copy of her driver's license and pushed his chair back. He almost forgot to turn the lights back on in the dark police station, but quickly reached for the switch. They illuminated a hallway that led to a back room filled with rows and rows of filing cabinets.

Impatiently, he turned on the lights in there and kept searching. For the year "2003." He found the correct filing cabinets and unlocked them, then looked for "C."

There! There it is. The "Collins Case" file. He put that file on the table in the middle of the room and opened it up. The first thing he saw was a picture of the little toddler. He had to hold on to the table as a wave of dizziness and surprise washed over him, threatened to wash his feet out right from under him.

The little girl in the picture smiled back at him with her reddish-brown hair, freckles on her straight nose, and exotic hazel eyes with a mosaic of golden-and-emerald-green flecks in the dark-brown center encircled by a blue rim. *Oh my gosh! No way!*

With shaking hands, he put the copy of Maria Sullivan's ID next to the picture of the toddler and compared them. The same eyes, the same freckles, the same straight nose. The same hair color! *No freaking way! Aaron Heikinnen is right. We'll still have to do genetic testing to absolutely verify, but there's no doubt about it: Maria Gabriella Sullivan is actually Moana Marie Collins.*

He felt as if he had made the mistake of his life sending away the parents this morning. *Well, we sure have every reason now to open up the case again. Obviously, the girl didn't drown. She's right here in Niceville.* His thoughts were spinning. *Oh my gosh! What did General Collins say? He has a new suspect. A Hispanic lady who worked at Eglin's TLF at that time. A Hispanic lady? No way!*

Chief Parlot closed the folder again and rushed out, only to turn back around and close the filing cabinet and turn off the lights. He then ran down the hallway to make a phone call. He needed to inform the police department in Miami immediately. They now needed to hold Martina Sullivan overnight and charge her in another crime, a much bigger crime than faking a legal document: kidnapping!

Sirens blaring, Chief Parlot arrived at the restaurant. He got out of the police car and ran inside, joining the idling group, the only people left at the Compass Rose. Everyone was standing around Maria's chair. She was rubbing her temples, her face pale, her eyes half closed. He greeted everyone.

"Chief," Brad Collins said with a big smile on his face. "Chief, we found her! She's alive! Our daughter's alive!" Mr. and Mrs. Collins beamed with happiness, smiling at each other, and holding hands.

"Yes, Aaron Heikinnen already informed me that you've found your daughter. I've already compared her toddler picture to her current ID and I'm ninety-five percent sure she's your daughter."

"'Ninety-five percent sure?' What?" Brad looked at him, his eyes narrow.

"Well, General Collins, we can only be one hundred percent sure after we do a genetic test, but I don't think anyone here doubts that the young lady sitting over there is your missing daughter," Chief Parlot said.

Both Collins nodded and everyone agreed.

Elisabeth turned to the chief and spoke softly. "Chief, I assume our request from this morning. . . ."

"Of course, we will take up the case again. We have new evidence now, and a suspect already in custody."

Everyone looked at him now. Jack asked the question on everyone's mind. "Suspect in custody?"

"Yes, sir. Martina Marie Sullivan is being held without bond in Miami."

Suddenly, Maria looked up at the Chief, her green eyes piercing through him. "*What* did you just say?" Before he could answer, a phone rang. Maria looked around. "That's my ringtone. Where's my phone?"

Aaron reached into his pocket and pulled out the ringing phone.

"That's mine, not yours," Maria barked at him and ripped it out of Aaron's hand to pick up.

"Hello? Tía Mariella? ¿Aló?" She held up a hand to signal to everyone that this call was important and just walked away as if nothing else had happened. Everyone's eyes followed her as she headed back toward the table they had eaten at earlier. She sat down talking, babbling away.

"What's that she's speaking?" Elisabeth asked. "Spanish?"

"Yes, it's Spanish. Her mamá is from Venezuela and raised her bilingual," Aaron said, and realized just a bit too late he probably shouldn't have said that.

"Her *mamá*?" Elisabeth looked furious. "*I'm* her Mama!"

"Elisabeth." Brad Collins took her hand. "Please, calm down!"

"Me? Calm down? No way!" She shook off his grip, now talking directly to Chief Parlot. "That lady who raised her belongs in *jail*. She has taken everything from me! *Everything*! My hope, my love, my marriage, my life, and twenty years with my own daughter! I gave birth to her and she is my daughter! Just mine!"

Everyone in the group looked down. The bartender brought out a round of whiskeys on ice. "On the house," he said and turned to Chief Parlot, "Our manager is willing to keep the restaurant open for as long as you need, Chief."

"Thank you," Chief Parlot said, then saw Sarah, Drew, and Jack grab one of the drinks. They all downed them immediately while watching Elisabeth sob.

"Mrs. Collins," Chief Parlot said calmly, "we understand how upset you are. I urge you to look on the bright side for now and focus on the remarkable fact that you've found your daughter. Focus on knowing she's alive. She's obviously well, a successful, young college student. Engaged to this young man over here. And she just learned that the lady she grew up knowing as her mother is not her mother. It's a lot to take in. We'll need everyone's patience and understanding at this moment as we try to figure out the whole story."

Brad nodded and put his arm around Elisabeth. "It'll be okay, hun. It'll be okay."

Elisabeth leaned on him. Through her tears, she looked over at the corner of the restaurant where her daughter was sitting, talking on the phone in a language she herself did not understand. She wiped her tears and sighed. "I'd always hoped to find her. Knew I would recognize her. And we have," she whispered. "But never in my life have I thought our daughter might feel differently. Feel affection for a woman other than me. A woman she spent all her life with. Never thought she wouldn't remember me." She started crying again. "All I want is to hold her, touch her, love her. Be with her, talk with her."

Brad hugged her now. "We will, hun. We will. Just give her time. And she *did* recognize you."

She sobbed. "But look at her. Look at our daughter, our now adult daughter, sitting over there having a conversation with a family member we don't even know! It's not fair, it's not."

Sarah had to hold back her tears, and Drew cleared his throat. Jack downed another whiskey.

Aaron looked to Maria and saw her hang up the phone. She came rushing back, phone in hand, tears in her eyes. "Aaron, they're holding her! She's behind bars! Oh my gosh! Tía Mariella told me. This is not good. It's not good, Aaron!"

They all looked at her, but Maria was only focused on Aaron. She needed to be. These other people confused her, and she still wasn't sure what was happening.

"Come here, Maria," Aaron just said, and hugged her.

Elisabeth was ready to jump in and give her daughter a big hug as well, but Brad held her back.

Maria sobbed on Aaron's shoulder now. "Tía Mariella said they increased her counts, her crimes. She said she's now being held for kidnapping! It's not right. I don't think she kidnapped anyone."

"It *is* right, because she *did* kidnap a child," Elisabeth screamed. "She did! Twenty years ago! She kidnapped my child! My baby girl! You!"

CHAPTER 104

M$^{e?}$ Over Aaron's shoulder, Maria stared at the woman with the pixie cut. The woman with the same nose and same freckles as her.

"I am your *mother* and that lady just took you from me!" Elisabeth pushed forward but was being held back by the man in uniform who had kept silent, just staring at Maria.

Something was happening within her—something strange was happening within Maria. She didn't know what it was, but something was brewing. She felt dizzy, but shook herself and wiggled out of Aaron's hug. She walked over to the woman and looked her in the face, angry, ready to defend her mamá, who was in jail for something Maria knew couldn't possibly be true.

But as she stared into this woman's face, her anger disappeared, all of a sudden, as if by magic. Looking at her, this woman she didn't even know, made her feel small. *I feel so little. And so loved. I feel loved.*

Her anger was gone and she was about to say something when the woman suddenly yelled again. "The woman you know as your mom kidnapped you! She just took you away. Away from me, from Brad, from both of us. She had *no right* to do so. And she will *pay* for it!"

The love was gone. Poof it went. Maria didn't know what to do, what to think, what to feel. Still, she felt there was something there with this woman she didn't know. *I feel drawn to her, want to hold and kiss her, but her words are cruel. So cruel and untrue. Not true.*

"*No,*" Maria snapped.

The woman looked at her, taken aback.

"Martina Sullivan saved me. She saved me in every way. She taught me everything, made me the woman I am today. I am *everything* I am because of *her*. I don't care what she's done, but she is and will always be my mamá. And I will fight for her like she fought for me all these years." Then she turned and said, "Chief Parlot, Martina Sullivan is innocent. You have to let her go!"

Maria heard a deep sob behind her and turned around again. The frail-looking woman that looked so much like her was crying, her little body shaken by violent sobs. She dropped to her knees. "Moana, nein, meine Moana. Ich kann dich nicht noch einmal verlieren. Nicht noch einmal!"

What? She can't lose me again, not again? Maria's heart felt as if it had been stabbed. She felt the pain of this woman so deeply but wasn't sure why. *Who is this lady?*

She squatted down to look at her face. Her face bathed in pain, tears streaming down. She looked at her and suddenly felt so sad herself. *I know this woman. I'm sure I know her. I know her well. I know that I love her, love her so much.*

And then she did it again: she heard herself, her own brain and her own mouth, form the most peculiar sentence. "Ich hab dich lieb, Mama!"

What? I love you, Mama? What language am I speaking?

The lady looked at her. "Ich hab dich auch lieb, Moana."

I love you, too, Moana? Moana? Who? Me?

"Und Enti hat dich auch lieb," the woman said, and smiled. She pulled something out of her purse. An old and ugly-looking toy. A little security blanket with a duck head on it.

Maria stared at it. *I know this toy.* She smiled. Her mind translated the unknown language. "*Ducky loves you, too.*" *Ducky?* She thought about it. *No, that's not right. That's not translatable. "Enti?" Yes, Enti. It's Enti! My beloved Enti!*

She smiled a wide smile and grabbed the toy from the woman. "Enti, hi, Enti!" She was so happy and excited, she fell on her bottom from her squatting position.

"Maria," she heard Aaron say, "are you okay?"

He looked down at her, still holding that strange-looking thing Elisabeth Collins had pulled out of her purse, and watched as she nodded her head in a trance. Her words came out slowly. "I know this woman. She is my mama. I love her."

Elisabeth smiled a wide smile. She looked at her long-lost daughter and her smile faded. Her daughter looked so very confused.

Clutching Enti, she spoke again. "But my ma*má* is in Miami. Mi mamá. Mi mamá saved me, helped me. Te amo, Mamá. Mamá is in jail. Not good. I need to go. Now."

And then, she got up, still clutching Enti, and walked over to get her purse—walked like a robot, mechanically, in a trance, past the group—and just left, left the restaurant and walked toward her car.

Just need to get away from here. Fast. Quick as possible. I need to leave. Leave right away. Get away from these weird people. This weird place.

She turned around and looked at the sign of the restaurant. It said "Compass Rose." Like a compass, it had spun Maria's life all around. *It keeps spinning and spinning and spinning, still trying to find its direction. Just like me. A now broken compass. Spinning helplessly.*

CHAPTER 105

Helplessly, Jonathan watched the scene in the restaurant unfold from behind the cover of a bush in the dark parking lot. He knew it was all over. He had already replayed in his mind countless times how thoroughly his life was about to be fucked, for good and forever—until he saw *her* come out of the restaurant all by herself. He watched her for a bit, standing there all alone by her car. So broken, so frail-looking.

So deep in thought.

And then he knew exactly what to do.

She was looking back at the restaurant where the people inside were standing in a circle, gesturing wildly, talking all over each other. Surprise was on his side. He jumped out of the bushes and put his strong, wide hand right over her mouth, used the other hand to hold down her arms that were in front of her belly, clutching a purse and something soft. He swept her legs out from under her and dragged her into the bushes behind the parking lot.

Maria's eyes went wide and her body limp. She dropped Enti and her purse in surprise. *What the heck?* She heard heavy breathing in her ear, felt the hot air coming from someone's mouth, smelled the alcohol in the breath, felt strong arms squeezing her tight, the big hand covering her mouth and part of her nose. Sweat formed on her forehead. *I can't breathe. Please let me go!*

But he didn't let go. He walked backward, dragging her across broken tree branches and rocks. Her ballerina shoe got caught on an old branch on the ground. He dragged her further along, jerked her body up, and she lost her shoe. The old palm leaves on the ground scratched her foot. For the first time, she started wiggling.

"Stop it," she heard a low, dark voice whisper in her ear. "Stop fucking resisting." The man's breathing was heavy. He was working hard to drag her through the woods.

Maria's head was spinning. *Who is this? Where is he taking me? What's happening?*

Her other shoe got caught on something, but he pulled so hard that she lost that one also. She could feel rotten palm leaves and pine needles under her bare feet. The way he was holding her started hurting her neck.

She was having a hard time breathing with that fat, sweaty hand across her mouth half-covering her nose, his other strong arm pressing into her chest while locking down her arms. She took a few quick breaths through her nose and closed her eyes. *Who is this? What's going on?*

For a brief second, she thought about it then came to a conclusion. *I don't care. I don't know who I am anyway. I just wanna get away. Just take me then.* Tears were forming in her closed eyes. *Who am I?*

She had no answer to that.

Whatever.

Her whole body went limp. She had given up.

"Good girl. Good to not resist, Maria. Or should I say *Moana?*" She heard his mean voice laugh.

Tears formed in her eyes that wanted to escape. Then something Aaron had said came back to her. *"Maria? Moana? You're just you."*

Suddenly, she opened her eyes. They had changed. Her tears were all dried up. *I don't care who I am. I am me. And they all love me! I need to get away from this guy!*

With her bare feet, she tried to get ahold of the ground. *I need to stand up!* He wasn't dragging her very fast, and it seemed like hard work just to carry her. She needed to find some leverage with her body to throw him off balance but her feet couldn't find a foothold along the ground.

There! A little rock! Quickly, she curled her toes around it, long enough to make him stumble. The grip loosened around her chest. *Now! Now's my chance!* Quickly, she wiggled one of her arms out of his hold, far enough to ram her elbow in his belly.

"Oof," she heard him grunt, and felt his hand loosen over her mouth.

She opened her mouth as much as she could and with all her might, bit his fat finger. "Ahhhh!" she heard him scream, and tasted blood.

His grip loosened, she rammed her elbow into his chest again, and as he curled up in pain, she wiggled her head, found enough footing beneath her, quickly extended her knees, and shot up, ramming her head into his face. She heard a cracking sound, then a wail.

"Ahhhh, you fucking bitch! You broke my nose!" He brought his hands up to his face and completely let go of Maria.

Now's my chance! Have to get away, have to get back to Aaron, to everyone who loves me.

To that lady. She can't lose me again!

She took a deep breath and started running but tripped on a tree branch and face-planted into the ground. Pine needles scratched her face and a tree branch poked her stomach badly. Before she could do anything else, he was by her side, grabbing her hair. He pulled her up by her hair, violently. Her eyes teared up again, her hands flailing to protect her head. It felt as if he would tear off her scalp and all she could think of was that pain, that immense pain. She closed her eyes.

"Don't do that again, you hear me, bitch?" He now stared at her, face-to-face with her, still holding her hair. Through her tears and the darkness, she still couldn't make out who was hurting her. Suddenly, she felt a smack on her cheek, so hard and so terrible, her head flew to the side. Some of her hair ripped out, but he held fast to her head. Her cheek was burning in pain. He had slapped her.

"You will *not* resist again! I don't *like* that!" he barked at her. "You understand me?"

Maria closed her eyes and held her burning cheek, her other hand on her head to protect her scalp from being ripped out. She had never felt anything this painful before in her life.

"*Mija, you fight when someone is mean to you,*" she heard her mamá's voice whisper in the breeze as if she was there with her.

He was still close to her, holding her by the hair. With all her might, she lifted her knee and rammed it into his groin. As he doubled over in pain, moaning, she felt his grip loosen.

"*Most vulnerable parts on a guy: groin, nose, foot,*" Aaron's voice made it to her ear, a ghost on the wind.

She took her elbow and rammed it into the man's face. His hand slipped down her long hair. She lifted her leg and smashed her heel down onto his foot. He moaned again and was now holding just the bottom of her hair with a weak grasp.

Now! I need to get away!

She started running and felt pieces of her hair getting ripped out. She ignored the pain and kept running, stumbling in the dark over old palm leaves, rocks, pine needles. She had no idea where to go, where to run to, but her eyes had adjusted to the gloom. *There! There's some light!*

She ran faster, focused on the light at the edge of the woods. *Don't look back! Never look back!* she reminded herself over and over again. Her ears were alert, straining to hear if her assailant would pursue. And then she heard him, heard his shoes pressing down the needles and palm leaves on the ground. She tried to run faster, stumbling through the thickness of the woods, when suddenly she felt something smack her on the head.

Hard.

She fell.

The edge of the woods was right there, just a few steps away. Her freedom a few breaths away. Then the sharpness of her vision blurred, the light disappeared, and everything went black around her. The darkness swallowed her up.

CHAPTER 106

Aaron swallowed hard. He tried to get the knot out of his throat as he watched Elisabeth Collins weep. *I feel so bad for her.* Tears were streaming down her face.

"My child, my baby girl. I just want to hold her, love her," she sobbed.

Aaron saw General Collins hug her. "It'll be okay, it'll be okay. We found her. We have to focus on that now. Focus on the amazing fact that she's alive and she's here."

With a heavy heart, Aaron looked outside but couldn't find Maria. *Where is she? Sitting inside her car?*

Aaron looked back at the group and heard Chief Parlot say, "Mr. and Mrs. Collins. I know tonight's been hard on you. Everyone is shocked, I'm sure. I suggest we all go home now. It's been a long night. The restaurant needs to close. Everyone needs some rest. We'll start our investigation in the morning."

They all nodded, except for Aaron.

He was still staring at Maria's car in the parking lot. It was parked next to his. And then it dawned on him. *I drove Maria's car here. My dad drove mine.* He felt something in his pocket. *The keys!* All color flushed from his face as he pulled the keys to Maria's car out of his pants pocket.

"Where is she?" he yelled out, his voice coarse.

"What?" The chief looked at him. They all stared at him.

"Where's Maria?" Aaron pointed at the parking lot. "I don't see her anywhere!"

"Are you sure she's not sitting in her car? Last I saw, she was standing over by the car door," Jack said, and looked at everyone. They all nodded.

"She *can't* be in her car. I have the keys." He held them up and jingled them for everyone to see.

And before anyone else could say anything, he ran out the restaurant, calling her name, his heart beating fast, so fast. *Where is she? I know she wouldn't just run away. I know that!*

He got to her car, and then he saw it. The cuddle toy with the duck head that Elisabeth had given to her was lying on the ground in the dirt, right next to her purse. *Oh my gosh! Something happened. Something happened to her.* A big knot formed in his mouth. He was unable to speak, to scream out for help. He swallowed hard to get that bad taste out of his mouth.

CHAPTER 107

She had a bad taste in her mouth and found herself choking on something. She was forced to swallow, and a cold, stinging liquid made its way down her esophagus. She coughed. Her head was hurting, her limbs numb. *Where am I?*

She felt that cold something on her lips again, something like a cold metal, then felt the liquid being poured down her throat again. She had to swallow it. More was coming. *It's disgusting! What is this? Why am I being forced to drink something?*

She opened her eyes and saw *him*. Her attacker. Quickly, she looked around, taking in her surroundings. They were still in the woods, but close to the edge of it. She could see a faint light shining through the palm and pine trees to her left. She was lying on the ground, on pine needles and old, broken palm leaves. Her throbbing head was in his lap, a cold metal at her lips. She now realized what it was.

A flask. *He's making me drink out of a flask? What's in it?* She tried to push the flask out of her mouth with her tongue, but he pinched her nose, and eventually she ran out of air and opened her mouth to breathe and was again forced to swallow. The liquid burned her throat. *Alcohol. He's feeding me alcohol?* She now wiggled, kicked her legs, tried to use her arms to push away the flask, his hands.

"Oh, I see someone's up," she heard him say. She looked at him. Thin lips, bloody nose, blonde-greyish mustache, bluish-grey eyes. She finally recognized him. *Sullivan. Jonathan Sullivan? What the heck is* he *doing here? And why is he attacking me?*

He looked down at her, amused. She had managed to bring her hands up and was trying to push the flask away, but she was so weak. He made her swallow another big gulp and stared into her eyes.

She almost choked. *Why am I so weak?*

"Well, that should do it," he said, then finally took away the flask and screwed on the lid, calmly. Her head was still in his lap.

Maria couldn't figure out why she seemed to be moving in slow motion. She tried to lift her head, but was unsuccessful.

"Aw, cute. Still can't move, huh?"

She stared at him. *Jonathan Sullivan? Why? And why can't I move?*

"Guess that big stick really got your number, huh?"

Big stick? And then she remembered. She remembered being hit on the head by something.

"Well, Moana, guess it's safe to say you won't be fighting back anymore, huh?" He laughed. "That smack on the head plus the alcohol should definitely make sure you fucking girl can't fight anymore. And I can finally finish what I should've twenty years ago!"

She stared at him, her tongue heavy, her head spinning. *What? Finish what?*

"Well, I guess they were right. It's best we get rid of you."

What? We? Who is "we?" Get rid of me? Why?

"I just couldn't do it back then. Just couldn't. You were too cute. Those big eyes of yours. Begging me. I just felt so bad. Couldn't do it."

Do what? Maria's head was spinning.

"But I have to do it. Finish it once and for all. I thought I had a good plan. A fucking good plan. I even convinced one of them to go along with it. But I realize now it was stupid. I was fucking stupid, fucking weak. Charmed by a toddler. Shit!"

She tried to move again, but she was so weak. She felt the alcohol streaming through her blood. All she could do was listen.

"I'm not a bad guy. I'm not! I shaped up, stopped living in sin, got sober. I built my fucking business, and I will *not* let anyone take it away from me. Neither you nor them!"

Them? Who? The people I found at the restaurant? The lady in the pixie cut? The guy in the uniform? My parents?

"I know they'll lawyer up. I know they'll make me their fall guy, all because of their plan, their fucking master plan that didn't even work out." He laughed now. "No, it didn't. I saved their shitty asses with my idea. I did. 'Cuz I'm not a bad guy."

She stared at him. *I need to keep him talking. If he talks, he can't hurt me. And maybe then, someone will come and help me.*

But she was having a hard time moving her tongue, forming words, but finally managed to speak. "No, you're not a bad guy," she whispered. "You're good."

He stared at her now. "What the fuck did you just say?"

She mustered all her strength and spoke louder. "You're not a bad guy. You're good. You mean well."

He stared at her, then nodded. "You're so fucking right! Yeah, I *am* a good guy."

"You don't want any of this. They just made you do it." She had no idea who "they" even were, but she had to keep him talking.

He looked down at her, her head still in his lap. "Yes, yes, you understand me! You know I didn't mean any of this. All I wanted was a new lease on life, a new chance."

"Yes, a new chance at life. You've built yourself a good life."

He nodded.

"You can't let anyone take that away from you," she said, repeating what she'd heard earlier. He nodded again, and she saw his eyes grow moist.

"That's right, girl. So right." He smiled, and Maria managed to smile back. Suddenly, he lifted her head and pushed her up into a sitting position. Her head was spinning, hurting, but she managed to remain upright.

"Come on, girl, we gotta go."

She stared at him. *What? Really? He changed his mind and wants to help out now?* A slight smile came over her.

"Come on, let's go."

He helped her stand up. Her legs were wobbly, she could barely stand up straight. He supported her while walking. They were walking toward the light, her feet dragging. Whenever she stumbled, he steadied her, lifted her up again. They didn't say anything and made it out of the wooded area into the open. It was lighter here. The moon shone down on the grass they were walking on.

"Come on, let's go! We're almost there."

"Where?" she managed to ask. "Where are you taking me?"

"To finish what I couldn't back then. 'Cuz you're right, I can't let anyone take this away from me." She stared at him. "And this time, I have a plan. A much better plan. This time, it'll work. It fucking will. 'Cuz I'm doing this for *me*, not for them." They kept walking, him supporting her. She felt the grass turn to sand beneath her feet.

Her eyes widened when she saw it. The dark water in front of them. They were right by the water, the dark, mucky, murky water of the bay. She managed to turn her head. She saw the restaurant on her right, the parking lot next to it. They weren't far from the restaurant. *They can help me! I bet they're all still there! They can help me!*

She tried to stop walking, but was too weak. She tried to scream, but only a quiet "help" escaped her throat.

She heard him laugh, a bitter, coarse laugh.

"Nobody will help you this time, Moana. Nobody. 'Cuz I have a master plan. And it all makes sense. It makes fucking sense! I can already see the headlines in the newspaper: 'Missing toddler from twenty years ago found. Drowned for real this time, whoops. Was so confused about her identity after meeting her parents that she drank too much and fell into the bay and drowned.'"

She stared at him, wanted to scream at him, stop him, but she couldn't. She was too weak, could feel the alcohol in her blood, her head pounding with pain from the blow and dizzy from the alcohol.

He laughed again. "Man, I'm a fucking genius!"

He dragged her further in. Her feet were now wet, surrounded by water. *No, no, no! Please, let me go! Please! I don't want to drown! I don't want to drown again!* Fear took over and froze her. She was paralyzed by fear, too weak to fight back.

They were knee-deep when she heard it, a faint noise in the distance. "Maria? Maria, where are you?"

She perked up. *I know that voice. I know it. It's Aaron. Aaron!*

"Come on, let's finish it," she heard Jonathan Sullivan say. He dragged her further, and then he suddenly let go of her. Her body was too weak to hold itself up and she fell headfirst into the cold, dark water. Panic rose in her as she felt him pushing her down.

She swallowed a big mouthful of water.

No, no, no! I don't want to drown, I don't want to drown. She closed her eyes and started saying goodbye to everyone she loved. *Aaron. Mamá. That lady in the pixie cut. The guy in the uniform. Jack. The Heikinnens. My friends. Aaron. Oh, I said that already. Bye, Aaron.*

She swallowed more water.

Bye, Mama and Daddy.

She sank deeper, was pushed down, swallowed more water. Felt like a little girl. Felt her engagement ring get caught on something. *Wait! I'm engaged! I want to marry Aaron. I want to live! I'm not a little girl anymore! I'm a grown woman.*

She swallowed more water.

"Mija, fight back if anyone ever hurts you."

She felt a rock, a sharp rock that her engagement ring had gotten caught on. *A rock! Yes!* As she was getting pushed deeper into the water, she got both hands around the rock and pulled as hard as she could. It wiggled.

She swallowed more and more water.

Come on, Maria, come on! You can do it! she encouraged herself, felt her arms being so weak, but she kept wiggling the rock. *There! It's loose, I got it loose! I'm not a little girl anymore. I can swim now, yes I can!*

With her last strength, she picked up the rock, kicked her legs, and dove away underwater—just slipped right out of the hands pushing her head down. She was free!

"What the fuck?" she heard Jonathan Sullivan scream when she came up again for air nearby. He saw her.

"You fucking bitch! You won't get away from me!" He dove into the deeper water where she was wading, the heavy rock in her hands. She kept it out of sight and under water, but moved her legs enough to stay above water and get more air into her strained lungs. She was breathing hard. The mucky taste in her mouth made her retch. He heard it and with a grin on his face, he swam toward the sound of her convulsing body. Maria realized he was getting closer, and gathered all her strength to swim away, her hands clutching the rock. Then, she waited.

This is the spot, this is the time! I can do it. Hopefully he doesn't realize how shallow it is here.

As Sullivan neared, water splashing all around, ready to grab her again, she pushed herself off the sandy ground and, with a loud scream, smashed the rock into his head. She saw a look of surprise in his eyes, then those eyes crossed, and he went down. She dropped the rock and crawled across the sand bar to the shore.

CHAPTER 108

"**O**ver by that little shore! I just heard a scream come from that direction. Wait, there's something in the water," Aaron yelled, and ran as fast as he could.

"I see it, too," Brad shouted, and ran after Aaron. The younger man sprinted so fast that both Brad and Chief Parlot could barely keep up with him.

While running, the chief yelled into the radio hanging from his police vest, "Requesting backup at the Compass Rose. Immediately!"

"It's Maria!" Aaron yelled and was the first one by her side. He kneeled down in the sand next to her. "Oh my gosh, Maria. Are you okay? What happened? Maria?"

She looked up at him, her head throbbing, her face scratched and bruised, blood trickling down.

Brad arrived at the shore. "Moana, my baby girl!" He plopped down next to her in the sand. "Oh my gosh, my baby girl."

She smiled at him, then pointed behind her.

Brad stood up and walked closer to the shoreline. Then he saw it. Someone floating in the water. Without thinking, he ran in. Chief Parlot finally arrived as Brad was dragging the person onto the shore. "Chief, this guy is unconscious but still alive, I think."

Chief Parlot came over and helped lay the unconscious guy into the recovery position, then started monitoring his pulse. Brad checked his breathing.

"Who is this?" Chief Parlot asked.

Brad shrugged his shoulders. "Don't know."

"Bad guy," Maria whispered to Aaron.

"Maria says he's a bad guy," Aaron yelled over, and helped Maria sit up. He sat behind her, holding her tight. "What happened, Maria?"

Her tongue was heavy. She choked a spurt of seawater and alcohol, then managed to whisper, "Attacked me. Tried to. Kill me. Finish what. He couldn't. Back then."

Aaron stared at her, then passed on the info. "She says that guy tried to kill her, 'to finish what he couldn't back then.'"

"What?" The two men looked at each other. Immediately, Brad stopped monitoring the unconscious man's breathing and stood up.

"Backup's on the way," the chief's radio blurted out.

"Good. I'll need two ambulances also. Immediately," Chief Parlot ordered while keeping an eye on the unknown man.

Brad looked back and forth between his daughter and the man on the shore, then saw Elisabeth, Jack, Drew, and Sarah running toward them. He waved them over.

Elisabeth was clutching Enti as she ran and arrived first. She looked at Brad, then saw her long-lost daughter sitting in the sand, dripping wet, bruises on her face and blood trickling out of her hair. Her face turned pale and she sank to her knees, right in front of her child. "Moana, du meine Güte! Mein Engel. Ist alles okay?"

Maria nodded. "Ja. Okay," she whispered.

"Mein Engel, meine arme, kleine Maus. Hier, hier ist Enti. I found her in the parking lot," Elisabeth said, and handed Enti to Maria, who weakly smiled back at her. Elisabeth started crying. "My poor baby girl. What's going on here?"

She turned to Chief Parlot and Brad, her face flushing and regaining its color. "What the heck happened to my daughter this time?" She noticed the man lying in the sand. "And who the heck is *that*?"

"Apparently a bad guy," Brad said, and walked over to Elisabeth. He joined her in kneeling before their daughter.

"Sullivan," Maria whispered.

"What?" they all asked.

Aaron felt her limbs go weak. *She's about to pass out.* He shook her gently. "Maria, stay with me, Maria."

"Yeah. I'm. Here. Sullivan out."

Aaron looked over to the man still lying unconscious in the sand and didn't move. The chief was still holding his hand, monitoring his pulse. Aaron took a closer look at the compact guy, looked past his bloodied face, and then it clicked. He recognized that greyish-blonde hair, the grey mustache, the straight nose, the thin lips.

"Oh my gosh, she's right. It's *Sullivan*. Jonathan Eric Sullivan!"

"Who?" they all asked, looking at Aaron.

"Jonathan Sullivan. Martina's ex-husband. The guy on the fake birth certificate!"

The chief stared at him. "Thank you, Mr. Heikinnen. Good to know." He nodded at Brad. "I assume we have another suspect on our hands, General Collins. Do you know this guy?"

Brad turned around and stared at the unconscious man lying in the sand. He studied his pale, bloody face, his strong stature, then shook his head. "No, Chief, I don't think I've ever seen this man before in my life. Do you know him, Elisabeth?"

She turned around and studied him. "No, I don't think I do." She stared at him. "Was this the guy at the restaurant? The coughing one who . . . well, I'm not sure either way. Why? What did he do?"

"He tried to kill our daughter," Brad grumbled, his voice low. He stood up and crossed his arms.

Elisabeth gasped and threw her hands up. "What? He did *what*?" She got up also and walked closer to the man. The sound of blaring sirens made them all turn toward the parking lot, but Elisabeth focused on Chief Parlot, who was still tending to the man's vitals. "Is he still alive?"

The chief looked up and saw both Collins standing there, their arms crossed. "Yes, Mrs. Collins, he is. Has a faint but stable pulse. Looks like he has a gushing head wound."

The Collins watched the blood trickle out of his head and run down his face and pool onto the sand. The backup and ambulances arrived then, and paramedics rushed over.

"Chief, he doesn't deserve to live," Elisabeth said, her voice cold as ice.

Chief Parlot looked at her, his eyebrows raised. Her face was bright red, tears streaming down. "He's a killer. He tried to take my child from me. Again. He deserves to die! Just let him die!" She started sobbing uncontrollably and noticed the paramedics kneel down next to the unconscious man.

"Elisabeth, don't you want to see him punished for this?" Brad gently put an arm around her and pulled her away. They both watched as the paramedics assessed the man's injuries and lifted him onto a stretcher.

"You're safe now. They'll help you," Maria heard Aaron say. He was still sitting behind her, holding her up. In a trance, she watched the light of the blaring sirens illuminate the dark water. She watched everything silently.

Is this real or am I dreaming again?

She saw the paramedics lift Jonathan Sullivan onto a stretcher and then into an ambulance, then noticed two others standing over her. They briefly spoke with Aaron, arguing about something, then Aaron lifted her and carried her into the other ambulance. Silently, she held on to him, clutching Enti, until he laid her onto the stretcher inside.

The paramedics got busy tending to her and gestured for Aaron to leave. Maria watched him go and smiled at him until she didn't see him anymore. She could feel IV fluids flowing into her body and closed her eyes.

I'm safe now, I think. At least I finally know who I am. The pieces of the past are coming together. She heard the doors to the ambulance close and drifted off to sleep.

Aaron watched them close the doors and stared at the ambulance. Brad, Elisabeth, Sarah, Drew, and Jack did the same. Nobody said a word. Jack put a hand on Aaron's shoulder and squeezed him tight.

Chief Parlot sent off the first ambulance, then came over to the little group. "Well, General and Mrs. Collins, Mr. Heikinnen, it's done. I'm glad she's safe now." Aaron and Brad nodded. Elisabeth cried silent tears.

"Chief, will you arrest that guy who tried to kill my daughter?" Brad asked, his voice low, his exotic eyes bright green.

"Yes, General Collins. Jonathan Sullivan will be arrested and charged with kidnapping and attempted murder." The whole group nodded and kept staring at the flashing ambulance lights.

They were silent for a bit until Elisabeth spoke. "Will he also be charged for the kidnapping twenty years ago?"

"Well, we have to figure out if he was involved, and if so, what role he played," Chief Parlot said.

Aaron now turned to him. "Chief, Mrs. Collins is right. You should charge him for that too. Maria told us he was here to finish what he couldn't back then. He's clearly guilty. But I don't think Martina Sullivan is."

"What?" Suddenly, Elisabeth's tears stopped and she now stared at Aaron. "Of course she's guilty. She and her ex-husband did this to us."

Jack looked up. "Well, we don't have a motive, and it's not clear—"

The chief cut him off with a wave of his hand, then looked at each and every one of them. "Please, I need you all to stay out of this. The police will handle the investigation. For now, I want you all to focus on the young lady's recovery."

Jack sighed. "He's right."

Drew nodded, then squeezed Brad's shoulder. "Well, Cave Man, two suspects in custody for your daughter's kidnapping. And she's alive! You actually found her. Unbelievable. Now, you have both your girls back. It's all you ever wanted. It's so great, Cave Man. I'm happy for you, happy for you all."

"Ja, I, too," Sarah said, and looked at Elisabeth.

Brad smiled and put an arm around his ex-wife, who smiled back. "That's right," they both said. "We're finally whole again!"

Aaron glanced at the happy couple and raised an eyebrow. "Yeah, all these pieces just seemed to fall into place, huh?" he grumbled, but nobody heard.

The ambulance driver signaled the chief, who looked at the group. "They're ready to go. Who will follow the girl to the hospital?"

"Me!" Aaron, Brad, and Elisabeth yelled simultaneously.

The chief smirked. "Fine then, all of you. Mr. Heikinnen, you can drive, right?"

Aaron nodded, keys already in hand.

"Excellent. Go ahead, Mr. Heikinnen, and take the Collins with you. Follow the ambulance closely and stay with your fiancée. I'll take care of everything else here."

They all looked at each other and nodded. Aaron, Elisabeth, and Brad jogged over to Maria's blue Oldsmobile and got in. Her parents sat in the back seat and Aaron behind the wheel. He started the car and set off after the ambulance, its sirens wailing shrill through the dark Florida night.

ACKNOWLEDGMENTS

There's a lot of people whom I'd like to thank for fulfilling this lifelong dream of mine: writing a novel!

Let me start out by thanking my amazing husband, Ben, who is always there for me, encouraging me to achieve my life goals. The inspiration for this story about true love comes from my love for him. I also thank him for sharing his expertise about the Air Force, especially for answering countless questions about ranks, civilian jobs, and bases around the country. His deep well of knowledge helped me immensely in writing this book. Thank you for encouraging me to finish what I started and for giving me the resources, time, and space to do so. Thanks for helping me become an author. Ben, you're the best husband and friend a woman could ever have.

Huge thanks as well to my two kids, Maila and Ayden, who not only listened to excerpts from my many drafts of this book, but also helped me understand the strength of a mother's love, the worries and the laughs that come with being a mom. You have given me a new perspective in life, a new purpose. Without both of you, I couldn't have written this book, especially the parts written from the perspective of a mother and her toddler.

Speaking of a toddler's perspective: thanks to all my 2Day2s Class students at SSDS for helping me understand the amazing minds of little human beings. And thanks to my former colleagues at SSDS for giving me the opportunity to learn more about little children and their development.

Thank you and Danke to my parents, Renate and Horst Preuß, and to my sister Inga, who all often listened to the numerous stories I wrote for fun as a child. A special thanks to my dad, who told me when I was fourteen that I have a special gift for writing. Took a while, Papi, but I've finally finished my first novel. Danke!

Big thanks go to my in-laws, Nancy and Charles, Will and Heather, Marasie and family. Appreciated your interest in the writing process. Thanks to Nancy for reading my whole book, and big thanks to Will for editing chapters and my ending. Special thanks to Marasie for helping me proofread my whole first draft. Appreciate the English-mother-tongue input and your help with the Spanish.

Thanks also to my friends, the Mizhquero-Miller family, and to Carolina for the mother-tongue input on Spanish words and sentences. Appreciate it!

A huge thanks goes out to David Termuhlen, my beta-reader, who pushed me to rethink my plot, rewrite my chapters, and dig down deep to tell the best possible yarn. Without your professional and constructive feedback, Elisabeth and Brad would be bitter characters only, there'd be tons of coincidences, and a lot of on-the-nose writing. I'm so thankful you were willing to read through my rough draft, line by line. Thank you for taking all this time out of your days to help me make this book much better. Without you, it would not be what it is now. I'm looking forward to many more discussions about the "big picture" and plot of future books.

Special thanks also to my editors at Motif Edits. Thank you, Jeff, for the fantastic line edits and thank you, Caroline, for proofreading my novel. You helped make it the best book it can possibly be. Thanks to Shavonne for the plot discussion calls that made me realize what I needed to do to write to-genre. Really appreciate everyone's feedback and professional edits. I'm looking forward to continuing my work with you.

Last but not least, thank you to Self-Publishing School (SPS) for teaching me how to be a self-published author—how to write, edit, publish, and market my novel. Without being a student at SPS, I wouldn't have been able to publish my first book. Thanks to my coach Barbara Hartzler for the helpful information, and thanks to all the SPS employees who run the online coaching calls. A big 'Thank You' to Dakota for being my SPS book production team manager, and for everyone else within that team. Really appreciate all of you for helping me with the finishing touches of the book. SPS offers a wonderful and supportive online community with an immense amount of knowledge. Happy to be a part of it!

WANT TO WRITE A BOOK OF YOUR OWN?

Self-Publishing School helped me, and I know they can help you!

Check them out now at: https://self-publishingschool.com/friend/

MEET THE AUTHOR

Greta Schumacher grew up in Bad Nenndorf, Germany. She immigrated to the United States in 2010 and has lived in and experienced numerous states and cities while following her husband's Air Force career. She currently lives in Ohio with her husband and two children.

As a child, Greta enjoyed reading and loved writing. She studied to be a secondary school teacher and taught English, German, and Physical Education. After having her own children, she switched to teaching preschool. Greta has always been interested in psychology, especially early childhood development, language acquisition, and young children's memories. She believes that toddlers' understanding of situations and feelings are often underestimated and loved exploring early childhood memories as a theme in her first novel.

Interested in learning more about the author?

Follow me on Facebook: GP Schumacher

Reach me via email at gpschumacher.author@gmail.com